PRAISE FOR MICHELLE FRANCES

'I tore through the pages . . . A high-speed chase of
a novel'
Louise Candlish

'Michelle Frances brings fresh energy to this age-old
theme of sibling rivalry and family secrets . . .
The finale doesn't disappoint'
Daily Mail

'Terrific . . . Twisted, fraught with suspense'
Jo Spain

'Toxic family relationships, sultry European settings
and an intricate plot which leaves you never knowing
who to trust'
Catherine Cooper

'Brilliantly twisty, a sharp, sinister and addictive read'
Sunday Mirror

'I was blown away. *The Girlfriend* is the most marvellous
psychological thriller'
Jilly Cooper

'Tension oozes from the pages'
i newspaper

THE BOYFRIEND

Michelle Frances has worked in television drama as a producer and script editor for several years, both for the independent sector and the BBC. *The Boyfriend* is her fifth novel, following *The Girlfriend*, *The Temp*, *The Daughter* and *Sisters*.

ALSO BY MICHELLE FRANCES

The Girlfriend
The Temp
The Daughter
Sisters

THE BOYFRIEND

MICHELLE FRANCES

PAN BOOKS

First published 2022 by Pan Books
an imprint of Pan Macmillan
The Smithson, 6 Briset Street, London EC1M 5NR
EU representative: Macmillan Publishers Ireland Ltd, 1st Floor,
The Liffey Trust Centre, 117–126 Sheriff Street Upper,
Dublin 1, D01 YC43
Associated companies throughout the world
www.panmacmillan.com

ISBN 978-1-5290-4965-7

1 3 5 7 9 8 6 4 2

A CIP catalogue record for this book is available from the British Library.

Typeset in Sabon by Palimpsest Book Production Ltd, Falkirk, Stirlingshire
Printed and bound by CPI Group (UK) Ltd, Croydon, CR0 4YY

Visit **www.panmacmillan.com** to read more about all our books
and to buy them. You will also find features, author interviews and
news of any author events, and you can sign up for e-newsletters
so that you're always first to hear about our new releases.

For Trisha Jackson. Thanks for everything.

ONE

19 February

'Hello? Hello? Can you hear me?'

A voice, deep, authoritative, was penetrating the oblivion Amy had been inhabiting.

'Hello? Come on now, open your eyes.'

This voice, whoever it belonged to, was persistent. She had an unwelcome sense of being targeted.

'You're in hospital. I'm Doctor Kunda. You've had an accident and hurt your head.'

Amy could feel pain, deep, all-encompassing pain that obliterated all other senses, including her willpower.

'I want you to try and open your eyes. Can you do it?'

A crack. There. A tiny, blurred line of light, too bright. Amy was aware of lying down; she was in a bed. Then shapes swam into view. Otherworldly figures moving like huge blobs in white and blue around her. They frightened her.

One of them spoke, although she couldn't tell which.

'That's it. Well done. Now can you tell me your name?'

It was too much. She closed her eyes again.

TWO

19 February

'Aha! So my patient is no longer ignoring me.'

Amy saw a giant of a man dressed in blue scrubs approach her bed, followed by a number of other medical professionals. The nurse who had attended to her when she'd first woken gave her a reassuring smile.

'I ignored you?' she said.

'You had a good excuse,' said the man. 'I'm Doctor Kunda. Nice to meet you, Amy.' He towered over her, and she was caught in the beam of his sharp brown eyes. 'I hear from Nurse Morgan here that you're unsure how you got to be in hospital?'

Amy glanced at the nurse with the red hair and freckles as she checked the machines Amy was wired up to. 'That's right.'

'We've already done a scan and I'm happy to report there's no evidence of intracranial bleeding,' said Dr Kunda. 'We'll be keeping a close eye on you over the next couple of days, just to make sure there's nothing we need to worry about.'

'Like what?' asked Amy, alarmed.

'We always like to monitor patients after a head injury,' said Dr Kunda. 'Most often it's fine, but we need to be sure before we can discharge you. Got a headache?'

'Yes. Awful.'

He smiled. 'It's to be expected. Now, what about this memory?'

'I still don't remember anything.'

'Do you know what day it is?'

'The nineteenth of February. I only know because Nurse Morgan told me.'

'Anything about the accident?'

She shook her head.

'Apparently you were found earlier this evening on some black ice in a street in Earlsfield. Completely knocked out.'

'It was near my flat,' said Amy. Nurse Morgan had told her how a passer-by had called an ambulance. Amy could recall nothing of the incident.

'So, when is your last memory, do you think?'

'About six months ago. The end of last summer. I remember the bank holiday in August. It was hot. I went to the beach.'

'And now it's minus one and snowing!' He laughed uproariously, as if he'd made a great joke. Nurse Morgan caught her eye and grimaced.

'Now, your brain has had a bit of a shake,' continued Dr Kunda. 'The amnesia is likely to be temporary. It will return, probably in fits and starts.'

'When?' asked Amy.

3

'Can't say. You might be lucky and get something in the next few days. Or it might be weeks . . .'

'What's the worst case . . .?' asked Amy in trepidation.

'Impossible to predict, I'm afraid. Months? Perhaps longer. And when your memories do return, they may not be complete. Some may be mixed with things that have happened to you at other times in your life, some may be distorted. Or,' he added cheerfully, seeing her despondent face, 'it may be like switching on the TV. Glorious technicolour before you.'

She gave a wan smile.

'Now,' said Dr Kunda. 'We need to talk about side effects.'

Amy paled.

'It's nothing to worry about. There'll be headaches, naturally. You might find yourself getting more irritable than usual. It's also very possible you will feel paranoid; the most ordinary of situations may appear threatening.' He smiled. 'So lay off the horror movies for a bit, eh?'

'Yeah, sure,' muttered Amy.

Dr Kunda flicked through the notes as if searching for something, then looked up at her inquisitively. 'Do you have a next of kin? Husband? Boyfriend?'

Amy hesitated. 'No,' she said, feeling the usual brush of shame. Nearly thirty and no significant other to contact about an emergency trip to hospital. She wondered if he was surprised, if he was judging her.

He clocked her reticence. 'Girlfriend?' he asked.

Amy sighed. 'No. Mother.'

'Great! Perhaps she will come and visit? Stay a while after you have been discharged?'

4

Amy murmured something non-committal. She would discourage it. Her mother lived in Dorset. It was too far and Amy was sure she would be able to take care of herself.

'Well, time for some rest,' said Dr Kunda. He straightened. 'Don't worry,' he said as he turned to go. 'You might remember you've won the lottery.'

Amy watched as he left. *Yeah, right*, she thought. *Thanks, Doctor Comedian.* God, her head hurt. Unable to bear it anymore, she closed her eyes.

THREE

20 February

The days dragged when you were in hospital. Amy had woken that morning, the bright hospital lights hurting her head. She'd had a utilitarian breakfast. She'd been wheeled off for more checks. During morning visiting she'd watched television, trying not to be aware of the buzz of warmth that emanated from the rest of the ward while their loved ones came by. There had been an unexpected highlight when one of the nurses had brought her handbag in. It was dirty, thrown to the ground during the fall, but a Good Samaritan had found it and handed it in at the hospital. She'd automatically checked it to see if anything was missing, but of course she couldn't remember what had been in there in the first place. Her phone, purse and keys were all present, and that was the main thing. Then it had been lunch, after which she'd fallen into an exhausted sleep.

On waking, the hospital lights were blinding as ever. She winced and did her best to look around without moving her head. Another burst of energy was coming into the ward with the afternoon visitors. She looked up, unable to bury her curiosity, tinged with longing. There was a nice woman across from her in her forties and Amy saw the woman's husband return for his second visit of the day. In fact, each of the other five women on the ward had a man at her bedside. Softly spoken individuals who brandished gifts of food and magazines, gave out kisses and entwined their wives' fingers with their own.

Amy tried to sit up, but her head was pounding. She squinted at her watch in hope, but it was at least another hour until she would be administered any more painkillers. It was too long, far too long. She reached out a hand to press the call button when a face she recognized came purposefully onto the ward.

'Look at the state of you,' said Lisa, not unkindly, as she leaned over Amy's bed, her practised GP's eye taking it all in.

Amy had studied herself in a mirror and was aware her left eye and cheekbone were swollen and the colour of an aubergine, but she was still mildly affronted. 'What's wrong with me?'

'It's mostly bruising, I'm sure. Wow, that is some black eye.'

'What are you doing here?' asked Amy, quietly delighted to see her friend. It was all very well thinking that you could just get on with it, but the reality was she'd felt desperately lonely.

'You left me a voicemail that you were in hospital. And despite the fact you said you were fine, I couldn't pass up a chance to take a look at you. You know how I love an injury. How are you feeling?'

'So much better now that my caring friend has treated me with her best bedside manner.'

'That's why I never went into hospital work,' said Lisa. 'I prefer to diagnose my patients in the practice and then move them on to the specialists.'

'You're all heart. So it looks really bad?' Amy was aware she was fishing for reassurance, that she was emotionally fragile. She'd tried to pull her long dark hair over her face, but it was like covering a broken window with a tea towel, so she'd given up.

'Like you've fallen onto the edge of a frozen pavement, landing face first.'

Exactly what she'd been told had happened. Amy felt a waft of chill on Lisa's coat as she peeled it off in the over-heated hospital. It must still be freezing outside. A scarf came off too, and Lisa shook free her practical ponytail, a few blonde strands escaping. She pulled up a chair, folded her coat over the back and sat down, crossing her legs and interlinking her hands around her knees.

'Headache?' she asked.

'Dire.'

'No, I'm not giving you anything,' said Lisa sternly, in response to Amy's best pathetic look. 'You're fully dosed up already.' She softened her tone. 'How's the memory?'

'Nothing from the last six months.' Amy's voice quietened as she spoke. She had found it deeply disconcerting to have woken in hospital and not remembered how she came to be there. When Nurse Morgan had asked probing questions, dressed up to sound matter-of-fact and reassuring, references to ordinary facts such as ages and dates and who was the prime minister, Amy had seen the look on the nurse's face when she'd claimed it was the end of August. It was the carefully controlled blankness, the silent nod that spoke volumes. *It was the lack of affirmation.* So Amy had known instantly that something was wrong. She'd challenged Nurse Morgan and discovered that in fact it was mid-February – almost six months later than the world in which she was living. Amy had been struck by a sudden and immediate sense of vertigo as a realization had thundered into her mind that she couldn't remember entire months of her life. A great gaping hole existed where there were meant to be memories.

Now, having had a few hours to come to terms with her affliction, she felt a strange emptiness; part of her was missing and the lack of familiarity that she usually took for granted made Amy anxious and vulnerable. Now Lisa was here, Amy was overwhelmed with gratitude.

'Hey, don't cry,' said Lisa, pulling a tissue from her bag and handing it over. 'It's only temporary, you know that, right?'

'So they tell me.'

'"They" are right. Any other injuries?'

'Not that I've noticed.' Earlier, Amy had lifted the blankets to check herself over, afraid she might find something serious that she couldn't remember from the fall. Everything had looked normal except for a scar on her knee. She couldn't remember how she'd got it, so assumed it had happened within the last six months. In the part of her life that she couldn't grasp. It felt strange not knowing what had happened to her.

Lisa was watching her, weighing something up. She cleared her throat. 'So . . . are you aware that you're going on holiday in four days' time?'

Amy was taken aback. 'I'm what?'

'You booked a week in Val d'Isère. You, me, Jenna and your mum. Staying at your aunt's mountain lodge. To celebrate your thirtieth birthday. We have train reservations, a couchette from Paris. With fold-down bunks!'

Amy tried to take it all in. 'My mother is sleeping on a train?' she eventually said.

'Er no. She's flying. Doesn't care about adding to the climate crisis. Something about, "what difference is one passenger going to make when the plane's going anyway?"'

Amy took a deep breath. It disturbed her that she could forget something as big as a holiday. Although, she supposed, her brain wasn't going to be selective about what it did and didn't remember. She wondered what else she didn't know.

She looked at Lisa. 'Did I really organize that?'

'Back in October,' said Lisa.

'Right. Well, it's a nice idea. A girls' trip away.'

Lisa gave a small shake of her head. 'David and Lewis are meant to be coming too,' she said. 'Meeting us the day after we arrive. Staying just for the weekend. You do remember David and Lewis?'

'Of course.' They were her friends' husbands. Amy had been bridesmaid at both of the weddings. They'd been friends since sharing a house at university, over a decade ago. Jenna the art student, Lisa in medicine and she in law. When they'd graduated, they'd all got jobs in London and decided to continue flat-sharing right through the early years of their careers, until both her friends had moved out with their boyfriends one after the other and Amy had opted to buy a small flat. Jenna now lived in a large, expensive house in leafy Richmond with Lewis, who had made a considerable amount of money in the city and now ran a gallery. Lisa was also part of the suburban dream in Epsom in Surrey, where she lived with David, a fellow GP. With the news of the men coming on the trip Amy felt the familiar stab of loneliness. Other than a couple of failed attempts on the dating apps it had been five long years since her last relationship. She covered quickly.

'Great. David and Lewis. Anyone else?'

'Jack's invited . . .' added Lisa.

'Jack?'

Lisa clapped a hand over her mouth. 'Oh my God . . . You don't remember that either.'

'Remember what? Who's Jack?'

Lisa grinned. 'Your boyfriend.'

Amy's mouth dropped open. 'My what?'

'Doctor Jack Stewart. Consultant paediatrician at St Thomas's hospital.'

'Are you winding me up?'

Lisa sat down on the bed. 'You met him three months ago. Outside Waterloo station. After you'd finished work at one of your ungodly late hours. He took you to a tapas restaurant in Wandsworth on your first date and you guys both went mad for the stuffed courgette flowers.' She sighed. 'You don't remember any of this, do you?'

Amy shook her head, stunned. It was as if Lisa was relaying someone else's life, not her own. She had a boyfriend? She felt lighter suddenly.

'What's he like?' she asked.

'Pretty cool. Well, at least he sounds it from what you've told us.'

'You haven't met him?'

'Not yet. That was the plan this weekend.'

Amy felt her stomach sink. '*Was* the plan?'

Lisa pulled a face. 'You seemed fine about it when you told us . . . He couldn't make it after all.'

'Oh.'

'It's his hospital shifts. They got changed at the last minute.' Lisa grinned and nudged Amy's arm. 'He's out there saving lives.'

'Course.'

'And not just any old lives, *children's* lives.'

Amy smiled and tried to be understanding but it was hard to understand anything properly in her current state.

'So if your tests rule out any serious brain injury you'll be discharged pretty quickly . . .' said Lisa, 'which I'm sure is what's going to happen, but if you're not feeling up for it and you want to cancel the trip anyway, that is absolutely fine.'

Amy nodded and Lisa left soon after, promising to check in the next day. When she'd gone, Amy lay back on the bed and tried to rationalize what she'd been told.

She had a boyfriend.

The word sounded alien to her. A strange word to be attached to her in any way. *Amy has a boyfriend.* His name is Jack. Jack Stewart. *Doctor* Jack Stewart. It was as if she'd been gifted him, out of the blue. *But we've been dating for three months*, Amy remembered. That's what Lisa had said. She tried to picture him but her mind drew a blank. It must have pleased her mother, thought Amy with a wry smile. Oh how she wished she could remember telling her. After all those years of disappointment.

Amy pulled her bag out of her bedside locker and opened up her phone. It took a couple of goes, as the screen seemed to have a habit of freezing. It was old and Amy supposed it must have been acting up for a while as the same thing had happened that morning when she'd called her mum and Lisa. At the time Amy hadn't looked at her messages. She'd been so overwhelmed by her memory loss and so tired, she hadn't had the energy.

She opened the app. The first few messages were from well-wishers: her mum, Jenna, Lisa. She scrolled down further past various groups, messages from her boss at the prestigious law firm where she worked, a client. Then her heart stopped as she saw his name. Jack Stewart. *Her boyfriend.* With a mixture of excitement and trepidation she clicked on his last message, which had been sent three days ago.

Only a few more days until your trip. Wish I could come but we'll do our own another time. Just the two of us.

Butterflies flit in Amy's stomach. He had suddenly come alive. She glanced down at the screen again, scrolled a bit further along the message chain, read some more:

Please tell your mum that I'm extremely sorry not to meet her tonight. I feel really awful about it as I was looking forward to it so much and she has come such a long way, but I know you two will have a fabulous night. Bentley's do the best crab cakes. Martha, for what it's worth, Amy has told me so many wonderful things about you and I'm dying to meet the woman who's produced such a fantastic daughter.

Crikey, he *was* keen. Then:

Amy, you're the most fabulous, smart, gorgeous girl I've ever met. And I think you look good in green.

None of them made much sense – she didn't remember what he was referring to but he was there, he *existed!* She held the phone to her chest and a smile appeared on her face. She was tickled. She had a boyfriend. Who would have thought it?

A notion struck her. Presumably he wouldn't even know she'd had an accident – no one would have his contact details to tell him.

It felt strange, composing a message to a person she didn't remember, and it took her several goes until she hit on the wording that felt right. She had a sudden positive thought. Hearing from him might help trigger her memory.

Hi, how are you? I'm in hospital, St George's. Don't worry, still intact. Except, weirdly, I've lost some of my memory. Be lovely to hear from you.

She didn't want to admit outright that she couldn't remember him; it was too hard to explain. And anyway, when he replied, they could speak on the phone, and the sound of his voice might bring everything back.

She pressed send and waited. After a few minutes, it felt silly to hold the phone in her hand so she put it on the cabinet. Glanced at it every so often but it remained silent.

It stayed silent the rest of the evening and the next day and the next.

FOUR

24 February

It felt strange going back into her flat. As Amy opened the door it was as still and quiet as a morgue. The air smelt stale and no wonder as the place had been empty for five days. She picked up the pile of post on the doormat and sifted through, seeing nothing that needed her immediate attention.

Some of the flat's musty smell came from a vase of dead crimson roses that were in the hallway. Amy went over to them, feeling despondent at the brown petals discarded all over the table and the floor. A card was propped up against the vase. She picked it up.

To the most beautiful woman in the world. I know you're weirdly cynical about Valentine's, but I couldn't resist. You're getting flowers whether you like it or not. Because I love you. Jack X

She held the card, staring at the words, taken aback by the strong sentiment, by the fact she'd been sent Valentine's

Day flowers. Her heart twisted. It was only ten days ago but a lifetime for these flowers and, it seemed, their relationship. She'd heard nothing from Jack since the text she'd sent at the hospital. She'd checked her phone several times until her hope had become pathetic and she'd forced herself not to do it anymore.

Amy picked up the flowers and disposed of them in the outside bin. She took a few breaths of the cold frosty air and delved in her pocket for her secret friends. It was only on rare occasions that she smoked – sometimes she felt as if it gave her a sense of solidarity. Her and the cigarette, the iconic symbol of a lone dissenter. *Who are you kidding*, she thought. *Lone maybe, not so sure about the dissenter.* Lighting one up, she exhaled heavily. *Forget about him*, she told herself. *He's a loser. He can't even be bothered to reply when you say you've had an accident.*

Everything she thought was true but it didn't stop it hurting. In some ways it was worse being ignored by a boyfriend she couldn't even remember. Maybe there was a reasonable explanation? Something he'd said that she now couldn't recall? Perhaps he'd lost his phone and was in the process of replacing it? Or had something happened to him? She got a momentary stab of worry before realizing she was scrabbling around for excuses. She had to face up to the fact she'd been ghosted. He'd vanished out of her life for reasons only known to himself.

Amy finished the cigarette and threw the butt into the bin. Maybe the trip to Val d'Isère would take her mind off it all. She'd decided to go ahead as, although she still felt a little fragile, there was no point moping around at home. She was also desperate to see her Aunt Esme.

Amy went into the kitchen to see if there was anything remotely edible to eat. It hadn't occurred to her until she'd got home that she couldn't remember the contents of her own fridge, but she was a very organized person, someone who planned. She was delighted to find that her old self had not let her new self down and there was a carton of soup still in date. She turned to get a pan to heat it up and then stopped, puzzled. On the kitchen worktop was a half-drunk cup of coffee, a film of greyish milk pooled in the centre, the beginnings of mould forming. She must have left it there before going to work on the day of her accident. Amy knew that she never usually left crockery unwashed, she didn't even leave things to drain; they were washed, dried and put away before she went to catch the train. She picked it up and poured its disgusting contents down the sink. She must have been distracted by something that morning.

After her lunch, Amy went to pack. She had to get to St Pancras station for later that afternoon, where she was meeting Lisa and Jenna. She threw her clothes into her suitcase then opened the top drawer of her dressing table and took out some jewellery, which she also put in the case. There was a box she didn't recognize, royal blue with a gold edging. Puzzled, she opened it and her eyes widened. A large diamond beamed back at her, hanging on a gold chain. She had no recollection of where it had come from and she smiled, mystified, as she took in the pendant, trying to remember. Of course, she didn't know.

She closed the box and put it in the suitcase with the rest. She might be the only one of her friends to be on holiday without a partner but at least she'd have a single carat around her neck, she thought defiantly.

FIVE

24 February

The champagne cork popped and Lisa poured three glasses, the last only a quarter full. Her hand wobbled as the train sped through the French countryside and she steadied the base of the glass against the tiny table.

'Whose is that?' asked Amy, eyeing the short-changed glass suspiciously, while already knowing the answer.

'You're not meant to be drinking at all,' said Lisa. 'Doctor's orders.'

'Are you going to be mothering me the whole trip?' asked Amy lightly. Lisa had offered to escort her home when she was discharged that morning but Amy had insisted she was fine. She lived so close to the hospital and it seemed crazy to drag Lisa all the way into London just to hold her hand for a ten-minute cab ride.

They were in the bar carriage of the overnight train to the Alps, perched on stools so small they were not made for human backsides. Amy took her tiny glass of champagne and looked over at Jenna, who was staring out of the window of the train, seemingly distracted by the view. The afternoon sun caught the gold in her mess of tawny curls and hazel, almost feline eyes. She had always been the most beautiful of the three of them.

'Are you having some, Jenna?' asked Lisa.

Jenna turned. 'Oh yes, why not?' She accepted the glass that Lisa handed to her.

'Everything OK?' asked Amy. Her friend had been quiet ever since they'd met at St Pancras.

'Sure, everything's fine,' said Jenna, a note of surprise in her voice. She peered at Amy, looking directly at the yellowing bruise on her face, and Amy raised her hand self-consciously. 'What about you?' asked Jenna. 'Are you sure you're feeling well enough to do this trip?'

'It's a bit late now,' smiled Amy. 'We're hurtling through France at one hundred and thirty miles per hour.'

'But you only left hospital this morning.'

'That's right.'

Jenna was looking at her as if she was waiting for a justification and Amy bit down a flicker of irritation. 'It's my birthday,' she said. Jenna still didn't look convinced. 'My thirtieth birthday,' said Amy.

Amy's doctors had no medical reason for her not to go, although they advised restraint, at least for the first few days, and had reminded her of the possible side effects to be aware of – a whole heap of ailments including headaches and paranoia. Amy assumed they couldn't *all* affect her. More to the point, her friends had booked time off and paid for tickets. And there was Aunt Esme. Wonderful, audacious Aunt Esme, who had offered her lodge. Amy had found an email from five months ago when she'd been planning the trip where Esme had generously given over her home. Although Amy was not really looking forward to being the gooseberry to her girlfriends and their husbands, along with dealing with her overbearing mother, she could do with spending some time with her aunt. It had been almost a year since she'd last seen her. And what was the alternative? Spending her birthday alone in her flat?

Lisa lifted her glass. 'Here's to our week in the Alps. To celebrating Amy's third decade.'

'Shame Jack couldn't make it,' said Jenna.

Amy looked up. Had she imagined it or did her friend sound a little . . . cool? She sighed. 'Actually, I think he's dumped me.'

Lisa scoffed. 'Come on, he's not dumped you.'

'Not in words, but in his silence.'

'He's busy, that's all.'

'I sent him a text saying I was in *hospital*. He's a doctor, for God's sake. You think this would blip on his radar.'

'He sent you flowers only the other weekend,' Lisa reminded her. 'A dozen roses.'

'Did I tell you?'

'You posted them on Facebook.' Lisa pulled out her phone and with a few swipes, turned it to face Amy. There they were. A dozen crimson roses with a post from herself that said: 'My Valentine's Day gift from Jack.'

Amy cringed. 'I really put that on there? Publicly?'

'You must have been pleased to get them.'

She suspected she had been. But Amy also knew she was

very private and secretly thought of the way other people displayed their love lives on social media in some sort of subtle one-upmanship as slightly needy. She couldn't believe she'd done the very same herself.

'It's not the only one.' Lisa swiped her phone some more. 'Look, here's the photo of your first meal out together. You remember, in Wandsworth. I told you about it. As I recall, you stood up me and David, Jenna and Lewis to go and eat tapas with Jack.'

Amy peered at the photo on Lisa's phone. There were three plates of olives, cheese and ham in close up. 'Oh God,' she said, 'Why did I think this would be interesting to anyone?'

'Well, you do when it comes to Jack,' said Lisa. She held up her phone to reveal a photo of a man sitting at a café table, the shot taken from the shoulders down. The caption said: 'Jack and I get Sunday brunch.'

Amy got a jolt when she saw it. So that was him. He had a good physique, and dark hair on his arms. 'Why didn't I get his head in?' she bemoaned.

'You were making a point about his socks,' said Lisa. She read out the rest of the caption. '"The new sunshine in my life and his matching socks."'

Amy grimaced. It was nauseating! She looked at the photo of Jack's socks. They were bright yellow. Cheerful.

'What else?' she asked.

'The Lakes,' said Lisa.

'Italian?' asked Amy hopefully.

'Cumbria. You went with Jack for Christmas.' She held

up her phone on which was a picture of a damp Lake Windermere. '"The most romantic lake in the world,"' she read out. '"The perfect place to spend Christmas with the perfect boyfriend."'

Amy tried to remember. She'd sounded happy, so in love. But none of it resonated with her.

'How old is he?' Jenna asked Amy.

'Thirty-two,' Lisa answered for her. 'And he's particularly talented at rugby.'

'How do you know?' asked Amy.

'You put it on here,' said Lisa, indicating her phone. She patted Amy's hand. 'Anything you want to know about your boyfriend, just let me know. He's fabulous. I wish he'd been able to make it.'

'I wish he'd answer my message,' said Amy.

As she glanced back up she caught Jenna watching her, except her friend turned away as soon as their eyes met.

'Why don't you call him now?' asked Lisa.

'What here? On the train?'

'Good a time as any.'

Amy shook her head. 'No thanks. I'm not in the mood to be officially dumped. Actually,' she said on reflection, 'he'll probably just reject my call.' She could see Jenna was staring absently out of the window again, but something made Amy think her friend was listening very carefully to what she was saying. What was up? Or was she imagining it? She remembered the doctor's warning of paranoia.

Then Jenna did something that Amy recognized, a tic that her friend did when she was troubled. She started clicking her fingers. Her hands were tucked under her chin so it was barely noticeable, but Amy caught the soft, restless sound. Something was up, thought Amy, something that Jenna didn't want to talk about.

Amy stood and picked up her bag. 'I'm just going to use the bathroom.'

As she walked down the carriages she tried to ignore the heavy stone in her stomach, but it nestled there, pinning her down with a sadness that she recognized only too well. Whatever it was, whatever the relationship with Jack had been, it hadn't been that successful. He hadn't been in touch and she was facing up to the knowledge she was single. Again.

The toilet was occupied and she had to wait. She gazed around the carriage, eyes resting briefly on the other passengers. There was a family; two small children deeply engrossed in some colouring books while their parents chatted away in French. A group of three young men, sporty looking, their legs sprawled and too long for the seats, lounging back, drinking beers, clearly heading for a ski holiday. There were a few single travellers too, a middle-aged woman reading a book, an older lady tapping on her phone. And then Amy's eyes lingered on someone else. He was sitting about seven rows down the carriage, a man in his twenties, wiry, bearded. He was wearing a cap pulled down low over his eyes. There was something about him that struck Amy as unusual but she couldn't quite work out what. He was hunched in his seat, right up against the window. A black rucksack lay on the table in front of him and he had one arm placed across the top of it. He seemed tense. He wasn't gazing out of the window and he wasn't occupying himself with a book or his phone or anything. It was as if he was waiting for something. She saw him check the time on his watch and this seemed to amplify his nerves. He tapped his spare hand against the arm of the seat, an agitated thrum of fingers. His other hand never left his rucksack.

Amy began to get jittery. She looked around, tried to see if anyone else had noticed the man but they were all occupied in their own lives. She thought of her friends just a carriage away. It was too close. None of them would survive, not if there was something in that man's bag. She glanced back over her shoulder into the next carriage, hoping to see a member of the train crew. She needed to get help. She needed to tell someone what was going on. There were no staff members behind her. She'd have to walk past the man, back through the carriage and into the bar and alert one of the crew there.

Amy started the walk back down the aisle, gripping the tops of the seats to keep her balance. She kept glancing at the man as she approached, getting more frightened as she got closer. She had a vision of herself being blown up, just as she drew level with him. He'd detonate the bomb and she'd be a mess of body parts and blood, unidentifiable. *Don't keep looking at him*, she told herself, as she got even closer. *Don't alert him.* Her heart was racing in her chest and then she felt the train slow. An announcement was made in French and Amy understood enough to know they were drawing into a station. This new information lodged itself into her brain and then she realized in horror that he intended to wait until they were at the next stop, wait for more people to get on in order to inflict maximum damage. Heart in mouth, she sped up until she was right upon him. She couldn't help herself, she looked again, saw his ruck-sack lying dangerously on the table. She hurried on and half ran towards the end of the carriage as the train came alongside the platform. She pushed at the buttons to open the interior carriage doors and rushed back into the bar. Jenna and Lisa looked round, their faces falling as they saw her.

'What's wrong?' asked Lisa.

Amy shot a look over to the barman. She had to tell him first, she couldn't afford to lose any time. She went up to him and blurted: 'There's a man in the next carriage. He's behaving very suspiciously. He has a bag. A rucksack, on the table in front of him.'

The barman looked alarmed. 'You think he is dangerous?'

She nodded. 'He's mid-twenties, navy cap, dark jeans, grey jacket.' The barman was already on the internal phone behind the bar and was talking to someone else in his crew.

Oh God, please let everyone be all right, thought Amy.

'What's going on?' asked Jenna. 'What man?'

'He's in there,' said Amy, pointing back at the carriage. 'Something's definitely not right. And he's got this rucksack. He won't let go of it.'

As she spoke she looked urgently out of the window,

seeing who was getting on. Her heart sank as she watched a number of people climb the steps into the train. And then she froze. Outside, walking down the platform was the man, the rucksack in his arms.

'That's him!' she exclaimed, pointing. She looked back at the barman and another member of the crew who'd just entered the carriage. They rushed over to the window as four gendarmes came running onto the platform. As soon as the police saw the man, they started shouting, their guns raised. Amy tensed, felt herself pull back, waiting for the explosion, but when she looked back at the man, he was crouched to the ground, the bag open at his feet, looking utterly stunned as the four police pointed their weapons at him. A woman in jeans and a green puffa jacket was next to him, dumbfounded and frightened, as the man held a wrapped gift for her in his hands, a gift he'd just taken from his rucksack.

'You weren't to know,' said Lisa. 'You did the right thing, reporting it.'

'I got completely the wrong end of the stick,' said Amy. She was utterly mortified and had apologized profusely. The police had been brusque and moved on their way. The whole experience had left Amy feeling very shaken, not just from thinking she was witnessing a terrorist attack but at the intensity in which she'd believed it. She'd patchworked together a nightmare scenario from nothing more than a man anxious about meeting up with his girlfriend. She'd let her imagination run away with her. She'd been *sweating* as she'd walked back down that carriage; her armpits still felt damp. It had all felt so real.

'You had to say something,' said Jenna. 'Imagine if you hadn't and you'd been right?'

'Anyway, it's fallout from that bump on your head. A bit of paranoia. Don't worry about it,' said Lisa. 'It can happen to anyone. I was at Heathrow once and someone had left their bag against a wall in departures. Imagine! At *Heathrow*. I was about to report it when the owner came back. He'd been in a queue in Pret. Idiot. I ended up going over to him, telling him what I thought, but he told me to fuck off.'

Amy smiled wanly. She knew her friend was only trying to cheer her up. The train staff had laughed, in a relieved way, and they'd gone on their journey. She'd be the talk of the week amongst their colleagues. The English girl and her paranoia. But it wasn't that she cared about. It was the way her mind had behaved in a way that she utterly did not recognize.

SIX

25 February

Amy lay in her bunk in the darkened couchette enjoying the peaceful rhythm of the train. She could see a thin line of light at the edge of the blind at the tiny window and, knowing her friends were still asleep, she quietly pulled herself up and lifted the corner of the navy, logo-marked fabric.

She gasped. The window framed a landscape of imposing snow-covered mountains set against pin-sharp azure skies. Amy stared at the sunlit jagged peaks, majestic and still, sleeping white giants. They dwarfed the forests that grew along their edges, identifiable by smudges of blackish green where snow had become too heavy for the firs and fallen to the ground, revealing glimpses of the trees underneath.

'You have to see this,' she said to the others, unable to contain her excitement.

As she rolled up the blind, Lisa and Jenna came to, blinking in the morning sunshine.

'Wow,' said Lisa, eyes agog.

Jenna pushed her sleep-scruffy hair away from her face

and stared out of the window. Amy noticed she had shadows under her eyes.

The train sped onwards, the scene from their window continually refreshing as they got out of bed and enjoyed a breakfast of croissants, coffee and orange juice in the dining car.

'Where did they get these?' asked Lisa in wonder, holding up the warm flaky pastry with not a cellophane wrap in sight.

'The train stopped at four a.m.,' said Jenna. The other two looked at her.

'You were awake?' asked Amy.

Jenna shrugged. 'Couldn't sleep. Took a stroll. The train crew picked up a delivery. They're freshly baked, apparently.'

At Bourg-St-Maurice, their station, the three women stepped onto the platform, their breath coming in plumes in the cold air. They found a taxi and gawped out of the window as it drove through the town. They crossed a viaduct and craned their necks for a view of the icy, frothing river as it cascaded over its rocky bed, snow stacked up on its banks.

Then the taxi wound its way up the mountain road, the drifts reaching two or three metres, far above the height of their car. On the other side, the road dropped away to a vista of peaks and plateaus, the sun reflecting off so many miles of white it was impossible to take it all in. Amy could feel a power in these mountains, a presence that was both silencing and humbling. Their beauty was seductive, but

Amy knew they were also dangerous. Her family had encountered tragedy here.

'The weather is good, no?' said the taxi driver.

The women murmured their agreement, mesmerized by the views out of the taxi windows.

'Tomorrow, more snow,' he said.

Dotted in the distance they spotted the occasional lodge, some traditionally wooden, the odd one more modern. Each looked tiny, perched on the side of the huge mountains, resplendent in the sun. They passed through Val d'Isère itself with all its tourist hotels and restaurants, and then drove back into the mountains on the other side, leaving the village behind.

'Where's your aunt's place?' asked Lisa.

'About another mile or so. It's a bit remote,' said Amy. 'But wait until you see the view.'

After ten minutes, the taxi driver slowed then turned up a narrow road, the wheels sliding a little on the snow. As the road curved around, a modern masterpiece of glass and steel came into view, nestled into the side of the mountain.

'This is it?' asked Jenna in wonder.

'Yes,' said Amy. Seeing the lodge again brought a smile to her face. It had been a year since she'd visited and her heart lifted at the thought of catching up with Aunt Esme.

'Oh my God,' said Lisa, eyes agog, 'how come you've never invited us here before?'

Amy shrugged. She had asked a few years ago. But both her friends had already booked ski trips with their husbands.

As they pulled into the driveway, Amy's mother, Martha, came to the front door. Amy looked up – it had been summer the previous year when she last remembered seeing her and she found herself curious, as if her mother might have changed and she had no memory of it. But she was the same, petite with expensive blonde highlights, currently covered with a sky-blue cashmere hat. She wore a matching jumper, which she hugged to herself as she welcomed them.

'Girls!' she beamed, her dimples creasing. She had a pretty, girlish look about her, despite being well into her fifth decade. 'It's so nice to see you all.'

Amy was last up the path and she paused as she noticed her mother appraise her.

'You look a little pale, Amy,' said Martha. 'How are you feeling after your accident?'

'Not bad,' said Amy. 'Did you find the keys OK?'

'Yes, in the key safe, as you directed,' said Martha. They kissed each other lightly on the cheek and Amy stiffened slightly when she caught the faint tell-tale aroma of alcohol. She immediately felt the familiar sense of heartbreak. *It's only eleven o'clock in the morning.*

'I'm sorry I didn't visit you in hospital,' said Martha.

Amy brushed off the apology. 'I've already told you, there was no need. I was only admitted for a few days and London is a long way from Dorset.'

'And your memory? Has it returned yet?'

'No.'

Martha put a hand on Amy's arm. 'You poor thing.' She

pulled Amy away from the open door. 'Come in out of the cold. It's positively freezing out there.'

'Well it is winter and we are in the Alps, Mum.'

'No need for sarcasm. Take off your coat.' She held out her hand and hung Amy's jacket in a cupboard in the hallway. Then she waved an arm in the general direction of the house. 'It hasn't changed,' she said. 'Not in ten years.'

'Are you feeling OK, now you're here?' asked Amy.

Martha inhaled bravely. 'It's fine,' she said.

Amy walked across the wooden floor into the living room where her friends were currently looking around wide-eyed, and it was no wonder. Aunt Esme's lodge was special, unique. A huge fireplace, where Martha had lit a fire, held court in the centre of the room. On one side an entire wall of the living room was fitted with floor-to-ceiling windows that framed the half dozen or so pines at the front of the lodge, the snow-covered tops teetering thirty metres out of view. Beyond them they could glimpse a vast landscape of white slopes, glistening in the sun.

'Wow,' exclaimed Lisa, who was walking around, touching the leather sofas and soft throws as she gaped out of the window. 'This house is incredible. Look at that view!'

Over in the far distance, some miles away, was the only slope they could see that was populated. A tiny handful of skiers were on it. Jenna stared. 'What's that?'

'La Face,' said Amy. 'The resort's notorious black run.'

Minute figures silently coursed down the mountain at some speed.

'Is it tough?' asked Jenna.

'Yes,' said Amy. 'Some of those angles are incredibly tight. It's right on the edge of a precipice too. You need to turn fast, it's hell on the thighs.'

'You've skied it?' asked Lisa, eyes agog.

Amy didn't need to look at her mother to know her face had darkened in disapproval.

'When I was thirteen,' she said. 'Esme took me up there.'

'You could have been killed,' muttered Martha.

'But I wasn't,' said Amy calmly.

'No, instead you broke your leg,' said Martha.

'Oh my God,' said Jenna. 'Seriously?'

'Yes. It was a helicopter-off-the-slopes job. Several days off school.' The incident had caused an almighty row when Martha discovered what her sister-in-law had done, taking her niece up to a run that Martha had already pronounced unsuitable, however good Amy's skiing had been. Amy knew her mother had had a point but still suspected she was looking for a reason to fall out with Esme. Martha had never liked her sister-in-law. They'd rubbed each other up the wrong way from the first time they'd met, over three decades ago. Esme thought Martha cared too much about appearances and what other people thought. She saw Martha as uptight, whereas Esme was a rebel and enjoyed breaking the rules. Martha had learned that her sister-in-law had eloped when she was nineteen and married a wealthy man several years older than her. The source of his income had never been disclosed and Martha had always sensed it had dubious origins. Martha had never met François as he'd died of a brain tumour the year before she got together with Peter, Esme's brother. All Martha saw was the spoils of François's wealth: the spectacular lodge, the beautiful classic two-seater sports car, the fine jewellery. And of course Esme's freedom to do as she liked, despite only being thirty years old. At the beginning of her own marriage, Martha and Peter had struggled with money but Peter had insisted they could manage without any help from Esme, even as Martha continued to quietly resent her sister-in-law's wealth.

As a child, Amy was irrepressibly drawn to Esme, not least because she was kind and generous. She welcomed them to her home and insisted they use it as their own. Yes, she might go skinny-dipping in the pool out on the deck on a starlit winter night, but Amy secretly admired her for this, even more so when Esme said she liked to think François was one of the stars she could see and it made her feel close to him. Life could be cruelly short, said Esme, and she'd never had children of her own. Amy always felt her aunt enjoyed taking her under her wing, introducing her to new experiences such as horse-riding, snowboarding or alcohol, or taking her on day trips, many of which Martha disapproved of. Peter had been caught in the middle, but he'd remained unruffled, gently persuading his wife that his sister meant no harm.

The black-run incident, however, was the last straw. Martha refused to visit Esme after that. And then, seven years later, the unthinkable had happened and Peter had died in an accident on the slopes. He'd been visiting Esme alone and it had been when they'd gone out skiing together.

Amy knew the last time her mother had seen Esme was

at her father's funeral. The two women had been worlds apart and there was no desire on Martha's part to resolve their differences. Worse still, Martha made no secret of the fact that she blamed Esme for Peter's death.

Amy continued to visit Esme every year and right now she was dying to catch up with her, but this time Esme had generously gone to stay with her boyfriend, Gabriel, in his lodge across the other side of the valley. To give Martha space, she'd said in her email, the one Amy had found from the previous October. Amy planned to go and see Esme very soon, perhaps when Lisa and Jenna's husbands arrived and she needed a break.

'So are you going to reattempt it while you're here?' asked Jenna, nodding towards La Face.

Amy felt her mother tense. She shook her head. 'Nah. It might not look that fast from here, but you can get up to ninety miles per hour on that run. And one fall is enough for the moment,' she said, gingerly touching the side of her head where it was still a little tender.

'Glad to hear it,' said Lisa, 'or I would've had to put my foot down.' She turned her head and her eyes were drawn to another picture window on the other side of the room. She walked over and gaped at something on the decking below. 'Good God, is that a swimming pool?'

'It certainly is,' said Amy. The lodge lay at the start of a narrow valley, mountains rising up on either side. Far down into the valley was a small wood, the massive pines covered with snow. Beyond that they could see a tiny traditional wooden house, the only other dwelling in sight. In this part of the mountains there were no lifts, no cable cars. The tourists kept away, entranced by all that was on offer in Val d'Isère itself.

'You want a tour of the rest of the house?' asked Amy.

'I'll fix some lunch,' said Martha, heading to the kitchen. 'I hope it's OK, I've already popped myself in one of the bedrooms,' she added lightly, but Amy saw her eyes cloud over and knew that her mother had placed herself at the front of the lodge where she couldn't look out over the valley.

'Are you OK?' she whispered.

Martha nodded. 'I might open us some wine for lunch.'

As Amy watched her mother leave the room, her stomach twisted with worry.

SEVEN

25 February

Each of the bedrooms had a balcony with a breathtaking view. From some of them the women could reach out and touch the pines, heavy with snow. Lisa grabbed a handful and threw it at Amy, hitting her full in the face.

'Truce!' yelled Lisa almost immediately, while Amy spluttered and laughed.

'I'll get you back,' Amy promised.

'These vistas,' said Jenna breathless, 'they're so inspiring.'

'Did you bring your camera?' asked Amy.

'Of course.'

'Jenna had an exhibition,' said Lisa. 'In January.'

'You did?' asked Amy, delighted. 'I'm sorry, I can't remember. Did I come? Was it amazing?'

It was a moment before Jenna answered. 'Yes, you came,' she said. 'And it was a success. Mostly,' she added coolly as she walked away, back into the bedroom.

Amy nodded but felt she was treading on dangerous ground and didn't understand why. She followed Jenna. 'So, are you happy to have this room?'

'It's perfect.'

Amy looked around. It had hand-built wardrobes, a soft carpet underfoot and luxurious throws on the bed. There was a view from every window – you could even look out at the slopes from the en-suite bathtub. Except, like the others, the room had a slightly unkempt feel to it. There was dust on more than one surface and Amy thought that Esme's cleaner must be getting a bit slack.

So now everyone had a place to sleep. The one room they'd left alone during the tour was Esme's. Amy had peeked in and seeing all her aunt's things there had made her miss her even more, but that reunion would have to come later. As with the other rooms, the curtains had been closed; Amy thought about opening them but decided against, reasoning that her aunt might prefer to leave them that way while she was away.

'Where's your aunt staying?' asked Jenna.

Amy pointed out of the landing window across the valley to the wooden lodge in the far distance, smoke rising from its chimney. 'Her boyfriend's. She and Gabriel have probably just got back from the slopes and they're on the fresh coffee and pain au chocolat right about now.'

'Talking of which,' said Lisa, 'I'm starving.'

Amy lingered at the window before going downstairs. Beyond Gabriel's lodge she could see the start of the Southern Slope, a three-kilometre run that went down into Val d'Isère. It was where her father had died, almost exactly ten years ago. It had been a terrible accident but, despite what her mother thought, Esme wasn't to blame.

Nevertheless, her aunt had not skied it since. Amy sighed and looked back at Gabriel's lodge. Part of her wished she could go and visit Esme now, but instead she turned and followed her friends down to lunch.

Martha had made some soup and served it with warm baguettes. 'There wasn't anything in at all,' she said, a note of disapproval in her voice. 'Not even milk! I had to call a taxi to take me back down to the resort.'

'Aren't there any shops nearby?' asked Jenna.

'Nothing within walking distance,' said Amy. 'Gabriel's lodge is our only human contact, and he's at least a mile away. Val d'Isère itself is a two-hour walk.'

After lunch they took a taxi into town to get kitted up with skis and boots, then they tried the slopes. Everyone was rusty and Amy was under strict instructions not to overdo it, so they stuck to the green runs. Fresh snow had fallen the night before and the sky was a pin-sharp azure blue. As Amy skied down the mountain, the sun lit the snow crystals ahead of her and her muscle memory began to reawaken. Soon she was becoming more fluent in her turns and relaxed into it, enjoying the crisp rasping sound of her skis as they cut into the snow. Exhilarated after several runs, they decided to head back to the lodge where Martha got out the large slices of *gateaux aux chocolat* that she had bought from the patisserie that morning. She also opened another bottle of wine, something that Amy tried to ignore.

'Oh dear,' said Lisa with faux concern as she looked into the empty cake box, 'there's none left for the boys tomorrow.'

Martha sat up in excitement. 'The boys! What time are they arriving?'

'Their flight gets in at six in the evening,' said Jenna.

'And then I'll finally get to meet . . .' Martha did a delicate drum roll on the coffee table and looked at Amy, 'Doctor Jack Stewart.'

Amy's forkful of cake paused halfway to her mouth. So when she'd told her friends her boyfriend couldn't make it, she'd omitted to fill in her mother. Somehow Amy knew why.

'Actually, Mum . . .' she started, noting both her friends had suddenly become very interested in the contents of their wine glasses, 'Jack can't make it after all.'

Her mother was confused. 'Can't make it how?'

'He had to work.'

'But it's your birthday. Your *thirtieth* birthday.'

I know, Amy wanted to say, *you'd have thought he could have sorted something,* but deep down she knew why. 'The fact is, he hasn't been in touch for over a week and I'm pretty certain he's broken up with me.'

'You don't know that,' said Lisa quickly.

Martha's face was flooded with shock. 'It's over *already?*' she said in dismay. 'But you've only been dating three months!'

Amy shrugged.

'But why has he broken up with you?' asked Martha.

'I've no idea, Mum. I don't remember.'

'Surely you can recollect *something?*'

'No. Nothing at all.'

'But that's impossible.'

'No, it's not. I've lost my memory.' Amy tapped the side of her head. 'Nothing there since late August. Jack and I got together some time in November.'

'You see, you do remember!' Martha was triumphant.

'No, Mum, I know because it's in my diary. *November twenty-first. Meet J for dinner.*'

'Anyone for more wine?' asked Lisa, getting up and heading over to the fridge.

'Thank you. I think I need one,' said Martha, holding out her glass. She looked at Lisa and Jenna in disbelief. 'Can you believe this?'

'It's quite normal to lose your memory after a head injury,' said Lisa. 'I'm sure Amy will remember everything over the next few weeks or so.'

'But by then it will be too late,' said Martha.

'Too late for what?' ventured Jenna, but Amy already knew where her mother's train of thought was going.

'To find out what went wrong and make it better,' said Martha.

'You mean, what *I* did wrong,' said Amy.

'That's not what I said.'

'It's what you meant though, isn't it?'

'I just think it's a shame. All those wasted years. It's a pity you didn't manage to hang on to Richard.'

'Mum, that was years ago. And I didn't want to hang on to him. It was me who broke up with him. As I've told you several times before,' she added under her breath.

'Richard,' mused Jenna. 'The erstwhile editor of the

student union paper. Didn't he go on to become some hotshot journalist?'

'He was the ambitious sort,' said Martha. 'I always think it's the little things that keep a relationship going. Small gestures that show you care. A love letter in a lunch box. An ironed shirt hanging in the wardrobe for work the next day.'

'You think if I'd ironed Richard's shirts we'd still be together?' drawled Amy.

'You're very scathing,' said Martha. 'But you'd be wise to listen sometimes.'

Amy was fizzing with irritation but bit her tongue.

'You know,' continued Martha, 'I met your father at university and we still made it work, despite being young.'

'I wasn't ready to settle down. You know this.'

Martha waved a hand. 'Well, it's too late now anyway.'

'Oh?' asked Jenna, ignoring Amy's warning frown.

'He married the daughter of a friend of mine,' said Martha. 'Harriet, her name is. And they've just had their first. Born last November.' She looked at Amy. 'You won't remember – I told you all this over one of our lunches – but their baby is an absolutely adorable little girl.'

'Good for them,' said Amy.

'Aren't you even a little bit . . .' started Martha.

'What?'

'Never mind.'

But Amy knew what she meant. Disappointed. Regretful. Wondering what might have been. The truth was there had been countless Saturday nights when Amy had been alone in her flat, while what seemed like every friend she had was out on a date with a boyfriend. She missed companionship. She missed touch. Sometimes she would go home from work on a Friday and know she'd not speak to another human being until the following Monday.

'Richard was too short for Amy anyway,' said Lisa, and Amy threw her a grateful look.

'Remind me again, how tall was he?' asked Jenna.

'Barely came up to my eyebrows,' said Amy, indicating.

'I've always envied your Amazonian stature,' said Lisa.

'She takes after her father,' said Martha.

'It must come in useful around all those men at work,' said Lisa. 'You can eyeball them when they behave particularly obnoxiously.'

Amy was one of only two women who worked in the small, Alpha male-dominated law firm that specialized in litigation. Her male colleagues got off on handling the clients with the biggest multimillion-pound settlements, but she preferred cases where she fought for the little guy. The one who'd been shafted by cutthroat corporations. She had a strong sense of righting an injustice, which carried over into her own life. In her first all-day company meeting, the lunch delivery had been late. The lawyers were starting to grumble and one wondered out loud when it was coming.

A brash, entitled man, as junior as her, had replied: 'Amy will know. What time are the sandwiches being delivered, Amy?'

It rankled. Amy felt her cheeks flush with fury and humiliation. No one else seemed to have noticed how sexist his comment was. In fact, when she failed to deliver a response, heads lifted from tablets and notepads, curious as to why she hadn't spoken.

'I don't know,' she said, 'but I will consult with my genitals as you seem to think they are blessed with a superior knowledge when it comes to catering.'

Their faces were a picture. Surprise, followed by a flash of humour – mostly. The lawyer who'd nominated her was deeply affronted, more so when his male colleagues laughed at him. But he was careful what he said from then on. Inevitably, there had been other incidents, but Amy always called them out on their bullshit. It had earned her a grudging respect. She took pride in knowing she could spot an idiot when she saw one. She might be perennially single but at least she never fell for a scumbag.

'I'm surprised you haven't found someone at work,' said Martha. 'Although you always wear such high heels, you must positively tower over most of them.'

'I don't think it's my heels that's stopped them asking me out,' said Amy.

'No, I don't suppose it is.'

Amy stiffened. 'What do you mean by that?'

'Sorry?'

'It sounded as if you thought there was another reason why the men I work with don't ask me out.'

Martha stayed silent.

'Go on, Mum. I want to know.'

'Well, it's hard for you. I understand.'

'What's hard for me?'

'All that business, all that having to be tough, cultivating a hard outer shell.'

'I have to be resilient, yes. But what does that have to do with my ability to be desirable?'

Martha threw her arms wide, spilling a drop of wine on the floor. She didn't notice. 'Darling, you're extremely desirable. Look at you. Beautiful. It's not what you look like, it's . . . well, sometimes I feel that you find it hard to let people – men – in.'

Amy bristled. 'Sorry?'

'You can be a bit cool, a bit closed off. Men prefer their women to be warm and inviting.'

'Hang on, these men I work with, are they not cool and closed off?'

'Well yes, but they have to be. More decisive, strong.'

'So a man is strong and decisive and I'm cool and closed off?' Amy was struggling to keep a lid on her temper. 'Mum, it sounds as if you've just stepped out of the nineteen fifties.'

'Well there's no need for that,' said Martha in an injured tone.

Amy clenched her teeth. She was furious but a part of what her mother had said had touched a raw nerve. She was who she was. But did that make her ineligible? Destined to be single? But why should she change? Why should a strong woman who knew her own mind be off-putting to a man?

In the silence, Lisa and Jenna, who had been pinned to their seats during the disagreement, suddenly roused themselves, keen to get some space. Jenna stood first.

'I think I'll go and get my camera. Take some shots before the light fades.'

'And I need to unpack,' said Lisa, following Jenna out of the room.

After they'd gone, Martha got to her feet, a tad unsteady. She came over to sit next to Amy, a distance between them on the sofa.

'I didn't mean to cause a row. I just want to see you happy, that's all.'

Amy looked at her mother, at her eyes clouded by disappointment – and was that pity? Oh God, now she had her mother feeling sorry for her. Amy quickly brushed any self-pity aside. There was no way she was heading down that slippery slope.

'I am happy, Mum.'

Martha pulled a sceptical face. 'And I really didn't mean to go on,' she said. 'I was a bit upset to hear about Jack, that's all. I liked him.'

'You never met him.'

Martha sounded wistful. 'But I liked who you talked to me about.'

And there it was. Amy realized the introduction of Jack must have opened a bridge between her mother and herself where conversation was less strained. They must have had chats that were doused with optimism, where Martha didn't see her daughter as a failure. She couldn't remember any of them, but the look of sadness on her mother's face told her everything.

Amy felt a tug to her heart – along with a sense of

deep-rooted exasperation. The lack of a son-in-law and potential grandchildren to talk about to her wide circle of friends was a constant source of loss for Martha. And of course it was exacerbated by the fact Amy was Martha's only immediate family since her father had died.

'Mum, I know it's hard being here . . . in this house but . . . do you think you could ease up a little on the wine?'

'I beg your pardon?'

'I don't mean to upset you, but it's not good for you.'

'This place brings back bad memories, you know that,' said Martha, indignant. 'And that woman is responsible for your father's death. Taking him on that awful slope.'

'Mum, it was Dad's decision. They both decided to race.'

'Esme probably persuaded him. You know how reckless she is.'

'He was a grown man. He could make up his own mind.'

Her mother looked at her, tight-lipped. 'Are we getting a visit from your aunt while we're here?'

'I think she's planning on giving us our space. Although I intend to go and see her, obviously.'

Martha nodded.

'I'm sorry,' said Amy rubbing her temples. 'I think I'll go and have a little lie-down. Do you mind? Only I feel the beginning of a headache coming on.'

'Of course. Can I get you anything? Some paracetamol?'

'I'm fine, thanks.'

As Amy climbed the stairs and walked along the landing, she could hear Lisa on the phone in her room. She heard her friend laugh softly, her voice full of intimacy, and Amy knew she must be on the phone to her husband, David. She couldn't hear what was being said but the tone conjured a whole world of togetherness that Amy didn't have.

Amy shut the door to her own room and lay on the bed. She looked over to the other side, laid her arm across its emptiness. Could she have done something to stop the relationship falling apart? Had she pushed Jack away? Been cool and closed off? She suddenly felt a wave of shame and self-loathing. She couldn't even keep a boyfriend in the first flush of romance. Amy rolled onto her other side and a thought struck her. She and Jack had been dating three months so *they must have had sex*. She sighed heavily. She couldn't even remember any sex. It was so bloody unfair!

Her eyes fell on the bedside cabinet, and her phone lying there. She picked it up and, despite telling herself no good would come of over-analysing, of trying to find something where there was nothing, she started to go through all her messages with Jack in the hope of ascertaining what might have caused his silence. There were no clues whatsoever. His last message had been the one he'd sent saying how sorry he was he couldn't make it to France. Amy was surprised they hadn't made arrangements to meet up the weekend before the trip. It seemed odd they hadn't even agreed to go for a drink or anything. She looked at her call log, aware she was being desperate but unable to stop herself. Were they supposed to have met but she was caught up in the accident instead?

There were no missed calls from Jack the Friday night

of her accident. She was about to fling the phone onto the bed when something caught her eye. Amy frowned at the screen, puzzled by what she saw. Friday, 19 February, 7.39 p.m. The time of her accident. She'd been making a call that had lasted only thirty seconds. So it more than likely hadn't been answered. It would have shown up as a missed call on the recipient's phone.

Why had she been calling Jenna the exact moment of her accident and, more to the point, why hadn't Jenna mentioned it?

EIGHT

25 February

The room was suffused with a fading light when Amy woke. She sat up with a start, taking a moment to recall where she was. She remembered having a headache, realized she must have fallen asleep.

She padded downstairs to the kitchen, where Lisa and Martha were making dinner.

'Good nap?' asked Martha.

'Great,' said Amy. 'The headache's gone. Where's Jenna?'

'Still out taking photos,' said Lisa. She nodded towards the window at the sunset turning the mountains pink. 'Don't they call this the golden hour?'

Amy put on the radio; an upbeat pop song was playing. 'Can I help?' she asked, observing the dinner preparations.

'Chop some spuds if you like,' said Lisa. 'So what shall we do tomorrow? It's only us girls until the boys arrive in the evening.'

'Isn't there snow forecast for tomorrow?' asked Martha.

'Not until later on,' said Amy. 'Do you know what I've always wanted to experience? Paragliding over the mountains.'

Martha inhaled sharply. 'Oh my goodness. Why do you always have to have a death wish?'

Lisa smiled. 'That sounds incredible.' She nudged Martha's arm. 'Come on, think of the views! I bet Jenna would be up for that too.'

'Talking of Jenna,' said Amy, noticing the rapidly darkening sky, 'shouldn't she be back by now?'

Lisa picked up her phone. 'I'll give her a call, see if she's on her way.' She dialled then frowned. 'It's gone straight to voicemail.'

'Weird,' said Amy.

'Maybe she's run out of battery,' said Martha. 'You know how they drain so much quicker in the cold.'

'If she's got no battery, the torch on her phone won't work.' Amy jumped down from the breakfast bar. 'I'll go and look outside.' In the hallway she pulled on her snow boots and jacket and opened the front door. There was no one coming up the driveway. The light was fading fast and Amy switched on the outside lamp. It didn't illuminate much beyond a few metres from the lodge. Amy glanced down at the snow. She saw footprints and the tyre marks from their arrival that morning. Further down she could just make out a set of footprints heading away from the lodge – Jenna's from when she set off. Amy shivered. It was at least minus five degrees outside.

'Jenna?' she called, but there was no reply. Her voice sounded muffled, absorbed by the snow. She tried again, louder, but there was no sign of her friend.

She went back inside.

'Any luck?' asked Lisa.

'No. Once it's dark, it's really easy to get lost. I think we should follow Jenna's footprints, see if we can find her.'

'It *is* getting dark,' said Martha, a worried glance at the window.

'I'll go,' said Lisa.

'It's all right,' said Amy, 'I know the terrain around here.'

'OK, I'll go with you.'

'Honestly—'

Lisa held up a hand in protest. 'You're not doing it alone.'

'I'll come too,' said Martha.

'No, Mum. Someone needs to stay here in case Jenna comes back.'

Amy went into the hall, Lisa following.

'You will be careful, won't you?' asked Martha. 'And call me the minute you find her. Or I'll just be sitting here worrying.'

'Course,' said Amy. She looked at Lisa, who was zipping up her jacket. 'You ready?'

At that moment the front door was flung open with a crash and a blast of cold air whorled around the hallway. Amy spun around to see Jenna in the doorway, her camera dangling from her neck, and a man's arm around her waist as she leaned on him. She looked exhausted and shaken.

'Hey guys,' she said. 'Guess who I found?' Jenna nodded towards the man holding her up. 'Seems like Doctor Jack Stewart could make it after all.'

NINE

25 February

There was a small hiatus while this announcement filtered through. Amy was too stunned to speak. He'd come? The boyfriend who'd not been able to make it, the guy she'd thought had dumped her; he'd actually come? Her brain couldn't keep up.

Martha was the first to break into a smile. 'Jack?' She looked over to her daughter, incredulous. 'Amy's Jack?'

'I would shake your hand, but I fear my patient's ankle won't hold up if I let go,' said Jack, smiling.

'You've hurt yourself,' said Lisa. She went to the other side of Jenna and together she and Jack helped her into the living room and into a chair.

'I think it's only a sprain,' said Jack.

'I'd tripped on a rock,' said Jenna, 'hidden by snow, just down the mountain there. I could barely get up, let alone walk. I guess it was lucky Jack came along – I tried to call you, but my battery's gone flat.'

'Nice to meet you, Jack,' said Lisa. 'I'd better go and get some ice for that ankle.' As she headed to the kitchen, she gave a surreptitious wink to Amy. A wink that said: *See! He hadn't broken up with you.*

'Well, what a stroke of luck,' said Martha, delighted. She turned to Jack. 'I thought you had to work.'

'Managed to change my shifts right at the last minute,' said Jack. 'I wasn't sure if I could get a flight and then . . .' he looked at Amy, a big smile on his face, 'well it was only a few hours so I thought I'd surprise you.'

Amy met his eyes. She took in the smile and the hat-flattened curly dark hair that he'd roughed back up again. The kind, open face, the bright blue eyes. The sporty physique and the six foot height of him.

She'd never seen this man before in her life.

TEN

25 February

'Well of course that's what it feels like,' whispered Lisa. The two women were huddled together on the other side of the kitchen to Martha and Jack. 'You've lost your memory,' she continued, 'you just don't remember him, that's all.' She snuck a look over. 'Although how you could forget *that* piece of handsomeness I don't know.'

'You're not helping,' said Amy.

'Sorry, sorry. What I'm trying to say in a professional, medical way is that your amnesia means there'll be a short-term period where things feel strange. Your memories will return in time. Maybe now Jack's here, it might trigger some of them to come back sooner.'

Amy looked across at Jack, who was setting the table under Martha's supervision. Jack. Her boyfriend. Lisa was right, he was very attractive. She felt a flutter of pride before dismissing it, embarrassed. But she couldn't take her eyes off him. This was the man she'd been going out with the last three months. If only she could remember *something*. Not a relayed tale from her girlfriends but something herself, a private recollection that only she herself owned. He looked over then and smiled and she felt herself blushing. Oh God, this was ridiculous! Lifting her head high, she smiled back.

'Right,' said Martha, 'we're ready.' She nodded across to Lisa. 'You want to help me get the injured party in?'

As her mother and friend left the room to help Jenna, Amy found herself alone with Jack. She felt awkward, shy even, not really knowing what to say to him.

'I'm a terrible oaf with bad hygiene who collects train engine numbers. Oh, and I snore loudly,' said Jack.

Amy looked at him in horror, then immediately saw the glint in his eye and burst out laughing.

'Sorry . . .' she said, not quite knowing how to explain her predicament.

'It's OK. I know you don't remember me,' he said.

Amy caught herself blushing for the second time that evening. 'I've tried,' she said, holding up her hands in defeat.

He came over to her and she caught the scent of his aftershave. It wasn't unpleasant. *Please*, she begged inwardly, *something. Anything?* But her mind stubbornly refused to relinquish its hidden knowledge.

'How are you?' he asked, a small frown appearing on his face as he took in her bruised cheekbone.

'Much better. Thanks.'

'I was so sorry to hear about your accident. Looks like you took quite a fall.'

Amy shrugged. 'I don't remember.'

'So would you have still asked me out?' asked Jack, smiling. 'Seeing me now, as if for the first time?'

'It was *me* who asked *you* out?'

'I was delighted. And if you hadn't, I wasn't coming off that phone call unless I'd asked you.'

Amy was puzzled. 'What phone call?'

'You have a scar on your right knee,' said Jack.

Amy looked down, recalled the scar whose history she couldn't place. 'Yes.'

'We met on Monday, sixteenth November. Outside Waterloo station. Both of us were heading home from work, it was busy, rush hour, you were a little ahead of me and I saw you trip and when I asked if you were OK, I noticed you'd cut your leg. Despite my medical advice that you could do with some stitches, you insisted you were fine. So I'm afraid I took advantage and, seeing as you refused to see your own doctor, I asked if I could call you in a couple of days to check you were all right. You gave me your number, I rang you, and during the conversation you asked me out.'

'I did? Wow.' Amy suddenly felt a little overwhelmed. It was strange hearing her life retold to her by a stranger.

He took her hand and gently squeezed it. It was a kind gesture but Amy couldn't help feeling a bit uncomfortable that this man she didn't recognize was holding her hand. *You know him*, she reminded herself.

'It's OK. Your memory will come back,' said Jack. 'And until it does, I can tell you everything. I'll get to relive all our dates.'

'Were they good?'

'The best. But this,' he indicated between them both, 'can go as slow as you like. I'm just really happy to be here for

59

your birthday. I know you said you didn't mind me having to work but . . .'

'Was I lying?'

'You were very gracious about it.'

Amy secretly felt enormously relieved. She wasn't the demanding career type her mother thought she was after all. At least not all the time.

'Tell me something . . .' She trailed off, unsure.

'What?'

'It's fine.'

'Please? Don't hold back.'

May as well then. Amy watched his face carefully as she spoke. 'Did I ever iron your shirts?'

He laughed – it was a nice laugh, loud and spontaneous. 'Why would you do that?'

She shrugged. 'I don't know.'

'No, you are a fully emancipated woman and that's one of the reasons I'm so attracted to you.'

She glowed inside then. It was one of the nicest compliments anyone had ever paid her.

'Make way for the invalid,' called Martha as Jenna hobbled through the door, escorted on both sides.

Amy noted how Jack jumped up, went over to help Jenna into her seat at the end of the table. Found her another chair to prop her ankle up on. *That's nice*, Amy thought, *nice he cares.*

As Martha prepared to serve up the beef casserole and mashed potatoes, she directed Jack to take the seat facing her, which meant he'd be next to Amy.

'Great casserole, Mrs Kennedy,' said Jack.

'Call me Martha, please.'

Jack smiled. 'It's so good to finally meet you all. Amy's told me so much about you.'

Martha was instantly wary, as was Amy herself. What had she said?

'Oh yes?' enquired Martha.

'It all relating to how great a mum you are.'

Martha was surprised, touched by his words. 'That's very kind.' She glanced at Amy, acknowledging the rare compliment from her daughter.

'In fact, now I get to meet you all,' continued Jack, 'I feel I owe you an apology.'

Eyebrows rose around the table, none more so than Amy's own.

'I know this meet has been a long time coming but, aside from my hospital shifts keeping me tied up at unsociable hours, whenever I did get a free weekend, I'm afraid I selfishly wanted Amy to myself.'

'Well, we're just delighted to finally meet you,' said Martha.

'And you've kept us hanging for so long, we want to know all about you,' said Lisa.

He laughed. 'Honestly, I'm not that interesting. You know I'm a doctor . . . I've been at St Thomas's for three years. I live in Battersea . . . got a small flat on the edge of the park. No pets, haven't got the time sadly, although I would like a dog one day. I like to play rugby at the weekend, if I get a chance . . .' he held out his hands modestly, reaching the end of his list.

'Family?' asked Lisa.

Amy was about to chastise her friend – this wasn't the Spanish Inquisition – and then she realized she didn't know the answer and wanted to.

'Both parents passed away,' said Jack.

'I'm sorry,' said Martha. 'Was it recent?'

'No, a few years ago.'

'Any siblings?' asked Jenna. 'Oh, hold on, Amy told us. Yes, that's right, you have a sister.'

He smiled. 'I do. Clara. She's three years younger than me.'

'Oh right,' said Jenna. 'Thought she was older.' She looked at Amy. 'Isn't that what you said?'

'Did I?' said Amy. She had no idea.

'That's what she likes to think sometimes,' said Jack. He picked up the bottle of wine. 'Anyone for a top-up?'

After dinner they played cards and Amy found moments to sneak a look at her boyfriend. She was relieved to realize that she fancied him. He was easy to get along with and she liked the way he made an effort to be a part of their group. He shuffled and dealt the cards, he teased Martha when he had a better hand than her, making her laugh. Lisa also seemed to get along with him but occasionally Amy would look up and catch Jenna watching both Jack and her. Then Jenna would glance away, avoiding eye contact.

Amy got up to put another log on the fire and Jack smiled at her. Suddenly it didn't matter that she couldn't remember their early dates; he knew her, even if she didn't know him – yet – and she was enjoying his company.

The game finished and Jenna won, for the third time in a row. Lisa stood and yawned, stretching her arms to the ceiling. 'Right, time to call it a night,' she said. 'I'm done in.'

Amy was brought up short by the prospect of bedtime. Where was Jack going to sleep?

Lisa hovered, looking at Amy; clearly the same thought about the sleeping arrangements had occurred to her.

'Er . . .' started Jack. 'A sofa will do me. I mean, I wouldn't expect—'

'There's a spare room,' said Amy decisively. And there was. It was a little smaller but perfectly serviceable. It was across the landing from her own.

'Great!'

'I'll show you,' said Amy.

She led the way upstairs, Jack following with his bag that he'd rescued from the mountain path after helping Jenna back.

Amy pushed open the door to Jack's bedroom. The bed was unmade but she went to look in the wardrobe and found sheets. As she moved over to the bed, Jack took them from her. 'I can do that.' They stood there for a moment, not knowing how to say goodnight.

'Thanks for not kicking me out in the snow,' he said, and she laughed. 'See you in the morning,' he added. She felt a tug of disappointment, but then he kissed her gently on the cheek.

'See you tomorrow,' she said, then pulled his door shut behind her as she left.

Lying in her own bed, she stretched out, still dazed by the evening's events. She seemed to have a boyfriend. No, she didn't *seem* to, she *did*. And he was quite a catch. She allowed a small grin to appear on her face. There was a newness to her thoughts, an optimism. It was a sensation she hadn't felt in a very long time and it was wonderful.

ELEVEN

26 February

'Amy should go first,' said Lisa. 'Seeing as this is her birthday trip.'

All eyes swivelled to Amy: Lisa, Jack, her mother and the paragliding instructor, Christophe. Amy felt a rush of excitement as she was strapped to Christophe for their tandem flight.

'You ready?' she called back to him.

'Hang on,' said Christophe, 'I'm supposed to ask you that.'

Amy grinned and then released her snow plough and they were gathering speed down the Solaise slope until the inflated canopy lifted them up and she was airborne. As the edge of the mountain fell away, she was suddenly rushed upwards into a thermal and her stomach flipped over. She glanced down below to see everyone craning their necks up at her, their faces becoming smaller and smaller. She could just make out Lisa getting ready to take off with the other instructor. Amy lifted her head. The sky was the most brilliant blue and it felt as if she could touch it. She soared over the snow-clad mountains with only the sound of the wind and a faint whistling from the wires that stretched up to the canopy for company.

'Everything OK?' asked Christophe.

Amy gave a thumbs up. She could see vast miles of slopes, pristine in their whiteness, that eventually dropped down to the village of Val d'Isère, its tiny houses held carefully in the valley bowl. The whole effect was so beautiful, the light so crystal clear she thought it might ring out if it were tapped by a celestial finger. The thermals tipped them and they dipped like a bird, Christophe expertly handling the canopy as they swirled over the white jagged canvas below.

Then something truly breathtaking happened. A bird of prey flew up from behind them, still a distance away but she could see its golden plumage, its amber eye as it hovered in the thermal, scouting for prey below.

'It's a golden eagle,' said Christophe in her ear, 'symbol of intelligence, courage, strength and immortality. She can detect her prey from three kilometres away.'

It was exhilarating. Amy soared alongside the eagle and it felt as if they were flying together.

'They're an endangered species,' continued Christophe, 'like many of the birds here in the mountains. Poachers,' he added ruefully.

Amy watched as it wheeled around in front of them, gradually getting closer. It was magnificent. Its wingspan must have been two metres and it glided effortlessly, belonging to the air. A few seconds later it turned and was gone, a mere speck in the distance.

'Hold tight,' said Christophe, and she saw they were descending. Gradually they sank towards the earth and Christophe reminded her about her skis and she straightened them and before she knew it she was touching the snow with a soft landing and they gently skied to a stop.

'You like?' asked Christophe.

Amy was breathless with wonder. 'It was amazing,' she said, knowing the words were completely inadequate for what she'd just experienced.

'You chose the right morning,' said Christophe. 'The snow is here later.'

Amy looked up as Lisa landed a short distance from them and then the two instructors took the cable car back up the mountain to fly down with Jack and Martha.

'It's such a shame Jenna's missing this,' said Lisa, her eyes shining.

'Yes. I feel bad leaving her,' said Amy.

'She insisted. She didn't expect us to cancel this because she's hurt her ankle. And she's got the luxurious lodge to herself for a couple of hours.'

Amy nodded. Chose her words carefully. 'Has she been a bit preoccupied since we've come away, do you think?'

'In what way?'

'I don't know. She just seemed a little distant on the train and once or twice at the lodge.'

'Not that I noticed. You think there's something up?'

Amy quickly brushed it off. 'No, I'm probably misreading it. You know Jack's hired a go-pro so he can record the flight for Jenna to see?'

Lisa looked at her. 'What a sweet thing to do. I like him, Amy, I really do. And all that stuff this morning . . .'

'What stuff?'

'Getting up and cleaning the kitchen from last night. He did the dishes,' she emphasized. 'Without being asked!'

'Is this something special?' asked Amy, a wry note in her voice.

Lisa patted her arm. 'Oh my dear girl. You have no idea. It's not that they don't want to, well, sometimes they don't, but it's also that they don't even *see*. Trust a woman who's been living with her husband for six long years.'

Amy pulled a sympathetic face. Sometimes it felt alien, the way her friends spoke about the day-to-day machinations of their relationships. Simple, monotonous things that she couldn't even begin to imagine. She'd never lived with a man, so didn't know what it was like. She hadn't even been on holiday with one, well, not until this trip. And the more the years had gone on without either of those things happening, the more she'd felt detached from her friends and the rest of the 'normal' population, until there had been times she'd felt she was so bent out of shape she'd never fit in.

'And then,' added Lisa, eyes agog, 'he made us all breakfast!' She looked up. 'Here he is, Superman himself,' she said in admiration.

Amy smiled and watched as her Superman came in to land, her mother close behind. But there was one thing about Jack that had occurred to her when she woke that morning that didn't quite add up. Something she couldn't make sense of that left her feeling uncomfortable. She wanted to bring it up with him but wasn't sure how to phrase it.

'That was easily the most terrifying thing I've ever done,' said Martha, as she skied over to them.

Amy thought her mother looked truly alive: her skin was glowing, her eyes were bright. 'But did you enjoy it, Mum?'

'I was flying,' she said. 'I was actually flying.'

Amy's heart lifted. She felt relief that perhaps this trip wasn't completely tainted for her mother after all.

They continued the holiday vibe back at the lodge, outside in the infinity pool, the air temperature minus nine but the water heated to forty degrees, steam rising off the surface.

Amy swam to the edge and gazed out over the valley, the mountains rising either side of her. It was a vast white wilderness, empty, desolate almost with folds of snow undulating over the slopes. Grey rock protruded where it was particularly jagged and the snow was unable to take hold. In the far distance anonymous, hostile peaks pierced the blue sky.

'This is amazing,' called Lisa from the other side of the pool. 'We're sandwiched between two stacks of mountains. Hey, you don't get avalanches here, do you? Only I don't fancy being in this pool with tonnes of snow thundering down towards me.'

Amy smiled. 'There have been a few, but nothing as dramatic as you're describing. Anyway, the weather's not right for an avalanche.'

'No? What is avalanche weather?'

'Big changes. A freeze followed by a thaw.'

'Well it had better stay cold then,' said Lisa. 'Cold and beautiful while I'm in this lovely warm pool.'

'Your aunt has very good taste in alpine lodges,' said Jack, swimming up beside Amy. She noticed his broad, muscled shoulders as he pulled himself up to the edge of the pool, felt herself staring, unused to being up close to male naked skin. God, he was attractive. He clocked her looking and she gave an embarrassed smile and found she was blushing like a gauche schoolgirl. *He is your boyfriend*, she reproached herself silently, *and you've seen it all before, even if you can't remember.*

'I'll tell her when I see her,' she said.

'Oh yes?'

'She's staying with her boyfriend.' Amy pointed across the valley at Gabriel's lodge, way off in the distance. 'For the week we're here. I'm planning on visiting, maybe in a day or two.'

'I'd love to meet her,' said Jack. 'If that's OK? Would you take me with you when you go?'

His request caught Amy on the hop, but then she thought, *why not?* 'Sure.'

'Thanks. Is there anything else you're planning while you're here?'

She looked at him, puzzled. 'Like what?'

'I don't know. Visiting any other friends or relatives?'

'There's only Aunt Esme and Gabriel. I don't know anyone else.' Amy sighed. 'At least, I don't think I do. I have no idea what happened in the last six months of my life.'

'Still no sign of your memory returning?'

Amy shook her head, despondent. Her gaze fell to the edge of the pool, where Jack was holding on to the side and she caught sight of something she'd noticed the night before, at dinner. 'Your finger,' she said. 'What happened?'

Jack lifted his hand, highlighting the missing tip of his ring finger. 'This?' he said. 'Frostbite. Way back before I started med school, I took a few months off to do a ski season as a chalet guy at Klosters. Got myself into a bit of trouble on the mountain.'

'Oh yeah?'

'One of my party went missing. His girlfriend came running to me, hysterical, so I went out to find him. I searched for hours, stupidly lost a glove in the dark. Mountain rescue ended up picking me off the mountain, not the guest.'

'So . . . what happened to the guest?'

Jack's eyes briefly darkened. 'Him? He was in the bar the entire time. On his second bottle of champagne by the time I was taken to hospital. Turns out the whole thing was a mistake. He'd forgotten to tell his girlfriend he'd arranged to meet up with some old school friends.'

'Oh my God. I hope he was grateful.'

'Never saw him again. He left the next day.'

'Bloody hell. Not even an acknowledgement?'

'Nope.' Jack shrugged. 'But on the bright side, I was lucky a bit of frostbite was the only injury I came away with.'

She looked at it again, finding it slightly unnerving now she was close up.

He laughed. 'Is it off-putting? You didn't mind before.'

'No, no,' she said quickly, then smiled. 'OK, so I'm a bit squeamish. But your finger is . . . lovely.'

'I wouldn't call it that,' he said. 'But it does have its uses.' He waggled it. 'Meet Smokey. Keeps the children distracted at the hospital. You've no idea the amount of tears it stops mid-flow when I hold it up.'

'Smokey?'

'Smokescreen.' He saw her face and held up his hands in defence. 'I was under pressure at the time. I'd drawn a face on it and a little girl wanted to know its name. Couldn't think of anything else.'

Amy smiled.

'Look, don't worry about your memory loss. It's only been a few days. What about your phone? Any messages on there that help you?'

'I've gone through everything. Lots of stuff from friends talking about the day-to-day or arranging to hook up for drinks or dinner, except I don't remember the bars or restaurants. Work emails with clients but I have no recollection of the meetings.' She paused. 'And of course a few from you.'

'Did I say anything remotely useful in terms of bringing your memory back?'

'Afraid not. In fact there's not that many messages.'

'We'd speak on the phone mostly.'

'There's not much of a history of calls either.'

He smiled ruefully. 'Life as a doctor, I'm sorry to say. I've lost count of the extra hours I've done at the end of a shift.'

He paused, seemed almost nervous. 'Does it bother you? That you're dating someone who's at the beck and call of the National Health Service?'

Amy saw the apprehension in his eyes. 'Not at all,' she said, and he gave her a grateful smile. A smile that also had relief about it and his eyes flooded with respect.

'Thanks,' he said. 'That means a lot. And always know I do put you first, it's just sometimes my life is not my own.'

She was on the verge of asking him about the thing that had been bothering her since she woke up that morning but she was distracted by soft, white flakes falling from the sky. She glanced up, saw clouds rolling in from the east, swallowing up the blue sky.

'Oh my gosh, it's snowing,' cried Martha.

Suddenly the pool didn't feel quite so inviting. A wind was picking up, throwing the ever-growing flurry of flakes into their faces. Amy looked to the side of the pool where she'd put her towel. It wasn't there.

'Anyone seen my towel?' she asked, puzzled.

Everyone else was already getting out, wrapping themselves up in soft fluffy cotton.

'Where did you leave it?' asked Jack.

'Right there,' said Amy, pointing. 'On that chair.'

The chair was conspicuously empty.

'Are you sure?' asked Lisa.

'Yes,' said Amy. She was certain. She remembered putting it there. 'Did one of you guys take it by mistake?'

No one seemed to have her towel, and there were no spares around the pool.

'I'll go grab you one,' said Jack, heading inside. He came back out a minute later, smiling, a large white towel in his hands. 'You left it on the sofa,' he said.

But she didn't, Amy was sure of it. She distinctly remembered putting it on the chair. She shivered; now wasn't the time to worry about it. She got out and went inside to dry off and change. By the time they all returned to the kitchen for lunch, the scene outside was unrecognizable. The snow was falling thick and fast, the sky a battleship grey. They couldn't see much beyond a couple of metres and the view of the mountains was obliterated by the blizzard.

They ate lunch, occasionally looking out of the window and being taken aback at how dense the snowfall was. Soon after, Lisa got a call and it came as no surprise to them when she hung up and reported, 'The airport's been closed. No flights allowed to land. In fact they didn't even take off from Gatwick.'

'Oh how disappointing,' exclaimed Martha. She turned to Jenna. 'I suppose that means Lewis too?'

'Probably.'

'Haven't you heard from him?'

Jenna hesitated. 'Actually he called me this morning. While you were all out. A client is over from the States. Only in London for a couple of days and Lewis has to stay behind. So he couldn't come anyway.'

'Oh. What a shame,' said Martha.

Amy frowned. It sounded a bit odd, bit last minute.

'It's a big client,' Jenna added, sensing their surprise. 'A big supporter of the gallery.'

'Let's keep our fingers crossed that the snow clears up tomorrow,' said Martha.

After lunch they played games by the fire, curled up in front of the burning embers. Amy sat next to Jack, feeling the warmth of his body against hers. It was a new sensation, unfamiliar but pleasant.

She saw the coffee pot was empty and headed into the kitchen to make some more. As she filled the machine with water she heard someone come in behind her.

'You need a hand?' asked Jack.

She passed him the milk and he poured some into a saucepan to heat.

'Jack . . .?' started Amy.

'Yes?'

It was her chance to ask him about what had been bothering her. 'When I was in hospital, I sent you a text. To let you know what had happened. Only you didn't reply. Nor did you come and visit me. I was wondering why that was?'

'I did come and see you.'

Amy was taken aback. 'You did?'

'Yes. Late Saturday afternoon. After you sent me the text. I rushed there as soon as I could, except I was held up at work and I was late. One of the nurses there, Nurse . . .' he thought back, '. . . Morgan, I think – red hair, freckles – well she wouldn't let me in. Told me I had to come back in the evening.' He smiled.

'But you didn't?'

He looked guilty then. 'I'm sorry. I got a page from one of the registrars at my hospital. One of my patients, a little boy of five, he had a severe infection. He became quite ill and they needed help. I got very involved with his care over the next few days. I'm so sorry I let you down.'

Amy nodded, but she still felt slightly aggrieved, remembering how she'd been left believing she'd been dumped. 'Couldn't you have called me?'

Jack hesitated. 'The little boy. It was sepsis. He died.'

Amy's hand flew to her face. She'd put two and two together and made five when all the while Jack had been caring for some poor sick child. It didn't bear thinking about. She felt a deep, burning shame.

'Hey,' said Jack softly, coming over to comfort her. 'You weren't to know. And I should have called you, texted you, anything. I'm truly sorry I didn't.' He smiled at her. 'Are you sure you're OK dating someone who's beholden to their job?'

She nodded. 'How else could you be?'

He put a hand on her arm. 'Thank God for you. Ever since we started dating, you've been . . . I don't know, my rock. You make everything in life better and the hard bits more bearable. I am very happy to have met you, Amy Kennedy.' Then he leaned in, very slowly, very respectfully and when she didn't pull away he gently brushed her lips with his.

It was nice. It was better than nice – much, much better. After a while, Amy pulled away. 'I think they might be missing us,' she said with a smile. She didn't mind about that, not really, but Jack instantly understood.

'Too soon . . . it's fine. I totally get it. Whoa . . .' He grabbed the pan of milk just as it was about to boil and poured it into a jug.

'I'll join you in a minute,' said Amy. 'Coffee's still brewing.'

As he left the room, Amy realized she felt happier than she had in years. She also felt lucky. All those years of feeling like she was never going to meet anyone. The wait had been worth it.

TWELVE

26 February

It had snowed all afternoon. They looked out of the huge windows at the silent attack of snowflakes. An army of millions, parachuting in as a thing of deadly beauty in its graceful flight, then landing, one on top of another, and another, and another, building up, higher and higher until they were surrounded on all sides, unable to escape, the white enemy wedged up against the glass windows, almost as if it were looking in on them. They were near the end of a mammoth game of Monopoly; Jenna had been the first out and was sitting in the chair by the picture window, staring out at the blizzard. Martha and Lisa had also gone bankrupt and were playing a game of cards on the other side of the room.

'I think I got lucky,' said Jack as he threw the dice.

'You've just landed on "Go To Jail",' said Amy.

'I mean with the weather. Another day and I wouldn't have made it either.'

Amy had a sudden thought. 'Do you need to be back anytime soon? I mean . . . are you due at work?'

'I've actually got the whole week off,' said Jack.

'You have?' Amy's eyes widened. She was pleased.

'We were going to do a bit of exploring around the area. You threatened to take me ice climbing.' He smiled at her blank face. 'You don't remember.'

Amy shook her head. It felt strange not knowing what she'd said, what had gone on between them.

Jack put his playing piece behind bars. 'We'd gone for a drink. Pub near your flat – the George and Dragon, I think it was called. You invited me here to Val d'Isère and I said yes immediately. You said we could try some other sports, like ice climbing where, apparently, armed with an ice axe, you can attempt to ascend a two-hundred-metre frozen waterfall.'

Amy smiled. 'That was nice of me.'

'Hmm. Debatable.'

She laughed. 'What else?'

'How do you mean?'

'Well, tell me about other stuff. Our trip.'

'Trip?'

'To the Lake District. We went over Christmas, didn't we?'

'It was amazing,' said Jack.

'What did we do?'

'Loads of walking. Countryside is something else.'

Amy lowered her voice and glanced back at Martha. 'How did I get out of Christmas with Mum?'

'I think she was pretty understanding,' said Jack.

'She was?'

'Does that surprise you?'

'She always insisted we spend it together. Ever since Dad died.'

Jack shrugged. 'You must have worked your magic.'

Or you did, thought Amy. *At least the idea of you. Maybe she let me off the hook because I'd finally got a boyfriend.* She smiled. 'Thanks for the flowers, by the way.'

'You mean Valentine's Day? You've already thanked me.'

'But I don't remember. So I'd like to say it again.'

Jack grinned. 'This is great. I'm getting double kudos.'

'Is that game over yet?' called Martha.

'Amy's cleaned me out of my last few quid,' said Jack, throwing a double three with the dice and landing on Bow Street, complete with hotel. He grabbed her hand and raised it in the air. 'She is officially the winner.'

Amy saw the look of approval on her mother's face.

'It's nice to see you happy for a change, Amy,' said Martha. 'You're good together.'

'Of course they are,' said Lisa. 'They're a couple.'

'I know that,' said Martha, 'but . . . they just seem to *fit*. Do you know what I mean?'

'Mum, do we have to?' asked Amy, throwing an apologetic look to Jack.

'It's lovely,' said Martha, carrying on as if her daughter hadn't spoken. 'Don't you think, Jenna?'

Jenna looked up from the window. 'Very lovely,' she said, but Amy thought she detected a brusque note to her voice.

'Amy's waited ages for someone like you, Jack,' said Martha. 'Years. I was beginning to give up hope.'

'Mum!' cried out Amy.

Jack put a calming hand on her arm. 'She's not the only one. I sometimes felt as if I was never going to meet the perfect girl either.'

'Aw,' said Lisa, flashing a grin. 'Did you hear that? The Perfect Girl.'

'Just saying it like it is,' said Jack.

'When did you know?' asked Lisa.

'Know what?'

'That she was the Perfect Girl?'

Jack turned to look at Amy. 'Second date.'

'Not first?' teased Lisa.

'First I was too busy thinking how lucky I was and making sure I didn't do anything stupid or embarrassing.'

'Go on, then,' prompted Lisa.

'We went ice-skating.'

'I know,' said Lisa.

'You do?'

'Amy put it on Facebook.'

Amy held up her hands apologetically. 'Sorry, no idea why. Doesn't seem like me at all.'

'You were excited,' said Lisa.

Amy saw Jack beam and it made her own heart swell with an unexpected happiness.

'Well . . .' said Jack. 'She's pretty good on a pair of skates, as you might imagine.'

'It's all those years of lessons her father and I paid for when she was young,' said Martha proudly.

'Whereas I fell on my face within five minutes of stepping

onto the rink. And then I couldn't get up. Every time I tried to get on my feet I slipped again. Amy, meanwhile, is laughing her head off.'

'Charming,' said Martha.

'She's hysterical, skating around me. Then she skids to a stop, covers me in ice shavings. Holds out her hand and the way she looks at me . . .' he tailed off, a soft smile on his face, '. . . full of mischief and warmth. That's when I knew. That's when I fell in love with her.'

A hush settled over the room, Martha and Lisa caught up in the romance of the story. Amy returned Jack's tender gaze, felt her stomach flip over. It sounded like such an important moment in their relationship, a memory that was part of who they were and yet, to her perpetual sadness, she couldn't remember it.

Jenna abruptly stood. 'I've had enough of being cooped up. I'm going out.'

Martha was aghast. 'In this weather?'

'Not far. Just around the lodge.'

'But your ankle!'

'I can get my snow boot over it. And I'll take some ski poles. Go slowly.'

'I really don't think this is a good idea . . .' started Martha, looking at everyone else for reinforcement, but Jenna had already limped out of the room.

Amy watched anxiously, sensing something was wrong. She got up to follow Jenna.

She came into the hall as Jenna opened the front door and a freezing gust blew in. Jenna turned and met Amy's eye and gave her a look of raw hostility that stopped Amy in her tracks. Then Jenna pulled the door shut and it slammed in the wind and Amy was suddenly awakened to an image of such clarity she stood bolt upright.

Only she wasn't seeing the door in front of her now in the lodge. In her mind's eye she was back home, outside a house in Richmond. A house that she knew, that she'd visited many times. And the door that had slammed in her face was Jenna's.

THIRTEEN

2 January

Harry thrust his hands deep into his pockets. It was cold enough to burn skin. He watched as yet another warm, heated bus roared past him, lights on against the darkening afternoon and he glared at those travelling inside, protected from the biting wind. It wasn't that long ago he had been travelling everywhere in a black cab – proper luxury – but his luck had changed and now he envied basic public transport.

Harry pulled his woollen beanie hat down tighter over his ears. He'd put his shoulder-length curly hair up in a ponytail, deeming it more appropriate for the occasion, but the wind was razoring off the tips of his earlobes. His coat was inadequate, a thin bomber jacket and underneath he was just wearing a T-shirt. Ridiculous in these temperatures, he knew, but at least his body was well-toned from the rowing machine he had at home, something the judge had been unable to take away from him when he'd lost nearly all of his other possessions. He looked up and saw the lights of Max's wine bar up ahead – and not a minute too soon. The walk from his rented flat in the arse end of Haydon's Road to well-heeled Putney had taken him almost an hour and his feet were like blocks of ice.

He pushed open the door into an upmarket polished-wood haven. His shoes clacked across the floor as he made his way towards the bar, behind which was a man, similar age to himself, who was polishing glasses with great purpose before placing them on subtly lit shelves behind him. The downlighters picked out the man's sandy-coloured hair and winter tan. He wore a white shirt with the sleeves rolled up to reveal his forearms, and to Harry's amusement, a yellow floral bow tie. The man looked round.

'Harry Clarke?' he asked and Harry smiled and held out his hand.

'Nice to meet you.'

'You're late,' said the man.

Harry's first instinct was to tell him where to go, then turn around and walk back out, but he couldn't. He needed the job.

'I'm sorry,' he said. 'The bus broke down. I had to walk the rest of the way.'

'OK, well I'm Max. You want to take a seat?' Max indicated one of the large wooden tables and Harry went to sit, hating the sense his future lay in this man's hands.

Max took the seat opposite, crossing his chino-clad legs at the ankle. At the end of them he was sporting a pair of designer tan leather brogues. Harry recognized expensive shoes when he saw them. Max held a sheet of paper. Harry realized it was his CV, emailed over a couple of days before.

'Your last job,' said Max, 'you were a sales executive at Dolce & Gabbana?'

'Yes, on New Bond Street,' said Harry.

'How long for?'

'A year.'

'Why did you leave?'

'I was laid off. Retail's taken such a hit,' said Harry. Of course it wasn't the truth. But if he told the truth Max's eyes would grow hard and unforgiving and this interview would come to a rapid and cool but polite end. Harry shrugged ruefully. 'It's a global problem.'

Max nodded and Harry knew he would have had his own fair share of economic hardship. It made things easier. There would be a certain amount of empathy, something Harry had been only too aware of when he'd fabricated the reason for no longer working at the designer clothing store.

'And you left there at the beginning of October? Why so long to find something else?'

'My mother was unwell. I took a few months off to look after her.'

Max hesitated, caught out, as Harry knew he'd be. 'She OK?' he asked, a tad gruffly.

She's six foot under and has been for the last eight years, thought Harry, but he smiled and said, 'Much better. Thanks.'

'So before Dolce & Gabbana. What did you do?'

'A mix of retail and bar work,' said Harry. 'I like interacting with other people, with customers. I like having a positive impact on someone's experience and making sure they're having a good time.'

Max nodded and Harry knew his answer had gone down well.

'How much do you know about wine?' asked Max.

Harry raised his eyes to the shelves behind the bar, where sentries of bottles were lined up, each full of dark, glowing ruby liquid, the labels tasteful and inviting. He sought one out, looking for what he'd seen on the website photo that morning. 'You have a nice Chilean Pinot Noir. From the Limari Valley. Very elegant. Notes of cranberries and black cherries.'

This time Max was visibly impressed. 'You've done your homework.' He glanced back at the CV. 'What are you, twenty-eight?'

'That's right.'

'You OK with unsociable hours?'

Harry nodded. 'I've always been more of a night owl than a morning lark.'

'OK. Pay is nine pounds twenty an hour. Tips shared equally amongst the staff at the end of the night.'

The salary was barely above minimum wage, but Harry couldn't afford to turn it down.

'When can you start?'

Harry raised his hands, palms upwards. 'Soon as.'

'Great. Subject to a satisfactory reference, I'll put you down for a shift next Thursday. Trial. Six until midnight.'

Harry smiled. 'Thank you very much,' he said and shook Max's outstretched hand as his new boss stood up. The reference would be fine as the email address for his last employer was a fake one and Harry himself would be writing the reference.

'See you next week,' said Max as he stepped forward to open the door.

'Great,' said Harry.

'And don't be late.'

'I won't,' assured Harry. As he closed the door behind him he thought: *Wanker.*

Harry started the long walk home feeling a mixture of relief and despair. He would finally be able to pay some rent. Only the week before, his landlord's lackey, Nick, had knocked on his door and Harry had been distracted and had stupidly answered. Nick was not impressed, not impressed at all at Harry's refusal to engage with the final notice emails and had threatened him with eviction. Harry had begged for another few days and these had been granted on condition he paid the rent within the next two weeks. And now Harry had a job, he could keep a roof over his head until he could figure out what to do. For he sure as hell wasn't going to spend his life working for some arsehole who wore a floral yellow bow tie and who looked down on him.

And that's when he felt the despair. *It's only temporary,* he reminded himself. *Until you get another opportunity.*

And there were always other opportunities.

FOURTEEN

26 February

Amy barely noticed Jack leave the house as well, hardly heard him say he was going to keep an eye out for her friend. All she could see in her mind was Jenna's look of pure venom and then the door slamming shut. *Jenna's* front door slamming shut.

She couldn't go back into the living room. She needed time to think, to make sense of what she'd just remembered. *Remembered*. Still shaken, Amy made her way upstairs as quietly as possible, praying that no one would follow her.

Her friend hated her. And all this time she'd been pretending, being polite. *My God*, thought Amy, *what have I done?*

She softly closed her bedroom door behind her, grateful to be alone. She was drawn to the window and approached the exposed glass hesitantly. Outside she could see Jenna marching off through the blizzard as fast as her injured ankle would allow. The light was dim and Jenna was a figure in shadow, masked by the falling snow. Amy caught the moment as Jack laid a hand on Jenna's shoulder and

Amy held back, peering at them in a way that made her feel as if she was spying. She saw Jack try and persuade Jenna to come back inside, saw her shake her head and then his resigned shrug as he realized he'd have to follow her. Just before he did, something made him look up and Amy found herself caught as she looked down on them. She started but he smiled and indicated he was going to stay with Jenna. Amy gave a tiny nod and then moved away from the window.

She lay down on her bed and rubbed her temples with the heels of her hands. She replayed the memory that had pulled the rug from under her feet. She had a sensation she was lower down and in her mind she saw Jenna at the top of the three steps that led to her front door. It was cold, a chilling fog hung in the air. Jenna was inside her house but the door was open. She was holding the glossy black wood as if it were a shield to keep her, Amy, away. Amy instinctively knew she wasn't welcome to go any further. One foot on the step and Jenna would go inside. Her memory replayed the look on Jenna's face: cold fury. Hatred even. And then the door had been slammed shut and Amy recalled the hopelessness she'd felt.

She screwed her eyes shut tight and tried to remember more. What had she said to Jenna to provoke such a reaction? Why had she been there? But the image stubbornly refused to play on – or rewind. She was stuck in a snippet that repeated on a loop. *Dammit!* There must be some other clue, something in her memory that would materialize if only she thought hard enough, but the harder she tried, the more she struggled and the image in her mind began to blur. She thumped a fist on the bed in frustration. Amy was not used to having her quick-fire lawyer brain ensnared in sinking mud. She hated it. It was exhausting and it made her fearful, as if she had lost a part of herself, as if she didn't know who she was anymore. Not yet in the mood to return downstairs, she switched on the side light and picked up her book. She read, trying to distract herself, but her mind kept returning to the awful image of Jenna's anger.

After a while there was a soft knock on the door and it cracked open. It was Jack.

'Hey, what are you doing up here?'

Amy raised herself onto an elbow. 'Came up for a change of scene.' She glanced at the clock. It was almost five. She'd only been upstairs for about forty minutes.

'Can I come in?' asked Jack.

'Sure.' Amy pulled herself up to sitting. Crossed her legs on the bed. 'Where's Jenna?'

'Downstairs. Watching a movie with Martha and Lisa.'

'She OK?'

'Yeah. Was determined to get some shots in the blizzard, no matter what I said.'

Amy nodded. 'She say anything?'

'Like what?'

'I don't know . . . About being here. About me?'

Jack came over to the bed. Sat down beside her. 'She didn't say anything about you. Why do you ask?'

Should she tell him? Amy looked into his kind, non-judgemental eyes and sighed.

'I had a memory flash.'

Those eyes of his lit up. 'You did?'

'But it wasn't a good one.'

'OK . . .?'

'I was at Jenna's house. *Outside* Jenna's house,' she corrected. She told him what she had remembered.

Jack took it all in. 'Anything else?'

'No. What do you think?'

'About what exactly?' he asked gently.

'Should I confront her?'

He thought for a moment, a small furrow appearing on his forehead. 'You're sure she's still angry with you?'

'She's been cool towards me a couple of times since we've come on this trip.'

'In what way?'

'It's really hard to pin down. But I don't think I'm imagining it. Yesterday I tried talking to her about her exhibition that she had last month. But she totally shut me down. Apparently I went, but I can't remember anything.' Amy looked at him, desperate to shine a light on something. 'Did you come with me by any chance?'

Jack shook his head ruefully. 'You invited me but I had to work.'

Amy deflated and he put a hand on her knee. 'If you think it will help, have a chat with her,' he said.

'Was she angry outside? When you went after her?'

'She seemed fine.'

Amy frowned. The look on her friend's face had been bitter, she was sure of it. Maybe she had hidden it from him.

92

Jack smiled encouragingly. 'Or wait. Now you've had one memory return, there are likely to be more. Often the frequency increases as they start to come back. So if you feel more comfortable getting a better understanding of what might have happened before you talk to her, why don't you wait a day or two?'

'Maybe I will.'

'If you remember anything else, you know you can talk it over with me. If it's helpful,' he added quickly.

She smiled. 'Thanks.' She had a sudden thought. 'Can we keep this to ourselves for a bit? If Mum knows my memory seems to be returning, she'll be on at me non-stop. I think it's likely to return sooner if there's less pressure.'

'Course.'

'Is it always like this?' asked Amy. 'Feeling as if there's a great gaping black hole in your life, as if you're teetering on the edge of it with no idea what you've said or done the last six months and yet everyone else has had a front-row seat and you have to rely on them to fill in the blanks?'

'You mean like a bad night out on the tequila and you're not sure if you ended up dancing on the tables naked?'

'Something like that.' She laughed. 'But there's the rest of it too: the worrying, the anxiety. Always expecting the worst.'

'That's the paranoia kicking in. It's really common after a traumatic brain injury.'

She leaned into him briefly, touched her head on his shoulder. He lifted a hand and gently placed it around her. It felt warm, comforting.

'Sounds like you and me had some good times over the last few months,' said Amy.

'We certainly did,' said Jack.

'Can't believe we only got to the Lake District though. Did I press for somewhere more sunny?'

'You didn't, actually. You were very satisfied.'

She smiled. 'Hmm. Doesn't sound like me. I'm more of a guaranteed sunshine person. Do you know the one place where I really want to go?'

'Tonga?'

She looked at him, stunned.

'How did you know?'

He affectionately touched her head with his own. 'You told me, of course.'

'Oh. It's the whale-watching. The beaches. And the fact pigs and chickens have right of way.'

He laughed. 'As they should. So why haven't you gone yet?'

'Never been able to take enough time off work to go. I'm usually in the thick of a case where it's only me standing between a colossal ruthless corporation and some poor person whose entire life is on the line.'

He was quiet for a moment. 'It's nice,' he said.

'What is?'

'That you champion the underdog.'

'They need someone to have their back.' She paused. 'It's not just work, though. I've never found the right person to go with. It's not a place I've wanted to visit alone. So it's still a dream. One day, maybe.'

'Nothing wrong with having a dream.'

She turned to smile at him and in doing so both of them realized their faces were very close together. It was the most natural thing in the world for their lips to meet.

They drew apart. Amy searched his eyes. She wanted to know if this was familiar territory. That would make it OK. Even if she couldn't remember, if it was something her old self had done before, that would make her feel more secure.

'Have we had sex?' she asked.

He was taken aback by the bluntness of her question. 'Yes,' he said, smiling. 'We have. And I won't make any cheesy jokes about how injured I am that you can't remember how mind-blowing it was.'

'Was it?' she asked, tentatively.

'If you're not ready . . .'

'It's not that. It's just I can't remember. And that feels a bit strange.'

He looked at her solemnly. 'I promise you, we're good together.'

She smiled and then in response he kissed her again. She thought about how it felt as if she only met him yesterday, when in reality they'd been dating for three months. She wondered if she'd remember his naked body.

Afterwards she lay in his arms. She still didn't remember any of their previous occasions but what had just happened had been good. All except for one little bit. After they'd made love, he'd held her close and she'd suddenly, unexpectedly felt herself tensing. It had felt intrusive, uncomfortable. She'd hidden it from him but it had unnerved her. Deeply buried fears had risen to the surface, playing on her mind while he slept quietly beside her. What if her mother was right? What if she was cold and closed off, if she couldn't let people get close to her?

She looked across at him and thought how peaceful he seemed. How relaxed. He is relaxed with *you*, she reminded herself and took a shred of comfort from her thoughts. He's real, he's there, right beside you. Stop being so paranoid that he's going to disappear. She snuggled into his arm and felt him tighten his embrace around her shoulders.

FIFTEEN

7 January

Harry looked at himself in the mirror. White shirt, black trousers, black waistcoat. No floral bow ties for him. Max had insisted on the outfit, although staff were expected to kit themselves out, much to Harry's disgust. He pulled his hair back into a ponytail and then, satisfied with his appearance, he left the bathroom and went into the bar. Max beckoned him over and lifted the wooden hatch.

'Let me run through the till with you,' said Max, and Harry listened while still letting his eye wander across the room. It was early and there were only a handful of customers in and they were mostly women. Successful women, judging by their clothes, bags and confidence. Career women. Most of them well into their thirties. Harry looked for rings but the first three hands he scoured had nothing on their third finger.

'Is that all clear?' asked Max.

'Crystal,' said Harry.

'And remember, don't try and pretend you know more about the wines just to impress. If someone wants a recommendation and you're not sure, ask.'

'Got it,' said Harry and then, finally, Max moved away. There was one other member of staff on duty – another guy called Alex whom Harry had been introduced to earlier. He was good-looking in a bookish sort of way, slight-framed with floppy hair and glasses. As two more women in their late thirties came in, he realized why the staff were exclusively male.

The two women came up to the bar and Harry stepped forward, produced his most dazzling smile.

'Good evening. What can I get you?'

The women stopped talking to each other and noticed him. He clocked their looks of approval. They each perched on a bar stool, removed their scarves. Cashmere, Harry noted. Under the overhead lights he saw they wore a lot of make-up – tastefully done but on one of the women it had cracked where her skin was lined. The other one wore a pair of classy stud earrings – clear stones that shone like fire and he knew they were real diamonds. Neither was wearing a wedding or engagement ring and yet he thought they had to be at least a decade older than him, maybe thirty-seven, thirty-eight?

'Are you new?' asked the one with the diamond earrings, looking him up and down. Harry knew his physique filled his uniform well.

'First night,' he said humbly. 'So be gentle with me.'

She responded immediately by giving him a flirtatious smile. He didn't flirt back, not yet. He knew her type. He needed to play it cool, let her look. Let her think she was in control.

The woman turned to indicate her friend. 'Rosie and I are celebrating. What do you recommend?'

'We have a nice pink Prosecco in. From an award-winning winemaker in Northern Italy.'

'That sounds great,' said the woman, her earrings flashing. 'What do you think, Rosie?'

'Perfect.'

Harry felt the woman watching him as he pulled a bottle of Prosecco from the fridge. 'What's your name?' she asked.

He also produced two flutes and a cooler. 'Harry.'

'I'm Ellen and this is Rosie.'

'Nice to meet you both. What are you celebrating?'

'A promotion,' said Ellen, her eyes shining.

'Congratulations,' said Harry. He opened the bottle and the women cheered as the cork popped.

'I beat three others to get it,' said Ellen. 'Going to be lots of travel, Far East, especially. I'm going to be building up some air miles!'

He smiled and said: 'Sounds very glamorous. What an amazing opportunity.'

The women toasted each other then and someone else came in and Harry had to serve so he moved away, but Ellen and Rosie stayed in the same spot all night and continued to talk to him as he moved up and down the bar.

He brought them a plate of sliced charcuterie.

'What's that for?' asked Ellen.

'On the house.'

They beamed as if he'd offered them an all-expenses-paid

trip to the Caribbean; he didn't mention that Max had suggested it, seeing as they were regulars and spent well.

By the end of the evening, the two women were as permanent a fixture as the bar itself. Neither had wanted to move and they'd lazily watched him as he'd gone about serving, wiping down the bar top, restocking the wine fridge, all the while continuing non-stop conversation between themselves, some of which he overheard: plans to book a yoga weekend in Sardinia, whether it was still worth investing in a second buy-to-let property, what percentage their annual bonuses were going to be. Then Max approached, began to close off the till and gave Harry instructions on the end-of-night tasks. Harry listened to Max's supercilious tone, his irritation exacerbated by the knowledge Ellen and Rosie could hear everything.

'When's your next shift?' asked Ellen, as she finished her wine.

'Not sure,' said Harry. 'Tonight was a trial.'

Ellen lowered her glass, pulled a face and swivelled her gaze to Max. 'You have to keep him,' she demanded. 'He's divine.'

'Did he look after you, ladies?' asked Max, and Harry felt his hackles rise. He was not for sale and they were discussing him as if he wasn't there, as if he was merely a commodity to serve and entertain. Which of course was exactly what Max expected of him.

Ellen and Rosie made to leave soon after, visiting the ladies first. When they came out and headed for the door, Harry fully expected them to look back at him as they left, but neither did. He watched the door shut and felt a meta-phorical slap in the face.

'You did well,' said Max, coming back over.

Harry pulled his attention to his boss. 'Thanks.'

'The job's yours if you want it.'

He had no choice. He managed to put on a deferential smile. Looked grateful. 'Yes please.'

'Great. I'll finish up here – you head off and I'll see you same time tomorrow.'

Harry went to retrieve his jacket from the back room then headed out of the door into the freezing night. He turned to walk up the road then stopped dead. Just a short way up was Ellen, looking into a jeweller's metal-grilled window. She turned round.

'Rosie got a cab.'

'You didn't share?' asked Harry.

'She lives in the opposite direction.'

'Oh.'

'You want to make sure I get home safely?'

He only hesitated a moment. 'Course.' He held out his arm in a gentlemanly manner and she tucked her hand in.

She lived in a first-floor Victorian conversion flat a few roads from Putney High Street. A prime location with what Harry suspected would be a price tag to match. As she opened the shared front door he felt the welcoming blast of central heating. She shut the door behind her and they did an awkward dance in the narrow entrance hall as she got past him again to lead the way up the stairs.

Inside, her flat was tastefully decorated in muted hues of

white and grey. The wooden floor gleamed. The windows were dressed with modern blinds that to Harry were a little stark. The cream sofa was all minimalist angles and he dubiously wondered how comfortable it would be.

'Fancy a nightcap?' asked Ellen. It was the first thing she'd said to him since they'd left the street outside the bar.

'Thanks,' he replied.

She left the room and he heard her rummaging in what must be the kitchen, heard the sound of glasses landing on an expensive marble worktop. He looked around the living room, saw books on a shelf: a couple written by uber-successful women, Sheryl Sandberg, Michelle Obama, and a novel he thought he'd seen on a high-brow fiction prize list. There were a few photos – mostly of Ellen in far-flung places. Atop an elephant in the jungle; holding onto the wheel of a yacht somewhere bright and blue and smiling at the camera. She was obviously very successful. He liked that, liked her ambition and her obvious focus on what she wanted to achieve. He found it attractive. He recognized something of himself in those very same traits. He might be in a bar now, but it wasn't what he had planned for his future.

He heard her come back in and he turned. She had a bottle of wine tucked under one arm and held two glasses and a corkscrew in her hands and he jumped forward to help. He took the bottle and corkscrew as she placed the wine glasses on the chrome coffee table, then he went to open the wine.

'Can you manage?' asked Ellen, looking at him holding the bottle in his hand.

'Course.' He recognized the corkscrew as a silver Elsa Peretti from Tiffany's. It retailed at £299. He'd seen them when he'd wandered around the store on many a lunch break at Dolce & Gabbana, it being just a bit further down Bond Street, when he'd fantasized about being able to afford their 1837 Makers gold cufflinks to go with the other fantasy of a silk shirt from his own store. Harry wanted to be the sort of person who could effortlessly walk into designer stores and buy nice things. He felt as if he had as much right to beauty and quality as anyone else. He didn't subscribe to the notion that the rich were somehow 'better', however much they might believe it themselves. And he had plenty of experience of their sense of superiority, having been on the receiving end of it more than once.

Despite all the odds being stacked against him, he'd managed, in what seemed like a previous life now, through charm, luck and intelligence, to get a place studying English at Oxford University. They'd probably let him through the doors to fulfil some quota or other. Once there, he'd found out very quickly that he didn't fit. He came from the wrong school and wore the wrong clothes. He had no contacts, no uncle who was a director at Goldman Sachs, no family pile in the country. He was also utterly skint as his mother had no money to help him out, and in any event, she had paid him very little attention for as long as he could remember. In order to get by, he'd fallen into writing essays for his contemporaries while they spent their weekends at each other's grand houses riding, gambling and partying. It had all gone well for the first two terms and then suspicions had been aroused. The boy whose essay he'd most recently written was more than happy to throw Harry under the bus. Harry was asked to leave. The boy stayed on. His father happened to be an eminent politician.

Harry poured them both a glass of wine. 'It's a nice place you've got here,' he said, and she nodded.

'Where do you live?' she asked.

He couldn't possibly tell her. 'Wimbledon,' he said, and it wasn't more than two miles from the truth, but somehow he thought she didn't believe him anyway.

She patted the sofa next to her. He obeyed and smelt her perfume as he sat down. He hadn't noticed it in the bar and thought she must have just applied some.

'So when do you start?' he asked.

'Start?'

'The new job.'

'Ah.' She smiled, allowing the self-congratulatory glow to infuse her again. 'In a couple of months.'

'Looking forward to it?'

She looked at him as if he'd asked a strange question. 'Of course.'

Harry took a sip of his wine. He still knew only the bare minimum about wines, and had tasted even less, but even to his unsophisticated palate he could feel how smooth it was. Expensive, probably. As the glass came away from his lips he felt a touch on his thigh. He looked down to see Ellen had placed her hand there. Harry put his glass down on the coffee table, met Ellen's eyes.

'Shall we?' she asked.

He was surprised at how fast she was moving but shrugged inwardly. He leaned in to kiss her.

She backed away. 'Not here,' she said, and he saw her eyes flicker down to the pristine cream sofa. She stood and so he followed her into her bedroom. More subtle greys on the walls, the bedding. A huge abstract painting hung over the headboard with streaks of red and purple paint that looked like a scene in an abattoir but was probably a pricey 'investment'. He liked it. He wished he knew the artist and made a mental note to take a closer look later and then google it.

She sat on the bed and he followed. As they kissed he felt her pulling at his clothes.

An alarm woke him at six thirty. It was still dark and he struggled to orientate himself as he came to then saw Ellen's slender back as she got out of bed and wrapped a robe around herself.

'I'm going to have a shower,' she said, 'then I'll need to come in here to get dressed.'

Even in his partial somnolent state, the meaning was clear: *I want you out of my bedroom.*

'Uh . . . good morning,' said Harry, wondering for a moment if he'd dreamed the previous night. She was holding her robe tight against her breasts and he frowned, puzzled. *I was sucking on those last night*, he thought. *We had sex. And now I can't see you naked?* He rubbed his eyes. When he opened them again he saw she was looking at him pointedly. It had the same effect as a cold shower and suddenly he felt much more awake. She turned into the en suite and he roused himself, pulled on his clothes. He went into the living room where the remainder of his glass of wine still sat on the table. He considered leaving, but that felt too abrupt somehow, too rude, even with Ellen's cool morning greeting. He moved into the kitchen, switched on the kettle and found two mugs and some teabags. Maybe a cuppa would help smooth over the start to the day.

He didn't hear her voice at first as the water was boiling. It was only after the kettle switched off that he caught it. She was on the phone to someone, a friend.

'Yeah, he was good,' she was saying. 'Cute piece of arse.'

Harry half-smiled, unsure of whether it was a compli-mentary comment or not. There was something about Ellen's tone that was derisive. Then he heard her laugh. A dismissive peel in which he sensed whatever had been said had amused her – briefly at least. 'Oh God, no,' he heard her say. 'Doesn't fit my brief at all. He works in a *bar*.'

Harry stopped the kettle mid-pour and placed it back on the stand. He looked at the cups; one was full, one still empty. He leaned forward and spat in the full one then turned and went quietly into the living room. He retrieved his jacket and scanned the room. On the table lay the Elsa Peretti corkscrew. He picked it up and pocketed it then went into the hall. He listened out for a moment but Ellen's conversation had moved on. He was so inconsequential he hadn't held more than three minutes of her attention.

Silently he let himself out of her flat.

SIXTEEN

26 February

Amy woke with a start, her heart thudding. She flailed out, feeling someone shaking her, then she realized it was Jack. He was beside her, a look of concern on his face.

'You were dreaming,' he said. 'Shouting in your sleep.'

She glanced over at the clock – it was gone seven and she could smell dinner being cooked downstairs. She felt the solid comfort of Jack's warm body next to her.

'You OK?' asked Jack.

'Just a dream,' she said, brushing it off.

'A bad one.'

She nodded.

'Want to tell me about it?'

Amy paused. This was what being in a relationship was about. Someone to talk to, someone on your side.

'It was about Jenna. She was running, chasing after me. I don't know where, it was someplace dark. Outside. On a street.'

'Go on,' he encouraged.

'It was cold. I couldn't run fast enough, I could feel her gaining on me.' She shuddered. 'I looked around. Her face . . . she was angry. But that wasn't what was frightening. It was her look of determination. She was going to catch up with me, no matter what. It was like those wildlife programmes, you know, when the lion is going to bring that wildebeest down. The wildebeest can run but it's all futile.'

Jack went to hug her. 'It's only a dream,' he said. 'I wonder where this is coming from? What's happened between you two?' He raised a conciliatory hand. 'Sorry. Stupid question. You OK?'

Amy sighed. 'Yeah.' She sniffed. 'Can you smell dinner?'

'I certainly can. Race you to the bathroom?'

Amy pushed him back on the bed and kissed him. 'Ladies first.'

After she'd showered, she took her time getting dressed, enjoying the knowledge that her boyfriend was getting ready at the same time. The two of them, together. It was funny how the small things could make you feel a part of a couple. She slipped on jeans and a shirt and then opened the dressing table drawer. Inside she saw the jewellery box that she'd packed, unaware of where it had come from. She opened it up and looked at the diamond pendant, seeing the stone catch in the light.

'That's beautiful,' said Jack, coming out of the shower, a towel wrapped around his waist.

'Thanks,' said Amy. 'Only I've no idea where I got it.'

He watched her for a moment then came over, rested his hands on her shoulders and looked at her in the mirror. He grinned. 'Me.'

Amy twisted around. 'What?' she said, open-mouthed. 'But
. . . it's so . . .' she didn't want to say expensive, '. . . generous.'

He shrugged modestly. 'I saw it and knew it would look
perfect on you.'

'When?'

'Christmas.'

'Oh my God,' said Amy, still taking it in. She closed up
the box and then turned and kissed him. 'Thank you,' she
said, moved. 'I absolutely love it.'

Downstairs, everyone was gathered in the kitchen. Lisa and
Jenna were at the table poring over Jenna's laptop, while
Martha was cooking. There were a few knowing looks as
Amy and Jack appeared together, but to Amy's relief, her
mother said nothing.

'Hey, come and look at these,' said Lisa.

Amy looked to Jenna first, but her friend was engrossed
in her laptop. There was no remnant of the tension from
earlier. She cautiously went over and peered at the screen,
on which was a photograph of the mountains. It was exquis-
ite – taken the day before, with the setting sun painting the
slopes gold.

'That's incredible,' said Amy.

Lisa nodded. 'Isn't it?'

Jenna continued to scroll through, shot after shot illuminating the screen. Those Jenna had taken in the blizzard
had an otherworldliness to them; they were claustrophobic
and eerie. As Amy watched, she felt a stuck cog dislodge

in her brain. Suddenly she had a memory of herself looking at other photos of Jenna's, photos in a gallery. She gave a small, involuntary gasp and her hand flew to her mouth.

'What is it?' asked Lisa.

Amy shook her head, unable to speak for a moment.

'Have you remembered something?' asked Jack.

Martha glanced up from the stove, on alert.

They were all looking at her. 'I remember being at Jenna's exhibition,' said Amy. Did she just imagine it or did Jenna flinch?

'Oh my God,' exclaimed Lisa. 'That's amazing. Amy's had a memory flash. Martha!'

'OK, OK,' said Amy, trying to play it down, although she was pleased. This was a pleasant memory, one where she was having a good time. She allowed herself to fall back into it, saw she was at Jenna's husband's art gallery. Lewis had only opened the place a few years before, but it had already made its name on the scene. Lewis had discovered a couple of artists who had hit the headlines and he'd showed their work to the great and the good, earning them inflated amounts. Amy could see him in her memory, walking a distance behind his wife, his closely cropped red hair and pale blue eyes marking him out from the crowd. He was a man who liked a challenge. He liked getting what he was told he couldn't have and this applied to his personal life as well as professional. Six years ago Jenna had been in his line of sight. After several months of intensive pursuit, she had capitulated and agreed to marry him.

Amy wandered around looking at her friend's collection

of photographs, a series of ethereal landscapes taken in Northumberland, which were getting a great reception from the press. Many of them had sold. Amy looked over at Jenna, who was on the other side of the gallery being introduced to yet more journalists. She caught a glimpse of her friend's face, her animated eyes as she talked about her work. Amy had on several occasions hoped to catch Jenna's attention so she could offer her own congratulations but there was a permanent wall of press and well-wishers around her.

Amy felt her mother's arms embrace her.

'I'm so happy for you, darling,' said Martha.

Amy smiled. Then she turned to Jenna, eyes bright. 'Wow,' she enthused. 'So many people there. And you . . . you were in your element.'

Jenna looked up at her but said nothing.

'This is great,' said Jack. 'Your memory's coming back.'

Martha clasped her hands to her chest. 'Finally, we're getting back to normal.'

Everyone was delighted for her, absorbed in their congratulations. Everyone except Jenna. Amy glanced over but her friend remained quiet, flicking through her photos.

'What else can you remember, darling?' asked Martha.

Amy turned, distracted by Jenna's silence. 'Um . . . nothing. Just the exhibition.'

'Come on, now they've started, there must be more.'

'They don't come on request, no matter how much I might want them to.'

Martha made a dismissive sound. 'But you're not even trying.'

'Trust me, I've tried.'

There was a pause and then Martha gave a tight smile. 'You never did like taking my advice.'

Amy bit her tongue. 'Mum, I do listen to you,' she said, forcing patience into her voice. 'But it's not the way it works.'

'I only ever have your best interests at heart,' said Martha, her voice infused with hurt.

Amy gave an inward sigh. It wasn't the first time she'd heard that. Since her mother had become prematurely and suddenly alone, she'd had nothing to distract herself from Amy's life. The protectiveness her mother had always felt towards her only daughter had at times crossed over the line to controlling. *With your fair skin you need at least factor fifty. If you're out on a date, don't leave your drink on the bar. Don't whatever you do walk home alone in the dark.* Over the years, Amy had been bombarded with 'advice'.

An atmosphere hovered over the room, threatening to spoil the evening.

'What the heck is that?' asked Lisa in sudden awe, noticing Jack was fiddling with a paper napkin. She picked it up. Jack had folded it into a delicate rose. 'Is there no end to your talents?' she said.

'It's no big deal,' said Jack modestly, taking it from her. 'For you,' he said, handing it to Martha.

Her face lit up. 'Really?'

Amy turned away with relief. Seemed her new boyfriend was so amazing he even knew how to diffuse a situation with her mother. 'Anyone need a drink?' she asked, moving away from the table.

As she walked across the kitchen, a new picture ambushed her. She was lying on the ground, a sharp pain in her knee. Amy was about to turn, to speak about this new memory when she was overpowered by a sense of loneliness. Puzzled, she stopped, her hand on the fridge door. Allowed the memory to take over. Amy got a sense she was embarrassed on that cold pavement, cross with herself but at the same time had a great sense of vulnerability. It was busy, peak commuter time and dozens of pairs of legs marched by heading for Waterloo station, most faces glued to their phone screens, but those few who glanced down allowed the urgency of their destinations to propel them forward and not one person stopped.

It was the time she'd fallen, just before she met Jack. Amy waited for the rest of the memory to return. The part where Jack came up to her, helped her to her feet. Spoke to her about her injury. But nothing happened. In her mind she picked herself up, got a tissue from her bag to wipe away the blood that had seeped through her tights and she stayed alone. She walked up the steps into the station and then the memory stopped.

Amy took a deep breath. That wasn't how it happened. Jack had come up to her. Told her he was a doctor. He was caring, insistent she get herself checked out and he asked for her number. *Christ, what was wrong with her head?* This fall had messed with her so much. She took some juice from the fridge and poured it into glasses and tried again. Forced herself to think harder. It was there somewhere, it had to be. To her frustration, nothing changed.

SEVENTEEN

26 February

The snow continued all evening. They closed the curtains against the weather, lit the fire. Opened more wine. Amy got up from the sofa and made her way into the kitchen where she immediately stopped in her tracks. *Not again!* She couldn't remember why she'd gone in there. She gazed around the room, looking for clues. Something was tugging at the corners of her mind, something dancing in the shadows, hiding out of sight whenever she went to look for it, tormenting her. Amy wondered about going back into the living room and retracing her steps, but she couldn't face the looks of sympathy and barrage of questions designed to help her remember.

Amy took a seat at the breakfast bar and rested her head in her hands. She was tired and had noticed that her mind was at its worst then. It seemed to disconnect more often, like a flickering bulb that was about to blow.

Breathe, she told herself. *Let your mind be quiet.* It was nice to let it go for a moment, to not be forever chasing it. She'd tried to relax over dinner but it had been hard. The image of herself falling outside Waterloo station had nagged at her, and had made her worry that the injury to her brain was greater than the consultants had spoken about. What if other memories were distorted? Things that she took to be fact but were twisted versions of the truth? A person was a collection of memories, that's what made up your life, made you who you were. If she was remembering something different to what had happened, how could she trust herself? Did she even truly know herself?

She screwed her eyes tight and then opened them again. Spoke out loud. 'OK. Why have I come into this room? Is it for a drink? Something to eat? Has anyone spilt anything?' She huffed in frustration. 'What am I doing here?'

'Talking to yourself is the first sign of madness, you know,' said a voice behind her.

Amy jumped in fright.

'Sorry,' said Jenna, coming into the room. 'I didn't mean to scare you.'

'It's fine,' said Amy. 'I was just . . . trying to remember.'

Jenna turned and closed the door softly behind her. She stood there for a moment, not moving further into the room. Then she folded her arms. 'It's good you're getting some of your memory back.'

Amy nodded, waited for her to say more.

'So you remember being at the exhibition?'

Amy smiled. 'Yes. It was a huge success,' she said, but to her surprise, Jenna didn't automatically agree.

'What exactly do you recall?' asked Jenna.

'Well, I was there – on my own. It was busy – lots of

people were milling around. It was a really buzzy atmosphere.'

'What else?' asked Jenna.

Amy frowned. 'I don't understand. I had a glass of wine . . . I thought your photos were brilliant . . . I ate too many mini Yorkshire puddings with roast beef . . .'

Jenna didn't smile. She walked further into the room, sat at a distance along the breakfast bar.

'Are you telling me everything?' she asked.

Amy was taken aback. 'What do you mean?'

Jenna didn't answer, she was watching Amy carefully.

'I'm telling you what I remember,' said Amy.

'So you say.'

'Hang on a minute . . . are you suggesting I'm making stuff up?'

A wave of fear overwhelmed Amy. Was her recollection of the exhibition different to Jenna's? Was her mind messing up *everything* that had happened in the last six months?

'Jenna, if you could please tell me exactly what it is that's bugging you, I'll try to help. I'll tell you everything I know, really I will,' said Amy.

Jenna did smile then but it was bitter, hurt. 'Will you?'

'Of course.'

'What else do you remember doing at my exhibition?'

Amy was bewildered. 'Doing?'

'Yes.'

What was she going on about? thought Amy. She shook her head. 'You're going to have to tell me.'

At that moment the door opened. Both women snapped their heads round to see Jack in the doorway.

'Sorry . . . have I interrupted something?' he asked.

Jenna slid off her stool. 'Not at all.'

'I was just thinking Amy had got lost finding a pen and paper,' said Jack.

That was it! Amy felt relieved. She'd come into the kitchen to get something to keep score with the card game they were playing. She took one from the counter, all the while glancing at Jenna as her friend left the room.

'What was that about?' asked Jack, once Jenna had gone.

Amy shrugged. 'I honestly don't know.'

'Any other memories come back?'

Amy thought about the station, lying on the ground alone. She didn't want to go into it. Not tonight. She was too exhausted with it all. 'None.'

In the living room, the game underway, Amy would glance at Jenna every so often. A heavy lump sat on her chest. It was obvious to Amy that something had happened to upset Jenna. Something bad. Something that she, Amy, appeared to be responsible for. What had she done? The frustration at not knowing threatened to chew her up inside. Along with a terrible sense of dread.

EIGHTEEN

27 February

Sometime in the night it had stopped snowing. Amy woke to an empty bed. She pushed her hand over to where Jack had been sleeping the night before. It was cold. He must have got up some time ago. She supposed it was nice that he hadn't woken her but at the same time she felt the sharp pang of disappointment. *You're still in the first flush of romance*, she reminded herself. Those heady early days where everything is new and explorative. *Jack's already got to know you quite well – he's just doing the considerate thing.*

They'd made love again last night and Amy had willed herself to remember previous nights with Jack. There had been a moment when she'd realized that there was something familiar about him and she was comforted by an underlying sense of recognition, yet when she tried to grasp at their history, it evaporated. It was like trying to grab fog. It left her feeling unsettled. He'd fallen asleep first, leaving her to listen to his gentle snores and she'd lain awake, wondering when she might remember something about him, about their relationship.

Amy got up and looked out of the window. The landscape was covered in billowing clouds of snow. She had seen it deep before but this was unusual. It must be several metres deep in the drifts.

After she'd showered, Amy went downstairs, following the voices coming from the kitchen. Her mother and Jack looked up as she came into the room. Immediately she could see her mother was in her element, was enjoying Jack's attention.

'There you are, sleepyhead,' said Martha.

'Morning, Mum.'

Jack came over and kissed Amy on the lips and she saw her mother beam with approval and delight.

'Have you seen the snow?' asked Martha. 'It's like Christmas. Talking of which,' she added, turning back to Jack, 'you must tell me more of your trip to the Lake District. I asked Amy back in December and she hardly said a word.'

Amy ignored the barb and went to cut some day-old baguette. 'Have you two eaten?' she asked.

'Yes, thanks,' said Martha impatiently. 'So where did you stay?' she asked Jack. 'Amy said it was somewhere in Bowness?'

'It was,' said Jack. 'A small hotel near Lake Windermere.'

'What was it called?' asked Martha. 'Amy's dad and I took a trip there once, before she was born.'

'Cedar Hall.'

'Oh, not the same then. Did it rain?'

'It was a bit of a mix. Luckily we got some dry spells.'

'And did you go out and about much?' asked Martha.

'Walks mostly.'

Amy listened from the other side of the room as she ate her breakfast, curious to hear more detail about her rare Christmas away from her mother.

'Isn't it glorious up there?' said Martha. 'The lake is so beautiful.'

'We took a boat and went out onto the lake on Christmas day itself.'

Amy looked up.

'You did?' asked Martha, surprised.

'Yes,' said Jack, looking from Martha to Amy.

'What kind of boat?' asked Martha.

Jack paused. 'You know, a standard rowboat. One you can rent.'

'Goodness me,' exclaimed Martha. 'You didn't tell me that, Amy.'

'Have I said something wrong?' asked Jack.

'Not at all,' said Martha. 'It's just Amy has always had a fear of deep water. About the only thing she is scared of. Ever since she nearly drowned when she was seven. It was awful. We were on holiday in Wales and she got caught in a current in the sea.' She shuddered. 'Thank God for the lifeguards.'

Jack was quiet for a moment. Then he looked up at Amy and smiled. 'You never told me that,' he said.

'It wasn't my finest moment,' said Amy.

'But to get her on a boat . . . I'm amazed,' said Martha. 'And a rowing boat! Whatever did you say to persuade her?'

Jack went to put his coffee cup in the dishwasher. 'It was a beautiful day. And it was only a short trip. Half an hour?'

'Half an hour!' exclaimed Martha.

'Maybe less.' He smiled. 'I hope you weren't doing it to please me,' he said to Amy.

Martha snorted. 'That doesn't sound like Amy at all.'

'Mum!' admonished Amy.

'I should go and get a shower,' said Jack, as he kissed Amy.

'Cool. Where are the others?'

'Jenna went out to take pictures, but she's promised to stay near the house. Lisa, we haven't seen yet.'

Amy nodded. So Jenna was alone. She knew what she wanted to do. 'See you in a bit,' she said as Jack left the room.

'Oh, he's so wonderful,' said Martha. 'Imagine getting you on a boat!'

'I'm just going to get a bit of fresh air,' said Amy, and she went into the hall. As she put on her snow gear she reflected on Jack's recounting of their trip. Imagined herself on a small rowing boat in the middle of a vast lake. As she pictured the small distance between the edge of the boat and the dark water she could feel her palms start to sweat. She shook her head, dispelling the image quickly. She couldn't imagine how she'd agreed to get in such a tiny vessel and head out across the water; perhaps she'd been trying to prove to herself she could do it. Amy opened the front door. A huge drift rested against the house, towering over her. She made her way outside onto the path. The snow was up to her knees in places.

Progress was slow as she followed Jenna's footsteps. They went around the back of the house then across the valley towards the pine woods. The drifts sparkled in the sunshine and the cold air filled Amy's lungs. As she neared the trees, Amy was reminded of a Narnian landscape: pines stretching up to the sky, heavy with snow, luring her onwards. She took a moment to take in the beauty of her surroundings. The untouched snow between the trees, its surface curved and unblemished. Sunlight flitted through the branches, beckoning the passer-by in further. It was as if it was an entrance to another world, thought Amy. One that would be easy to get lost in.

A voice brought her out of her reverie. It was Jenna. She was talking to someone, angrily, thought Amy, although she couldn't make out the words. She moved towards the sound, passing a heavily laden tree and a pile of snow thudded to the ground.

Up ahead she saw Jenna, saw her turn and her face darken. She was on the phone, but she finished the call quickly.

Amy went up to her. 'I wasn't eavesdropping.'

'What did you hear?'

'Nothing.'

'Very convenient. You remember anything yet?'

'Are you talking about the exhibition?' asked Amy. 'You have to tell me what you know. Whatever it was I did.'

Jenna looked pained then but she shook her head. 'I'm cold.'

'Don't go,' said Amy.

Jenna stopped, looked Amy in the eye. 'I *can't* tell you. Because I don't fully understand it myself. I need you to remember the truth.'

'Please—' Amy started, but Jenna had already walked away.

NINETEEN

27 February

Amy let herself back into the house. Her head throbbed, tight with frustration, from poking around in her brain, niggling, pleading, searching. Looking for answers. Trying to figure out what was there, what had happened. Amy still couldn't come to terms with the fact she couldn't simply access something as normal and natural as a memory. She looked up as Jack came down the stairs.

'Where have you been?' he asked as she hung up her coat.

Amy sighed. 'Out. I went to find Jenna.'

'Did you have a chat with her?'

'She won't tell me what it is that's upsetting her. I feel as if I've done something awful.'

'Have you remembered anything else?' asked Jack.

'No. But I keep thinking about that dream I had. When she was chasing me. Do you think it's a recollection of something that actually happened?'

He wrapped his arms around her and rested his cheek against her head. 'I don't know.'

Amy smelt his freshly showered skin. It was comforting. 'Why would she be chasing after me?' she wondered.

'It will all come back,' said Jack. 'Have you had any more thoughts on when you're going to visit Esme?'

'No, sorry. I've been a bit preoccupied.' Amy pulled away. 'What have I told you about her?'

'I don't know,' he said. 'Lots.'

'I don't mean it as a test. It's so I don't bore you with saying anything I've mentioned before.'

Jack smiled. 'I wouldn't mind.'

Amy rubbed her temples. 'I've got a splitting headache.'

'Again? Right, go and have a lie-down. A proper rest.'

'But I've not long got up.'

'You need to get better. Right?' he said, searching her eyes for confirmation.

'I know, I know.'

'I'll make sure the others know. So you're not disturbed. And you should give me your phone, no distractions. Just forget about everything and try and sleep.'

Amy smiled. It was nice to be looked after for a change. She handed over her phone and allowed herself to be enveloped in his warm hug. 'Thanks.'

She went up to her room to get some painkillers. Popping them out into her hand, she stared in the bathroom mirror. Her eyes seemed vacant to her, lost. She blinked, then pulled herself together. Swallowed the tablets. *It will all come back*, she told herself. Little things already had. It would just be a matter of time. She blocked the uncomfortable thought that it wasn't coming back quickly enough for her.

She went into the bedroom, smiled as she noticed that Jack had tidied the room. He was something to be cheerful about. She lay down, thought she could feel the tablets starting to take hold. This relaxed her and she took an easy breath. Maybe if she lay there quietly for a bit, didn't force herself to think, something would skirt around the fringes of her memory. Something that would tell her what had happened between herself and Jenna.

She let her mind drift and gazed out of the window at the mountains. Monolithic rocks that had been there for millions of years. They seemed so solid: unmoving, permanent fixtures, but even they were subject to forces out of their control. Minuscule movements every year from nature's shifting patterns. She kept her gaze on the mountains, their immense presence and allowed herself to feel small.

A picture began to emerge. Amy saw herself rubbing her dirty hands together as she got up from the wet pavement. Brushing off the grit. At first she was frustrated, this wasn't a memory about Jenna or the exhibition. She tried to refocus but the memory of her lying on the pavement filled her mind and she let herself go with it.

She felt a pain in her leg and looked down to see blood oozing through her tights, a hole in the thin fabric. She saw herself blotting it, felt the urge to be away, out of the rain, away from the humiliation of the dirty pavement where she'd lain as others had flowed past in a river of bodies.

Keep still, keep calm. Don't search, let it happen, her inner voice soothed, understanding instinctively that if she did, more might follow.

Amy saw the wide flight of steps in front of her. She climbed them, slowly, her sore knee putting paid to her usual run up. She glanced down – it was still bleeding quite heavily. She noticed her clothes were messy where she'd fallen in the dirt. She limped into the dry cover of the station. Amy got the bloodstained tissue and dabbed again but she was unable to walk while simultaneously bending over attending to her knee. She was going to miss her train so she pressed hard, once, then just went for it, hurrying across the concourse, feeling the stabbing pain and the blood seeping as she did so. She knew her platform, saw the train listed on the overhead board. Her travel pass rested on the yellow circle on the gate and beeped. The barrier burst open. Through Amy went, hobbling as she headed to her usual carriage. She stepped onto the train and turned down the corridor to find her usual seat, where she could collapse and feel a sense of familiarity, of order restored.

Someone else was sitting there. They didn't look up; they were engrossed in their phone. It wasn't *her* seat, Amy knew, but still it threw her that somebody else was there.

She found somewhere else and as she sat down she felt the wetness had run further down her leg. She got a clean tissue from her bag and pressed it against the wound. Rested her head against the window as the train pulled out of the station and took a breath. *Bloody bastards, walking past her without offering to help. Not one person had stopped!* She was angry – but also upset. It seemed so inhuman, so callous. It made her feel insignificant, uncared for. It made her feel lonely. She felt herself wobble, thought she might burst into tears, and she swallowed down hard.

When the train stopped at Earlsfield Amy got off, tentatively stepping onto the platform. It was only a short walk to her flat and she suddenly felt an irresistible urge to be home. The rain had stopped but the streets were slicked wet. Amy needed to stop in the shop to get something to eat but couldn't face it. It was too much on her own. She just wanted to get home. Dinner would have to be baked beans on toast tonight.

As she let herself into her flat, she thought it felt cold. She turned up the thermostat, switched on some lights. She found herself putting on the TV, needing the sound of other human voices. Then she sat and inspected the damage to her knee. Slipping off her tights, she saw a nasty gash. Peeling off the fabric had started the bleeding again, so Amy took a quick shower, watching the water run red down the plughole, then she dried her knee with toilet paper and stuck on a massive plaster. Figured if she kept still for most of the evening with her leg up she wouldn't bleed to death.

Sitting in the living room with her basic supper, Amy heard her phone beep. It was a group WhatsApp message from Lisa and Jenna, inviting her to dinner that Friday at Lisa's house. It was going to be her two best friends and their husbands – and her.

Immediately Amy knew she couldn't face it. She'd done so many events: parties, dinners, birthdays, and every single one of them on her own. She loved her friends dearly and got on with David – Lewis too, mostly, though sometimes when the wine was flowing his sense of entitlement came out. Although Amy wouldn't ever say anything to Jenna, Lewis could be a bit boorish. She sighed. It would be easier if she had a boyfriend to take with her. Life was so much simpler when you were part of a couple. Two people to share the jokes, the laughs, the post-dinner chat when you got home. Someone to stand your corner if the conversations became too personal or exhausting. Someone else to be a part of your life, to know you, to share an experience so you weren't yet again having to cover up how much of the weekend you spent alone. Someone to cook for you when you were late home from work, to leave a light on so you walked up to a bright, welcoming flat. Someone to talk to when you fell outside a train station and cut your leg open.

Who is this person? thought Amy. *And where the bloody hell is he? Cos I could sure do with you; I've been waiting for years.*

She looked again at the invitation on her phone, knowing she should accept, knowing she didn't want to. Not this time. Her finger hovered. When you were single, you were the only real witness to your life. You had no one else to add to your stories, or yours to theirs.

Sod it, she thought. *I deserve someone too. And I'm just too tired to go to another dinner party where I'm the unbalanced person at the table.* Four seats fit so nicely, a fifth threw everything out of kilter.

She composed a message back.

Hey guys, dinner sounds wonderful but I can't make it.
Got a date.

As soon as she pressed the send arrow, Amy felt a sense of relief. An easing of the pressure that had sat on her shoulders for so long and of the awful hollow feeling in her chest.

A message pinged back from both friends immediately, demanding to know more. Amy smiled. It was only a harmless white lie. Something to get her off the hook for Friday. She'd come clean the following week, she thought. Or then again, maybe she wouldn't. Not yet. Maybe her new date could hang around for a bit – get her mother off her back for a few weeks. Just to give her a breather.

She and her boyfriend would have to split up before too long, obviously, as no one would be able to meet him, but it would mean her mother would stop looking at her in that way that made Amy feel as if she was damaged goods. She got a mischievous thought. He could be anything, anyone, her own creation. He would treat her spectacularly well. Buy her extravagant gifts. Maybe some of this would end up on Facebook in that way so many people felt compelled to publicly display highlights of their personal life. She would see. But as she lay back on the sofa, she felt an unexpected and particularly pleasing two fingers up at the world.

She looked again at the messages from Jenna and Lisa, both wanting to know who her new man was.

She began to type: 'His name is'. She glanced around the

room, took some names randomly off the spines of books on the shelf: a first and a surname. 'Jack Stewart', she messaged back.

> He's a doctor and I met him outside Waterloo station.
> He picked me up when I fell over and cut my leg –
> very heroic!

Lying on her bed, in the snow-bound lodge, Amy was frozen with shock.

She'd made up a *boyfriend*?

Because she couldn't bear playing gooseberry at a dinner party?

Was it true? She swallowed, revisited her memory. It felt as clear and real as anything that she knew had truly happened in her life.

Then she felt goosebumps spring up on her arms as another thought harpooned her, right through the gut.

If she'd invented Dr Jack Stewart, then who was the man downstairs?

TWENTY

27 February

Amy tried to steady her breathing. She must have got it wrong. None of it made any sense. It must be her bloody head injury again, causing problems, messing everything up. She was so confused. She rubbed her face with her hands. It was a mind blip, it had to be.

Amy was suddenly swamped with relief as she realized something. All those dates she'd had with Jack, all those photos on Facebook. There was her evidence! And Christmas! They'd been to the Lake District. He'd bought her a beautiful gift. She quickly went over to the dressing table, opened the drawer. Laid her hand on the jewellery box with an overwhelming sense of validation. She hadn't made it up. It was real, *he* was real.

Fucking hell, she was *hallucinating*.

Amy slid off the stool and went over to the window. She stared out at the solid mountains, tried to absorb their strength. She still felt a little shaken from the false memory – maybe her mind was mixing up experiences from before she'd met Jack with those after they'd got together. There had certainly been plenty of times she'd come home to a dark, empty flat. And the consultant had warned her this might happen.

The door softly opened behind her and she spun around.

'Sorry, didn't mean to startle you,' said Jack. 'I came to see how you are. Aren't you supposed to be resting?' he teased. 'How's the head?'

Amy smiled. 'A little better.'

He came into the room and moved over to her, wrapping his arms around her as he looked over her shoulder out of the window.

'It's breathtaking, isn't it,' he said, absorbed by the view.

Amy murmured her agreement.

'I thought we could go for a walk in a bit, all of us. A short one, so as not to strain Jenna's ankle. What do you think?'

Amy turned. Smiled. 'Sounds good. You know, I was trying to remember something.'

'Oh yeah?'

'About Christmas.'

'Go on.'

'You got me my lovely necklace . . .'

'Yes.'

'What did I get you?'

Did she imagine it or did he stall for the tiniest moment?

'A watch,' he said.

Amy pulled up the cuff of his jumper. His wrist was bare.

'Now I feel like I'm in trouble,' he said sheepishly. 'Only you were very understanding the last time I explained,' he added hopefully.

'Where is it?'

'The face cracked, remember?'

Amy shook her head.

'At rugby. Got in a rough tackle.' He paused. 'It's at the repairers.'

'Oh right.' She thought. 'What does it look like?'

'It's a G-Shock. Sports. Should've survived the tackle really.'

She nodded. 'What else happened?'

'How do you mean?'

'At Christmas.'

'We went for lots of walks . . .'

'Boat trips?'

He smiled. 'Only the one. I couldn't persuade you to do it again.'

'What did we eat? For Christmas dinner?'

'We went full traditional. Turkey and all the trimmings.'

Amy was surprised. 'Oh right. I always swore if I ever had a Christmas away from my mum, I'd do something completely different for dinner.'

'I know what you mean – it can get a bit tedious, can't it. But that was all that was on the menu. Unless you were vegetarian. Listen, I'll see if the others are free – we should go out while the weather's good.'

'I'll meet you down there.'

Jack kissed her and left. Amy looked again at the dressing table, gripped by a sudden fear that she'd imagined the necklace. She went over and sat on the stool. Opened the drawer. The jewellery box was definitely there. This time she took it out and opened it up. The diamond shone. She lifted it out and put it on, fastening the clasp at the back of her neck. The action felt familiar.

Suddenly she froze. She heard a voice in her head.

'It looks amazing on you.'

But it wasn't Jack's voice or one of her friends or anyone she knew. It was an older, well-dressed woman in a smart navy suit and a tangerine silk scarf. She was a jeweller: the owner of the shop. It was an upmarket place near her office. Apart from the woman, Amy was alone in the store.

Amy tried to calm her breathing, still the cold rush of panic. She must have it wrong. She shook her head, tried to settle her thoughts but the memory was clear. She could see the wooden panelled display cabinets. The bright lights inside them, illuminating the cream satin stands. The woman with the auburn chignon smiling at her, and then Amy remembered her name: Ruth Wood. She'd introduced herself when Amy had come in, the bell ringing as Ruth had pressed the buzzer to unlock the door.

Amy saw the image of herself in the mirror; a single-carat solitaire diamond nestled in the hollow of her neck.

'What's the occasion?' asked Ruth.

Amy stalled. She felt a stab of guilt and then banished it.

'Thought I'd treat myself, that's all.'

A little of Ruth's polished sales veneer slipped as she allowed true admiration to warm her eyes. 'For Christmas?'

'Yes.' Amy touched the diamond. 'Why wait for a man to give you something like this? It's a little gift. From me to me.'

Ruth smiled. 'I think this will have just as much meaning,' she said, 'as anything you might get from a man.'

Amy watched as Ruth carefully wrapped the necklace. As she left the store, she felt as if she had done something incredibly extravagant and naughty – she'd never spent so much money on herself in one go before – but she also felt as if there was someone looking out for her for a change. *And it's me!* she thought, giggling to herself, still high on her purchase.

She sobered up as she neared the brasserie where she was meeting her mother for lunch. Time spent with Martha was often strained, with Amy on edge, waiting for the questions about her private life, questions she dreaded. Martha always wanted to know whether she'd met anyone. Every time they got together a tense expectation hung in the air between them until finally Martha would ask and Amy would be forced to admit, once again, she'd failed as a daughter, as a fully functioning member of society. She wasn't right, wasn't attractive or desirable enough, and hadn't been for five long years. Facing up to her shortcomings cut deeply and sometimes Amy wanted to shout: Do you not realize I *want* to meet someone? That I am as lonely as you?

Amy knew her mother wanted the fun and the fulfilment of a wider family, of grandchildren. Martha recognized these things as achievements rather than her daughter's career or ability to stand on her own two feet financially. And the more Martha held out for that pinnacle of accomplishments, the boyfriend, the more Amy resented being made to feel like a failure.

This meeting was even more laden with heavy-heartedness as she was going to be discussing their Christmas plans. Amy always went to her mother's house, had done ever since her father had died, where they followed a series of stale traditions, traditions that were so familiar they didn't even think about them, and they certainly held no excitement or sparkle. Amy would sleep in her old childhood bed and feel as if she was never going to experience anything different on this day that she had long grown out of. Her mother would drink too much and reminisce about when Amy's dad was alive, going off into her own little world somewhere in the past, leaving Amy feeling increasingly lonely. Amy would get up early on Boxing Day for the journey back to London on the train, leaving her mother in bed with a hangover. With every mile Amy would feel weighed down with sadness and a sense that her life was wasting away.

She arrived at the brasserie to find her mother already seated. No sooner had Amy sat down than Martha pulled out her phone.

'I have to show you this,' she said, enthusiastically tapping the screen. 'Sally – you remember, my old friend from Weybridge – well she's just got her second grandchild. A girl. Beautiful she is, look.' And Amy was forced to peer at her mother's phone screen where a tiny baby, fast asleep, was wrapped in a crocus-yellow cotton blanket.

'She's cute,' said Amy.

Martha gazed at the picture, her face a mix of admiration and longing. 'She certainly is. And, oh, you need to see this too.' Martha swiped away. 'Caroline – you know, my friend from Pilates – her daughter Harriet's just had her first.'

Amy tensed. What her mother hadn't yet mentioned was that Harriet had married an ex-boyfriend of Amy's, Richard. Martha often gave the impression that she thought Amy had let Richard slip through her fingers – a sentiment that had been reinforced by Amy's failure to find a long-term boyfriend.

Martha held up her phone. 'Here she is, look. In her baby bouncer.'

Amy didn't really want to see but there was no getting away from it. With a jolt she realized she could see Richard in the baby's face. *That could've been you*, her inner voice told her, *could be your child*. Amy looked away. She wanted children, yes, but not with Richard, she reminded herself sternly.

'Very nice. Congratulations to all involved,' she said briskly.

Martha pulled a face. 'Well, you could sound as if you mean it.'

'Mum, I do. But you must realize I don't know this Harriet or her child. I don't even know Richard anymore.'

Martha sniffed. A sniff that Amy knew masked what she really wanted to say: *You could have known him. You could be the one who'd married him and given birth to that wonderful grandchild.*

'Well, you don't want to leave it too long.' Martha paused. 'I saw this article in the paper. It was about fertility in older women. Not *older*,' she hurriedly corrected, seeing Amy's face, 'but, you know, not in their twenties. It said that by thirty most women had lost ninety per cent of their eggs.' Martha looked at her daughter worriedly.

Amy felt a stab of panic, which she forced down irritably. She'd read the same article. But it wasn't as if she was deliberately *not* meeting a man just to defy her mother and test her eggs to the limit. A scientific experiment to see if her reproductive system could beat the odds.

As she tried to come up with a response that would steer her mother away from the subject, knowing from experience that Martha would keep relentlessly circling back to it, it dawned on Amy that there was one piece of 'news' that would give her the freedom she craved like a caged bird.

'Actually, Mum, I've met someone.'

It took a moment for it to register. Probably because it had been so long coming, thought Amy. Then Martha's face broke into a delighted smile. The sun coming through the clouds.

'Who?' she exclaimed. 'When? Oh my goodness, I want to know everything!'

'Jack Stewart. A doctor. Just last week,' said Amy, making sure her story tallied with the one she'd told Lisa and Jenna. 'At Waterloo station.' As she furnished her mother with the details, playing it down where she could as an undercurrent of guilt sat uneasily in her stomach, she knew she was about to do something that she could never have dreamed of before. Put it down to the giddiness of buying the necklace earlier, mixed with the desperate need for some space, but she couldn't stop the words as they came out of her mouth.

'He's asked me to go to the Lake District with him for Christmas.'

As Amy dropped the bombshell, she felt light-headed with possibilities. She'd go away. Someplace where Christmas – which she'd grown to loathe, with all its emphasis on couples and families and children – would be pretty much non-existent. *Istanbul!* She'd go to Istanbul.

'He has?' Martha's face was conflicted – joy her daughter was going to spend this special time of year with a boyfriend mixed with a realization they wouldn't be doing what they always did. 'Darling, you must go. Don't worry about me. Funnily enough, I was having coffee with Beth the other day and you know her son's in Australia and she's all alone and we did say it might be fun to do something together one year.'

'Are you absolutely sure?' asked Amy, speared with guilt and debating whether to take it all back, tell her mum she'd spend Christmas with her after all.

'Positive. It'll do us both good to do something a little different.'

And so it was sealed.

'So when am I going to meet him?' asked Martha.

Amy smiled. 'All in good time, Mum. We've not been together very long.' She mentally calculated when she and Jack might split up – she didn't want to break her mum's heart any more than necessary. It would have to be after Christmas now. Impossible before Valentine's Day – the sympathy would be unbearable. It would also be too much hassle just before her birthday, which was a couple of weeks later. March. It would be in March. Amy would invent some mutually agreed reason why they'd decided to amicably part.

Martha would be devastated, Amy thought nervously. Then again, she might be doing her mother a favour. Jack could be the warm-up, let her mum know her daughter was capable of meeting a man.

Amy sat rooted to the stool. There had been no Christmas in the Lake District. The necklace had not been from Jack; she had bought it herself.

Or was her mind playing yet more tricks on her? The idea of escaping to Istanbul to avoid Christmas with her mother seemed inconceivable.

Amy's mind darted to her phone, which Jack had dropped back on the bed. She grabbed it, looked through the posts on Facebook. Every photo referencing their relationship was something innocuous – a plate of food, a scenic spot for a walk. There was not one picture of his face, and now she knew why. And if she had made up a boyfriend then how the hell did the imposter downstairs find her? Who was he? He'd gone along with her fiction – how did he know everything? *What did he want?*

Unless . . . unless she was going mad. Which was the truth?

TWENTY-ONE

27 February

Amy paced the room, aware Jack was waiting for her downstairs. She could hear everyone else gathering, getting ready for the walk.

'Amy?' called Martha from the hallway. 'Are you ready?'

Amy opened her door and cautiously walked down the stairs. She stopped halfway, seeing four faces looking up at her. Jenna turned away first, bent down to adjust her boots.

'Chop, chop,' said Martha.

Amy's insides churned. She could see Jack looking up at her and somehow sensed, for now, she had to keep her new-found fears to herself.

'I'm actually going to give this one a miss,' she said.

'What's wrong?' asked Jack, concern creasing his face. 'I thought you said the headache was better?'

'It is,' said Amy quickly. She took a breath. 'I'm a bit tired, that's all. Thought I might sit and read a book for a while.'

'The fresh air will help,' said Jack.

'He's right,' said Lisa.

'That's mother's advice too,' said Martha.

Jenna watched in silence.

Why are they all ganging up on me? thought Amy. She fought back the irritation, smiled as calmly as she could. 'I'll go out later,' she said. 'You guys have fun. You're not going to be long anyway, are you?' She needed to know how much time she had alone.

'Half an hour?' said Lisa. 'We won't go far in case it irritates Jenna's ankle.'

'There you go. I won't be missing out on much,' said Amy. 'I'll see you in a bit.' And she turned and walked back upstairs to avoid any further protests.

Amy went into her room but stood just inside, the door cracked open. She heard the last-minute gathering of hats and gloves, then the front door open. One by one the voices disappeared and then the door banged shut. As soon as the voices faded, Amy slipped out of her room. She crossed the landing and put her hand on the door handle of the room where Jack had spent his first night. She pushed it downwards, and then slunk inside.

The bed was made neatly. His holdall was on the floor next to the wardrobe, unzipped, and Amy could see clothes inside. She went over and carefully pulled the bag open. She lifted the clothes, making sure she didn't mess up their tidy folds. Underneath the T-shirts, jumpers and jeans were a book and a spare plug adaptor. Nothing to identify Jack Stewart. She stood up and looked around. Next to the bed was a phone charger. She opened the bedside table the charger rested on but it was empty. So were the drawers and the wardrobe, except for a single shirt hanging.

Maybe the bathroom. She opened the door to the en suite and found Jack's toothbrush, his razor and deodorant. A washbag lay by the sink – it seemed unlikely but she rummaged through, just in case. It contained nothing except bathroom products.

Amy gave a sigh of frustration. *There must be something.* She had to look again. This time she checked under the bed, the pockets of all his clothes, the bin, even under the mattress. There was nothing. It was possible he had his wallet with him and naturally, his phone. But what about his passport?

Amy looked around the room again. It *had* to be in here. Who took their passport on a walk in the snow? She was about to restart the search when she heard a sound. Someone was coming up the stairs.

She froze. Panicked, she glanced at her watch. It had only been fifteen minutes – why was someone back so soon? Maybe it was Jenna, she thought, needing to rest her ankle. But the footsteps continued down the corridor away from Jenna's room and towards Jack's. Amy looked around frantically and then dived into the en suite. She heard the bedroom door open and she looked through the crack by the door hinge. She saw Jack was standing in the room. He put his wallet down on the bedside cabinet, looked around. Then Amy stepped out, a big smile on her face.

'Oh hiya,' she said. 'You're back early.'

'Your mum's hands are cold,' said Jack. 'I thought I had some of those warmers, you know, that you slip inside your gloves.' He looked at her quizzically. 'Everything all right?'

Amy lifted the toilet roll she had in her hand. 'Ran out in my room. Knew there were some spares over here. Hope it's OK . . . me coming in.'

'Course!' said Jack, brushing away her concerns.

They looked at each other then. *Who are you?* thought Amy. *Where did you come from?*

'Come on,' he said, turning back towards the door. 'Why don't you come back out with me? It's not the same without you.'

Amy's eyes slid over to his holdall. 'What about the warmers?'

'Sorry?'

'For Mum.'

He slapped his forehead. 'Of course.' He went over to his bag, rummaged through. Amy watched. She knew there was no such thing in there and she wondered if Jack knew that too.

'I could've sworn . . .' he said, then shrugged. 'Maybe I didn't bring them.'

He stood up. Downstairs the front door went.

'Jack?' called up Martha. 'We're back. So don't worry. Lisa threw a snowball and it went down the back of my neck, so I'm soaked through anyway!'

'It was revenge for pushing me into that drift,' Amy heard Lisa say.

'I'm hungry,' said Jack. 'Fancy some lunch?'

He let her leave the room first and she tensed as he fell in step behind her. She suddenly wanted to be in the company of the others.

TWENTY-TWO

27 February

Amy tensed every time Jack's arm brushed against hers at lunch. She'd intended to sit away from him, further down the table. It would've given her time to think, to pause. To watch him and see if he gave anything away. But Jack had sat down first and then, seeing her coming over to the table with her bowl of pasta, he'd pulled out the chair next to him. She'd stopped but could think of no reasonable explanation as to why she should pick another seat.

The wine was open again and everyone was drinking – everyone except Amy. She wanted to keep a clear head, try and work out what had happened. Try and make sense of how this man had inveigled his way into her life. Her mother, lubricated on two glasses of red, was still going on about how Jack had got Amy onto a boat during their trip away at Christmas. She was regaling Jenna and Lisa with the story, and Jack was coming across even more heroic than he had that morning.

'And then he got her *aboard*,' said Martha. 'Can you imagine? Once Amy's made her mind up about something, it's very difficult, nay *impossible* to change it.' She beamed at Jack.

'She was wearing a buoyancy aid,' said Jack modestly, 'maybe that was what gave her the confidence.'

No, I wasn't, thought Amy, getting an image of herself in her mind. *I was wearing a jumper and jeans and walking around the Grand Bazaar in Istanbul shopping for a ceramic lamp.*

Was she? Had she remembered that right? Suddenly she didn't know.

'Maybe you do yourself a disservice,' said Jenna, and Amy thought she detected a touch of sarcasm. 'Maybe you're what Amy really needs.'

'Well, she's certainly been happier since you've come along,' said Martha.

Amy felt her pasta sit queasily in her stomach.

'What else did you get up to?' asked Lisa. 'Amy's told us so little about her trip.'

'We climbed Scafell Pike,' said Jack. 'Boxing Day.'

'Seriously?' asked Lisa. 'Wasn't it icy?'

'We got ice spikes. They fit over your boots.'

'Oh right, cool,' said Lisa. 'So what's it like?'

'Steep! But she's fitter than me. Amy was leading most of the time.'

'Get you, darling,' said Martha, nudging Amy's elbow.

Amy forced a smile. It sounded like her, like it could've been her.

'How was the view at the top?' asked Jenna.

'Mountains at your feet every which way you look,' said

Jack. 'It was windy, though. I took a flask and we stopped for some hot chocolate before coming back down.'

No we didn't, thought Amy desperately. She didn't remember that at all.

'I always think it's worse coming down than going up,' said Martha. 'Something about those loose rocks under your feet.'

'Amy's like a mountain goat,' smiled Jack.

'How do you know?' blurted Amy, dropping her fork into the bowl with a clatter.

Everyone turned to her in surprise.

'Sorry . . . did I say something wrong?' said Jack, taken aback.

'Amy this, Amy that . . . You know nothing about me.'

Jack gave an awkward smile. 'Well, I know we've only been dating a few months but—'

'Stop,' said Amy. 'Please stop.'

'I'm sorry,' said Jack, crestfallen. 'I didn't mean to upset you or anything.' He went to put an arm around her shoulders but Amy stood abruptly.

'I've lost my appetite,' she said and left the room.

TWENTY-THREE

27 February

'What's up?' asked Lisa, putting her head around the door.

Agitated, Amy turned around, saw her friend close the door of the living room and come to join her by the fire. Amy had put on another log and the flames crackled and spit. Her stomach was in knots. There was something else about the fragments of memories of when she was in Istanbul. She was in a beautiful place but she was aware of a heaviness that hung over her. An unexplained sense of a terrible loss. She didn't know what or why, only that it filled her with dread. She didn't even really know if any of it was real. She looked into the white-hot light, knowing she had to tell someone.

'I've had another memory come back to me,' she said. 'Several, in fact.'

Lisa's face lit up. 'That's amazing. Isn't it?' she added, when Amy didn't smile back.

'It's Jack,' she said, her voice hushed. Then she took a deep breath. 'I'm pretty sure I made him up.'

Lisa frowned. 'Pardon?'

'I made him up, invented him. And he's sitting there, in that kitchen, as casual as you like having lunch with us all.'

Lisa was utterly baffled. 'You what?'

Amy didn't repeat herself a third time.

'But he's there,' said Lisa, pointing vaguely in the direction of the kitchen.

'Yes, but that's not Jack Stewart. Because Jack Stewart doesn't exist. The *real* Jack Stewart, who isn't real at all, is a figment of my imagination. A man that I plucked out of my head and told you all was my boyfriend.'

Lisa laughed, once, then closed her mouth. 'So . . . he's not real.'

'That's what I keep telling you.'

'You fabricated a person and made out he was your boyfriend?'

'Lisa, you really need to keep up.'

'But . . . *why*?'

'For a joke.'

'A *joke*?' spluttered Lisa.

Amy exhaled. 'Partly. I was fed up with all the twee Facebook posts. People putting up photos of their perfect weekends; hand-holding in the park, autumn leaves, playing board games together in the gastro pub . . .'

Lisa thought. 'Me and David play games in the pub. Were you taking the piss out of our Sundays?'

'I prefer to think of it as satire.'

Lisa paused, shook her head. 'I'm still not quite getting this. How can Jack be made up? You *showed* us everything. The dinners . . . the Valentine flowers!'

'The dinners were close-ups of things I ate at home. I probably bought the flowers myself. Look, he was only meant to be temporary. I was going to "break up" with him right after my birthday. He wasn't even meant to be on this trip – I pretended he had to work, remember?'

'Yes, that's what you told me.' Lisa rubbed her face with her hands, looked carefully at Amy.

'You don't believe me,' said Amy.

'It's not that . . . Look, a head injury can cause all sorts of side effects.'

'I'm not deluded,' said Amy.

'I didn't say you were. But if Jack Stewart doesn't exist, who's that in the kitchen?'

'That's the thing. I don't know.'

'He seems so nice . . .'

'He can't be,' said Amy. 'He's an imposter.' She paused. 'At least, I think so.'

Lisa thought for a moment. 'How certain are you? How clear are your memories of . . . inventing a boyfriend?'

'Pretty clear.'

'You do know this all sounds . . .' said Lisa.

'Totally mad. Yes.' Amy laid a hand on her friend's arm. 'Look, I'm worried. I'm pretty sure I'm right. So whoever he is, he's a liar. That terrifies me. He is a stranger and he has found a way to wheedle his way here, into this lodge, with all of us.'

'Maybe he just needed a holiday,' said Lisa.

'This isn't a joke,' said Amy darkly.

'I know, I'm sorry. I'm finding it hard to take it all in.'

Lisa paused. 'There is one thing you can do, you know that, don't you?'

Amy nodded. 'I have to confront him.'

TWENTY-FOUR

15 January

Harry was already beyond bored. A little over a week into his new job and the tedium of polishing glasses, filling them with wine, collecting them then cleaning them again felt like a relentless cycle from which he would never escape. The hardest part was the sense of servitude, the knowledge that he was there to obediently wait on people. It wasn't unlike the job in Dolce & Gabbana, where he'd had to bow and scrape to some of the wealthiest individuals in the city, men with more money than Harry would ever see in a lifetime who barely blinked as they handed him thousand-pound jackets, items they discarded as they tried on another, not seeing him other than as a human clothes horse. He'd hated it and knew he shouldn't have got another job that was working at the beck and call of other people richer than him, but what choice did he have? None, he reminded himself as he cast his eyes over the early Friday evening crowd.

He saw Max moving amongst the tables, offering to replace empty bottles with full ones, schmoozing with the customers, chatting to the newer clientele in the hope they would become regulars. There was no sign of Ellen and Rosie; he hadn't seen either of them since his encounter a week ago.

Max moved to another table. Harry watched. He was looking for the right moment to take his boss to one side. He had a request for him, one that he was a little nervous about. Then Max came over, leaned against the bar and cast his eyes approvingly over the room. Harry could tell that his boss was filled with a sense of well-being; safe in the knowledge it would be another successful night.

It was a good time. Alex, the other staff member working that night, was in the cellar pulling out more stock. Harry made sure he had something in his hands, that he looked busy.

He spoke to his boss's back. 'Max, could I have a quick word?'

Max turned briskly. 'What's up?'

Harry had already clocked Max's minuscule frown, but it was too late to back out now. 'I wondered . . . I'm a bit strapped. Would I be able to get an advance on my wages?'

'I'm afraid that's not company policy.'

Harry bristled. What did Max think this was, a multinational with zero flexibility? It was a single wine bar, for God's sake, with a staff of less than four. Where was the man's humanity?

'I appreciate that but, well, it's a long time until payday and I have a little cash-flow issue. For basic necessities,' he added, hoping Max would understand this wasn't beer money he was asking for, it was some cash to keep his landlord off his back. Or rather his landlord's collection man.

Harry had been sleeping off his shift early Wednesday morning when there had been a persistent and increasingly loud knock on his door. He'd done his best to ignore it but then a familiar voice had boomed through the letterbox that had seeped into his stomach with dread.

'Open this door, you lazy fucker! You've got ten seconds.'

It was enough to make Harry scramble out of bed. He knew Nick had a key and knew he would use it. Harry did not want a six-foot, eighteen-stone bear of a man bursting into his bedsit while he was lying there in his underpants. He pulled on a sweatshirt and joggers and hurried to the front door.

'You took your time,' said Nick.

'Nice to see you too,' said Harry, not opening the door fully. Nick clocked this and shoved his foot against it – hard – and it bounced out of Harry's hand and back against the wall.

Harry shoved his hands in his pockets and silently wished for Nick to get it over and done with. He knew why he was there; the unknown was what Nick had come to do about it.

'You owe rent,' said Nick.

Harry nodded.

'The boss agreed two weeks.'

Harry had never met his landlord but had read about him online. He'd been investigated for renting out places with dodgy fire safety regulations but despite all the evidence he'd somehow got away with it. His response had been to put the complaining tenants' rents up.

'I've got a job,' said Harry. 'He can have his money.'

'He wants it now.'

'I only started a few days ago. I don't get paid until next month.'

'Tell you what, you get four hundred by Saturday and I'll make sure he's happy until next month.'

'But that's only three days away!'

'Five hundred.'

'I can't—'

'Six,' said Nick, stony-faced.

Harry bit his tongue in fury but knew not to say anything else. Three days to find six hundred quid! It was impossible.

'You make sure you're up nice and early mind, cos I'll be along same time Saturday morning. And unlike today, I won't be knocking. If you're not here, door open, red carpet welcome, cash fanning out from those beautiful unbroken fingers of yours, I'll be coming into your bedroom as your own personal alarm clock. Do you hear what I'm saying?'

Harry stared at him. Nodded.

'Good. Then we have an agreement.'

Harry watched as Nick turned and walked back down the path then disappeared down the road.

Shit.

*

'I can't change the rules for one person,' said Max, 'otherwise it'll soon get out of hand.'

Harry felt a panic start to rise in his chest. Nick was going to be at his place in less than twelve hours. If he wasn't ready with the money, things were going to get a whole lot worse. This he knew from experience. He'd been struggling to pay his rent after he'd lost his job at Dolce & Gabbana, and when he'd tried to charm his way out of it he'd received a fist in his face. Nick did not like 'lip' and if Harry 'wanted to come to an arrangement' he needed to say so, not treat his landlord, and therefore by extension, Nick, like 'a dick'.

'Please, Max,' said Harry, hating his boss at that moment, hating himself for begging. He saw the other barman, Alex, come from the back of the room, arms full with a box of wine. Time was running out. 'It's kind of an emergency.'

Max looked at him and Harry forced himself not to stare back in anger.

'How much?'

'Eight hundred.'

'That's over two week's wages. You've only worked here one.'

Harry fought down the desperation. He smiled. 'I'm not going anywhere. I like it here.'

After what felt like an age, Max reluctantly nodded.

'OK. But just this once. I mean it.'

'Thank you, Max. I appreciate it.' Harry's smile dropped the minute Max moved away. Jesus, he was a tight bastard. It was always the same with those who had money. Harry had seen the till receipts at the end of the night. This place cleared over ten grand a week. He knew his boss was loaded, knew he lived with his wife and two kids in an Edwardian house in Fulham that was worth three million. The wife had come in one afternoon, the two kids trailing behind in private school uniforms. Harry had been tasked with getting the kids orange juices, which the wife had made a point of paying for, presumably so as not to look too privileged, even as she sat there in her yoga gear, clearly not having to work for a living. When she'd gone for her bank card, her driving licence had fallen to the floor. Harry had retrieved it for her, clocked the address. Later he'd googled it, his heart shrivelling as he saw the elitist street, the house's eye-popping value.

Harry wiped the resentment from his face as a woman came to the bar. She sat down, shrugged off her coat and placed her expensive leather bag on the brass bar top with a sigh.

'Hard day?' asked Harry.

'Christ, how did you know?' the woman replied. 'A glass of Malbec, please. Large one.'

He went to get a bottle of the Malbec and a clean glass, carefully poured the wine and slid it over to her, glancing at her as he did so.

She was looking at him. 'Yes, I am.'

'You are what?'

'Drinking alone.'

Harry held up both hands, palms out. 'I didn't say a word.'

'I could see it in your eyes. It's a well-earned glass after a stressful week.' She pointed down to a larger bag by her feet, documents poking out at the top. 'Which isn't yet over. So don't judge.'

'Wouldn't dream of it,' said Harry. He surreptitiously took her in as he wiped down the bar. Late thirties, well-tailored suit, expensive watch. No ring.

She took a large gulp of the wine, set it down and smiled. 'Better already.'

'What's so important it needs finishing on a Friday night?' asked Harry.

'Tax. Only two weeks until the deadline. Clients get later and later sending me their info. I'd like to tell them to go jump, but as director I need to suck it up. At least until I can sell the company and swan off into early retirement.'

'Oh yes? That's possible?'

'God, yeah. Or I wouldn't be doing it.'

'Nice,' said Harry. 'It's going to take me a bit longer, but I totally get you.'

The woman smiled indulgently. 'You want to retire?'

Harry had no idea why he'd said what he did. Envy perhaps or a wistful dream forming itself into words. A sense of not wanting to feel inferior to this woman who was clearly very focused. What did it matter? It was a nice idea that amused him. He decided to continue with it.

'I'm in the process of buying a bar. Got a redundancy payout from my corporate job, needed a total change of scene. I've an offer on a place in Putney Bridge. Should be through by spring.'

'Oh right. I thought you just worked here.'

'Because I'm behind the bar, dressed in this get-up?'

She shrugged.

He leaned over, spoke softly. 'You shouldn't judge.'

She smiled. 'Touché.'

'I'm not one for just saying I'll do something. Need to get my feet wet. And Max is a mate. He gets help and I get to learn the ropes.' He grinned. 'And I make my mistakes on someone else's time.'

She laughed and raised her eyebrows, clearly more impressed with him now. Harry deliberately moved away to serve someone else. Let her ponder that for a bit, he thought, before he went back and talked some more. He kept up the persona; like-minded entrepreneurs, sparring off each other. For the first time in months he wasn't bored to the point of destruction. He was using his brain. Harry was too intelligent for this job, but he hadn't had the opportunities that others had and, with a few bad choices, had ended up on a path that didn't go anywhere near filling his potential. Sometimes he despaired at finding a way out. It was little moments like this though, that reminded him he was smart. It was moments like this that made him feel there could be an alternative narrative to his life. Harry felt a buzz return, a high he hadn't had since before things had gone very wrong a few months ago, when everything had unravelled to the point he'd been fired from Dolce & Gabbana and ended up in court. He brushed these reminders away – what he was doing now was harmless. This was keeping him sane while he worked his mind-numbing job.

He learned her name was Nina and she was the director and owner of a boutique accountancy firm. When he went for a bathroom break, he looked her up at Companies' House – turnover for her business was seven figures. Nina stayed for a second glass of wine and then reluctantly stood.

'It's been nice talking to you.'

'Likewise,' said Harry.

She paused and then opened her purse and put a business card on the bar. 'You ever in need of an accountant, give me a call.'

'I've already got someone lined up,' said Harry.

'Oh.' She went to take her card back, but he put his hand over hers. 'It's good to know more than one,' he said, smiling.

She smiled back at him. 'I need to go home, get this work done.'

He nodded. 'Lot to do?'

'Couple of hours.'

Harry glanced at the clock. 'We'll finish shift at the same time then.'

He saw her hesitate.

'Nightcap?' she suggested.

'I can't tonight. Sorry.'

She covered her disappointment and put her coat back on. 'Another time then.'

'Hope so.'

He watched as she left, feeling the power of being in control. He wasn't going to get chucked out like the trash again.

After work ended, Harry pocketed his envelope stuffed with twenty-pound notes, withdrawing two hundred first. He left the bar and walked towards Wimbledon, to the affluent streets on the edge of the Village that flanked the beginnings of the common overlooking Rushmere pond. He turned up one of the large driveways and walked past the centrally placed fountain: a Cupid atop a set of tiered stones. He went up to the front door and the security light burst on. It was late now, past midnight and all the lights inside the house were off. He took the envelope out of his pocket and posted it through the letterbox, hearing the soft thud as it landed on the floor. His landlord might not like the direct route but now the rent was paid, Harry could avoid the humiliation of dealing with Nick in the morning. And he'd be left alone for a couple more weeks at least. As he walked back down the driveway he passed the fountain again. He unzipped his flies, emptied his bladder. Then with a last look at the house, he headed back to his bedsit.

As he did so, he pulled out the card Nina had given him earlier, clocked the mobile number. He composed a text. Minutes later he got a reply. He smiled. This time he was going to play it much more carefully.

TWENTY-FIVE

27 February

Amy took a determined breath as she stepped into the hall, Lisa following.

'Everyone's in there,' said Lisa, putting a hand on Amy's arm.

'So?' said Amy. 'It's better that way. Then they can all witness him flounder when I catch him out.' She saw her friend look dubious. 'Trust me, Lisa. I'm a lawyer. I can handle confrontation. I'm trained to sniff out bullshit.'

Lisa hesitated. 'But what if you're wrong?'

'What if I'm *right*? I have to confront him. How am I meant to let something like this go on?'

Amy led the way across the hall. She could hear the others talking softly. Talking about her, no doubt. About how she'd seemed a little unhinged before getting all upset and storming out of the room. Well, they too would be upset when they heard what she had to say. They would be outraged and her mother would go pale with trepidation. She wasn't going to let him lie to them any longer. She boldly went into the kitchen and everyone immediately quietened. She stared hard at Jack, at his faux look of anxiety. She paused, put aside any nerves. She was aware that everyone was looking at her, wondering what she was going to say.

'This man,' said Amy, 'is not who you think he is.'

She saw Jack pull a quizzical face, baffled by her statement. *Let him*, thought Amy. *He can act as much as he wants.* 'He is not Doctor Jack Stewart. He's an imposter.'

Jack's mouth dropped open in part-amusement, part confusion. 'Sorry, is this some sort of joke? On me?'

'Who are you?' asked Amy, watching him carefully.

'Pardon?'

'Because I know you're not Jack Stewart. You're not a doctor and you're not my boyfriend.'

'Amy, are you OK?' asked Martha, stepping forward.

Amy put an arm out to keep her back. 'Don't get too close to him, Mum. We don't know who he is.'

Jack was quiet for a moment, frowning, thinking. 'OK, I don't get it. Where's all this come from, Amy?'

She tapped the side of her head. Gave a small triumphant smile. 'The memories are coming back,' she said. 'More and more frequently. And I now know exactly what happened at Christmas. I was nowhere near the Lake District, I was in Istanbul.'

'You went to Istanbul with Jack?' asked Martha, confused.

'No, Mum. I didn't go anywhere with Jack. This man is not Jack.' She pointed a finger at him. 'I don't even know him. I made up my boyfriend.' She looked hard at him. 'As you well know. Somehow you found this out. You decided to become Jack Stewart and lie your way here. And I want to know why.'

'Amy . . .?' said Martha, putting a hand on her arm, her eyes full of concern.

'Mum, please,' said Amy, not taking her eyes off the man in front of her. 'I need him to tell me who he is.'

'Oh God,' said Martha, under her breath.

Jack ran his hands through his hair. 'I don't know what to say . . .'

'Just tell the truth,' said Amy. 'Then maybe there's a chance I won't call the police.'

'I am Jack,' he pleaded softly. 'Jack Stewart. Your boy-friend.'

'Stop lying,' said Amy. 'You're not getting away with this any longer.'

Jack held out his hands helplessly. 'I'm not lying. I promise you.' He looked to the side, appealed to Martha and the others.

'Maybe there's some sort of misunderstanding,' said Jenna.

Amy wheeled. 'Misunderstanding? There's a man in this house that none of us know. I think we should be just a little bit worried, don't you?'

'OK, OK,' said Martha soothingly. 'Tell us more, Amy. This is a lot to take in. What makes you so convinced that Jack here' – she gestured and to Amy's irritation she saw her mother throw him an apologetic smile – 'is not your boyfriend?'

'Because, Mum,' said Amy, 'I *remember*.'

Jack's face lit up. 'It's OK, I think I can solve this.'

Amy resisted rolling her eyes.

Jack indicated the door, seeking permission. 'If I can just go . . .'

Amy thought. If he was going to do a runner, maybe that would do them all a favour. She stepped to one side. 'Be my guest.'

Jack walked past her and out of the room.

'Amy, what's all this about?' cried Martha, as soon as he'd left.

'Look, Mum, I'm sorry for lying to you, for pretending I had a boyfriend. It was only meant to be for a short time, something harmless. I certainly never intended for any of this,' she said, biting her lip.

Amy had heard him go upstairs and it had now gone quiet. Doubt was creeping into her mind and she realized she shouldn't have let him be alone after all. What if he was intending to hurt them? What if he'd gone to get a weapon? She cast her eyes over the kitchen; saw the knife block. She moved closer to it.

'We should never have come here,' Martha said sorrowfully.

'What?' said Amy, distracted.

Her mother was looking at her, despondent. 'This place. It brings nothing but bad luck.'

'That's not true, Mum. It's not this place.'

'No?'

Amy tried to stay tactful. 'Even Dad had many happy memories here.'

'He died here! These mountains claim lives.'

They heard sounds then, of footsteps running down the stairs. Amy tensed. While everyone stared in anticipation at

the door, Amy softly pulled a knife out of the block, laid it on the counter next to her.

'Got it,' said Jack, as he came back in the room. He was holding up a small, pink plastic card.

'There you go,' said Martha, relieved. 'It's Jack's driving licence.'

Jenna stepped forward and held out her hand. Jack passed it over and she studied it, turning it over. She shrugged. 'It looks genuine enough.'

'Are you an expert?' snapped Amy.

'Well, no but . . . take a look for yourself.'

Amy took the driving licence that Jenna held out. It looked real. Jack's photo and name and address were on it: *2A Foxmore Crescent, Battersea, London*. She put it on the counter.

'Where's your passport?' she demanded.

'Really?' said Jenna.

'Why not?' said Amy. 'It's easy to fake a licence, notoriously difficult to get a passport. Let's see what he's got.'

'Amy . . .' said Lisa. 'I understand you've got a clear memory of who you think Jack is—'

'I don't think, I *know*,' said Amy, but even she sounded a little unsure now.

'Please don't do this to yourself, love,' said Martha, deeply upset.

Amy looked around at the doubt and concern on everyone's faces. Suddenly she had to get out of the room. She walked past them all, grabbed her coat and boots from the hallway and, dragging them on, escaped outside.

TWENTY-SIX

27 February

Amy stumbled through the thick snow, breathing deeply, letting the freezing cold air sting her senses. She went around the back of the house, her legs working hard, the snow coming up to her knees, sometimes higher. She passed the pool and headed further into the valley. Mountains surrounded her on all sides, an infinite wilderness where she was but a speck in a sea of towering white.

She tried to clear her mind. Jack had a driving licence. But so what? It was true what she'd said – they were incredibly easy to get hold of online. It was not proof he was Jack Stewart. *There is no Jack Stewart*, she reminded herself.

But how had that man back in the house figured out that she'd made up a boyfriend?

She didn't know. She walked a bit further. Gazed up at the mountains and felt their density bearing down on her.

And how did that man in the house know all the details of her and Jack Stewart's fictitious relationship?

She didn't know.

How did that man know she and her friends would be away in Val d'Isère this week?

She didn't know.

What did he want?

Exhausted, her legs gave way and she sat down heavily in the thick snow. *Why can't you remember?* The frustration was unbearable. She grabbed a handful of snow in her gloves and threw it into her face. *Why has your mind left you?* She picked up more snow, rubbed it on her cheeks, her eyes. *Why are you letting yourself down like this?* Skin burning from the cold, she suddenly stopped. Tried to rub it off but her gloves were caked in snow and it made it worse. She used her upper arms to get the worst off, felt the rawness where the snow had melted on her face.

The sun dipped further behind one of the mountains, throwing a swathe of pink-gold on the opposite peak. It was incredibly beautiful but at the same time its fleeting nature stirred a deep loneliness in Amy. In a matter of a few minutes the light would have changed again. Even as she looked at it, the intensity of the colours was waning, taking on a more subdued hue.

If Amy was right about the imposter back at the house then she had to accept another fact too. There was no boyfriend. There never had been. She was as single and unwanted as she'd been for the last five years. Amy was hit by a sense of failure and undesirability that was brutal in its intensity. She felt her throat thicken but fought back the tears. *No*, she told herself sternly, *no self-pity. You've only known this man two days and look how you lost your heart to him.* It was even worse than that, she thought, because she, Amy Kennedy, had always prided herself on being able to identify the liars and the cheats. If that man back in the lodge was an imposter, as she believed, she'd fallen for him hook, line and sinker. She hadn't spotted a thing. Her hand suddenly flew to her face. She'd even slept with him. Gone along with his tale of how good their sex life was and let him into her bed. She felt sick.

A sound above, a high-pitched piercing cry, made her look up. She saw a bird wheel on the thermals and with a lurch saw it was an eagle. She squinted up into the fading light, desperate to see if it was a golden eagle, and then she saw the mighty wingspan, caught a glimmer of the gold plumage in the last of the sun. Energized, she stood, gazed skyward. Maybe it was even *her* eagle, the one she'd seen up close when she herself had flown up in that free air. She felt it was. She felt less alone. She watched it, taking comfort from its presence, until it became just a darkened shadow against the sky. And then the light all but completely faded away and she could no longer see it.

It was time to go back.

No more, she thought. Now her memory was returning, Jack couldn't dupe her anymore.

TWENTY-SEVEN

27 February

Dinner was an awkward affair. Jack was quiet, glancing at her every now and then as if to gauge her feelings towards him. It made her angry. She'd had enough of his charade and the obvious effect it was having on everyone else. Her friends kept up light, meaningless chat, but it was clear they were unsure of what to do for the best. Her mother would give pained looks in her direction, followed by a flickering sympathetic glance at Jack.

Amy felt that everyone was feeling sorry for Jack. It got her back up. None of them seemed to want to believe her. It was too strange and too complicated. It was easier for them to go along with the path of least resistance. They were sleepwalking into God knew what. It frightened her how they were all so willing to give him the benefit of the doubt, even if only until they'd fully made up their minds. *Anything* could happen in that time. He was a stranger living amongst them, a cuckoo in the nest. She looked up at him herself then. He was sitting at the other end of the table and she was struck again by how good-looking he was. She watched as he politely twirled a forkful of spaghetti and placed it in his mouth. The mouth that had touched hers, the hands that had been on her body.

He looked up and she glowered at him. His eyes locked with hers, crestfallen.

'Please excuse me for a moment,' he said, standing. Visibly upset, he left the table and went out of the kitchen.

Amy saw everyone watch him go, felt their collective exhale as he closed the door. The polite pretence came down, the tension finally allowed a release.

'He was worried about you,' said Martha.

Amy looked round at her mother. 'What?'

'Earlier, when you went out into the snow and it was getting dark. He wanted to come after you.'

'Well, I'm glad he didn't.'

'What's wrong with you? Isn't it nice to have someone who cares?'

'Mum, he's faking it.'

'Why would someone go to the trouble of pretending to be your boyfriend' – Amy didn't like her mother's emphasis on 'your', as if it were a difficult thing to be her boyfriend – 'and then act for several days now as if they cared about you deeply?'

'Look, I understand your exasperation. I know it's a hard thing to get your head around. But he's a fraud.'

Martha lay down her fork, her face clouding with sadness. 'You're going to push him away,' she said. 'Like Richard.'

Amy inhaled sharply. 'Have you been listening to a word

I've said?' She turned to her friends. 'Lisa, Jenna, you believe me, right?'

Neither of them answered immediately.

'Great,' said Amy. 'That's great.'

'You don't always make it easy to know what to believe,' said Jenna quietly.

'What's that supposed to mean?'

Lisa, who was sitting next to her, laid a calming hand on her arm. 'Amy, it's not that we don't believe you. It's just . . . there are lots of factors to take into consideration. And I know it's hard to hear but there is the possibility that the fall has caused your brain to reimagine your memories.'

Amy pulled her arm free. She stared at them all, crushed. 'Nice to know you're all on my side.'

'It's not about taking sides, it's—'

All eyes swivelled to the door. Jack had come into the room.

'Look, guys,' he said, 'I think I should leave.'

'What?' cried Martha.

'I don't want to cause any upset, least of all to Amy, so it would be better if I took a flight back to the UK. Gave Amy some space. This can all be worked out back home. There's no rush – I'm going to be there for her for as long as it takes.'

There was a silence. Everyone looked at Amy.

'That's very thoughtful of you,' she said. 'Especially when you know the airport is closed.'

'Amy!' said Martha. 'He's at least trying to do the right thing.'

'The right thing, Mum, would be to tell the truth. Or better yet, to never have invented a persona for himself.'

'I thought it was you inventing the persona . . .' muttered Martha.

Upset, Amy scraped her chair back. 'I'm going upstairs.'

She barrelled out of the room, ignoring the looks behind her. She went into her bedroom, shut the door. Then she stood back from it, half expecting to hear a sound on the other side, for Jack to have followed.

Her heart was hammering.

She put her hand on the key and turned the lock with a loud *thunk*.

TWENTY-EIGHT

28 February

Amy stirred, her sleep interrupted by a tapping sound. She opened her eyes. There it is was again, a soft knock on her bedroom door. She tensed, aware of how tired she felt. She'd stayed awake for hours the night before, her mind going over and over what she knew, what she didn't know. There was another tap. Amy sat up, checked the time on her phone and was taken aback to realize it was past nine o'clock.

The knock came again, this time with a soft calling of her name. It was Lisa.

Amy got out of bed. She went over to the door and opened it.

Lisa's face registered surprise and Amy tried to smooth her dishevelled hair.

'I've only just woken up,' she said.

'Bad night?'

'Didn't sleep well at all.' Amy tensed as she looked over Lisa's shoulder. 'Where's Jack?'

Lisa shrugged. 'Don't know.'

'He stayed?'

'Well, we couldn't really kick him out. It started snowing again last night. It was dark. There were no cabs, no flights.'

Amy stiffened. God, she felt tired. She stifled a yawn. 'Have you come to tell me how mad I am?' she said defensively.

'Not at all. I thought we could do a bit of digging, make a few phone calls. If you say you made Jack up, there must be some evidence somewhere.' Lisa pushed her in the direction of the bathroom. 'Go on, get a shower and we'll get started.'

'See,' said Lisa, pointing at the photo on Amy's phone. It was the picture of the Valentine's Day flowers that Amy had loaded up onto Facebook – the flowers she'd proudly said had been sent by Jack.

Lisa expanded the image. 'You can just see it – look.'

Amy took the phone and there was a blurred image of a tiny envelope on a stick in the middle of the bouquet. The message that the florist had added. Printed on the envelope was the florist's company name.

'What about it?'

'Well, they might have a record of who bought them.'

Amy looked up at her friend in hope. Her hands shaking, she googled the company but then the screen on her phone froze. She made a sound of impatience.

'What is it?'

'My phone's packed up again.'

Lisa offered her own. 'Use mine.'

Amy took it gratefully and found the florist's number.

She held the phone to her ear, waiting. Her heart leapt as it was answered.

'Hello . . . my name is Amy Kennedy. I wonder if you can help me with something . . . You sent me some flowers on the fourteenth of February. Yes, that's right, Cedar Street in Earlsfield.' She paused. 'Could you tell me who paid for them?' She looked at Lisa nervously. 'It was cash?' Her face fell. 'Do you remember who came into the shop? Was it a man or a woman?' She covered the receiver, spoke to Lisa. 'She wasn't working that day. She's checking with her colleague. Yes, I'm here. Oh. Are you sure? Well, thank you anyway.' She hung up.

'Well?' asked Lisa.

'Her colleague doesn't remember. So many orders for Valentine's.'

'Let's try something else,' said Lisa. 'What about the hotel in the Lakes? Surely they'd have a record of your stay. What was the name of it again?'

Amy told her and they looked up the number. She rang it and asked the receptionist if there was a booking over Christmas in her name. 'She says not,' Amy relayed to Lisa.

'What about Jack's name?'

Amy asked. She listened to the reply, thanked the receptionist and hung up.

'Go on,' prompted Lisa.

'There was a booking in the name of Mr Stewart *but*,' she quickly added at Lisa's raised eyebrows, 'spelled the other way. S. T. U. A. R. T. So it's not him. Which means we didn't stay there.'

'It's hardly cast-iron proof though, is it?' said Lisa. 'What if they spelled his name wrong?'

'It wasn't us,' repeated Amy.

'Did they give you an address?'

'Not allowed to,' said Amy. 'Data protection.'

She tossed the phone on the bed in frustration and paced over to the window, unwilling to meet what she knew would be Lisa's consoling gaze. She could physically feel the waves of sympathy coming across the room from her friend, sympathy for Amy's desperation to verify something that was becoming impossible to prove.

But Amy was convinced she was right. She felt caught in a trap of her own making. One little lie she'd told, one little fib designed to make her life easier, but look how it had spun out of control. She felt tense, realized she was clenching her fists and forced herself to release them. There had to be something else that proved he was someone she'd fabricated. She gazed out of the window, a sense of helplessness threatening to over-whelm her. She felt her mood plummet, felt a reminder of the deeply buried fearful sensation that had spooked her before.

'There's something else,' she said to Lisa.

'Go on.'

'My memories . . . the ones that have returned. In them I sometimes get an awful feeling . . .'

'About what?'

'That's just it, I don't know. All I can be sure of is that something really bad has happened.'

'OK . . .' Lisa shrugged. 'I guess it will come back to you in time.'

Amy nodded. She didn't like the way it hung over her like a bad omen. She was frightened of what it was.

'Oh my God,' exclaimed Lisa. 'Your phone. Of course! How could we have forgotten? The messages. From Jack.'

Amy looked over at her phone. *The messages.* Who the bloody hell had sent them if it wasn't Jack? Suddenly she felt unsure.

'You need to call the number,' said Lisa.

Did she? Amy's mind was scrambling around, trying to think of an explanation. How had she sent and received messages to a person who didn't exist? A memory flickered then, a feeling of familiarity that died as soon as it appeared. *What was that?* She looked for it again but it wouldn't reappear. Lisa was waiting expectantly and Amy knew she had to do it.

She pressed the call button on Jack's number. In her ear, a phone rang. Then slowly, a dawning realization. There was another phone ringing. There, in the lodge. Lisa got off the bed and opened the bedroom door. The ringing sound immediately got louder. It was coming from Jack's room across the landing.

Amy quickly hung up.

'It's Jack's phone,' said Lisa. 'In his room.'

'It can't be,' said Amy. 'Jack doesn't exist.'

Another flicker, the memory scraping at the window of her mind again, but to her frustration it wouldn't appear.

'Amy . . .' said Lisa, reaching over to her.

'I'm telling you, Lisa, it's true. I made him up. I *remember*.'

Lisa's face radiated concern.

Amy glowered. 'Don't say it.'

179

'What?'

'The P word,' she growled.

'I'm sorry, Amy,' said Lisa gently. 'Look, it's common, loads of head injury victims suffer with issues of trust after an injury.'

'I'm not paranoid,' said Amy. 'And I'm not a victim.'

Lisa left then, saying she was going downstairs to make everyone some breakfast.

Amy flopped back on the bed, feeling more alone than ever. It was obvious that none of them believed her. Her story was hard to believe, this Amy acknowledged, but there had to be some proof out there somewhere. She took in a deep breath, closed her eyes. *Think*, she told herself. And then it came to her.

The nurse from the hospital. Jack had said he'd visited. He said he'd spoken to Nurse Morgan. Amy could remember her vividly, her red hair, her rigorous manner. If that man downstairs really had gone to the hospital, then maybe there was something about him that Nurse Morgan could throw some light on.

Amy called St George's switchboard and told herself not to be disappointed if Nurse Morgan wasn't on shift. But to her excitement, she was. Amy sat up straight, explained who she was.

'Yes, I remember,' said Nurse Morgan. 'How are you getting on?'

'Memory is starting to return in small pieces,' said Amy. 'But I wanted to ask you about something that happened when I was in hospital.'

'I'll try and help,' said Nurse Morgan.

'My boyfriend came to see me,' said Amy. 'Jack Stewart. On the day after I was admitted, the Saturday. He told me he came by but it was out of visiting hours so he wasn't able to see me.'

'Let me think. Yes, I remember. He was only a few minutes late but we have to be sticklers for the rules. It was the morning, so I reckoned he could come back later.'

Amy frowned. 'The morning? I thought he came in the afternoon.'

'No, definitely the morning.'

'Are you sure?'

'Absolutely. I went off shift after lunch so I wouldn't have seen him if it was the afternoon.'

Amy muttered something about being mistaken and then thanked the nurse and hung up.

She lay back on the bed and tried to make sense of what she'd heard. Jack had told her he'd come to the hospital on Saturday afternoon. What was it he'd said? She thought back to their conversation from a couple of days ago, after they'd come in from the pool. They'd been talking in the kitchen. He'd told her he'd come to St George's to see her. *Late Saturday afternoon. After you sent me the text. I rushed there as soon as I could . . .*

But the nurse was adamant Jack had come to the hospital in the morning. She sounded so sure.

But he didn't even know of her accident at that point.

Amy knew she hadn't texted him to let him know what had happened until Saturday afternoon.

So how had he known to get there in the morning? At that point only three people knew she was in hospital. Her mother, Lisa and Jenna.

TWENTY-NINE

1 February

Harry felt someone kiss him on the lips. He stirred, coming to, enjoying the sensation of smooth sheets against his skin. He opened his eyes to see Nina looking down at him. Nina dressed in one of her business suits, hair arranged, make-up on.

'Morning, sleepyhead,' she said.

He reached up and tried to pull her down onto the bed with him but she slipped out of his grasp.

'No way. I need to go. Got a client meeting to get to.'

Harry rubbed his eyes. 'Why didn't you wake me?'

'You've been working until late all week. Thought you could do with a lie-in.'

Harry took this in. It meant she was happy to leave him alone in her flat. It would be the first time. They were gradually moving through the litany of firsts in their relationship. First date, first kiss, first sex. They'd met up five times since the night in the bar – each time Harry had been careful not to be too keen. He got it: most people were put off if someone was too available but successful career women who'd dedicated most of their working lives to chasing big money and status positively recoiled if they didn't feel there was some sort of fight in getting what they wanted.

He stretched. 'You sure?'

'Course.'

Except he detected a note of uncertainty in her voice. He knew exactly how to respond to it.

'Thank you.' He looked at his watch. 'But I've got a meeting with a potential supplier at ten.' He threw off the covers. 'I'd best jump in the shower.'

She smiled, reassured, as he knew she would be. She slapped his backside as he walked towards the en suite.

'Just pull the door closed when you leave,' she said, picking up her jacket and bag.

He kissed her. 'Have a great day.'

'You too.' And she left.

Harry listened until he heard the front door close. Then he pulled aside a fraction of the curtain and watched Nina stride down the road in the early morning frost.

He looked back at the bed. Tempting . . . but there was something more important to do.

After a shower, Harry went into the kitchen. He saw a high-end coffee machine on the counter and thought it would be nice to make himself a cup. In the bread bin he found an artisan loaf. He cut two slices and toasted them, adding butter and marmalade from the fridge.

Taking his breakfast with him, he made his way into the living room. It was only the second time he'd stayed over in Nina's flat and he thought it very trusting of her to leave him there by himself. He ran his fingers along the shelves, taking in the photos, books and ornaments. There was a desk calendar that he flicked through, noting people's birthdays, 'Kirsty', 'Amelia', 'Mum', and then a 'ME!' in caps. She would be turning another year older in a couple of months. He looked around the room. There was a wooden cabinet tucked into the alcove beside the fireplace. He bent down and opened the doors. Concertina files were stacked against one another. He pulled one out and found documents, details of investments. He flicked through, his eyes widening at the amounts. And there were so many of them. He did a rough calculation and totalled a sum well into six figures. Then he found bank interest statements and premium bond certificates – Nina had invested the maximum possible, fifty thousand pounds. All in all there was about half a million pounds' worth of capital. On top of that there was her business and her flat that he was in now. He wondered how much mortgage was left to pay on it and decided to look in another file in case there was a statement. When he found it, he smiled. Seemed she'd paid nearly all of it off – only thirty grand remained and it was worth twenty times that.

Harry carefully put everything back and then stood and stretched. Might be time for that nap after all.

He woke to the sound of a key in the lock. It took him a second to realize where he was, then he leapt out of bed as if he'd been scalded. Fuck. *Fuck!* What the hell was she doing back so early? He thought she'd be gone for the day. He smoothed down his hair, threw the duvet back on straight. He grabbed his phone and went into the bathroom. Two minutes later he flushed the toilet. As he came out, Nina was standing in the bedroom, perturbed.

'Hi,' he said warmly. 'How was your client meeting?'

'Fine,' said Nina. 'I thought you had to meet a supplier at ten?'

'They rang to cancel. Got the diary mixed up or something – double-booked. Their loss – I'll probably go with the competition now, since they can't fit in another meet in time.' He was aware he was waffling, giving too much unnecessary detail.

She was looking at him suspiciously. She threw her jacket on the bed and he glanced down, hoped when she picked it up, she wouldn't feel the warmth from where he'd been lying only five minutes before.

'It's nearly one o'clock,' she said.

'I know. I hope you don't mind, I've got another meeting at two but it's this end of town. I've been in the kitchen, catching up on emails. You know how it is after a weekend.'

She didn't say anything.

Harry threw his arms up in apology. 'I've outstayed my welcome, I'm sorry. Or at the very least I should've checked it was OK. Sent you a text or something. I apologize.'

He saw her soften slightly. 'It's not that, it's . . . I wasn't expecting to see you, that's all.'

Me and you both, thought Harry. 'Like I said, if I'd had the forethought to message you, it wouldn't have been a surprise.' He took a chance and walked over to her. Placed a hand on her cheek and kissed her. She didn't back away. 'Talking of surprises,' he said, 'I've managed to get tickets for the Globe theatre for the weekend of tenth April. I'd love it if you came with me.'

'The tenth?' She smiled. 'That's my birthday.'

He affected surprise. 'Seriously? Wow.' He kissed her again. 'So, shall we do it?'

'OK. Thanks.' She leaned over and pecked him on the cheek. 'Stay for some lunch?'

'I'd love to, but my meeting beckons.'

As he heard Nina's front door close behind him, he got a surge of triumph. He took in a deep breath of the cold air then exhaled slowly. Grinned. A man was sitting on a bench a little way down the road dressed in a sharp suit, his brown curly hair neatly styled. He caught Harry's eye as he looked over. Harry nodded, sharing his sense of well-being with everyone. The man looked away. Harry walked down the road in the opposite direction, energy flooding through his limbs. He'd almost been caught but he hadn't, *he hadn't!* He was bionic, he was untouchable. This was what he'd been craving, this was how it had felt before. The excitement that made a mundane existence tolerable. He looked up at the bright, cold blue sky and for the first time in months felt truly alive.

THIRTY

28 February

Amy stepped downstairs, listening as she went. She could hear voices in the kitchen and the smell of bacon wafted under her nose, making her realize how hungry she was.

When she opened the door, Lisa and Jenna immediately went quiet. She glanced over, knowing they'd been talking about her. She wondered if they were keeping secrets, what they knew. Had one of them somehow been in touch with Jack after her accident? How? Why? Had Lisa already known that they wouldn't have drawn any conclusions to that morning's investigations about Jack?

'Any bacon going spare?' asked Amy.

Jenna, who was standing at the stove, looked in the pan. 'Sure. You want ketchup?'

'Yes please. Where are Mum and Jack?'

'Don't know,' said Lisa.

'Haven't seen either of them this morning,' said Jenna.

'Are they in their rooms?' asked Amy.

'Don't think so. Your mum's door was open when I came down earlier.'

'So . . . have they gone somewhere together?' asked Amy, unable to contain her anxiety at this notion.

Lisa was looking at her. 'Is it a problem if they have?' she said carefully.

'Yes!' said Amy. 'We don't know anything about him.'

She saw Jenna and Lisa exchange a brief look.

'I'm sure everything's fine,' said Lisa.

'Sandwich is ready,' deflected Jenna, holding out a plate with a bacon baguette.

They were treating her as if she was erratic, unhinged. Gingerly tiptoeing around her. She took the plate and went to the breakfast bar, where she sat silently and ate. Her mother was missing from the house. So was Jack. If that didn't make Lisa and Jenna alarmed, then it was clear that neither of them believed her story. She thought again of how Jack had somehow known of her accident before she had texted him from the hospital. Had someone else in this house told him? Why? How had they got his number?

Amy resolved to call her mother as soon as she finished her breakfast. She'd go up to her room and ring her from there. Out of the corner of her eye she saw Jenna share another look with Lisa. Their concern was obvious, but they were focusing on the wrong person. It was Jack they should be thinking about, Jack they had to be wary of. *It's Jack!* she wanted to scream. *I'm of sound mind!*

She took another bite of her sandwich, its saltiness breaking through her thoughts. Nagging at her. Its taste pulling her backwards, to what? A vision swam into her mind. She was in her flat. Amy recognized a sense of not having to rush, of downtime. It was the weekend. She was making breakfast, dry-frying some bacon and putting it between two slices of buttered bread. She took her sandwich into the living room and sat on the sofa, still in her pyjamas. It was late as she'd had a lie-in after a monstrously busy week, working until ten, eleven o'clock at night.

As she ate, she wondered what she might do that day. It was a bright, cold January morning but she hadn't made any plans as she'd hardly had time to think all week. There was a contemporary art exhibition on at the Tate Modern and she thought about calling Lisa and Jenna, seeing if either of them wanted to join her. She hesitated. Sometimes she felt as if she were encroaching on their home lives, the single girl still relying solely on her friends for company, while they had more full lives, juggling time with their husbands as well. She was the only one of the three of them who still regularly found herself at a loose end and was wary of coming across as too needy. Anyway, she thought, she was supposed to be dating Jack now and still in the first flush of romance. She would have some explaining to do if she called Lisa and Jenna to see if they were free.

Amy sighed. Having a fictitious boyfriend had its pros and cons. Probably a bit like the real thing, she thought, aware of the irony. Maybe she'd go to the exhibition by herself. It would mean dragging herself back into central London, something she didn't relish, having spent all week commuting. She'd sit alone on the train, then the Underground. There would be no one to talk to as she wandered around the exhibition. No one to discuss the paintings with.

But the alternative was what? Going to see a film alone? Staying at home and watching TV while the short burst of winter sunlight disappeared, wasted by not getting out? Amy realized she was still tired from her week and felt like doing very little but sometimes doing nothing on your own in the silence of your flat was incredibly isolating. Go out or not go out? Amy recognized she was stuck in a circle of indecision, something that happened with alarming frequency when she was the sole person responsible for motivating herself to get out and do stuff.

Her phone rang. She sat up, intrigued. Perhaps this was the answer to her impasse. But as she looked at the screen she saw it was her mother. She couldn't help but feel a little stab of disappointment.

'Hi, Mum,' she said brightly.

'Morning,' said Martha, 'or is it afternoon?'

Her mother's tone was almost accusatory, thought Amy, perplexed. For a moment she thought her mother could see she'd had a long lie-in, but that was impossible. And anyway, what did it matter? She decided to ignore it.

'How's your weekend going?' asked Amy. She thought she felt her mother hesitate.

'It's OK', said Martha. 'I suppose you're with Jack?'

Amy considered. If she was, she could invent a reason not to stay on the phone too long. But she actually felt bad about lying.

'Not at the moment,' she said.

'Oh.' There was an expectation in the silence that followed. 'When am I going to meet him then?'

'Soon.'

'How soon?'

'I don't know, Mum.'

'It's been over a month since you started dating.'

Did she imagine it or had Amy caught the faintest hint of slurring in her mum's words? Her heart sank. 'That's not that long, Mum.'

'I understand he's new and it's all very exciting, but other life still goes on, you know.'

What was her mother talking about? 'Yes . . . of course it does,' said Amy. 'What's up?'

Martha paused. 'It's the ninth.'

'Yes,' said Amy casually, then realized too late that she'd messed up. Ice flooded down the back of her neck. *Shit.* She had forgotten. No, that wasn't entirely true. She'd never forget, not where it counted, in her heart, in her very psyche but the actual date, yes, for a few days with work eclipsing everything else, it had slipped her mind.

'It's ten years ago today, Amy.'

Amy put her head in her hand. Ten years. That would make it worse in her mother's eyes. A big anniversary. Something to bring the pain home even greater.

'Your dad died ten years ago today.'

'I know, Mum,' Amy said softly.

'Only you didn't call.'

'I'm sorry, really I am.' Amy knew that whatever she said it wouldn't make it better, wouldn't undo what she'd done, that she had been a Bad Daughter. 'Are you OK? What are you doing?'

'I'm at home. Alone.'

'Do you want company?'

'No, no, don't change your plans. I'm OK today. I could do with seeing you soon, though.'

'Of course. Next weekend?'

'That would be wonderful.'

'Great. It's a date. Friday night. I'm taking you for dinner. Bentley's, my treat.'

'Bring Jack.'

'Sorry?'

'I'd love to meet him.'

Oh for God's sake, thought Amy. How was she going to get out of this now?

'Your dad would've liked to meet him too.'

'I know, Mum, but—'

'Don't say no. Please, Amy,' said Martha and hearing the sadness in her mother's voice, Amy couldn't bear to. Conscious she would have to undo this at some point, for now she was caught.

Martha wrote it in her diary, brightened and thanked her daughter with genuine excitement.

Shit, thought Amy as she walked down the streets of Mayfair, *shit, shit, SHIT*! How had she managed to totally neglect telling her mother, apologetically, that unfortunately Jack couldn't make their dinner date so please could they rearrange? How the hell could she have let something so huge with the capacity to become so monumentally awful, slip her mind? She'd only remembered herself that morning when her mother had texted to say how much she was looking forward to it and Amy's heart had plummeted. Her mother had arranged a whole weekend in London based around meeting Jack. But Amy hadn't been able to do anything as she'd been late for a client meeting. Which had run on, beyond the afternoon and now here she was, on her way to meet her very excited mother, for dinner, with a non-existent boyfriend.

Amy's phone buzzed. It was a message from Martha saying the train was delayed as it was being held at a signal. For a moment Amy entertained the glorious idea that her mother would never arrive at the central London terminal, she'd be stuck for hours in a suburban train nightmare until it was too late and she had to turn back. Her phone buzzed again: *'We're on the move!'*

Amy exhaled. She now had half an hour to kill before her mother would be at the restaurant. She saw the lights of a phone shop up ahead; she might as well at least solve one problem, her dodgy phone that kept playing up. Maybe she would think of something to let her mother down while she was at it.

As Amy browsed the smartphones she thought about how she'd have to invent an excuse and short of Jack being involved in an accident, which was far too full of pitfalls, it would have to be work-related. He was held up at the hospital. Some crisis or other. You couldn't argue with it but it would still be devastatingly disappointing. Amy knew that Martha would blame her and it would ruin their evening. It would be so much better if Jack were able to apologize to Martha directly. She would be so much more understanding.

Amy went to the till with her purchase and fervently wished she could soften the blow somehow. Then as her new phone was being rung into the till, she had an idea. Mad, desperate, but it might help. Just for tonight. And then somehow she'd wing it for the next couple of months before she and Jack broke up.

Amy looked at the shop assistant. 'I need a number for it,' she said. 'Pay as you go.'

The table in the restaurant had been set for three. Martha was already there, wearing a new silk blouse, noted Amy. She kissed her mother on both cheeks, feeling guilty at the glow of excitement that radiated from her.

'You look lovely, Mum.'

'Thank you, darling.' Martha plucked at her blouse. 'I got it specially.' She looked across at her daughter. 'Is that a new suit? Unusual green colour.'

It had been a brave choice, one Amy had recently treated herself to in an attempt to boost her low morale, but now she couldn't help wondering if she'd made a mistake.

'Do you like it?'

Martha smiled self-deprecatingly. 'Not for me. Better on a younger person.'

Did she mean better on Amy as a younger person, or that Amy was getting on in her years and it would be better on someone younger? Amy didn't know. She didn't have the energy to pursue it, instead excused herself to the toilet.

When she came back, she had a look of deep disappointment on her face.

'What's happened?' asked Martha.

Amy ruefully held out her phone. The old, temperamental one. 'I just got a text. It's Jack. He's been held up at the hospital.'

Martha's face fell. 'What, *now*?'

'Afraid so.'

'But he's coming later?'

Amy shook her head.

'But I was looking forward to meeting him. He can't just cancel!'

'It's his job, Mum. He's a doctor, he's saving lives.'

'That's all well and good, but we've booked this place. I've come all the way from Dorset! Arranged to stay at Beth's and everything!'

Inwardly, Amy once again cursed the fact she hadn't managed to deal with this before.

'Now what shall we do?' asked Martha huffily.

'We could still eat?'

'I've half a mind to call him.'

'He won't be able to answer. But he sent you a message.'

Martha sat up. 'What message?'

Amy opened the message she'd sent herself from the new phone, the one she had temporarily dubbed as 'Jack's' and read aloud.

'*Please tell your mum that I'm extremely sorry not to meet her tonight. I feel really awful about it as I was looking forward to it so much and she has come such a long way but I know you two will have a fabulous night. Bentley's do the best crab cakes. Martha, for what it's worth, Amy has told me so many wonderful things about you and I'm dying to meet the woman who's produced such a fantastic daughter.'*

Martha went pink. 'He said all that?'

Amy held up her phone. 'Yep.'

'That's nice.'

'Cheesy, if you ask me,' said Amy.

'It's very noble. OK, I forgive him.'

Thank God for that, thought Amy.

Later, when she got home she collapsed on the sofa, exhausted. Her mum had wanted to talk about Jack through much of the meal and although Amy had tried to change tack more than once, she'd still found herself agreeing with Martha on how unselfish and honourable his work was, and answered the questions on whether or not he could cook with a comment on his excellent chicken pie. She nodded as Martha had enthused about how much she thought Amy's dad, Peter, would have got on with him, and told her mother how yes, Jack enjoyed sport and they'd played tennis together (she had won). Martha had been delighted, and finally Amy had fulfilled her mother's dream about a man who would look after her daughter, all the while feeling more and more lonely as she spoke.

She gazed around her empty flat and understood how people got a pet to keep themselves company. She called Lisa but her friend was busy: 'Sorry, but David's just got in. Can I call you back?'

She told her not to worry and hung up, putting her phone on the coffee table in front of her.

Then Amy took 'Jack's' new phone out of her bag and placed it next to hers. Smiled ruefully as it sank in what she'd started. She had a sense she was digging herself into a hole. Only a few more weeks, she reminded herself, and then she'd call it all off. She thought she'd probably be safer keeping the new phone as Jack's for those weeks, in case there was another crisis she had to get out of.

She opened up his phone. Typed. She pressed send and then went to put the phone away in her desk drawer.

Her own phone announced the arrival of a new message. She smiled sadly as she looked over. Yes, she knew what it said, of course she did, but she still went back and read it anyway.

Amy, you're the most fabulous, smart, gorgeous girl I've ever met. And I think you look good in green.

If only it had been genuine.

Sitting at the breakfast bar in the lodge, Amy put down her bacon sandwich and stared wide-eyed at her friends.

'It's my phone,' she burst out.

'What?' asked Lisa.

'This morning. You told me to call Jack's phone. We heard it ringing. It's not his though, it's mine. I bought it for myself. Because my old one was so ropey.' Amy explained about buying the new phone, about how she'd also got a temporary SIM card so that she could send a message from 'Jack', make her mother feel better about being stood up by him. 'It was a thought I had on a whim,' she said. 'Probably not my best idea, to be honest, but I was in a hurry, wasn't thinking straight and desperate for a quick fix.'

'Seems a bit extreme,' said Lisa.

'I have an extreme mother. It's my phone,' repeated Amy. 'It was in the drawer in my desk back at the flat.'

'Yes, but how on earth did Jack here in this house get your phone from your flat?' asked Jenna.

'Jesus . . . he must have got in somehow.' Amy had a sudden thought. 'Maybe when I was in hospital . . .'

'Were there any signs of a break-in?' asked Lisa.

'No.' She sat up straight. 'Wait! There was something weird.'

'Go on.'

'When I got back from the hospital, there was a mug on the kitchen counter. It had dregs of coffee in it. It hadn't been washed up, it had gone mouldy.'

'So . . . you forgot to wash it up?'

Amy looked at her askance. 'You know that's not me.'

'OK,' said Lisa. 'But it still doesn't explain how someone got in. And why would they help themselves to a cup of coffee and not steal anything? Did you look for the phone before you came to France? Was it still in the drawer?'

'I didn't check,' said Amy.

Jenna was looking at her, waiting for her to say something else to prop up her story, but Amy could think of nothing.

The front door opened and they heard Martha and Jack coming in, voices bright. Amy jumped up. She went into the hall, Jenna and Lisa following. Martha's face was rosy from the cold, her eyes shining, yet also red-rimmed.

'Where have you been?' demanded Amy.

Martha was taken aback. 'Out. With Jack.'

'Did you not think to let anyone know?' As Amy spoke she felt her anger rise – it was irresponsible for her mother to just disappear with a man that she'd explicitly told her was an imposter.

'I left a note,' said Martha.

'What note?'

'Here, on the hall table.'

There was no note. Amy watched as Martha poked around, looking on the floor. 'Here!' she exclaimed, holding up a piece of paper in triumph. 'It must have blown off when we closed the door.'

It was still foolhardy, thought Amy. *Going off with a strange man*. She folded her arms.

'I don't know why you're looking so cross,' said Martha. 'Jack's actually done a wonderful thing.'

For the first time since he'd come in, Amy looked at him.

'It was nothing,' he said modestly.

'Not at all,' said Martha. She turned back to Amy, spoke softly. 'He took me to the Southern Slope.'

Amy bristled. That was her place, her family's place, only for them.

'We walked together. I laid some roses,' said Martha. 'Pink ones. You know how your dad always loved them.

Reminded him of our wedding. Not real ones, obviously; paper ones. Jack made them,' she added.

Of course he did, seethed Amy.

'It was lovely. Meant a lot to me.'

Amy was furious. Who was this man, lying not just to her but also to her mother? Inveigling his way into their lives, pulling emotional strings? 'He shouldn't be doing that,' she said.

'Oh come on, Amy,' said Martha, irritated at her daughter's lack of enthusiasm. 'Stop being such a sourpuss. It's a nice thing to do and you know it.'

No, it's not! Amy wanted to scream. *It's manipulative and devious. He's making you like him. He's putting blinkers over your eyes.*

'I didn't mean to upset anyone,' said Jack awkwardly.

Martha patted his arm. 'Nonsense. Now come on, we deserve a coffee after all that snow,' she said, pulling him towards the kitchen.

Lisa came to stand next to Amy. 'He's wearing the socks,' she murmured.

'What?'

Lisa pointed down to the floor, at Jack's feet as he walked into the kitchen. 'The yellow socks. The ones that made you smile, remember?'

Amy looked. On Jack's feet were bright yellow socks. *The new sunshine in my life and his matching socks.* Exactly as she'd posted on Facebook. She narrowed her eyes, hating them, hating it all, the confusion, the continuous, exhausting effort of having to convince everyone of the truth.

'He's made up,' she said. 'I keep telling you, Jack doesn't exist.'

She went up to her room. As she lay on her bed, listening to everyone else downstairs laughing and chatting in the kitchen, she suddenly knew what she had to do. She couldn't believe she hadn't thought of it earlier.

She would go and see Esme. Esme would believe her.

THIRTY-ONE

28 February

Amy pulled on her snow boots as quickly and silently as possible. She'd have to walk to Gabriel's house. It would be quicker to ski but the skis were in the boot room and the only way to get to it was through the kitchen and she didn't want any of them to know she was going. She fastened her jacket, tensing against what sounded to her like the loudest zip teeth in the world. But the voices stayed in the kitchen. She looked around for her phone – it hadn't been in her room and she thought she might have left it on the hall table but it wasn't there. She couldn't afford to spend any more time looking and would have to go without it. Very carefully, Amy opened the front door, slipped outside and then quietly closed it behind her.

She immediately felt a sense of freedom. The sun and the miles of bright snow lifted her spirits. She started to make her way around the side of the house, creeping underneath the kitchen window. Once she was at the back of the lodge she knew they couldn't see her. She headed across the valley, towards Gabriel's lodge in the distance. She went as fast as she could, anxious to get to Esme, and then it occurred to her that they may not be in. She faltered but her heart lifted when she saw an encouraging wisp of smoke escape from the chimney.

Knowing that her aunt was inside gave her a new-found energy. She trudged through the thick snow, her leg muscles soon burning. It was so deep still – up to her knees in most places. Occasionally she found her feet falling into a drift that was even deeper, where she'd lose her balance and find herself in snow up to her thighs. Then it would take a moment to right herself, to try and gauge the snow to see where it was more passable. She longed to see Esme and chastised herself for leaving it so long. She needed her aunt's reassuring voice of reason, needed to be able to tell her what had happened. Instinctively she felt that her aunt would believe her.

Despite her determination, progress was slow. It took her an age to reach the pine woods. She decided to walk through rather than around them, as there was less snow where the trees had given cover and she would be able to speed up. As she entered the woods, she felt the relief in her legs of not having to expend so much effort. She continued at a quicker pace, dodging around the pines, always keeping an eye on her direction so she would exit the woods near to Gabriel's house.

A sound behind her made her stop. She turned, her heart beating. There was nothing there. *Maybe it was snow falling off the trees*, she thought, but it hadn't sounded like that. It had sounded as if someone else was walking through the woods. She stared again, focusing carefully but it was just her and the trees. Monster pines towering over her, their branches blocking out the blue skies. Suddenly she wanted to get out of there, be back in the sunshine. She continued onwards, quickening her pace, all the while feeling as if someone was following her. She half ran, half stumbled through the snow, face-planting once but then picking herself up and not looking back until she burst out of the trees into the light and ahead of her was Gabriel's lodge. She took a deep breath and laughed at herself for getting so spooked. *Fool*, she told herself sternly. *You need to pull yourself together.*

As she headed to the house she couldn't help glancing to her right where she knew the start of the Southern Slope lay a few hundred metres beyond Gabriel's place. She knew Esme didn't use it anymore, not since the accident ten years ago. Her aunt preferred to take another route with fewer memories.

Amy continued up to the lodge and, stomping the snow off her boots, she knocked on the door. Her heartbeat quickened as she heard footsteps approach inside. The front door opened and Gabriel's brown eyes lit up as he saw her.

'Amy!' he exclaimed and kissed her on both cheeks. 'How wonderful to see you. *Entrez.*'

She did, gratefully, and then once he'd closed the door he stood and appraised her. 'You look so well,' he said.

'So do you,' said Amy, although it wasn't entirely true. She thought her aunt's boyfriend looked tired and his usual astute, lined face kept tanned by a lifestyle outdoors was paler than she remembered. His frame seemed smaller too, not quite as athletic in a green woollen jumper and navy chinos.

'I was hoping you'd come and pay me a visit,' said Gabriel. 'Can I get you a coffee?'

'Yes, please,' said Amy. But there was something he'd said that was niggling her, something she couldn't put her finger on. She looked around, expecting her aunt. 'Where's Esme?' she asked.

Gabriel's face creased into a frown, confusion flooded his eyes. 'Esme?' he asked.

'Yeah . . .' said Amy, and then she realized what had been bothering her. Gabriel had said: 'I was hoping you'd come and pay *me* a visit'. Not us.

'Esme's not here,' said Gabriel slowly.

Amy smiled. 'I haven't gone and forgotten she's away or something have I? Only . . . of course . . . you don't know. I had an accident a few days ago. Hit my head. I'm afraid I've got amnesia. Can't remember anything from the last six months. Has she gone on one of her shopping trips to Milan or something?'

Gabriel wasn't smiling back at her. His face was full of pain and worry. 'No,' he said, 'she hasn't.' He paused. 'I'm so sorry, Amy, but Esme is dead.'

THIRTY-TWO

28 February

A thousand tiny pinpricks erupted over her body. All the heat abruptly left it and she began to shiver uncontrollably. She felt herself sway, felt Gabriel take her hand and lead her into the kitchen.

'Sit,' he instructed, helping her into the wooden kitchen chair. She was aware of warmth, of sitting near the wood burner. Her eyes were cast to the ground, and she saw Gabriel's slippered feet; brown leather with white stitching that she remembered Esme had bought him two Christmases ago. Esme had laughed when he'd asked for slippers but then sought out the most stylish ones she could find. Gabriel opened the burner door and threw in another log. Amy watched, wordless, as he turned to the coffee machine on the counter. He took two cups and saucers from a cupboard, one teal, one red, and poured two coffees. She saw him add two teaspoons of sugar to one of the cups, knowing that was hers, not having the strength to protest. She didn't have sugar in her drinks, didn't like it.

He put the cups on the table, sat down opposite her.

'You must have some,' he said, pointing.

She looked at the bright-red cup, forced herself to pick it up and gagged on the sweet drink. She put it down again.

Gabriel put his hand on hers. 'I know,' he said softly. 'I understand the shock.'

She still couldn't take it in. Esme: beautiful, vivacious, rebellious Aunt Esme was dead.

'You need to drink more,' Gabriel said gently, nudging her cup closer. He took a bottle of brandy from the dresser behind him and, unscrewing the cap, poured some in. Then he watched her until she put the cup to her lips. The alcohol burned her throat and stomach, jolting her out of her shock.

'When?' asked Amy.

'Four months ago.'

Amy was shaken. 'Four *months*?'

'I'm afraid so.'

'How did it happen?'

'A car. It was an accident. We were in Geneva for a few days. Esme stepped into the road, he didn't see her . . .' Gabriel shrugged. 'There was nothing anyone could have done. Do you remember . . .' he started carefully.

'What?'

'The funeral?'

'I came?'

'Of course you did. You loved your aunt deeply.'

Tears streamed down Amy's face. Gabriel came over to her, put his arms around her while she wept.

'I'm so sorry,' he said. 'If I had had any idea of your accident, I would have got in touch.'

Amy blew her nose, tried to compose herself when she was hit by a bolt of recognition. This was the same awful feeling that had been hovering over her like a cloud, she realized. This was the buried memory that had caused her such a deep sense of sadness.

'Your memory will come back, though?' asked Gabriel.

'Hopefully. I'm already getting the odd sign.'

He smiled. 'That is good. Now, you need to stay for lunch. I am not going to take no for an answer,' he added quickly as he saw her start to protest. He got up and went over to the fridge, where he extracted two or three small boxes and some packets of waxed paper.

'I have the best cheese,' he said, holding them up. 'Abbaye de Tamié? It's made by the monks. You will like it, I think. And Emmental. I have bread too. And there is *jambon*.'

He busied himself and Amy watched as he fetched plates and knives and set the food on the table. She still felt a raw sense of utter disbelief, as if she had woken from a nightmare but the darkness had followed her into the real world. She half-expected her aunt to walk in the back door, face glowing from the cold, eyes bright, as she had done so many times before. She would tease Gabriel for the amount of cheese he was putting out, knowing they could never eat it all. He would take it good-naturedly, ignoring her, safe in his superior French knowledge about all things *fromage*. They would all sit together; Esme would ask her about her life back in London, listen with genuine interest in her work, and be puzzled and indignant about her continuing single status. She would try to entice Amy to stay in

France and meet a Frenchman like Gabriel, her tongue firmly set in her cheek. Most of all she would make Amy feel as if it didn't matter, as if it was something inconsequential because Amy had so much else going for her. Then she would talk of local gossip, and make Amy laugh with her stories of her social clumsiness: the eccentric English woman who was once tolerated, now loved.

'Try some,' said Gabriel, pushing some *jambon* towards her.

Amy looked down. She needed to; he had gone to so much trouble. She took a piece of bread, put it on her plate.

'So, other than your accident, I hope life has been good to you?' asked Gabriel.

She looked up at him, wondered whether to confide. But he looked older, greyer, sadder and she didn't want to burden him. 'Fine,' she said.

He studied her face. 'You're keeping something from me.'

She looked down. 'Nothing I can't handle.'

'Are you sure?'

'Yeah. Man trouble, you know.' She paused. 'He's not quite the guy I thought he was.' She stopped, suddenly realizing something. 'Smokey . . .' she said. 'It's all a bloody smokescreen.'

'What are you talking about?'

She shook her head, gave a wry laugh. 'Nothing. Story he told me about his finger. The tip's missing . . . an old injury. Think I was the one made to look in the wrong direction.'

Gabriel frowned. 'Should I be worried about this guy?'

'No . . . honestly.'

He wouldn't let it go. He stared hard into her eyes. 'Are you frightened of him?'

It made her catch her breath. Was she? Aware Gabriel was watching her carefully she broke into a smile. 'No, nothing like that,' she said. 'Just . . . I don't know. I was going to have a girlie heart-to-heart with Esme.'

Gabriel seemed to know she was covering but he didn't push it any further. 'Well, if you change your mind . . .'

'I know where to find you,' said Amy.

He nodded. Looked down at her plate, at the half-eaten bread and ham. The untouched cheese. 'Not hungry?'

'Sorry . . .' she said guiltily.

He smiled. 'Please do not worry.' He stood and cleared the plates, topped up their coffees. 'How is the lodge?'

'Fine. Great, as always.' Amy got a lump in her throat as she realized that Esme would never again return to it.

'And your mother?'

'She's doing OK. Considering.'

'She does not know about Esme's accident,' said Gabriel.

Amy looked up sharply. 'What? But . . . didn't she come to the funeral?' Even as she said it, she knew the answer. If Martha had known about her sister-in-law, she wouldn't have spoken about Esme as if she was still alive.

Gabriel shook his head, looked a little embarrassed. 'No. You see . . . It's no secret that your mother and Esme didn't get on. Esme had decided she didn't want Martha there. At least, that was her stipulation when she amended her will, shortly after your father died.'

'Oh.' Amy was taken aback.

'I think there is something else that you don't remember,' said Gabriel slowly.

A sense of dread ran down Amy's spine. 'What?'

But Gabriel was smiling. 'Your aunt . . . Like I say, her will set out a few things that now, after many years might seem a little . . . irrelevant. But back when she was putting her affairs in order, there was a particular reason why Esme didn't want your mother made aware if she died. Not until everything was settled.'

'Settled?'

'Esme was a very wealthy woman. She wanted her will to be fully executed with no chance of any disruption.'

'I still don't understand.'

'You are a beneficiary. The lodge she left to me, but all her capital . . . she wanted you to have it – and only you. The condition was that you kept the news of her death to yourself until the money was in your bank account. I know it seems silly now, but those are the terms of the will and so that is what has to take place. I think the amount is in excess of three million euros,' added Gabriel.

Amy was dumbfounded. '*Three million*? She left to *me*?' she stuttered.

'Why not? You're her only surviving blood relative.' He patted her hand. 'Are you aware that probate has been granted?'

'It has?' asked Amy, unable to take it all in.

'Yes. Surely you have emails?'

'No, yes, I must have. Somewhere. It's been hard keeping

track of everything. Not knowing what I'm supposed to be doing. You know, with the memory loss.'

'The funds should be transferred very soon. You should call the solicitors,' said Gabriel. 'They're based in Geneva. In fact, I have their details somewhere.' He stood, intending to search, but Amy pulled him back down.

'Wait,' she said, holding his hand. He saw then how shaken and fragile she was. He cupped her hand in his and smiled.

'She lived life to the full,' he said. 'And she loved you so very much. You were never alone if you knew Esme.'

Except, thought Amy, now that Esme was dead she was absolutely alone.

THIRTY-THREE

5 February

It had been a good week. Harry had seen Nina twice. He'd
stayed over at her flat on both occasions and had learned
a lot more about her. She was an only child, with a father
deceased and a mother in a care home. (Which Nina wasn't
funding as the mother had a decent pension.) She'd been
single for three years and was ready for a new relationship. She didn't mind that he was nine years younger than
her. She had sat him down after dinner one night and told
him that she wanted a family and as she was already
thirty-seven, this would have to be quite soon – within
the next couple of years. She didn't want to sound
demanding but there was no point in wasting each other's
time if he didn't want them too. Harry had reassured her
that he adored children and had always wanted some of
his own. He'd told her how much he admired her honesty.
Privately, he genuinely didn't mind a kid – she could
certainly afford them.

All in all, things were progressing nicely. They got on
well and he was fond of her. He reckoned he could spin

out the bar set-up story for at least another three months and then he harboured a growing hope that they might be so close he could even come clean. Explain how he'd always been judged for being poor, when in reality he was only trying to make ends meet. A little part of him dared to hope she might understand. Maybe by then, she might even be so attached to him they would decide to move in together. Whatever happened, he would have found a way to make their relationship continue. There would be a way. There was always a way.

Harry glanced at his watch. It was almost time to go home – just one more load of glasses to go in the washer and then he could leave. Alex came in from dumping the last of the wine bottles in the recycling bin and Harry saw Max look up from the till, a frown on his face. Whatever it was, Harry didn't want to know. He shoved the wire basket of glasses into the machine, pressed the button to switch it on and left the bar to go and get his coat.

'Just a minute,' called out Max.

Harry stopped. Turned around.

'If I could have a quick word with you and Alex,' said Max.

Harry pointedly looked at his watch.

'It won't take long,' Max insisted.

It didn't seem like he had any choice. Harry knew that Max expected him to jump to attention, return to the bar, but he stayed where he was, enjoying the look of irritation that flitted across Max's face.

'There seems to be a discrepancy with the takings,' said

Max. 'The receipts don't add up to the cash in the till. It's about sixty quid short.'

Harry said nothing. Kept his face blank.

'I want you to keep an eye on what you're keying in,' said Max, 'in case someone's making a mistake with the amounts.'

Max looked at them both, but Harry felt that his boss's eyes lingered on him longer. It riled. Just because he was the new guy. Hell, it was probably Max himself making a mistake totalling up. Or the till. It could easily be a glitch with the software.

There was a knock on the glass frontage and all three men turned to see.

Harry's eyes lit up. Nina! She mimed at her watch, tipped her hand back and forth in question – was he finished?

Damn right he was. He grabbed his coat and, without looking back, left the bar.

As he stepped out into the cold, he thought how pleased he was to see her. Her lips tasted of booze.

'This is a nice surprise,' he said.

'I wasn't sure if you'd still be here. I was going to call but I was passing by anyway, so thought I'd see if you were free.'

'For you, always,' he said, and he held her hand all the way back to her flat.

In the morning he got up while she was still asleep to make her breakfast. She'd had one too many glasses of wine with her friend the night before. The same friend was coming over shortly so they could go to the gym together, then have lunch. Nina sat up in bed, looked at the fruit salad, cheese toastie and strong coffee that Harry had on a tray and sighed.

'This is exactly what I need. How did you know?'

'It's my job to know,' he said. 'I like to look after you.'

'No one's done that before,' said Nina.

'Even more reason for me to do it now.'

She lifted a hand to his face, felt his cheek and he knew he'd touched on a vulnerable point, had made her fall for him a little bit more. And what he'd said was true, he did like taking care of her. She was a good person, someone who deserved a helping hand, like he deserved a helping hand in life too. He thought they complemented one another.

'Thank you,' said Nina, taking a bite of the toastie and groaning with ecstasy as she pulled the strings of cheese apart. 'You put in mozzarella,' she said. 'No one knows how to do that.'

'Of course I did. A toastie isn't a toastie without mozzarella.'

She grinned and he kissed her.

'What are you up to today?' she asked.

'Meeting a friend for a bike ride in Richmond Park.' He wasn't, he was going home to watch TV and wash his work uniform, but that was not something that made him sound sporty and driven. The door buzzer went.

Nina looked at the clock in alarm. 'Is that Kirsty?' She groaned and slumped back on the pillows. 'My God, it's nine o'clock already!'

'You're not up for the gym?'

'I'd rather spend the day with you. Is it bad of me to say that?'

'No. I'm very good company.'

She slapped him playfully on the arm. 'You know that's not what I mean. Kirsty's great but . . . well, she's very protective of me and it can get a bit exhausting.'

'Protective?' asked Harry.

Nina went quiet.

'Go on, you can tell me.'

She sighed. 'I had an ex who . . . well, he wasn't always very kind to me.'

Harry looked at her in horror. 'He was violent?'

'Only once,' she said. 'Then I left him.'

'The bastard,' said Harry, and he meant it. He felt a surge of white-hot anger and for a moment wished that man, whoever he was, was there right now so he could smash his face in. Harry hated bullying, hated when people who were bigger and stronger attacked the weak and vulnerable. Knowing they couldn't fight back. It was cowardly and thuggish. There had been a man who'd lived with them, back when Harry was nine. His mother's boyfriend. She'd been happy for a few weeks, she had laughed more, had noticed Harry more and asked about his schoolwork. Then one night Harry had woken to the sound of muffled cries and thumps. He'd padded down-stairs into the living room to see his mother cowering on the floor, her hands across her face. His mother's boyfriend had his fist raised, had a look of wild fury about him. Harry had opened his mouth to speak but the man had told him to face the wall. He hadn't seen anything, but the sounds he'd heard that night still had the power to give him nightmares, even now. The slaps and thuds, the cries of anguish. Once he'd turned in terror, but he'd barely glimpsed a thing when he'd received a blow across the head. He hadn't dared turn around again, not on any of the nights. He could still remember the wallpaper, that patch he'd stared at in frozen fear and hatred. Those deep red and grey poppies, crowding every bit of space. The man had left shortly before his tenth birthday and his mother hadn't invited anyone to live in their home again.

'Tell you what,' said Harry, 'I'm free later, if you want to meet up? We could go and see a movie or, if you're too tired, just hang out and watch TV.'

'I'd love that,' said Nina. 'Shall I come to yours?'

'It's a bit cold,' said Harry, ruefully. 'The boiler broke yesterday. Plumber can't come until Monday.'

'What?'

'It's fine. I boil kettles for a bath. And it's only for a day or two. Do you want to get in the shower and I'll let your friend in?'

'Would you?' Nina kissed him, then stuffed the rest of the sandwich in her mouth and went into the bathroom.

Harry enjoyed seeing Kirsty's face when he opened the door. Surprised and put out it wasn't Nina greeting her.

'You must be Harry,' said Kirsty.

'Would you like to come in?' asked Harry, opening the door wider, enjoying the feeling of being the self-appointed gatekeeper to Nina's home.

Kirsty walked into the flat and placed her bag and coat down on the sofa. 'Where's Nina?'

'In the shower,' said Harry. Kirsty nodded. 'Coffee?' asked Harry.

Kirsty hesitated before answering. She looked at him as if to say: 'who the hell are you, offering me coffee in my best friend's home?' and Harry could detect a hint of annoyance in her voice when she spoke: 'No thank you.'

Kirsty sat, ran her hands over the fabric of the sofa cushions. 'Nina and I are going to get lunch after the gym,' she announced.

'She said.' Harry was beginning to find her possessiveness irritating.

'Nina said you work in a bar,' said Kirsty.

He knew that wasn't how Nina would have put it. 'Yes. I'm opening my own.'

'So I hear. Where?'

'Putney Bridge.'

'Where, exactly?'

He didn't want to answer. But she was looking at him expectantly. What the hell. 'Chelverton Road.' It was time to change the subject. 'What about you?'

'I'm not opening any bars.'

'No,' he said, biting back the irritation. 'I meant, what do you do?'

'I'm an estate agent. Local.'

Of course she fucking was. She probably knew all the properties around that were available. Shit, why had he given her the name of a road? Although he thought hopefully, there was a chance she wasn't familiar with commercial leases.

'You've swept her off her feet,' said Kirsty.

'I have?'

'And I think you know it.'

He smiled modestly. 'More like the other way around.' He crossed his arms, uncrossed them again. 'She's told me so much about you. I'm so pleased to meet you.'

It was as if he hadn't spoken. 'I like to look out for her,' said Kirsty.

'Me too.'

She ignored that as well. 'I don't like men who turn out to be something different to what they claim to be.'

She was talking about Nina's ex, the one who'd hit her, but Harry still felt his insides squirm, as if Kirsty could see right through him, read his mind, know the truth. He held her gaze.

'Hey! So you've met,' said Nina, coming into the room dressed in her gym gear.

'Just getting to know one another,' said Kirsty with a warm smile. Harry smiled too.

'I'm going to leave you to it,' said Harry. He got his coat and felt Kirsty's eyes on him as he kissed Nina. He made sure it was a long, slow kiss.

'See you later,' he murmured under his breath. He then said goodbye to Kirsty and left the flat.

It was four in the afternoon and Harry was just wondering whether to send Nina a text to find out when would be a good time to go over, when his phone beeped. He sat up from the crummy sofa and opened up his messages.

Feeling a bit tired after last night and gym session. Can we take a rain check on this afternoon? We'll do something else soon X

He stared at the screen, alarm flooding through him. This was not good. Not good at all. He swore – this was down to that bitch Kirsty pouring spiteful things in Nina's ear. God knows what poisonous thoughts she'd planted over lunch, what doubt she'd set in motion. Damn her! He had to get back control. He looked at the message again. No mention of just hanging out and watching TV as they'd talked about that morning. No suggestion of meeting up in the future. Just a vague, 'We'll do something else soon.' He thought carefully before composing his reply. *Play hard to get*. No attempt at persuasion, no begging her to change her mind.

Completely understand. Try and get a nap! Harry X

Then he put his phone down and made a plan.

Harry wondered how long it would take for the door to be answered or if it even would. Then, finally, from inside the flat he heard footsteps.

'Harry!' said Nina, opening the door.

'Surprise!' he said, holding up two hessian eco supermarket bags.

'I er . . . wasn't expecting you.'

'Did you get any rest?'

'Not really. I was just catching up on some work.' She looked over her shoulder as if she needed to get back to it.

He spoke quickly. 'So you need Bag A,' he said, holding up the bag in his left hand.

Despite herself, she smiled. 'What's Bag A?'

'Let me in and I'll show you.'

She hesitated but then, out of politeness, he thought, she stepped aside.

'No coming in the kitchen!' called Harry, making his way into her flat. He placed the bag on the counter and pulled out fresh apples, kale, ginger. Chopped and tipped into the blender and whizzed it up. Poured it into a glass and took it into the living room where she was sitting at her desk.

She looked up. 'What's that?'

'Energy-boosting juice.' He handed it to her. 'Drink,' he instructed, standing over her to make sure she did.

She took a sip and her eyes lit up. 'Actually, that's really good.'

'It's my secret ingredient.'

'Which is?'

'Secret.'

She snorted. Paused and indicated her drink. 'You should sell these in your bar . . . when you open up.'

Harry tensed but kept smiling. 'I might do. I'm keen on a diverse non-alcoholic list.'

She nodded. 'I'd be interested to see your plans.'

He sat down beside her with enthusiasm. 'That would be great. In fact, I'd love your input.'

He saw some of the doubt clear from her eyes. 'Really?' she said.

'Yes. So, you wanna know what's in Bag B?'

'Sure.'

He pulled out a buff folder and opened it up. Inside were printed sheets showing mock-up websites and computer-generated design frontages of a bar, all with variations on a 'Harry's' branding.

'Wow,' she said, picking them up. She looked at him and it was with a new respect. He was relieved. Kirsty had unnerved him earlier and part of him wished he'd been smarter right at the start. When he'd first told Nina he was opening up a bar he'd meant it as a joke, something he expected to be challenged on. But she'd gone along with it and now he realized he should have made up something that was less easy to check.

He saw her studying the printouts that he'd generated on the internet. It had been fairly easy to do, hadn't taken him that long.

'You like?' he asked.

'I do.'

'Great. The designer and I have narrowed it down to three styles and I want to know which you think works best. In the meantime, I shall get on with the contents of Bag A.'

She looked up, puzzled. 'I thought we'd done Bag A?'

'Only part of it,' he said. 'The rest is dinner. Homemade lasagne OK?'

She grinned. 'You're full of surprises.'

As he chopped onions in Nina's kitchen, he thought about Kirsty. She was a pain, a real spanner in the works. No doubt she'd try and disrupt things again. He wondered how he might manage her in the future. Nina was everything he'd been looking for and he didn't want anyone messing it up.

THIRTY-FOUR

28 February

The walk back up to the lodge was one of the hardest Amy had ever done. Gabriel had offered to come with her, but Amy knew that would have only raised questions once she'd got home – why was Gabriel there and not Esme? She'd graciously declined, promising to visit again the next day. As she'd left Gabriel's house and heard the door shut behind her, she'd been surrounded by the silence of the mountains. Amy looked over to the woods but the thought of going back through the trees didn't appeal. She'd rather stay out in the open, even though it would be hard going.

She trudged through the snow, each step taking her further from the sanctuary of Gabriel's house. Perhaps it had been a mistake to walk back alone; after all, she'd only just learned of her aunt's death. And yet it had happened so long ago. Months. Her aunt's body was long cold in the ground. Amy couldn't remember her goodbyes, her grieving. Had she seen her aunt after she'd died? Had she held her hand, told her how much she loved her? She was hit with such an overwhelming sense of loss she stopped dead in her tracks, unable to find the energy to continue. Gazing around at the mountains, she was mesmerized by their unforgiving size and power. She stood there, not minding about anything, about what happened to her or what might be waiting for her at the lodge. She didn't want to go back. She wasn't sure how she could go back there and pretend everything was OK. To go about the rest of her day and not mention Esme. She wanted to stay out here in the cold and the harsh environment until her pain was numbed. She sank down into the snow on her knees, sat back on her haunches. She considered lying down. The snow looked so sparkling and enticing. It would be cold but she knew she wouldn't feel it. Just for a moment, just to rest.

A shadow fell over the snow some way ahead of her, the grey shape undulating across the whiteness. Amy looked up sharply and gasped as she saw the eagle flying above her. It soared and wheeled over her head, around and around. She stared, unable to believe its presence. Then Amy slowly got back to her feet, her eyes never leaving the bird as she watched, entranced. *Symbol of intelligence, courage, strength and immortality*, she remembered. Her cheeks stung and Amy was surprised by the pain on her skin and then realized she was crying, even while she felt her spirits soar. She wiped the tears away, a strangled laugh escaping. *Esme*. It was as if she was looking on, telling her to get up and stop wallowing in her own misery. Amy watched until her neck hurt and then lowered her head, knowing she had to move on.

Amy continued with a renewed, determined energy. After a while she pulled back her glove and checked her watch.

She was taken aback to see she'd been away from the lodge for several hours. She could see it up ahead, the windows reflected bright in the late afternoon sun. She could see the balconies off the bedrooms and knew which one belonged to Esme's room. She remembered when she'd come back from an afternoon's skiing and Esme had been sitting outside in layers of clothing, her face tilted towards the sun. Amy had shouted up and Esme had smiled down at her, telling her to hurry up so they could drink a glass of wine together and watch the sun go down.

The image suddenly evaporated. The balcony was empty.

She let herself into the lodge and took off her jacket and boots. As she placed everything away in the cupboard, pieces of snow fell off her boots, instantly dissolving into a wet puddle on the marble floor. Everyone else's boots were lined up along from hers, and at the end was a pair that were also sitting in a puddle of melted snow.

They were Jack's. Amy stared at them, her brain ticking over.

The kitchen door opened and Jack came into the hall.

'Where have you been?' asked Amy.

He was taken aback by the abruptness of her question.

'We were about to ask you the same question,' said Lisa, who'd come through behind Jack.

'Were you following me?' demanded Amy.

The look of surprise on his face was almost comedic. 'What? No,' he said.

Amy glared at him. 'Your boots are wet,' she said. 'Someone was following me. It was you, wasn't it.'

He looked at her and held out his hands, palms facing upwards. 'I went down to the town, to the shops. To get some groceries.'

'It's true, Amy,' said Lisa. 'We were running low on food. It's still impossible to get a taxi up here so Jack offered to walk through the snow.'

'Nearly got swallowed up by a drift,' said Jack, smiling, 'but made it back in the end.'

Amy narrowed her eyes. 'You're lying,' she said. She stalked past him into the kitchen and up to the fridge. She flung open the door and stopped abruptly.

The shelves were packed with food. Vegetables, cheese, yoghurts. Bread lay stacked on the counter. She felt as if she'd seen it before but that was impossible. The fridge had been empty that morning. She remembered as much herself.

But something didn't feel right. *It's your paranoia*, a voice said in her head.

'Amy,' said Lisa gently. 'Jack's been to the shops and that's it. Where have you been? We didn't know where you were. You didn't leave a note,' she added pointedly.

Amy swung her gaze to her friend. 'Out,' she said. 'For a walk.' And then she made her way upstairs.

On the landing she took a deep breath, tried to regain her composure. Ahead of her was a closed doorway: Esme's room.

Quietly, Amy opened it and went inside. She felt a lump in her throat as she gazed around, now understanding why the house had been left to gather dust.

The curtains were still closed and Amy felt a sudden urge

to fling them open, to break up the suffocating sense of loss and sadness that hung over the room. She strode over, purposefully grabbing the luxurious material with both hands and yanked it aside. Her hands hurried to turn the lock on the balcony window, slipping in their haste, then she opened those too and stepped out. The instant blast of cold air gripped her body mercilessly but she embraced it, holding her shoulders back and staring out at the snowy landscape in the fading light. Her hands were on the balcony ledge, the freezing metal burning her palms until the pain throbbed right up her arms, but still she hung on, tears pricking at her eyes. She looked down to where she'd been standing a few minutes ago, remembering her aunt where she, Amy, was standing now, and grief threatened to over-whelm her, when she saw something that made everything stop.

Down in the snow, going away from the house towards the woods and Gabriel's house she could see her tracks.

And right behind them was another set of footprints.

THIRTY-FIVE

28 February

Amy stared, no longer feeling the pain in her hands. She shook her head, frowning as she tried to see in the growing shadows, then quickly turned back into the room, locking the windows. She hurried downstairs and, checking no one was around, pulled on her boots and coat and went outside.

She saw where she'd started her walk to Gabriel's and how there was another set of prints following the same path. She continued to walk across the valley, following both sets of prints. But then the second set stopped abruptly, whereas her own continued. She frowned, puzzled for a moment but then she saw a ski track. Whoever had followed her had put on a pair of skis. She looked ahead. Both sets of prints, her boots and the skis, continued all the way to the woods. Amy looked down at the snow. She placed a foot exactly where she had walked a few hours ago. Her boot fit the imprint perfectly. Then she put her foot in the other set. The imprint in the snow went beyond her boot. A larger foot had trodden there. A man's foot.

They were lying to her. Jack might have gone to the shops

but she'd been out of the house for hours. He could still have found time to follow her.

She had to be careful. She had to find out more. She stood there a moment and felt the cold start to seep in through her clothes. It was utterly silent. She looked up at the darkening sky that was turning the mountains black. It was time to go back.

THIRTY-SIX

28 February

Amy stood under a hot shower waiting for the water to warm her right through. Her mind was pinballing around in a state of confusion: Jack, the footsteps, how he had followed her, *why* he had followed her. She felt no sense of security being inside the lodge; Jack had lied his way inside the house with her, had made himself comfortable. He was in her mother's affections, her friends' trust. He was everywhere.

She gave up with the water; being naked in the shower made her feel vulnerable anyway so she got out and dried herself. She went back into her bedroom and gazed around, listless and disheartened and then her eyes fell on something lying on the bed.

Her phone.

She went over, picked it up. How odd that she hadn't noticed it when she was looking for it earlier, before she went to Gabriel's. As she got dressed she realized she'd forgotten to get the solicitor details from him. She made a mental note to get them when she went back in the morning.

Thinking of Gabriel made her think of Esme, and Amy felt her chest tighten. She sat down at the dressing table and looked in the mirror. It was time for a stern talking to. Esme wouldn't fall apart, thought Amy. Esme would be strong and would banish fear and doubt. She would fight on until she'd convinced the naysayers in this house of Jack's false identity. Amy made herself sit up straight. She applied some make-up and it gave her courage. She would not cower. Looking again in the mirror, she decided she needed more armour. *The necklace,* she thought, *the diamond that I bought for myself.* She was removing it from its box when there was a soft knock on the door.

Amy tensed. 'Yes?'

'Can I come in?' asked Jack, opening the door a crack.

You already are, thought Amy as she turned on her stool to face him.

'Sorry, I didn't mean to disturb you,' said Jack as he stepped into the room. He stayed by the door. 'You look nice,' he said.

Amy didn't reply.

'Um . . . look, are you OK? Only I was thinking downstairs . . . if you thought someone was following you on your walk that must have been pretty scary.'

He was waiting for her to respond but still Amy said nothing.

'Did you go anywhere in particular?'

'No,' said Amy. 'Just for some air.'

'To clear your head?'

She frowned. 'What do you mean?'

'The headaches. Are you still getting them?'

'Yes, I am. What of it?'

'I was hoping they would have subsided a bit by now. I don't like the idea of them . . .' He looked concerned and it made Amy's heart beat a little faster – was there something wrong with her, something more serious than she'd thought? Then he smiled, covered it up. 'I want to keep an eye on you, that's all. The doctor in me never goes away, especially when it comes to my girlfriend. Are you sleeping?'

Her gaze lowered briefly. She wasn't, not properly, but she didn't want to tell him that. She didn't want him to have any more ammunition against her. He knew the answer anyway, she could tell by the way he was looking at her.

Jack saw the necklace in Amy's hands and his face lit up. 'Are you going to wear it?' he asked, walking over to her. It was too late to stop him and before Amy could do anything he was reaching out to take it.

'It's OK,' she said quickly. 'I can do it.' But he was so close she could feel the heat from his skin, smell his after-shave. It made her nervous and her hands couldn't fasten the clasp.

'Let me,' he said, and he took it from her and fastened it around her neck. Her skin crawled as his fingers brushed against her.

'It looks beautiful,' he said softly. 'As good as the first time I put it on you.'

Amy's stomach curdled. *You're a liar*, she thought. *I bought it, for me.*

'I know you have . . . reservations about us,' said Jack,

'and a different version of events to what really happened, but I want you to know that it means a lot to me that you're still wearing the necklace. Even with everything that's going on.' His voice was steeped in emotion. Amy watched him, her eyes flinty.

'And I promise I didn't follow you on your walk today.' He took a breath. 'I know how hard it is for you with your accident and everything, but I know we can get through this.' He paused. 'I've made dinner tonight. I got some chicken while I was out earlier, roasted it with garlic. See you downstairs?' he asked hopefully.

Amy nodded then watched as he left the room.

He was convincing, that much she'd give him. She looked again in the mirror and touched the diamond lying at her throat. *Stay strong*, she reminded herself. *Remember what you know.*

THIRTY-SEVEN

10 February

Harry carried a fresh cup of tea into Nina's living room. He placed it down gently on her desk and picked up the empty one, careful not to disturb her, as he knew she was trying to get her head round a particularly complex set of figures. He was about to tiptoe back out when she looked up from her screen and caught hold of his hand. She pulled herself up out of the chair and stretched.

'You are amazing,' she said.

'It was a toss-up between tea or a glass of red,' said Harry.

Nina groaned. 'I'd kill for a glass of wine. Maybe with dinner?'

'Of course. It'll be ready in fifteen minutes. That OK with you?'

Nina reached her arms around his neck and kissed him. 'You really know how to look after a girl, don't you?' She glanced down at her laptop. 'I'm almost done, thank goodness, then I'm all yours.'

'Is that a promise?'

She kissed him again. 'You try and stop me.' She plucked at the pink-and-blue striped apron he was wearing, one that he'd found in her kitchen drawer, and ran her hands over his chest. 'Very fetching,' she said flirtatiously. 'What's for dinner?'

'Sausage casserole and mash,' said Harry, pushing her back down into her chair. 'Get on with it,' he added mock sternly, 'and then we can eat.'

He left the room and headed back into the kitchen. He realized he enjoyed cooking, enjoyed making meals for Nina when she was on one of her tight deadlines. As he drained the potatoes he heard the doorbell ring and Nina get up to answer it. The radio started to play a track he loved and he turned it up and began to mash the spuds.

Harry could see a future where he cooked and stayed home to take care of things. And Nina clearly enjoyed being taken care of. He could be whatever she needed him to be, whatever made her life run smoothly. He was respectful of what she did, didn't mind when she blew him out for last-minute client demands. He was mindful of her need for space and the way she wanted to live her life. They could be a very successful partnership, and so what if he was the one who came with less wealth? No one batted an eyelid if it was the other way around, if it was the woman who didn't have the fattened bank account but was willing to keep the domestic side of life running smoothly and to be an attractive asset to a financially successful man. Harry knew he could fulfil his side of the bargain.

He took out some plates, set cutlery on the table. Then

a thought came to him. He slipped out of his clothes, leaving on just the pink-and-blue striped apron. The track on the radio ended and Harry turned it back down again. It was then he heard the noise. He frowned. It sounded like a muffled cry. Puzzled, Harry made his way into the hall. The front door was wide open. Held up against the wall was Nina, a man's hand across her mouth, his face in hers. She was trying to shake her head, to deny something, her eyes registering absolute terror.

'Let go of her,' Harry said icily.

The man turned around and Harry frowned. He'd seen him before. *The man on the bench*, he thought, *the man hanging around Nina's flat*. He suddenly knew exactly who he was.

'I said let go of her,' he repeated, wishing he'd brought a knife with him from the kitchen.

The man took in Harry, naked, except for his apron and laughed. He dropped Nina and turned, swaying as he did.

'You fucking liar,' he said to Nina, his voice slurred with drink. 'You're screwing this prick? A prick in a pinny?' He laughed again, amused by his own joke. He stared at Harry again, standing there, hands by his sides. 'Stupid fucking prick—'

Before Harry knew what he was doing he strode forward and landed a heavy right hook on Nina's ex-boyfriend's nose. Blood spurted. Harry's fist screamed in pain but he lifted his arm again, threw another punch at the man's jaw.

'You fucking cunt,' screamed the ex, holding his face, trying, but failing to fight back.

'Get out of here,' said Harry, 'and never, ever, come back.'

The man hesitated a moment and then thought better of taking Harry on. 'I'm gonna get you, you prick. I'm going to come back and fucking kill you.' He staggered towards the doorway and stumbled out onto the path as Harry shut and locked the door.

Harry turned back to Nina, who was sitting on the floor, her back against the wall, head in her hands.

'Are you OK?' he asked, crouching down to her, placing his hands on her shoulders.

She looked up at him. 'Thank you,' she said quietly.

They held each other for a moment, heads together. Then Harry heard Nina crying, her voice muffled in his hair. He pulled away to reassure her, but when he did he saw she wasn't crying, she was laughing.

'You're naked,' she said, the words spluttering through her laughter. 'You kicked his arse wearing nothing but an apron.'

He smiled.

She wiped her face. 'Will you stay? Tonight?'

He promised he would.

Later, over dinner, Nina told him the whole story. About how she'd met Rob, her ex, at a charity dinner, set up by his employer. He was charming, successful and it had been good at first. Then little things had started to creep in. A comment on the clothes she was wearing, a strong suggestion she didn't go out with her friends but stay in and have a romantic night with him instead. She was alert to it early and finished the relationship with a clean cut, but Rob wasn't accepting of it. He'd come around to her flat one evening, drunk with remorse it seemed. She'd reluctantly let him in, thinking that allowing him to talk would help him understand it was over. But he'd got aggressive and she'd managed to call the police. There was now a restraining order against him.

Harry washed up while Nina called the police again. He heard her talking to them about how they'd be paying Rob a visit and they would check in on her too, the next day. She reassured them she was fine tonight, she had someone to look after her, and he felt pleased. He imagined her saying it to Kirsty too, at least a version of it and knew he didn't have to imagine it, that she would do it. She would tell her friend about how he had protected her, how he had saved the day. He smiled.

THIRTY-EIGHT

28 February

Everyone else was already in the kitchen. They looked up when Amy came in and tentatively welcomed her, then made an effort to continue with a show of normality, their focus returning to the dinner preparations. Jenna and Martha were busy helping Jack, but Lisa peeled away, two glasses of wine in her hand. She came over, offered one to Amy.

It was the smallest, noticed Amy, not even half full. They were treating her like an irrational child, one whose behaviour couldn't be trusted. She took the glass without comment, had a sip.

'Smells good, eh?' said Lisa of the chicken roasting in the oven.

It did and Amy realized she was ravenous. She hadn't eaten properly since breakfast. A plate of chicken and vegetables was exactly what she needed. She felt her mouth salivate, until she was hit with an alarming thought – Jack was doing the cooking. What if he had done something to the food? Her heart was pounding but as soon as the thought had exploded, it fell back down to earth, dwindled to nothing.

You're being ridiculous, she told herself. *Why's he going to poison everyone? That really is paranoia talking.*

'How are you feeling?' asked Lisa.

Amy felt herself tense. This obsession with her well-being was beginning to get on her nerves.

'Great!' she said.

'That's good to hear,' said Lisa carefully. 'How are the headaches?'

'The headaches,' said Amy tightly, 'are still giving me a headache.' She saw Lisa's face cloud with worry. 'But I am *fine*,' she reiterated through clenched teeth.

Lisa was not convinced. 'Are they any worse? More frequent?'

'Oh for God's sake,' growled Amy, under her breath. 'What is this? Have you and Jack been discussing me?'

'No—'

'Only it sounds as if you're conspiring against me.'

Lisa was taken aback. 'Conspiring? What are you talking ab—'

'The pair of you going on about my health, my headaches, ganging up on me, making me feel as if there's something very seriously wrong. If I'm paranoid, as you both seem so keen to suggest I am, then it's because you two are set on some campaign to make me feel that way.'

Amy took a breath. She hadn't meant to explode like that. Lisa was looking at her, hurt etched over her face. *Don't feel bad*, Amy told herself. *You must stay strong, stay focused. Remember, you're the only one who realizes that Jack is not who he says he is.*

Lisa moved away and quietly began to set the table on her own. Amy looked around – no one else seemed to have noticed their disagreement. Jack was carving the chicken; Martha and Jenna were serving up.

As everyone sat down to eat, Amy tried not to notice that Lisa was a little subdued. The food was delicious and she ate hungrily. Then the conversation turned to her. Jack was speaking, a smile on his face.

'So, Amy, what would you like to do to celebrate your birthday?'

Amy paused mid-forkful, shocked. She'd completely forgotten that the following day was her big day – the reason they'd all come out here. She looked at him, doing his best to pretend that everything was normal. As they all were. They were all mad. Going ahead with a party while ignoring the burning building around them. What did they think she was going to do? Put her knowledge and fears aside while she wore a party hat and ate cake?

'Nothing,' she said curtly.

'Oh come on, surely we can have a little bit of fun,' said Martha.

'Mum, I know you mean well, but this is crazy. Have you forgotten that you are sitting next to a man who is pretending to be someone other than who he really is?'

Embarrassment cut a swathe around the table and knives and forks were placed down awkwardly.

'I'll tell you what I would like for my birthday,' said Amy. 'I would like Jack to tell us all the truth.'

'Amy, stop—' said Martha, getting upset.

'It's OK,' said Jack, placing a comforting arm on Martha's shoulder. He stood up and walked around the table to Amy, everyone watching, holding their breath.

Amy stiffened as he got closer, then at her chair he dropped to his knees. He took her hands, looked up into her face imploringly. 'Amy, please believe me. I beg you. I'm Jack. Your boyfriend. The idiot who always loses his car keys just when we're about to go out. I have no agenda other than to love you.'

It was a fervent speech, of this Amy was vaguely aware, but the thing that struck her most was his claim about always losing his car keys. Did he? She had no idea. She couldn't bloody remember! This ridiculous notion was threatening to make her burst out with inappropriate laughter. She did her utmost to contain it and pulled her hands away.

She got up from the table and aware of four sets of eyes on her back, left the room, closing the door behind her.

She was about to walk off when she heard her name mentioned. Jack was talking about her. She stopped still, listening.

'. . . feel like I've ruined her birthday,' Jack was saying. 'I'm so sorry about all of this.' He paused then spoke softly and she had to strain to hear. 'I want you to know I'm telling the truth . . .' he continued, his voice hollow with emotion, '. . . and I'm really worried about her.' She heard sympathetic murmurings.

She couldn't listen to a word more.

THIRTY-NINE

28 February

Amy paced the living room, furious with them all. Why couldn't they see what she could see? Why were they so happy to go along with Jack's lies? *How the bloody hell was she going to make them see that he was an imposter?*

She sat down on the sofa heavily, the air squishing out of it as she, too, exhaled. She felt overcome by a sense of failure. She was a lawyer – she was supposed to be able to examine every angle of an argument, devise a strategy to flush out the truth, but her brain felt like cotton wool. She couldn't remember enough of the last few months to grasp anything that was real and stable. If only Esme were still here. Tears pricked at Amy's eyes. Esme would ask Jack questions. Clever questions that would catch him out. Questions Amy was too exhausted to think of.

She rested her head on the back of the sofa feeling utterly abandoned.

Esme was gone. The house was now Gabriel's, or at least it would be once the deeds were passed into his name. And she had been left the money. Amy supposed she must have received an email from the solicitors at some point over the last few months but when she'd checked her phone for all clues of her memory loss, she hadn't seen any. She made a mental note to check again.

And what of Jack? Should she fear him? Why had he been following her? His little speech at the table had made her cringe: '*I have no agenda other than to love you.*' Was that the sort of thing boyfriends said? If only she knew, she thought ruefully. Even with her near-zero experience, it sounded weird. An agenda to love someone? Hardly the stuff of romance.

Amy sat bolt upright, a strange sensation creeping down her spine. His agenda. She'd been trying to work it out for two days now, ever since she'd remembered she'd made him up.

He wanted her money.

He knew about the inheritance. He knew she was due money and somehow he was planning to get it.

Amy shook her head, her mind spinning.

But how? she reasoned. How on earth had Jack discovered such a thing? Doubt crept in as Amy understood she'd landed on an idea that was outlandish . . . and yet it wasn't entirely out of the question. It would explain why he was so insistent he was her boyfriend. Why he supposedly loved her so much. Why he was keeping such a close eye on her.

Amy jumped as the door opened behind her. It was her mother.

Martha hesitated before coming in. 'Is everything OK? Only you look as if you've seen a ghost.'

If only you knew, Mum, thought Amy but she couldn't say a thing. Nothing about Esme. Nothing about the moment of clarity over Jack. She made a concerted effort to appear calm, collected.

'No ghost,' she said. 'It's just a demon in this house.'

'About that,' said Martha, sitting on the sofa next to Amy. 'I feel as if I've been letting you down.'

Amy's heart did a little flip. Was this finally an indication that her mother was taking her seriously?

'I haven't supported you as much as I should have done – your *mother*. I realize I haven't listened properly. I haven't taken your allegations about Jack as seriously as I should have done.'

A wave of tentative relief rolled over Amy. 'Thank you, Mum. You see I've been trying to explain and I know it's hard to believe and my story sounds fantastical but I can't tell you how glad I am that you're starting to take on board what I've been trying to say all along.'

Martha looked startled. 'No . . . oh . . . I'm sorry. Perhaps I've given you the wrong end of the stick. I meant to say . . . your injury . . . I haven't understood how serious the implications are, what it's led you to think, how it's affected you.'

Amy felt panic flutter inside her. 'It hasn't affected me at all, Mum,' she insisted, 'beyond a few headaches.'

Upset, Martha placed a hand on Amy's. 'That's not true, darling. Look, this is so hard for me, you're my only daughter and you mean everything to me. I can't stand by anymore and watch you get so upset.'

Amy pulled her hand away. 'So believe me when I tell you that Jack is a liar.'

'Is he, though? I can only go on what I see. How good he's been to you. All those messages from him, the flowers. He was *there*, Amy. He's been in your life for months.'

'Has he hell,' said Amy.

Martha's eyes were filling with tears. 'Please. You've had a serious head injury and I've neglected to understand what that's done to you.' She took a deep breath. 'All of us have.'

Alarm bells starting ringing in Amy's ears. '"All?"'

Martha stood slowly then went to the door. Amy watched, puzzled, and then Martha nodded to someone outside. Amy's eyes widened as Lisa, Jenna and Jack came in. She recoiled back into the sofa.

'We've been talking . . .' said Martha gently. 'We all care about you so much and we're worried about you. I know the weather is difficult at the moment but I'm sure we could find a doctor to go and visit. A specialist. Just to check you out again, maybe get another scan. After all, it's been a few days since you left hospital, it would be a good idea to make sure everything is as it should be.' Martha finished with an overly bright, brittle smile.

Amy stared, breathless with astonishment. It took a moment before she could speak, her eyes bouncing around them all, their grave expressions. 'Are you having a laugh?'

'Think of it as a check-up,' said Lisa quickly. 'If everything's fine, then there's nothing to worry about.'

Amy stood, too fast, and she was aware she toppled ever so slightly. 'How dare you?' she said, her voice cracking.

'All of you, ganging up on me.' She pointed at Jack. 'Believing him, over me. You're all plotting against me. You think I've gone mad. How dare you treat me like some hysterical woman? I'm sound of mind,' she ranted, realizing too late she sounded anything but.

'Amy, please at least consider it,' said Jack.

'I will not,' snapped Amy.

'You're tired,' said Lisa. 'You're not sleeping.'

'Oh you told her that, did you?' snarled Amy as she glared at Jack.

A tear was running down Martha's cheek. 'I don't know what else to do,' she whispered. 'I feel like I don't know you anymore. I don't know my own daughter.'

'Open your eyes, Mum. Take off the rose-tinted Jack glasses and open your bloody eyes.'

FORTY

28 February

It was late but Martha didn't want to go to her room. It felt wrong somehow, taking herself away when her daughter was in such an obvious state of distress. She stood in the doorway of the empty kitchen, the only light coming from the glowing wine fridge, and contemplated a glass. She'd probably already had her quota for the day but then who cared, she thought angrily. She wished she'd never agreed to come to this house, this place that held so many devastating memories and seemed determined to destroy her family. Her sister-in-law had a lot to answer for, she thought bitterly, and where was Esme anyway? It was very convenient of her to hide away while she, Martha, was left to deal with the nightmare of Amy's paranoia.

She got a glass from the cupboard and opened the fridge, taking the bottle closest to her. Unscrewing it, she poured herself a large quantity, the sound of the air glugging back into the bottle already beginning to offer some comfort. She was vaguely aware she was a little unsteady and inadvertently splashed some wine on the counter. She wiped it up and then, clutching the glass close to her chest, left the kitchen and wondered where to go. She drifted aimlessly into the living room but didn't want to sit there in front of the fire, not by herself. There were too many old memories of being with Peter, the two of them cuddled together on the same plump leather sofa that still sat there, while a young Amy had slept upstairs. She smiled as she remembered how she and her husband had once filled Amy's Christmas stocking and hung it over the fireplace that she was standing in front of right now – and how Amy's face had lit up when she'd come down in the morning. If she closed her eyes, she could picture the look she and Peter had exchanged as their six-year-old daughter had gasped in wonder; that of a parents' mutually kept secret of delight. Happier times. She still missed her husband every single day and being in this house seemed to exacerbate her loneliness.

Martha took another gulp of her wine. She moved to the back of the room where the sliding doors opened to the terrace and beyond that, the pool. As she peered out she saw the outside lights were on and someone was sitting there in the freezing cold.

Martha grabbed the throw from the sofa and wrapped it around her. She opened the door, shivering against the brisk wind then carefully slid it closed again behind her. The mountains in the distance were looming shadows. Martha could sense their domineering presence as the scudding clouds grew thicker and hid the half moon, casting a blackness over the landscape. It was Jack sitting in the chair, his jacket pulled tightly up around his ears. He looked up and Martha thought she saw him quickly wipe away a tear.

'What are you doing out here?' he reprimanded gently. 'You haven't got a coat on, you'll catch your death.'

He was right, it was cold, and the wind was cutting right through her. But she couldn't just leave him out here by himself. Especially not now she'd seen he was upset.

'I know what it's like,' she said. 'To lose someone you love.'

He was quiet for a moment and Martha could see the pain in his eyes.

'I've spent so long looking for someone like Amy,' he said. 'It was the happiest day of my life when I met her at Waterloo station. My whole world changed. She brightened every day. Even when I wasn't seeing her, just thinking about her made me smile.' He laughed to himself. 'At work they teased me mercilessly – asked me when they were going to meet this woman who had put a spring in my step even at four in the morning in the graveyard shift.'

'I know it's hard . . .' said Martha.

He looked up at her. 'For you too. Sorry, I've been thinking only of myself when you're worried about her too.'

'I can't lose her,' said Martha, her voice breaking. 'She's everything to me. All I've got in the world.'

'It's going to be OK, Martha.'

She gave a broken smile. 'You remind me of my husband. He was very caring. Always looking out for me. And I know you're saying nice things to cheer me up.' She sighed heavily. 'I wish she'd agree to see a doctor.'

He bit his lip. 'Me too.'

'Do you think . . .' started Martha fearfully. 'Can brain injuries have lasting effects on people's personalities?'

He gave a single reluctant nod.

'Are they irreversible?'

'Let's not think like that,' said Jack quickly. 'We'll be home in a couple of days anyway, fingers crossed. It'll be easier to persuade her to see a neurologist then.'

Martha gazed up at the night sky, blinked so that the moon went back in focus. 'Except a lot can happen in two days. And she's not been sleeping properly.'

'No. And that can make the problem worse. I don't like the idea of her being awake half the night. It's not helping her state of mind, or her recovery.'

Martha thought. She was well aware of the impact sleep deprivation had on the mind. She'd gone half mad after Peter had died, never being able to close her eyes without imagining him hitting that rock. It had tormented her for nights. In the end she'd been prescribed tablets. She'd eventually stopped having nightmares and stopped taking the pills, but with a return to Val d'Isère, she'd gone back to them. Nothing much, half a tablet at bedtime, while she was out here. Without them the memories would have gotten the better of her, as she'd lain in her bed alone at night.

'I have some tablets,' she said.

'Do you?' asked Jack, a glimmer of hope on his face. Then his shoulders slumped. 'She probably won't agree to take them, though.'

'No,' said Martha. 'She won't.' She shivered, overwhelmed

with a sense of helplessness and despair. 'She's the only person left in the world to me,' she said. 'I don't know what I'd do if something happened to her.' Martha felt herself well up, gulped some wine. She laughed sadly. 'She gets her stubbornness from me. If she'd taken after her father more, she'd have taken a sleeping tablet, anything to get a proper night's rest. He was the practical one of the two of us.' She sighed, memories pulling her backwards in time. 'She was always contrary. When she was little she'd do the opposite of what I said was good for her, simply to defy me. The number of times I had to lie to her, tell her, "No, there are absolutely no vegetables in your pasta sauce", even though I'd grated in half a carrot . . .'

She paused mid-sentence, catching Jack's eye as she realized what she'd just said.

FORTY-ONE

13 February

There was the tiniest glimmer of warmth in the sun. Harry could feel it briefly touching his face as he walked through Green Park with Nina. The trees were still leafless but small buds were visible if you took the trouble to look up. The ice cream van had ventured out despite the twelve-degree air temperature and people were giddy enough to buy them. Harry had bought two soft whips, each with a chocolate flake and it felt joyously impulsive as they strolled along in thick jackets and jeans.

They'd come into town as it was the first day it hadn't rained in a week. The park was a welcome blast of green rolling lawns and the sunlight glinted off the lake. Harry was pleased to find Nina enthusiastic to see him when he met her at the Tube station. There had been no mention of Kirsty amongst the friends she'd been out with the night before and he hoped Nina was giving her a wide berth for a while. Things were going well. Nina messaged him every day and they met up at least three times a week, often staying the night together at Nina's. She had told him he could leave a toothbrush in her bathroom if he liked. She'd allocated him towels. She'd asked about coming to his flat, and Harry had said that she was more than welcome but he'd got new neighbours upstairs who had a habit of playing loud music until the early hours, which she agreed wasn't great when she had to be up early for client meetings. She hadn't bothered bringing it up again and it became an accepted understanding that they would be better at her place. There had been talk of taking a short break together in the spring. Rome perhaps, or Barcelona. Harry was going to ask Max for some extra shifts so that he could pay his way.

As they finished their ice creams they left the park and headed along Piccadilly, crossing the road at the Royal Academy of Arts to see the installation in the grand entrance. A giant treehouse, built entirely of wood with several rooms and staircases that disappeared around huge trunks. It must have been at least four metres high and twice as wide. Secret doorways and terraces beckoned, a mystical, living hideout that wouldn't be out of place in *Lord of the Rings*.

'I would've loved something like that when I was a child,' said Nina.

Harry was blown away by it. 'Me too.' He hadn't had a garden in the house where he'd grown up and while his mother worked in an office in town he'd been left alone for hours on end. Harry would come home from school and spend a lot of time in front of the television where he'd discovered movies. He'd lost himself in different worlds and had imagined his house populated by other characters that often seemed more real to him than his absent mother.

They wandered around, looking up at the wooden branches that beckoned them into concealed portals, sharing the wonder of escapism and then, sighing for the last time, they tore themselves away and continued walking down Piccadilly. Harry grabbed Nina's hand.

'Lunch is on me today,' he said.

She smiled. 'Wow, thank you. Where are we going?'

'Shall we find a place off the main drag?'

'Sounds great.' Nina went to turn up the next road and too late, Harry realized which one it was – Old Bond Street.

'Come on,' he said, indicating. 'Let's go a bit further along, head down one of the narrower lanes.'

'We can do that from up here, look,' said Nina and she pulled him further up the road.

Ahead, Harry could see the white ornate stone frontage of Dolce & Gabbana. He stiffened but told himself to remain calm. It would only be a few seconds and they would pass it. Probably before anyone inside even noticed.

Nina came to a halt right outside the shop. She looked in the window. 'Oh my God, that's the dress.'

'What?'

'You know, the dress I told you I saw on the TV, worn by that feminist newsreader. God, I love her so much.'

'It's great.' He kept his back to the window.

'You're not even looking. Come on, turn around!'

Jesus! He turned quickly. Saw the dress. Looked beyond it into the shop. There was Elliot. His former boss. Attending to a rich customer. Harry's heart skipped a beat. He turned back before Elliot could look up. Then he took Nina's hand. 'Come on, I'm starving.'

She pulled free. 'You've just had ice cream. Come on, I want to try it on.'

He couldn't step foot in there. The police would be called. The truth would come out. Everything would come crashing down. He glanced in. The customer inside was not dissimilar to Freddie Canning. Tall, angular. Entitled. The first time he'd met Freddie had been during his second week working at the store. Harry had initially been excited when Freddie had come in with his girlfriend, a very thin, fashionably beautiful girl, who took a seat with her phone. It became obvious that Freddie was a serious shopper and it was a chance to earn some commission. Harry had approached and offered his assistance and then talked Freddie through the design elements of several pairs of jeans, all the while thinking there was a rather disgusting smell emanating from somewhere nearby. Then Freddie noticed it too.

'What's that stink?' he said, looking at Harry first, then around the shop. Then there was a sudden dawning and Freddie glanced down at his shoe. Lifted it. 'Fucking hell,' he said. He looked back at Harry. 'Can you get a cloth or something?'

Harry was still smarting at the initial intimation that the smell was coming from him. 'Pardon?'

'Whatever you use to clean off shit.' He gazed down at the black snakeskin leather. 'Fucking hell,' he moaned, 'these are Pradas.'

I don't use anything to clean off shit, thought Harry, rankling. This twat seemed to think he, Harry, was a shit expert, whereas he was too superior to brush up against shit. *Whoever wipes his arse?* thought Harry.

By now, Elliot had clocked the disturbance. He was over in a flash, all soothing smiles.

'Harry, can you go and get some kitchen roll from the staff room, please?'

Harry reluctantly did as he was bid. When he returned, the offending shoe had been removed and Freddie was in the changing room. He came out, donning a pair of jeans for approval.

'What do you think, babe?' he asked his girlfriend, who looked up from her phone.

'You look good,' she said.

Then Freddie noticed the kitchen roll in Harry's hands. 'It's there,' he said, pointing at the shoe on the floor.

Harry froze to the spot; surely this man didn't seriously think he, Harry, was going to clean his shoe?

He saw Elliot stymied, wondering how best to handle the situation.

'I wanna try on that jacket,' said Freddie, pointing across the shop at a black leather jacket with a shearing collar.

Elliot wavered, looking subtly from Freddie to Harry. 'I'll just get it,' said Elliot. Then he gave an infinitesimal jerk of the head towards the shoe, a silent instruction. It was as if by not saying it out loud, Elliot wasn't actually asking Harry to do it.

Harry was taken aback. *Was he taking the piss?* Judging

by the look on his boss's face, evidently not. Stunned, Harry found himself doing what was being asked of him. He gingerly picked up the shoe and with another look back at Freddie and his boss, neither of whom were paying any attention to him, he made his way to the staff room. It was only when he was cleaning the shoe that it hit him. He was wiping crap off a rich man's shoe because he, Harry, was the poor one of the two. It was humiliating. Harry was fuming but felt power-less to do anything about it. He chucked the offending kitchen roll in the bin, knowing it would stink out the staff room for the rest of the day, something that wouldn't ever occur to Freddie. Then he took the shoe back out to the shop floor.

Freddie was dressed again and Elliot was holding several pairs of jeans that Freddie had tried on, along with the jacket. He handed them to Harry and Harry knew this meant he could ring them up and get the commission, even though Elliot had consulted with the customer. Harry supposed it was Elliot's way of paying him off.

Harry moved to the till and rang in the jeans. One thousand, eight hundred and seventy-five pounds for three pairs of jeans and five grand for the jacket. He went to put them in luxury branded bags.

'Hey, you've washed your hands, right?'

Harry looked up to see Freddie grinning at him.

Harry frowned. 'What?'

'Your hands. You're touching my jeans. Oh, never mind,' said Freddie impatiently. 'It was meant to be a joke.'

Harry looked down at the desk where Freddie's wallet lay open. He saw Freddie's name embossed on the black leather, knew he'd never forget it. Harry slid the bag of jeans over the desk and deliberately knocked the wallet to the floor behind the counter.

'My apologies,' he said.

Freddie's girlfriend was hanging onto his arm, whining about how thirsty she was. Harry knelt down behind the counter, picked up the wallet. A neat line of plastic, all filed away in pockets one above the other. There had to be at least a dozen credit cards. He quickly slipped one out and put it in his pocket. Then he stood and handed the wallet over and waited anxiously while Freddie extracted a card to pay for his clothes but Freddie didn't seem to notice one of the pockets was empty. Harry flickered his eyes down to the card machine as Freddie keyed in his PIN, then quickly looked away again. He handed Freddie the till receipt then watched him leave the shop, feeling for the first time in the last thirty minutes as if he had gained back a part of himself.

It had started small at first. A few beers and a bag of crisps from a corner store, some distance from home. He touched the screen with Freddie's card, everything worked fine and he walked out of the shop, elated. Then the next big test. He went into a supermarket, piled up some groceries, but made sure the total still came to less than the touch payment limit, just in case he needed to tap the card again.

At the checkout, this time he inserted the card, then keyed in the PIN he'd seen Freddie use in the shop. Harry surmised that no one with a dozen credit cards could remember a dozen different PINs. He thought it was very likely that Freddie had the same number for them all. He'd held his breath while the screen flashed to 'Transaction in progress' and then processed the sale. A spat-out receipt and everything was his. No one batted an eyelid. Harry left the store buzzing with excitement. He moved on to clothing – he needed new T-shirts and a jacket. He was hungry after the shopping trip and stopped for lunch. Feeling emboldened he chose a restaurant that was upmarket. He made sure to ask for a table near the entrance in case he needed to run. But again the card worked, his bill was paid, he tipped heavily and the waiter thanked him whole-heartedly as he left. On the way back to the Tube, Harry passed a swanky sunglasses shop. He bought a pair of designer aviator shades and put them on straight away, strolling down the sunlit street. He tossed his new jacket over his shoulder and realized he felt different. As if he'd made it. He had become Freddie Canning. He had gained a swagger and a confidence and with that, people now treated him differently. He got served quicker in bars, was attended to in high-end clothing stores. One night he stayed over in a central London hotel with a rooftop pool, just to see what it felt like. He signed in as Freddie Canning. He got a buzz when the staff addressed him by Freddie's name. He felt as if he had left the old Harry, the skint Harry, the exploited Harry behind. He was careful though – he made sure not to spend too much in any given day and he never ever got anything sent to his home address.

A couple of months went by and the card was still

working. Harry figured that Freddie likely never even checked his statements. He had so many cards he probably had a direct debit set up to pay them off monthly and wouldn't ever bother to look through the transactions. Curious one day, Harry googled Freddie Canning on his new phone that Freddie had unwittingly bought him. He discovered a small article in a London paper from the previous year. A photo of a premiere of a high-end TV show. Freddie lined up outside a movie theatre with some girls and an actor from the show, all of them grinning at the camera. The article name-checked them and referenced Freddie as heir to a smoothie company fortune.

Just a spoiled rich kid, thought Harry. *Spends his father's money and doesn't lift a finger.* He felt envious and then reminded himself he was as good as the real Freddie now anyway. He scrolled through the newspaper's current articles and saw that a new cocktail bar was going to open in Mayfair that night. Freddie wasn't the only one who could attend high-class events, thought Harry. He would go to one too.

Later, Harry moved through the crowd of scantily clad flesh, inhaling myriad perfumes. For the first time in his life he felt at home among the bright young things, and he held his head high, looked the girls in the eye. He went to the bar and ordered a mojito cocktail and pulled out his card to pay. He tapped it on the card machine but instead of the usual comforting beep, the machine emanated a different sound. The barman frowned at the machine, as if it was the machine's fault. He held his hand out for Harry's card, and caught off guard, Harry handed it over. The barman wiped it clean and handed it back.

'Machine can be a bit funny,' he shouted above the music. 'Try again, Mr Canning.'

Harry sensed a man along the bar look around, his ears pricked at the barman's raised voice. Harry was about to retry the card when he raised his eyes, met the man's.

It was Freddie Canning. His heart racing, Harry turned quickly and started to make his way out, pushing through the crowd, which had become denser now and women were protesting as he shoved them. He heard a man's voice shout – Freddie's presumably – and he quickened his pace. Just as he was about to get to the exit, a bouncer stepped into his path. Harry looked up into his eyes and knew it was all about to come tumbling down.

He was arrested, charged and bailed. It turned out Freddie's accountant had quite by chance noticed that Freddie had used two different cards in two entirely different countries on the same day (Freddie had been holidaying in Italy) – and the card had been stopped.

Harry appeared in court and was handed a custodial sentence of one year, suspended for two. He had to keep his nose spotlessly clean for those entire two years to avoid going to prison. Of course he also lost his job and Elliot kicked up such a fuss, brand trustworthiness, customer confidence, blah, blah that Harry was banned from going into the Dolce & Gabbana store as well. Part of the conditions to avoid being banged up.

Harry looked in the shop window again and saw Elliot

ring up the sale. As soon as the customer no longer held Elliot's attention, there was a much greater chance Elliot would spot Harry loitering outside. He had to get away. But Nina was tugging on his hand to persuade him in.

'Come on,' she said, 'Let me try it on. I want to know what you think.'

Harry resisted. 'It's a bit . . .' He hesitated, looked again at the dress.

'What?' asked Nina.

'Tarty?' Jesus, he was on dangerous ground here but he had no choice.

Nina stopped, the wind taken out of her sails.

'*Tarty?*' she repeated.

'What I mean is, you're a really classy lady. That's your natural look, whereas there's something about that dress which is a bit . . . downmarket.' There wasn't, it was stunning, but he wasn't going to admit that.

Nina pulled her hand free. Folded her arms. She was hurt, Harry could tell.

'Great,' she said.

'Sorry.'

'You've completely ruined it. Even if I tried it on and liked it, how am I meant to wear it with your words ringing in my ears? Tarty? Is that your way of saying I'm too old for it?'

'No! God, no,' said Harry. He put his arm around her, encouraged when she didn't shrug him off. 'You look about twenty-five, for God's sake. You'll be able to pull off a bikini when you're seventy. It's not you, it's that dress.'

She narrowed her eyes, checking he was being genuine then suddenly deflated. 'I've gone off it now. Come on, you owe me lunch. A bloody nice one too.'

She began to walk away and he breathed a huge, silent sigh of relief.

FORTY-TWO

28 February

Amy sat in the chair in her bedroom on her phone, methodically going through every email she'd received since 28 October – the day of Esme's accident – looking for any correspondence from a firm of solicitors. There were none. She also looked through her sent folder but there was nothing there either. Had Gabriel made a mistake? No, she thought, he had been so sure, so clear about it. Esme had left money to her. Amy supposed she might have received an old-fashioned letter to begin with, setting out the terms of the will, perhaps even including a copy, but surely all further correspondence would have been conducted by email? It was then that she remembered she hadn't been able to find her phone earlier. Had someone else taken it? Had they accessed her emails, read and then deleted them? *Jack*, she thought darkly. He'd been sleeping in her room for that one night. Perhaps he'd taken it on other occasions, he would have had plenty of opportunity. She had a sudden rush of clarity: *he'd actually made her hand her phone over to him that time. Said she needed to rest without any distractions!* Amy didn't think too much about how he had got her screen unlock code. She brushed over this inconvenience, convincing herself he was devious enough to have found a way.

She looked at her watch. It was late but perhaps Gabriel was still up. In fact, she could see the exterior lights on outside his house across the valley. She wanted the solicitor details so she could call them first thing in the morning. There was no more time to waste, not now she understood what was really going on, that Jack was trying to steal her inheritance. She called Gabriel's mobile but it rang out. She tried again, but got his answerphone a second time. Frustrated, she hung up. *Why aren't you answering?* she wondered, as she looked over at the lights of his house, glowing in the distant pitch-black landscape.

There was nothing else for it. She'd have to go back there, tonight. Get the solicitor's details from Gabriel in person.

It wasn't the wisest idea she'd ever had, she thought, as she walked away from the lodge and got swallowed up by the gloom. The wind cut into any exposed skin and she felt her cheeks burn. She could barely see her hand in front of her face. She gazed upwards, knew there was complete cloud cover, no stars, no moon. She didn't dare put her phone torch on, not yet. She was still too close to the lodge. Someone might see and she was in no mood to be told to abandon her mad idea, to be questioned as to what she was doing.

She strode on, unaware that someone had already seen. Someone was watching her disappear into the darkness.

FORTY-THREE

28 February

Amy tried to follow her tracks from earlier that day but even with the light from her phone it was difficult, and the wind was catching the tops of the drifts and throwing them into her face. After a while she realized nearly every step she was making was into fresh snow. It was impossible to see how high the snow came up so she'd misjudge her footing, find herself tipping forwards and losing her balance. She decided to check her progress. She looked up but could no longer see Gabriel's house. She grimaced – she'd spent so long looking at the ground and trying not to fall, she'd taken her eye off her goal. She turned, looked all around and was perturbed to discover she couldn't see Esme's lodge either. She stood still for a moment, hugging herself against the cold, wondering where she had gone wrong. All she could hear was the wind as it raced across the valley.

Shit. Amy held up her phone. Flashed the light around. Closest to her, the snow lit up as the beam caught it, the crystals sparkling. But the torch could only illuminate a few metres, before its reach faded into a never-ending blackness.

With a creeping fear, Amy realized she had no idea where she was.

She noticed the time on her phone – it was past ten. How had she been out here an hour? A thought struck her – had Gabriel gone to bed? Switched off the lights on his house, which was why she could no longer see it?

Panic began to gather in the pit of her stomach. She tried to buoy herself but with no clue which way she should be heading, found fear getting the better of her. *Well, you can't stay here*, she told herself sternly. *You'll freeze to death. You'll also freeze to death if you get lost out on this mountain all night*, her inner voice pointed out.

Amy took a deep breath. Stared into the darkness. Was that a more solid patch of black further ahead? Could it be the woods? She decided to head in that direction; a long-shot plan was better than no plan at all. She thought about keeping her phone torch on as she walked but then noticed she had less than fifteen per cent of battery left. A cold fear spread through her limbs. She was behaving like a total amateur. Going out in sub-zero temperatures on a mountain without a reliable form of communication. She switched the torch off, told herself it was better for her night vision anyway. If she kept walking and she *was* heading for the woods, then Gabriel's house wasn't much further from there.

She clung to this hope as she lurched forward. Above the whistling wind she could hear the continued crunch and squeak as her boots made contact with the snow. She tuned into it, trying to keep a regular rhythm, using it to calm her beating heart. *Crunch, crunch, left, right, left, right.* It had to be this way. She wanted to get to Gabriel's so badly. Once she was there it would be warm, it would be light. She would be safe. She could probably even stay the night if she wanted to. Get the number and call the solicitor from Gabriel's house. Stop Jack. He was a liar, dangerous; he could be capable of anything.

She didn't hear it until it was almost upon her. Another set of footsteps interrupting her tempo, these quicker, heavier. She turned to see a torch light flashing, approaching faster and faster. Amy was petrified, caught in its beam. She wanted to call out but her throat had dried up. And then a figure, looming in the shadows. She instinctively held up her arms to protect herself from whoever was bearing down on her. She heard herself let out a sound of terror, just as that person, a man, took hold of her arms firmly. She flailed around, screaming, trying to get away.

'Stop, will you, just stop! Please! I'm not going to hurt you.'

Amy recognized his voice. *Jack.* She froze, confused, wary, despite his reassuring claims.

He let go of her then and she backed away, unsure of what he was going to do.

'I'm so sorry, I didn't mean to frighten you.' Jack held his hands out in apology. 'What in God's name are you doing out here?'

She couldn't speak. Fear had robbed her of her voice.

'Come on, let's get you home.'

Amy felt a gentle tug on her arm. For a second she allowed herself to be led away, then she resisted. *Where is he taking me?*

Jack was confused. 'What are you doing? We need to get you back home in the warm. Have you any idea how worried we've all been? Your mum's about to call mountain rescue.'

'I got lost,' said Amy. That was all she'd tell him. He didn't need to know where she was heading and why.

'You don't say,' said Jack, unable to hide a hint of exasperation. 'Next time take a torch – or a St Bernard. Or better still, wait until morning. Where were you going anyway?'

Amy didn't answer. He sighed. 'Look, the lodge is this way.' He indicated back the way he'd come. 'About twenty minutes.'

Was that all? She must have been going around in circles.

'You think you can manage it?'

Of course she could. And to prove it, Amy set off ahead of him.

FORTY-FOUR

28 February

'But what were you doing going out in the dark by yourself?' asked Martha. 'My God, it's minus fifteen degrees out there, what on earth were you thinking?'

'Please, Mum, I'm tired. Can this wait until morning?' Amy wasn't just tired, she was cold too. Colder than she'd realized. She was aware her speech sounded a little slurred and she couldn't stop shivering. She'd hoped to be able to simply go to bed when she got in, but although Jack had left her alone and Jenna and Lisa had tactfully returned to their rooms, her mother was demanding an explanation. Amy had made herself some tea and was sitting at the breakfast bar, her hands wrapped around her cup. She took another sip, aware her mother was watching her.

'Your lips are blue as well,' said Martha.

Amy closed her eyes. 'Anything else?'

'This isn't a joke, you know. You could have died out there.'

'Oh for God's sake, Mum,' snapped Amy, but then she stopped, surprised. Her mother was openly weeping.

'Do you ever stop to think about what all this is doing to me?' asked Martha. 'I was terrified, thinking the worst had happened to you. It's not enough that I get a phone call a week ago saying that you've hit your head and you're in hospital but now, here we are in this godforsaken place that has already claimed one member of our family and yet you seem to enjoy putting yourself in as much danger as possible!'

Ashamed, Amy was quiet. She hadn't meant to upset her mother. But there was something bigger at stake that she couldn't ignore.

'I'm sorry, Mum. I didn't mean to worry you.'

'How can I *not* be worried?' said Martha, exasperated. 'It's not normal behaviour, going outside in the freezing cold in the middle of the night. And then not even telling me what you were *doing* out there!' Martha sighed. 'You do realize that what you're doing is . . . irrational, don't you?'

Amy bristled. She was the sane one, the one who could see through all the smoke and mirrors. 'I am perfectly clear-headed,' she said.

She saw her mother stiffen.

'I want you to promise me,' said Martha. 'No more night-time jaunts in the snow.'

'I'm a grown woman, Mum. I will do what I like.'

'You're not thinking of going back out there, are you?' asked Martha, horrified.

'Mum, please stop.'

'You're putting yourself at risk. I want you to promise,' repeated Martha.

Amy rubbed her temples. She was gagging for a cigarette. If she refused her mother's request, she wouldn't leave her alone. It was easier to say what Martha wanted to hear.

'OK,' said Amy. 'I promise.' She looked up to see Martha watching her carefully, a frown on her face. Her mother didn't believe her. Amy had run out of energy. She stood up. 'I think I'll go to bed,' she said. 'Night, Mum.'

Up in her room, Amy looked out of the window across the valley towards Gabriel's house. The lights were still on, so he hadn't gone to bed. Amy checked her watch – it was almost midnight. Strange that he was staying up so late. She resolved to get up early and call him to get the solicitor details first thing.

As she undressed and wrapped herself in a dressing gown, there was a tap on the door. Amy opened it to see Martha there, a steaming mug of hot chocolate in her hands.

'I'm sorry for going on at you downstairs,' said Martha. 'One day you'll understand, you know, if . . .' she tailed off awkwardly.

If you ever get around to having children, filled in Amy silently. Her mother thrust the mug at her.

'I thought a hot chocolate would help you recover,' said Martha. 'Will you please drink it?'

Her mother looked so piteous, Amy took the drink. It was a small thing she could do. She took a sip. It was delicious. Then she pointedly waited for her mother to go.

'Oh right. You must be tired,' said Martha, realizing.

'I am a bit,' admitted Amy.

'You will finish it?' asked Martha, of the hot chocolate.

'Yes, Mum. Now stop worrying and go and get some sleep. You look tired yourself.'

As Martha lay in bed, the covers tucked up to her chin, she felt invaded by a crawling sensation of guilt. She hadn't seriously thought about hiding a sleeping tablet in her daughter's hot chocolate, not until Jack had found her lost outside in the snow in the middle of the night. It had frightened Martha to death. She couldn't let her daughter die in the same mountains as her husband had done. What if Amy had fallen? What if she'd got hypothermia and died? It didn't bear thinking about. Her actions were for the best.

FORTY-FIVE

19 February

Harry was annoyed. He'd missed the bus and the live-time indicator told him the next one wasn't for another twenty-eight minutes. It was a freezing cold night and he was due at work. He decided it was quicker to walk but it would be impossible to avoid being late. As he strolled up Garrett Lane, he envisaged the holier than thou attitude he was going to get from Max and it wound him up further with every step he took. If only he didn't have to do this stupid, menial job, bowing and scraping just to earn a pittance. He wanted a different life, one where he lived with Nina in her modern, more central flat. He would look after it, look after her. He'd cook for her, have a meal ready when she came home from work. He'd take away the stresses and strains of her pressurized job. Then maybe, when a child came along, he would look after that too, take it out for walks in the park.

Harry turned into the road where Max's bar was. It was busy as usual, despite the weather. He saw a group of people stand back and wait for a woman to leave before going in.

He made his own way to the door and then braced himself before going inside.

Max was on him in seconds.

'Sorry,' said Harry, 'the buses seem to be delayed. I had to walk.'

'Right,' said Max and his tone indicated he didn't believe the excuse. Harry found himself getting affronted, as for once he was telling the truth. But he couldn't be bothered and went to hang up his coat.

As he came back into the bar and started serving, he noticed Max's strange behaviour almost immediately. Max would look up from across the room whenever Harry or Alex were serving, drift past in a faux casual way when they were ringing up the sale. It was as subtle as a brick. Clearly there were still issues with the takings and Max was hoping to catch one of them out. Harry laughed to himself – his boss would never find any dirty money on him. He idly wondered if it was Alex and silently cheered him if it was. They barely got paid a living wage and Harry wouldn't blame his co-worker for topping up his salary.

The bar was heaving. Friday always brought out the fun seekers, those who embraced the weekend. All the tables were full and people had come in high on the Friday-night vibe. Harry finished serving a couple of guys and their girlfriends and then felt the brief blast of cold air that meant the front door had opened. In walked Nina, swiftly followed by Kirsty.

Harry's heart sank but he fixed a delighted smile on his face. Truth was, it was more hassle when Nina was in the bar, he had to watch what he said, especially when Max was in earshot. And the sight of Kirsty frankly wound him up.

Both women took a seat at the bar and Harry leaned over to peck Nina on the lips. He nodded at Kirsty and got the women their wine and two glasses. He also placed a dish of mini chorizo and garlic bread on the bar.

'On the house,' he said, hoping it would soften Kirsty's mood. 'Good day?' he asked.

'Not bad at all,' said Kirsty. There was something about her tone that rankled him; it was cool, knowing.

'I'm knackered,' declared Nina. 'Glad it's Friday.'

'I wasn't expecting to see you tonight,' said Harry.

'It was Nina's idea,' said Kirsty, frosty. 'We're getting a take-out at her flat later but she wanted to come in for a glass of wine first.'

'And to see me?' teased Harry.

'Course,' said Nina, grinning.

Kirsty said nothing, just looked at him hard.

What is your problem? thought Harry. She was still looking at him, as if she knew something he didn't. She could go shove it, he thought. He found her to be one of the most judgemental, narrow-minded people he'd ever had the misfortune to meet.

He felt a tap on his arm. Max beckoned him to one side.

'What's up,' snapped Harry, still annoyed, then saw too late Max's affront. As much as Harry hated kowtowing, he knew he had to rein it in. No point making life more difficult for himself.

'The group over there,' said Max, subtly indicating the people Harry had served before Nina. 'Did they buy a bottle of the New Zealand Sauvignon and the Chilean Pinot Noir?'

'That's right,' said Harry.

'Thought so,' said Max. He paused. 'Did you ask them how they wanted to pay?'

'Er . . . yes. It was cash. Thirty quid each bottle.'

Max nodded. 'The till is getting full. I've just emptied it out and checked the cash against the receipts.'

Harry frowned. 'And?'

'They don't add up.'

Harry stared at him. He looked back over his shoulder and was relieved to see Nina and Kirsty were deep in conversation. 'What are you insinuating?'

'There's exactly thirty pounds missing,' said Max.

Harry felt a sweat break out on his forehead. He hadn't taken the money but this wasn't a conversation he wanted to be having here, right now, with Nina only a few metres away.

He lowered his voice, tried to stay calm. 'So what, it's me? Maybe you've made a mistake. If you want, I'll count it. Double-check.'

Harry went to move away from the bar but Max put an arm out to stop him.

'No,' said Max.

Harry could hear the silence of Nina and Kirsty behind him, knew they'd stopped their conversation and were listening in.

'I'm afraid we can't have . . . mistakes like that,' said Max.

Harry was suddenly aware of Alex standing near a table that he was wiping down. He was watching, listening and then he quickly moved away, his head down guiltily. The little bastard . . . But Harry didn't like a grass, knew he didn't want to point the finger. He looked back to Max and grit his teeth. 'This is unfair. I haven't done anything wrong.'

'The till doesn't tally,' repeated Max pointedly. 'And it's not the first time. I can't have staff I don't trust.'

What? A growing panic was rising up through Harry – he needed this job. And worse, his girlfriend was in hearing distance. He took a deep breath.

'Perhaps we should talk this over later? After my shift?' he pleaded softly. He saw Max waver.

'Could I have a word?'

Harry turned to see Kirsty had moved up the bar closer to him. A sense of dread gripped him. Nina was looking on puzzled, concerned.

'We're a bit busy,' said Harry, trying to close Kirsty down.

'I think this is important. You see, I couldn't help overhearing some of that. And I think I'm right about you. You're nothing but a fraud.' Kirsty pointed a finger at Max. 'This your best buddy? Cos it sure as hell doesn't sound like it, the way he's been talking to you. But that's what you told Nina, isn't it? Not the only thing you told her either.'

'Keep your nose out,' said Harry.

'Bet you'd like that,' said Kirsty, barraging on. 'But I'm not going to watch my friend get caught up again in a relationship with a useless bastard. This bar you're supposedly opening. It's all a bunch of lies, isn't it?'

Max stood straighter, folded his arms, interested in what he was hearing.

'I've phoned every estate agent in Putney. No one has any sites for rent in Chelverton Road. What do you want from my friend? Her money? Cos you've sure as hell not got any.' She turned and looked back at Nina apologetically. 'Sorry, I didn't mean for this to come out here. I wanted to talk to you back at the flat.'

'Get your things,' said Max. 'I think it's better all round if we terminate your employment here.'

'This is insane,' said Harry. He looked to his girlfriend. 'Nina?'

Her face was full of doubt and consternation. 'I don't understand,' she said. 'I've seen your plans . . .'

'Fake, probably,' said Kirsty.

'Nina, please,' said Harry, desperation creeping into his voice. 'OK, so what if it's true—'

'You want her money,' said Kirsty.

'I was going to tell you—'

'Yeah, right,' said Kirsty.

Harry tried to ignore her, kept his focus on Nina. 'Genuinely I was. We're good together, aren't we? And if I'd told you the truth from the start, that I was a barman on minimum wage, would you have even been interested?'

He saw confusion and guilt flit across her eyes.

'It was a stupid little game I started that got out of control,' continued Harry. 'One little lie – before we were even an item, remember? At the time I was only trying to hold up to the beautiful, successful woman in the bar.' He gave a small smile. 'I was intimidated.' He saw Nina waver. 'And romance isn't always about roses and sunsets. Each of us brings something different to the table.'

'Don't listen,' said Kirsty. 'He's a scheming little bastard. Whatever he says is bound to be a lie.'

Harry couldn't stop himself. He lunged over the bar and grabbed Kirsty by the front of her blouse, his eyes blazing. 'You're nothing but poison, you know that?'

'Get off me,' she said calmly.

'Let go of her immediately,' said Max. 'And get out of here. You've got five seconds or I'm calling the police.'

Harry opened his hand and Kirsty fell against the bar. He grabbed his coat and stormed out, ignoring the stares, ignoring everyone. Fury burned through him. He was blinded by it, consumed with it. He was a fired bullet, moving like lightning down the street.

How dare that bitch set out to get him like that, how fucking *dare* she. She'd decided right from the start that she didn't like him. And would've done anything to bring him down. He walked onwards, down Garrett Lane towards Earlsfield, his anger stoked by the injustice of it all.

FORTY-SIX

1 March

Amy woke feeling totally disoriented. Alarmed, she put her hand out on the bedside table, scrabbling for her phone so she could check the time, knocking her book and then the lamp to the floor as she did so. Irritated, she tried to sit up so she could see but as she did so she was aware of how groggy she felt. It was light, lighter than she expected it to be. She'd set an alarm for seven, knowing Gabriel was an early riser. She peered over the side of the bed and retrieved her phone from the carpet. Pressed the side button and saw the time light up.

It was eight forty-five in the morning.

Shocked, Amy sat upright. She'd slept through her alarm. She flung off the duvet and swung her legs to the floor, stumbling as she did so. Her body didn't seem to want to keep up with her. She tapped the side of her head with the palm of her hand, *wake up, wake up,* and then calling Gabriel's number on her phone, she made her way over to the window.

She stood looking down at his house, listening to the

ringing in her ear. But it went to voicemail. She called again, but he didn't answer. Amy flung her phone down on the chair in frustration. There was nothing else for it – she'd have to go back to his lodge. She was about to turn away from the window when she noticed something odd. His exterior lights were still on. She could see them quite clearly. It seemed strange, unnecessary. The weather wasn't great, but it didn't warrant the lights on. Maybe he too had over-slept.

Amy was cross with herself as she quickly showered. Of all mornings, why did she have to miss her alarm today? The hot water didn't seem to be clearing her mind and Amy wondered if she was getting the flu, perhaps from being out in the snow for so long the night before. She vaguely recalled being incredibly tired and lying back on her pillows after her mother had left. She couldn't remember falling asleep. Maybe she *was* sickening for something.

As soon as she was dressed, Amy went downstairs and quickly fixed herself a makeshift breakfast. Fuel really, as she wanted to get going. Everything seemed to take longer than usual, she was clumsy, dropped the butter knife and it clattered onto the floor. She swore under her breath and waited for someone to hear but no one came in. She was intending on getting out before anyone noticed and yet she was doing a very good job of signalling her every move. What she needed was a fresh cup of coffee to wake her up, but she daren't risk it. For one thing it would take too long, and the aroma would be sure to draw hungry people in so she settled for a glass of water instead.

Amy still had a piece of baguette in her mouth as she hurried into the hall and was pulling her coat from the cupboard when—

'Amy?'

She stopped dead. Turned. Lisa was halfway down the stairs, a look of consternation on her face.

'Are you going out?'

Amy attempted to remain breezy. 'Just for a bit.'

'But it's about to snow.'

Irritated at being held up, Amy looked towards the window. Tiny flakes were appearing, drifting haphazardly to the ground. The sky was that peculiar yellow-grey that signalled the beginnings of a significant fall of snow.

'I won't be long!' Desperate to get out, Amy shoved her feet into her boots but in that time Lisa had come all the way downstairs and was blocking the front door.

'I really don't think it's a good idea,' said Lisa. 'I think there's a storm coming.'

Amy could feel a sense of rage building through the fogginess in her head. She had to keep her cool, keep this all nice and calm and make it no big deal. Then an alarming thought struck her. She unzipped her jacket pockets, searching, but they were empty.

'What's up?' asked Lisa.

'I forgot something,' said Amy, eyes skyward as she racked her brains. She must have left her phone on the chair upstairs in her room. She smiled nonchalantly. 'Just my phone.'

'You were thinking of going out in this weather without a phone?' asked Lisa.

'No,' said Amy through gritted teeth. What was the matter with her brain? Why couldn't she remember the simplest of things?

Lisa was unconvinced. 'Honest, Amy, I think it's better if you stay in for a bit. Snow's really coming down now.'

Amy glanced to the window. In the few minutes they'd been talking the small flurries had already turned into a steady downfall of thick flakes. The sky was now leaden and visibility would be barely a couple of metres.

'Why don't I make us a coffee?' asked Lisa. 'Storm might pass in a bit.'

Amy could hear others walking around upstairs then her mother and Jenna talking. In a moment they'd be down and she'd have three of them to contend with. Better to diffuse this situation and make it look as if it didn't matter when she went out. A coffee might be a good idea anyway. She just couldn't seem to wake up properly this morning.

She fixed on a smile. 'Sounds great,' she said. She slipped off her boots and jacket, put them back.

Jenna and Martha came downstairs, their conversation stopping as they saw Lisa and Amy in the hall.

'I'm making coffee,' said Lisa. 'Martha, why don't you give me a hand and Jenna, you and Amy could light the fire.'

Amy frowned. Did she imagine it or were there hidden, conspiratorial looks between them?

She followed Jenna into the living room.

'I'll clean, you build?' asked Jenna, starting to shovel away the previous night's ash.

Amy nodded. After Jenna had cleared the fireplace, Amy scrunched up some old newspaper and placed some kindling on top. She took the box of matches from the mantelpiece and struck one, watching the flame balloon and then die back. She placed the match to the paper and it caught alight. In seconds the flames were rollicking through, sparking off the kindling wood. Amy added a log and watched as the growing flames rolled around it.

Behind her, Martha and Lisa came in with a tray of coffee. Lisa poured from the cafetiere as they all made small talk about the snow:

'I hope it doesn't last too long.'

'We're meant to be going home in two days.'

'It's a nice place to be if we're snowed in.'

Amy took the cup of coffee offered to her and had a sip. Its bitterness made her wince today. She stood. Everyone looked at her.

'I'm only going to get some sugar,' she said, wondering why she felt as if she had to explain her every move.

They nodded and she left the room. As she crossed the hall she looked out of the window again, heavy hearted. It wasn't the weather to be trudging through the valley, however much she wanted to speak to Gabriel. She turned away from the blizzard and went into the kitchen. There she stopped. What on earth had she gone in there for? Amy looked around, waiting for it to come back to her but her mind remained stubbornly foggy. *What do I need? Why am I here?*

Someone came in behind her. 'Everything OK?' asked Lisa.

Amy shrugged. 'I forgot what I was doing.'

Lisa smiled. 'Sugar.' She took the bag from the cupboard and handed it to her. 'I'm glad you stayed in this morning. You have to be careful.'

Amy said nothing. This wasn't the same as all the other times she'd lost her thread. It felt like a different kind of confusion. This was more . . . she didn't know how to describe it. It was as if she were bone-tired, wading through treacle.

'You need to go back in there,' said Lisa, pointing towards the living room, a secret look of glee on her face.

'Why?'

Lisa pushed her towards the door. 'Just go.'

Amy did as she was told. Two minutes later she looked up to see Lisa come back into the living room, a plate in her hands on which was a large cake with candles. They all broke into song.

Amy was taken aback. She had completely forgotten it was her birthday. It shocked her but then she reasoned there was so much else to think about, so much to be concerned about.

She made herself smile along at the singing. It was a nice gesture but she didn't really feel like celebrating her birthday.

'Make a wish,' said Martha as Amy blew out the candles.

Amy closed her eyes and thought about what she wanted. *I wish the snow would stop so I can go and see Gabriel.*

She opened her eyes.

'What was it?' asked Lisa.

'Can't say or it won't come true.'

The cake was chocolate. Lisa and Jenna had made it the

day before when she'd been out. Amy cut them all a slice, which they ate with the coffee. There was a small pile of gifts on the table.

'Open mine first,' said Martha, pushing a large, sumptuously wrapped box forward. Amy took it, pulled off the cerise ribbon. She slowed as she saw what was inside. A handmade cuckoo clock. Tiny, exquisitely carved people chopped logs and played instruments amongst miniature wooden pine trees. Amy looked up in awe. When she was small she'd always wanted one. 'I love it. Thanks, Mum.'

The others thrust their gifts forward then. Jenna had given her a framed photograph of a London skyline, Lisa a designer silk scarf.

There was one present left. A small box sitting alone on the table.

'Jack left it. He didn't want to crowd you,' said Martha. 'You should open it.'

Amy didn't want to.

'Go on,' said Lisa.

Under pressure, she did. As she peeled off the paper a small box was revealed. It was the size and shape that would contain jewellery. Then Amy saw the company branding. It was the same jewellers as where she'd bought her necklace. She frowned and then flipped the lid of the box. Inside was a pair of earrings. Tiny drop diamonds set in gold.

A sound made her look up. Jack had come into the room, was standing back by the door.

'I wanted to get you the earrings as well,' he said. 'To match your necklace.'

Amy tensed. *She* had bought herself the necklace.

'Do you like them?'

She looked at him, tried to read his face, find signs he was lying. Maybe a flicker in his eyes, or a twitch on his face.

'Who served you?' she asked.

'In the shop?' Jack was surprised by her question.

'Was it a woman? In her fifties? Stylish? Hair in a chignon?'

'No . . . it was a younger woman. About thirty.'

This wasn't right. He was lying.

She thought frantically, landing triumphantly on something. 'But the owner of the shop,' she said. 'Her name is Ruth, right? Ruth Wood.'

'I don't know who that is,' he said gently.

'It's the woman with the chignon!' she said furiously.

Jack looked embarrassed. 'It's owned by a man,' he said. 'I remember he was working close by.'

No . . . thought Amy. The woman who'd served her had told her she owned the shop. She hadn't imagined her. She remembered her as real; she remembered their conversation. She put the box back down on the table, ignoring Jack's look of hurt. When she said nothing, no 'thank you', no comment on how much she liked them, she was aware of him slipping back out of the room. She stiffened against criticism from her friends or her mother, but mercifully they stayed silent.

She lay back on the sofa. God, she felt tired. She tried to recapture the image of Ruth. Saw her. Saw her chignon, her smart navy suit, her tangerine scarf. But was it memory?

Or was it invention? Amy tried to stay awake. But the sofa cushions were too comfortable and then there was the fire and she had a belly full of cake, and so she found herself submitting to the drowsiness that had clawed at her all morning and drifted off to sleep.

FORTY-SEVEN

1 March

Amy was aware she was dreaming but was unable to wake herself up. It was the same dream as before. She was being chased down a dark street. The fear was rising up in her chest as she realized there was no one else around. It was cold; her feet were slipping on the ice. She slid, almost falling again and again. She was running for what seemed like minutes, always conscious Jenna was getting closer and closer. In a matter of moments she'd catch up—

Suddenly her eyes shot open. Heart racing, Amy took some deep breaths. *It's only a dream*, she told herself. *Same dream*.

Slowly she became aware of a clicking on a keyboard. She looked up to see Jenna sitting on the chair across the other side of the room, working on her laptop.

Amy sat up. 'Have I been asleep long?'

'Only a couple of hours.'

'A couple of *hours*?' Amy felt herself panic. It would be nearly lunchtime. She had to get up, had to go and see Gabriel.

Jenna was looking at her. 'You want anything?'

Amy shook her head. She wondered why Jenna was in the room with her and not editing her photos at the kitchen table as she usually did. She stood. The groggy feeling had lessened but was still there.

'You OK?' asked Jenna.

'Think I'm coming down with something,' said Amy. 'Feel a bit fuzzy-headed.'

Jenna glanced away. A moment passed.

'You get any more memories?' asked Jenna.

'No,' said Amy.

Jenna took this in. 'Can I get you a drink?'

'No thanks.' In actual fact she could do with a glass of water but she was fed up with being treated like an invalid. If she wanted something she could get it herself. And anyway, it could wait. She needed to get to Gabriel's.

'Where is everyone?' asked Amy.

Jenna shrugged. 'Around the house.'

Amy went to go to the door, aware that Jenna was watching her again.

'What's up?' asked Amy.

Jenna quickly looked away. 'Nothing.' Amy looked back at her friend, saw she was staring at her screen pretending to be engrossed with her photos but she was softly clicking her fingers. *Fibber*, thought Amy. *What is it that's bothering you?*

A picture flashed into Amy's brain, a memory. She was at Jenna's exhibition. *I know this*, thought Amy. *I know I was there*. But this reveal felt bigger, felt ominous.

Trepidation filled the pit of Amy's stomach. She shook her

head. But the image that had appeared in her mind wouldn't go away. A part of her was holding back, didn't want to know the whole of what was threatening to reveal itself but with the certainty of a falling tree, it came crashing down. Amy had been wandering around the gallery for over an hour, not having a chance to congratulate her friend, as she was so busy with the press and potential buyers. It was getting late and Amy was tired after a long day at work. She had glanced up at Jenna again but she was still surrounded by admirers and so she'd decided to go outside to the front steps. A moment's respite. A sneaky cigarette before attempting one last time to talk to Jenna. If she couldn't get close to her she'd have to go home and send her a text.

She wrapped her coat around herself against the cold and pulling her cigarettes from her bag, extracted one. Lit it and took a long drag. She blew the smoke out into the cold air and heard a sound behind her. She turned and saw it was Lewis.

'Caught you,' he teased.

'No one knows,' said Amy. 'Not even my mother. Actually, especially not my mother.'

'I won't tell,' he said conspiratorially. 'Taking a breather from the adoring crowd?'

Amy noticed his words were a little slurred. She stiffened, knowing he was drunk. 'She's getting the attention she deserves,' she said.

'She certainly is,' said Lewis. 'About time too.'

Amy wasn't sure if she detected a note of impatience in his voice. It had taken years of graft and at some points

Jenna had been on the verge of giving up. But that was the nature of all art, wasn't it? A hell of a lot of hard work and a bit of luck before you got any success? Amy knew that Jenna had tried to make it without Lewis's help and in the end he had sort of bullied her into showing in his gallery. Part of Jenna didn't want the leg-up; she'd said that if she was successful she wouldn't know if it was because of her husband or on her own merits.

'You on your own?' asked Lewis.

She'd had to answer this question so many times over the years in so many guises it had the power to bring her down. But now she was with Jack – or at least that was what she'd told everyone. Somehow the fact of his not existing had become worse than being single. It seemed to cement her failure. Every time someone mentioned him it was a reminder of how she had never attracted such a man. The amusement she'd got out of it at first had tarnished into sadness. She bolstered herself. Only a couple of weeks to go; get past Valentine's and her birthday and she'd break up with him.

'Jack couldn't make it,' she said.

'We never see him,' said Lewis. 'You guys are still newly dating, aren't you? In that honeymoon period? Surprised he doesn't want to spend every waking hour with you.'

'He has a job,' said Amy curtly, 'a very demanding one.' She ignored Lewis's smile, knowing he'd riled her.

'You sharing?' asked Lewis, indicating the cigarette.

She didn't like to really, she'd rather he had his own but he had a commanding presence about him. She shrugged. She'd had her fix anyway – he could have it.

He took it from her, his fingers brushing hers.

'I should go back in,' said Amy. 'Try and talk to Jenna before I go. It's been impossible before now.'

She was about to move but he spoke firmly. 'She's still surrounded. They're in thrall.'

Amy hesitated. 'Well . . . maybe it's time for me to go home then. I'll catch up with her tomorrow.'

She smiled and turned to leave but Lewis put his hand on her arm. He pulled her back towards him and put his lips on hers hard.

It took a few seconds for Amy to register what was happening. When she did, she stared at him in shock, looking for an explanation. 'What the hell . . .?' she started but then her gaze slid to the entrance where Jenna was standing, open-mouthed, her hands by her side, her fingers moving rhythmically together. They were locked in a silent moment of horror.

'Jenna . . .' said Amy, but her friend turned and went back inside. Amy looked back at Lewis, expecting remorse, embarrassment, but he just cut her an oddly remote look, threw the cigarette on the ground and followed Jenna inside.

Back in the lodge, Jenna was watching Amy from the other side of the room. 'Is everything OK?' she asked, frowning.

Amy looked up, startled.

'No,' she said. 'I know why you've been so angry with me.'

Jenna stiffened.

'It's Lewis. Lewis kissed me.'

FORTY-EIGHT

1 March

Amy moved back into the room. 'You know I had nothing to do with it, don't you?'

It was the wrong thing to say. Jenna's face hardened.

A new wave of horror engulfed Amy. 'Did Lewis say something different?'

'It wasn't the first time, he said. You'd flirted with him before,' said Jenna.

'That's not true,' said Amy, shaking her head vehemently. 'I promise you. And that night at your exhibition . . . I'd gone out for a break. You were busy and I hadn't managed to speak to you – he came outside and we were only talking for a few minutes when he pulled me over to him. He kissed me.'

Jenna made a sceptical sound. 'And at the time you were dating Jack,' she said accusingly.

'Jack's made up,' repeated Amy. 'I was *pretending* to date Jack.'

'So you were so fed up of being single you thought you'd steal my husband?'

It was a cruel thing to say. 'No!' exclaimed Amy. 'I promise you, Jenna, it's nothing like that. I'm sorry that Lewis has . . . disappointed you, but I'm your friend. I'm telling you the truth.' She saw a flicker of uncertainty in Jenna's face. 'Did we talk about this much?' she asked. 'Afterwards? Only I can't remember.'

'You tried. You came to my house. I didn't know what to believe and I wouldn't let you in.'

The slammed door, Amy thought.

'But then I agreed to meet. We were supposed to have a drink,' said Jenna. 'The night of your accident.'

Amy was surprised. 'We were?'

'But it never happened. You were delayed at work.'

'I'm so sorry,' said Amy. Then it all fell into place. 'I rang you,' she said. 'I saw it on my call log. I was calling you at around the time I fell on the ice and hit my head.'

'We didn't speak,' said Jenna shrugging, 'I missed your call.'

'I promise you,' repeated Amy. 'I didn't want Lewis. I've never wanted Lewis. I don't know why he kissed me; I certainly didn't invite it.'

Jenna was looking at her. There was still hostility in her eyes but also doubt and an element of exhaustion. Amy turned to go. 'I'm really sorry, Jenna, but there's something I need to do.' Ignoring her friend's look of incredulity, Amy left the room and headed upstairs. She had to get her phone, try Gabriel again, tell him she was coming over. She couldn't believe she'd fallen asleep for so long. Anything could have happened. It was now well into Monday – she'd lost the whole morning. She had a horrible sense of time slipping out of her control. As she hurried along the landing, she glanced out of the window. It was still snowing heavily.

She opened the door to her room and went straight over to the chair by the window, where she'd thrown her phone that morning. It wasn't on the seat.

She looked around. Maybe it had slipped to the floor? But it wasn't there either. Amy frowned – had she moved it somewhere else? Forgotten that she'd done so? But a search around the room revealed nothing. It wasn't on the bed, or the bedside cabinet, or the chest of drawers. *Jesus!* She had to call. She felt herself break out into a sweat. All she wanted to do was make a call. Everything was conspiring against her. She rested her head in her hands, tried to think. *The bathroom!* She hurried in and searched everywhere: the towel shelf, the windowsill, the cabinet but it wasn't there. *No . . . no, please. I need my phone . . .* Where the bloody hell was it?

She stiffened, suspicions rising. She went onto the landing, mind in overdrive.

'Are you OK?' asked Martha, coming out of her room.

'Have you seen my phone?' asked Amy.

Martha looked surprised. 'No. Where did you last have it?'

Amy pointed back into the room. 'On the chair. But it's not there anymore.'

Jenna had come upstairs now; Lisa and Jack too had come out of their rooms, drawn by the voices.

'Amy's lost her phone,' declared Martha.

Amy bristled. She hadn't lost it. Someone had taken it. And she thought she knew who.

'I left it on the chair in my room,' she said, her hands shaking with frustration. 'Has anyone moved it?'

'No one's been in there,' said Martha.

'How do you know?'

Martha was taken aback. 'It's your room. No one would go in there.'

Amy looked across the landing at the person standing furthest back. 'What about you, Jack? Do you know where my phone is?'

He gave a sympathetic shrug. 'I'm sorry, I haven't seen it.'

'Are you sure? Only I think you might have taken it.'

'Amy,' admonished Martha. 'It's probably still in here.' She walked past Amy into the bedroom, looked at the chair.

'You see? Not there,' said Amy. 'And I think Jack knows why.'

'I promise you, I haven't taken it. I haven't been near your room.'

'And I know you're a liar.'

'Amy . . .' said Lisa awkwardly.

'It's not the first time,' said Amy. 'He's taken it before. Yesterday. I couldn't find it and—'

'It's here,' said Martha from inside the room. She had her hand aloft, the phone clutched in her fingers. 'It had fallen down the side of the cushion,' she explained.

Amy stared.

'Maybe you owe Jack an apology?' asked Lisa gently.

'It definitely wasn't there earlier,' said Amy, defiant. She looked at him. 'Did you sneak in and put it back? You did, didn't you. While I was looking for it in the bathroom!'

'Amy, it's been here all along,' said Jenna. 'You just didn't see it.'

Amy looked around. Her mother, Jenna and Lisa were wearing expressions in varying degrees of embarrassment and impatience.

You are wrong, she wanted to shout. *He is lying to all of us.*

But it was pointless. Not when she didn't have any proof.

FORTY-NINE

1 March

Lisa had enlisted Amy to help make the lunch, a gesture of pity, Amy had felt, something to break the tension. But Amy *knew* that Jack had taken her phone, knew it in the very depths of her being. She'd called Gabriel as soon as she'd got it back, but again he hadn't answered. It was still snowing outside but starting to ease. Amy was going to sneak out after lunch. She was desperate to get to Gabriel's but she knew it was better to wait until they'd eaten when she wouldn't be missed so much. It would only be another hour. Plenty of time, she reassured herself anxiously.

She grimly chopped onions for some soup as her mind whirled with thoughts. How was she going to catch Jack out? She needed something that would smash his carefully built wall of innocence. Maybe she needed to lay a trap, something that would make the others sit up and take notice. What could it be? Her mind raced and spun, no ideas settling, nothing becoming clear.

'What shall we do this afternoon?' asked Lisa.

Amy looked up. Lisa was working at the other end of the counter, mixing butter and garlic for the bread.

'There are some board games in the living room. Fancy a bit of Monopoly?'

Amy kept her voice casual. 'I might get a bit of air, actually. It's almost stopped snowing.'

Lisa's head jerked up to the window. 'OK. We should all go out. Set up a snowball fight.'

'Mmm,' said Amy, non-committal. She was intending on doing her own thing.

The onions were softening and Amy added a couple of tins of tomatoes. She forced herself to relax into her task, even though she wanted to throw down the pan and race out of the house. She looked up at the kitchen clock. The seconds were ticking by, every one of them wasted as she kept up this charade to keep them all at bay. She had such a strong urge to get to Gabriel's, it was like a physical wrench.

An image was tugging at the fringes of her mind and Amy became very still, allowing it to blossom. She was on a train, a Tube but it was overground. She was late, that she was aware of and she was calling someone to let them know. *Jenna.* Amy realized her memory was as Jenna had told her that morning – she was supposed to be meeting Jenna but had been held up at work. She could remember the knot of frustration when Jenna didn't answer, the urge to get to the bar. The worry of not being able to let her friend know she wasn't going to be there in time. It was important that she told her; Jenna had finally agreed to meet so they could talk about the fateful night at the exhibition.

Amy was first off the train and ran to the ticket barriers at Putney Bridge then out onto the streets. She had her phone in her hand, the map on the screen so she could see where she was going, running all the way. She could also see the time and swore under her breath. She was supposed to have been there half an hour ago. She dodged other commuters making their way home in the dark, faces hidden by scarves pulled high against the cold. As she turned into the road, she could see the lights and the overhanging sign of the bar: MAX'S. She ran to the door and pushed it open, feeling the welcome blast of warm air on her face.

She looked around for Jenna but couldn't see her. Amy made her way into the room, towards the bar. She was conscious of a woman sitting at the bar crying. She was doing that thing when you tried not to, holding her breath and blowing her nose furiously. Another woman was comforting her and Amy overheard a few words: 'He's got some sort of problem, some psychotic need to make himself sound more important than he is . . .'

A man with a yellow floral bow tie was working behind the bar. He handed the two women each a glass of wine. 'On the house,' he said apologetically and then he turned to Amy. 'Can I help you?'

'I'm looking for my friend,' said Amy. 'I was supposed to meet her here half an hour ago.'

'Brown curly hair? Pretty?'

'Yes, that's right.'

'I'm afraid she's gone.'

'*Shit*. Sorry,' added Amy, to the man in the bow tie.

He smiled sympathetically. 'No problem.'

Amy turned and left. She stood outside for a moment, wondering what Jenna was thinking. Of all the times to be late . . . Amy shivered; it was not a night to be standing outside in the cold. She'd get the bus home then try and call Jenna and explain. She walked towards the bus stop and—

'Are you going to blend that soup or just look at it?' asked Lisa.

Amy jolted, brought out of her memory. She glanced around the kitchen for the hand-held blender then, grabbing it, reduced the tomatoes to a smooth liquid.

'Mmm, smells delicious,' said Martha, coming into the room. 'I'll serve up.'

Amy moved away, happy to let her mother take over. She set some spoons on the table and went to pick up a bowl of soup from the counter.

'This one's yours,' said Martha, handing her another bowl.

'Does it matter?' asked Amy. She was faintly aware of Lisa turning away, a tight grimace on her face.

'Not really,' said Martha. 'I was keeping the smaller one for myself. I'm not that hungry.'

Out of the window, Amy saw something that lifted her spirits. The snow had finally stopped. *Thank God!* Just had to get through lunch and then she would escape outside.

Amy took the bowl her mother offered and went to sit at the table. She ate quickly, keen to get to Gabriel's.

After lunch, Amy felt unwell. That bug, she thought again, it's rearing its ugly head again. She took a packet of paracetamol and went into the living room. She'd take the tablets and then the worst of it would go. At least she didn't have a temperature, she thought.

She popped two pills out of the blister pack and washed them down with water. Her head spun. She rested it against the back of the cushions, waiting for the dizziness to go. It stubbornly refused to dissipate. Frustrated, Amy got up. She really couldn't wait any longer. She went into the hall and was about to put on her coat when she heard voices from the kitchen. Low, heated voices. The door was open a crack and she stopped and listened. Lisa and her mother were talking.

'I understand your concern but there must be another way,' said Lisa.

'Such as?' said Martha.

'She's an adult. You can't do something like that without her permission.'

'She's acting irrationally. Has been for days. She's consumed with paranoia. I'm worried about how far it's going to push her. She won't see a neurologist. I just want to know she's safe. It's only for a couple of days and nothing too much. Not in the daytime anyway.'

'I still don't like it.'

Amy pushed open the door and the two women inside jumped in alarm.

'Good gracious, Amy, you'll give me a heart attack,' stuttered Martha.

'What's going on?' asked Amy.

Her mother attempted a smile. 'What do you mean?'

'Are you talking about me? What's "only for a couple of days"?'

Her mother hesitated. 'Until we go home.'

'That's not all of it.'

Martha relented. 'Until you can see a doctor.' She held up a placating hand. 'Now I know you don't believe there's an issue but once we get home, all I'm saying is that if you see a specialist then you can rule it out and tell us all how wrong we were, can't you?'

Amy frowned. Her mother's explanation didn't add up but she couldn't be bothered to argue. She was *too tired* to argue. Suddenly a walk across the valley didn't seem like something she could deal with right now. Maybe she'd give the paracetamol another few minutes to kick in. She left the kitchen and went upstairs to her room and lay down on the bed.

FIFTY

1 March

She was running, running as fast as she could. Her feet were slipping on the ice. She gasped, aware of the gap closing, in a few moments they would be grabbing her—

A *click*.

Amy's eyes flew open, her breath coming fast. What was that noise? She looked wildly around the room, still halfway between dream and reality. Had someone come in?

There was no one there. Amy sat bolt upright: had someone just left? She looked over to the door but it was a blank. A silent piece of wood giving no answers. And in any case, she'd locked it. Hadn't she?

She threw off the duvet, desperate to check. She rattled the handle but it *was* locked. Her mind swam. She grasped the handle more tightly, trying to steady herself. *Dammit*, she thought as she screwed her eyes up tight, *there's something important I need to do. Gabriel, I need to go and see Gabriel.*

The handle twisted in her hands. Someone was trying to get in from the other side.

'Who is it?' she said sharply.

'It's me,' said Martha.

Amy opened the door.

'You're awake,' said Martha, switching on the light. 'I've brought you a cheese sandwich.'

Amy covered her eyes from the light. The idea of food made her feel nauseous. 'I'm fine thanks, Mum.'

'But you should eat.'

God, it was all so tiring. She couldn't be bothered to argue. 'Just leave it on the side. Thanks.'

Amy watched as Martha put the plate on the bedside cabinet. 'Did you try to come in earlier?' she asked.

Martha turned. 'No, why?'

'I thought heard the door go. It woke me up.'

Martha looked at her. 'Why do you lock it?'

'You know why.'

'None of the rest of us do.'

Amy tensed. She didn't need her mother telling her how paranoid she was being. 'So did you? Try and get in?'

'Not me,' said Martha. 'Perhaps you dreamed it.'

Amy said nothing. Someone had tried to come in her room. Deep down she knew this. *Jack*, she thought. She felt an urge to lie back down again. 'God I feel so tired. I must be coming down with something.'

Her mother didn't answer at first and Amy looked up to see if she'd heard.

'Yes,' said Martha, 'perhaps you are.'

Martha wasn't looking her in the eye. 'Maybe a little more rest,' her mother said, backing out, then she closed the door softly behind her.

Amy got up to lock the door after her mother had left and then collapsed back down on the bed. She lay there, wondering if she could muster the energy to go and see Gabriel. It was dark outside now and she checked her watch – saw it was past five o'clock. The solicitor's office would be closed by the time she'd reached Gabriel's and got the telephone number. She felt a surge of panic, of having missed her opportunity. But also a sense she couldn't fight it.

She lay her head back on the pillows and closed her eyes.

FIFTY-ONE

2 March

Amy could see a thin line of light through the curtains. Not any old light. *Sunlight.* Today was different. The storm had gone. Amy sat up. Today felt different in another way too. She tested it out, blinking, tipping her head from side to side. Waited for the tiredness, the feelings of lethargy and the heavy limbs. But there weren't any. Just a new invigoration. She was better. Whatever bug she'd been harbouring the last twenty-four hours had gone. And she was starving. Amy saw a plate on the bedside cabinet with a curled cheese sandwich on it. She put out a hand, hungry enough to be tempted but then decided to get something fresh instead.

Energized, Amy got out of bed. As she sat on the toilet she tried to remember the night before. She'd come up to her room for a nap after lunch then vaguely remembered her mother coming upstairs later on with the cheese sandwich. Then she must have crashed out again. Amy washed her hands, peering at her face in the mirror. The cloudiness had gone from her eyes. Never before had she felt so good. This was what happened after an illness – you didn't ever realize how exhilarating it was to be well until you'd experienced the alternative.

Funny how there had been no other symptoms though. No temperature, no runny nose. Just that awful, debilitating tiredness.

Amy went back into her room and pushed open the heavy curtains, feeling the sunlight soar through her. What an incredible day it was. She gazed out at the sweeping white landscape, the miles and miles of snow. It was so beautiful. There was something so innocent and untouched in all that smooth whiteness but at the same time it belied a ruthless hostility.

Something caught her eye and she frowned. She wasn't sure . . . the sun was so bright. She looked again, squinting. She was pretty certain Gabriel's lights were *still* on. That was two days now. It didn't seem right.

She jumped at a knock at the door.

'Are you decent?' called Martha.

Amy went over and after turning the key, let her mother in.

'I've brought you a cup of tea,' said Martha, holding out a steaming mug.

'Thanks, Mum.' Amy took it and placed it on the chest of drawers as her mother came into the room.

'How are you feeling?' asked Martha.

'Much better.'

'You look brighter.'

Amy smiled.

'Only got today and then we go home tomorrow. Thought we could go for a little walk, all of us. Stick close to the house.'

Amy had the feeling she was being babysat again. Her mother had been on edge with her ever since the night she'd got lost in the snow. It was deeply frustrating but this time she bit her tongue. She didn't want to waste time getting into an argument with her mother, she wanted to get a shower and go over to Gabriel's. Martha was waiting for an answer.

'I'm not going anywhere with Jack.'

Martha gave her best look of understanding. 'I get that. Maybe just us girls then.'

'Sure,' Amy lied. She would find a way to slip away.

Martha smiled. 'Are you going to drink your tea?'

'Not yet.' Amy thought she saw her mother's face briefly twist in alarm. 'I'll have it later,' she said. 'I need a shower.'

'But I've just made it. Have it now, while it's hot.'

Amy looked at her mother. 'Why are you so desperate for me to have the tea?'

Martha smiled quickly. 'I'm not.'

'Yes, you are. You're fussing.'

'I'm not fussing,' said Martha.

'You've always fussed. Ever since that time on La Face when I broke my leg.' Amy stopped abruptly. That was stupid. She knew she was only adding fuel to the flames. She should have kept her mouth shut so she could get into the shower. She waited for the fallout.

Martha paused. 'Sorry,' she said. 'I don't mean to.'

Amy's mouth dropped open.

'You have the tea when you like. I'll see you downstairs,' said Martha and she left, closing the door behind her.

Amy shook her head, astounded at her mother backing down. It was so out of character. She wondered whether there was something else going on but time was ticking and she wanted to get to Gabriel's.

After she'd showered and dressed, Amy saw the tea still sitting on the chest of drawers. She picked it up but it had gone cold. She took it into the bathroom and tipped it down the sink. As the last of the liquid poured away, Amy saw a granular substance right at the bottom of the mug. *Odd*, she thought. *Mum knows I don't like sugar.* But it didn't look like sugar. She sniffed; it was odourless. She dipped her finger in and licked it; tasted a chemical tinge on the edge of her tongue.

Amy frowned. She couldn't make out what it was. But it tasted familiar – recent. She felt as if she'd had it in something else. But she hadn't eaten anything out of the ordinary. In fact, it had been simple stuff: cheese toasties, tomato soup . . . A slow dawning was beginning to creep over her. Her mother had told her which was her bowl of soup, had been very particular about it, made her swap. Amy suddenly realized she'd been fed by other people the last couple of days. And she'd felt so under the weather. So bloody tired . . . She gasped. Had they been *drugging* her?

Stunned, Amy sat down on the edge of the bath. *Why?* She knew, of course she knew. They didn't trust her, they thought she was acting irrationally, putting herself at risk. The night jaunt in the snow, her mother's fear she was going to come to harm. Amy lurched at another realization. Her mother and Lisa had been *discussing* it! The day before when she'd walked into the kitchen. *Only a couple of days.* Was that how long her mother was planning on keeping her docile?

Amy sat quietly for a moment, letting the sense of betrayal wash over her. So they really did think she'd lost it. They didn't trust her at all. They thought she was so paranoid she needed restraining.

She was utterly alone.

She looked at the mug still in her hand. She couldn't let them know what she'd found out. Determinedly, Amy stood. She couldn't believe she'd wasted a whole day. She needed to get to Gabriel's urgently.

She hurried back into her bedroom and looked for her phone then swore when she couldn't find it. She glanced over at her bedroom door, realized she'd been distracted by Martha's visit. She hadn't relocked it. *Jack*, she thought darkly. And every single one of them was hypnotized by his lies.

She went downstairs where her mother was in the kitchen.

'Lovely tea,' Mum,' she said, doing her utmost to keep the tremor out of her voice.

Her mother looked at her with barely concealed relief. 'A pleasure.'

Amy left the room and listened out carefully. Her mother didn't follow. The others must all be upstairs. There was no sound of any of them.

She put on her coat and boots and slipped out of the house.

FIFTY-TWO

2 March

Amy trudged as fast as she could through the thigh-deep snow. It was impossible to get up any real speed and yet she was desperate to get away from the house as quickly as possible. She kept glancing back at the lodge, looking to see if anyone was watching but no one called her back; no one came to follow her. Her footsteps from two days ago had completely disappeared – covered by fresh snow with no evidence of her ever having been there before. She was soon getting hot in her clothes; for once the sun had a real warmth to it. Breathless, Amy looked up at the sky, searching for the eagle, its familiar soaring above her, its wings spread dark against the blue. But the space above her remained empty and cloudless. She waited a while but there was nothing. She felt a pang of disappointment. She'd grown used to seeing it, marvelling at its ability to survive in such a desolate environment. Today of all days she would have welcomed its companionship.

By the time she reached the woods her leg muscles were screaming. The snow was now thick in the woods too but not as bad as in the open terrain. Amy made her way through the trees as quickly as she could and then came back out into the sunshine where she could see Gabriel's lodge only a short distance away. As she approached she could see the exterior lights – she was right, they *were* on. An unsettled feeling fluttered around her stomach. It wasn't the only odd thing about the place. There was no smoke coming from the chimney. Gabriel had central heating but Amy knew how much he loved a fire.

She knocked on the front door, the heavy brass ring thudding against the thick wooden door. There was no answer. Amy lifted it again, really hammering it down this time. The sound echoed across the valley before getting lost in the cold air. Still no answer. Amy told herself she hadn't waited long enough. He needed time to come to the door. Or he was out, perhaps. She walked around the house but there were no tracks in the snow showing that anyone in skis or boots had left the building. Then as the minutes ticked by, Amy's nerves started to kick in. She went back around the house, peering into all the ground-floor windows. Gabriel wasn't in the living room and the fireplace was empty. The dining room was lifeless, as was the study. She looked through the kitchen window and with relief saw two coffee cups on the table. At least he was around. She went to the front door and knocked one last time, before she tentatively tried the handle. It turned and with a click it was open. Amy frowned. But it was so remote he probably didn't bother locking it.

Amy stepped inside. 'Gabriel?' she called. 'Hello?'

It was silent. The house was warm, the heating had kicked in. She shouted out for him again, wondering if he was asleep. It felt intrusive to go upstairs but she thought she would anyway, in case he was unwell or something. The doors to the two bedrooms were both open. As Amy peered around the first, the spare, she could see it was unoccupied. The second room was the one Gabriel had shared with her aunt. The bed was made, the quilt pulled up neatly to the pillows.

Amy slumped. Where on earth was he? He hadn't gone out and he wasn't in the house. She slowly went back downstairs wondering what to do next.

She headed back to the kitchen, and was coming to the conclusion that she had no choice but to go back to the lodge when she saw a piece of paper tucked under the coffee machine on the kitchen worktop. She went closer and plucked it out. It had her name on it. She unfolded it and inside was written the name and phone number of a solicitor firm in Geneva. Esme's solicitor, she thought, pleased.

Amy glanced around, looking for a landline phone. She may as well call them from here. It was private and in any case she didn't have her mobile with her. She lifted the receiver from the wall and punched in the number. Put the phone to her ear. But there was no sound. Amy frowned. She pressed the dial tone button a few times but the phone remained dead. Slowly, she replaced it in the cradle. The line wasn't working. Was it the snowstorm? Or something else?

Amy then turned and her glance caught the cups on the

table. One teal, one red. She remembered when she'd seen those two cups before. Remembered sitting at that table with Gabriel, her drink in the red cup, his in the teal cup.

That had been a full two days ago.

FIFTY-THREE

2 March

Goosebumps crawled over Amy's skin. She tried to think. Maybe Gabriel hadn't had time to clear up after she'd left on Sunday afternoon. Maybe he'd decided to go and stay with a friend for a couple of days.

No, she suddenly knew with utter conviction. Because she'd arranged to meet up with him the next day.

So where was he?

She had to find him. She wouldn't be able to go back until she did. She'd be sitting in that lodge, fidgeting, wondering, unable to do anything.

She had to look harder.

She rechecked every room in the house. Then she walked through the kitchen into the boot room where she found his boots and skis. So he definitely hadn't gone out, not on foot anyway. She opened the door to the outside, the sunlight blinding her. Across the pathway was a garage but when Amy peered in the window, Gabriel's car was still inside.

At a loss, she gazed around. The snow lay over Gabriel's garden, a pristine white blanket. There was no hint as to what it contained in the summer: the lavender near the front path, the roses against the stone wall. Where the plants lay dormant, a white hillock hinted at their presence underneath.

It was then she noticed the hillock of snow near the front door. It was quite long, about six foot, and slightly higher than the surrounding snow. Amy hadn't paid much attention to it when she was standing there knocking on the door half an hour ago. One end faced directly into the sun and where the morning's rays had beamed down, a small amount had melted. Protruding through the snow was a piece of brown leather with white stitching along the edge. It was a slipper.

FIFTY-FOUR

2 March

Amy was frozen to the spot, terror trickling through her. *No, please God, no,* she begged as she went over to the mound. She pulled away at the snow with her bare hands, slowly at first, too scared of what she might find. The slipper revealed itself further – it was attached to a foot. Amy cried out in agony and then forced herself to go to the other end of the mound. It was almost unbearable but she scraped away more snow until she could see what she'd known all along would be there.

Gabriel. His white face frozen in death.

FIFTY-FIVE

2 March

She knew it was futile, but she checked for a pulse anyway. Her fingers were numb and could barely feel a thing. His skin was cold and lifeless.

Amy slowly stood. He'd obviously been out here some time – from before the blizzard as he was covered in such deep snow. She tried to work out when that was. Recently everything had been so hazy for her, but she remembered the snow had started yesterday morning. So he had to have been out here for at least twenty-four hours – maybe longer.

But why? Why go out in thick snow in a pair of slippers? Amy wondered if he was wearing a coat. She knew she'd have to uncover a little more of him to find out. She bent back down and scraped away some more snow from his body. He was in the same green woollen jumper that he'd been wearing when she'd left. No coat.

And then she saw something else. A bit of plastic, the corner of a bag. She raked away more snow and found a packet of birdseed on Gabriel's chest. Amy stared. He'd been feeding the birds? Was that why he'd come outside? She supposed it was possible, but in his slippers? She looked back at the front door. It had been shut when she'd arrived. Why close the door behind him? Surely if he'd stepped out for a minute to put food out for the birds, he'd have left it open?

She looked at his still face again and this time she wiped more of the snow away. At least he was with Esme now, she thought sadly, brushing snow off his forehead. It was then that she noticed the mark. A red contusion, right below the hairline. She stopped and wondered. Had Gabriel tripped and fallen onto something? Knocked himself out and then been buried in the snow? But surely the packet of birdseed would have gone flying, not fallen neatly onto his chest. And there was the phone . . . why was the line down?

Then she remembered something. She'd been so certain that she was being followed the day she came to see Gabriel. Had someone else been to the house? Someone who Gabriel didn't want around, someone threatening? Had that person struck Gabriel on the head and left him to die in the cold? *Jack*, she remembered, it was Jack she'd accused of following her two days ago, when she'd last been here. Was Jack responsible for Gabriel's death?

She needed to call the police. Frustrated, she was reminded again of not being able to find her phone that morning. Amy stood up and considered walking to the town. But it was at least two hours – much further than going back to Esme's lodge and using a phone there.

And Jack was at the lodge. He was living amongst them. Alone right now with her mother and friends. A murderer. *You don't know he's a murderer,* her inner voice said.

Gabriel's death could easily have been an accident. Am I going mad? Has the paranoia sent me over the edge?

Desperate to be on her way, Amy set off down the path and retraced her steps through the woods and back along the valley. As she saw Esme's lodge come into view she felt her pace slow. She realized she was scared.

Amy continued up to the lodge and then opened the front door. She shook off the snow, placed her boots in the cupboard and hung up her coat.

She could hear voices in the living room. She stopped and listened. They were all in there: Lisa, Jenna, Jack and her mum.

Amy went across the hall and opened the door. They all turned to look at her.

'There you are,' said Lisa over brightly. 'We saw your footsteps and were about to join you for a walk.'

Why weren't they angry with her? Amy was so certain they'd been babysitting her the last day or so, keeping her in the house. They were all watching her, on tenterhooks, scrutinizing her almost. She supposed they expected her to be tired, to have drunk the doctored tea.

'It's a beautiful day,' said Jack. 'We should make the most of it. It's snowing again later, and then tomorrow we go home.'

She watched him carefully, looking for signs that he suspected where she'd been. He'd tried to stop her two nights ago, made her abandon her journey and come back to the lodge. Had he guessed where she'd been heading? Was he nervous of what he knew she'd find there?

'I've been to see Gabriel,' she said.

'You aunt's boyfriend?' asked Jenna. 'How are they both?'

'Dead,' said Amy. 'They're both dead.'

A stunned silence descended over the room.

Martha was the first to speak. 'What do you mean?' she stammered.

'Esme died some months ago. In a car accident. But Gabriel, well he died recently. As little as a day or so.'

Lisa stood and came to her, placed an arm around her shoulders. 'Come and sit down,' she encouraged and Amy caught the puzzled glances thrown over her head. She was led to a chair and she sank into it.

Lisa perched on the arm beside her. 'Are you sure?' she asked.

'Absolutely certain,' said Amy. 'I've just found Gabriel's body. In fact,' she went to rise, 'I need to call the police.'

Lisa placed a hand firmly on her shoulder. 'You stay there. You're in shock. One of us can call.'

'What happened?' asked Jack gently.

Amy held his gaze, watching for his reaction. 'He was outside,' she said. 'Had been for a day or so. He's buried in snow.'

Martha's hand flew to her mouth.

Jack stood. 'I'll go and check, see if there's anything I can do.'

'You stay away,' snapped Amy.

'He's a doctor,' said Jenna. 'Maybe he can help.'

'I told you. It's too late.'

Nobody knew what to say. Amy noticed more awkward looks exchanged amongst them.

'Tell us everything,' said Jenna.

Amy spoke of the house being empty, her searching for Gabriel. Of how she'd almost missed him except for the toe of his slipper visible in the snow. She omitted the part about the bruise on his head.

'Oh my God, it's awful,' said Martha.

'We need to call the police,' repeated Amy.

'I'll do it,' said Jack. He stood and left the room. Amy waited until he'd gone and then looked at her friends and her mother.

'I think Jack is involved in this,' she said, keeping her voice low.

They all looked at her, astounded, dismayed.

'There's a bruise on Gabriel's forehead. It looks as if he was hit and then he fell. He was left to die in the freezing temperatures.' Amy looked at her audience but not one of them was agreeing with her.

Jenna spoke awkwardly. 'But it was an accident, surely. Poor Gabriel, well he must have slipped and hit his head.'

Amy shook her head. 'I went to see him another time, on Sunday. Two days ago.'

Martha was surprised. 'You never said.'

'Someone was following me,' continued Amy. 'It must have been Jack.'

'But he's never been there before,' said Martha.

'How do you know, Mum?' asked Amy impatiently. 'Because that's what he's *said*? I think he followed me and then after I left Gabriel's, Jack went inside. I think he's the one who hurt Gabriel.'

'Is this the day he went to the shops?' asked Lisa.

'Oh it was!' said Martha in relief. 'So it can't have been him.'

Of course that was what her mother would say, what they'd all say. She didn't blame them; it was hard to believe.

But what the hell did she have to do to make them take her seriously?

'Why are you all so ready to believe a virtual stranger and not me, your daughter, your best friend? You've only met Jack a few days ago and as far as you're all concerned he's the perfect man, the perfect boyfriend who can do no wrong. What on earth makes you all so sure?'

They all looked at one another but it was Martha who spoke.

'Well, you told us he was,' she said. 'For months. On Facebook, when we met up with you. On the phone, when you texted us. You told us how amazing he was.'

FIFTY-SIX

2 March

'I've spoken to the police,' said Jack, coming back into the room. 'They'll send an ambulance as well.'

Amy looked up at the man she'd seemingly invited into their lives. The man who'd captivated her friends and mother. His face was full of concern and warmth. He was practical, caring and kept his head in a crisis. He could cook, he was tidy. He was, she remembered, good in bed.

Am I hysterical? she asked herself. *Have I totally lost it? Has this head injury made my life a living nightmare where I suspect everyone of harm?*

She was suddenly exhausted.

'Thank you,' she said to Jack. 'For calling the authorities.'

She could feel the palpable relief from everyone in the room.

FIFTY-SEVEN

2 March

Unable to bear everyone's scrutiny, their looks of pity and concern, Amy had escaped for a moment by herself. Even that had been an ordeal – they hadn't wanted her to leave but she'd got tetchy in the end, insisted she needed some space until eventually, to her immense relief, she'd been allowed to go outside without interference.

She didn't go far, she couldn't bear the thought of them coming after her and she suspected they were keeping an eye on her from one of the windows. She took a short walk along the valley, enough to feel a part of the mountains and then she stopped and let herself fall into a drift, her body making an upright seat of sorts in the snow. She looked up to the sky. *Please? Just a glimpse?* But the eagle didn't appear. That niggling fear again, that sense that something bad had happened to it, but it was too much to bear.

She felt herself teetering on the edge of madness.

I can't go on like this.

She kept very still for a moment, allowed herself to breathe. Then for the first time in what felt like a long time she asked herself some difficult questions. To examine what she believed. Amy had always prided herself on her sharp mind, her infallible ability to know what was fact and truth. But she also knew her friends, her mother, were undeniably capable. And they were utterly convinced she was not in a secure state of mind.

One of them was wrong. Her friends and her mother? Or herself?

Amy had to admit that since her injury she hadn't been herself, forgetting where she'd put things, walking into a room and not knowing why.

So what if she'd been wrong all this time? What if Jack was real and it was her memory that was the problem? It wasn't beyond the realms of possibility. Amy knew that all sorts of strange outcomes had come from brain injuries. It was well documented that people had woken from comas fluent in a new language, or had been able to play the piano at concert hall standard, even though they'd never previously touched a keyboard. If only that had been her side effect. Become a musical genius. She let out a sad laugh that died on her lips. No genius here. Just Amy on her own.

Loneliness was a funny thing, she thought. It followed you everywhere, yet you remained in an utterly solitary state. It played tricks on your subconscious, making you question whether you were good enough, why you didn't attract someone to share your life with. Maybe that was what had happened. Maybe, in a reflection of the desperation she'd felt, her mind had invented a desperate scenario. Perhaps her subconscious had *thought* it had invented a boyfriend because that was what she'd desperately craved.

Amy gazed out at the snow. *Had she made up the fact that she'd made him up?*

This theory sat heavily on her shoulders, becoming ever more weighty and solid. Now she had seen a credible justification, it was as clear as day. That was the explanation. That was what had happened. All this time she'd been played by her own mind.

She swallowed, then got up and walked back to the lodge.

FIFTY-EIGHT

2 March

Amy closed the front door behind her. She hung up her coat to a resounding quiet but it was the sort of quiet that had ears. The others were listening, whispering to each other no doubt, waiting for her to appear. Her skin prickled with the weight of their expectation.

She walked into the kitchen. They were all there; each of them was looking at her, all as nervous as her, waiting for her to say something.

There was a stretched silence.

Amy took a breath. She had to get this over and done with. She opened her mouth but no words came out. Her stomach fluttered with anxiety.

What should she say? *I'm sorry, I was wrong.* No, it was too big, too shattering. It was admitting to the loss of herself. Her perception of reality was tied intrinsically to her own sanity. She'd lost both. She could no longer trust herself.

She tried again. 'I wanted to . . .' She trailed off and unable to stop them, tears rolled down her cheeks. She stood there, hands hanging limply by her sides.

Jack's face crumpled in sympathy and he came over to her, tentatively at first. He gently raised his arms and when she didn't protest, he wrapped them around her.

She let herself be held, unable to fight. There was nothing left to fight against.

'It's OK,' he whispered in her ear, as the tears streamed down her face.

There was a sense of safety in succumbing, a sense of relief. The opposite of being scared, she supposed, now there was nothing to be scared of. And they were all so convinced: Lisa, Jenna and her mother. Not just convinced, never really dubious, just glad he was normal, he was nice, he was such a good person. A catch.

She pushed away any last dregs of the habitual resistance. *Let go*, she instructed herself. *Stop torturing yourself.*

FIFTY-NINE

2 March

Out of the corner of her eye, Amy saw Lisa nod to the others and they slipped out of the room.

Jack gently pulled away, looked her in the eyes. 'Are you OK?'

She nodded, because it was the right thing to do. In reality she didn't know when she would ever be OK again.

'I understand,' said Jack. 'Losing your memory . . . it's an awful, debilitating thing. It goes much deeper than forgetting a few facts about your life.'

Amy was quiet.

'We'll go somewhere,' said Jack. 'Just the two of us. Somewhere you can do nothing except lie on a beach in the sunshine. In fact . . .' he smiled, excited by an idea, 'we'll go somewhere really special. Somewhere you've always wanted to go.' He looked at her knowingly and her forehead creased as she wondered if he meant her dream.

'Yes, Tonga,' he said excitedly. 'And it's my treat. I'd like to take you,' he continued, seeing her about to protest. 'I'd like to be the one who gets to go to such a special place with you. If you'll have me?' He smiled, warming to his idea. 'I'm going to call my boss at the hospital now, see when I can next take some annual leave.'

'Now?' she asked, puzzled by the urgency.

'Why not? Why wait? I want you to feel better. I want to look after you. Tonga would be a place where we can forget about everything. Slow down, unwind, you and me. What do you think? Are you able to take more time off work?'

Amy shrugged. 'I'm off indefinitely. Until . . .' she pointed at her head, '. . . you know.'

'It'll come back. Even quicker if we have some relaxing time in the sun.' He put his hands on her shoulders, gazed into her eyes. 'You do trust me? I promise, everything's going to be OK. No more running off, no more doubts, OK?'

Amy exhaled. Nodded.

'What made you change your mind?' Jack asked quietly.

She didn't answer at first. It was hard to explain.

'It doesn't matter, I'm just glad you did,' said Jack. 'Why don't you go and chill out by the fire and I'll come and join you once I've spoken to my boss.'

She let him guide her out of the room.

SIXTY

2 March

Amy lay on the sofa watching the flames, seduced by the way they flickered in such a random pattern. Short eruptions followed by sudden bursts of power; every colour from white through the spectrum of yellows and oranges to an occasional chemical blue. Jenna was the only other person in the room, once again at her laptop. Amy had borrowed Jenna's phone and quietly called the number on the piece of paper that was tucked into her pocket. But the solicitor who was handling her aunt's estate was in a meeting. Her secretary had said she would pass on the message.

Amy got up from the sofa and wandered over to the window. It had started to sleet. The temperature was above freezing for the first time in days. She gazed across the valley to Gabriel's house. There was no sign of the police or the ambulance, just as there had been no sign the last two times she'd got up to look. It seemed to be taking a long time. There again, perhaps the deep snow was hampering their journey.

'They there yet?' asked Jenna, looking up from her laptop.

Amy shook her head. Gabriel was still alone, lying in the snow.

'Roads are blocked,' said Jenna. 'Must be difficult to get up there.'

Amy turned. 'What are you doing?'

'Going through some of my pictures over the last few days.'

'Are you pleased with them?'

Jenna considered. 'There's quite a few that cut it, yes. These mountains . . . they're incredible.'

'Another exhibition?'

Jenna looked at her sharply. 'Perhaps. Although I won't be using Lewis's gallery,' she added quietly.

Amy's heart began to beat faster. 'No?'

'He and I . . . we've spoken. He's moving out.'

Amy swallowed. 'I'm sorry.'

'Not your fault.'

'Are you OK?'

'I will be.' Jenna paused. 'I'm sorry he put you in such a difficult position. Actually . . . it wasn't just you. There was a time, a year ago. It was a one-off he told me. A stupid mistake he'd made when he was drunk. His assistant at the gallery.'

'I'm so sorry,' said Amy.

Jenna nodded, then looked back at her screen and Amy understood that her friend didn't want to talk anymore. She listened to the click on the keyboard as Jenna flicked through her pictures. *Click*, another. *Click, click, click*. Jenna looked at her screen, seemingly deep in concentration and Amy turned her gaze back to the window. The mountains were powerful. Treacherous even. *Click, click.* Her own father had died out there. She found herself wondering what had gone through his mind as he'd fallen when racing his sister down the mountain. She'd never asked herself that before. It made her shudder. *Click, click.* She hoped he hadn't known in that split second as he lost control that he was about to die. Amy pulled her cardigan around herself. She was suddenly aware that something had changed. The clicking had stopped. She turned her head back to Jenna, saw she was staring wide-eyed at her screen.

'What is it?' asked Amy.

'Oh my God,' said Jenna quietly, turning to look at her, trepidation etched across her face.

Amy crossed the room, looked over Jenna's shoulder at her laptop. There was a shot of the valley on the screen. The photo captured the desolate nature of the space, the mountains rising up either side. In the far right of the screen there was a building and with a pang, Amy recognized it.

'Can you see?' asked Jenna, her voice low.

'Yes, it's Gabriel's place,' said Amy.

'Shush,' said Jenna, patting her hand in the air to tell Amy to be quiet. 'Wait.' Jenna zoomed in on her screen and a tiny shape began to emerge. A figure. Larger and larger. A person outside Gabriel's house. But it wasn't Gabriel.

It was Jack.

Amy stared, checking and rechecking in her mind. Even though the expanded picture was pixelated, the identity of the figure was clear. The door opened behind her and she jumped. It was Lisa.

'When did you take this photo?' Amy asked Jenna in a hushed voice. 'It's Jack,' she whispered to Lisa, as her friend came over to them. 'Jenna's got a picture of him outside Gabriel's house.'

'What?' asked Lisa.

Jenna checked the date at the bottom of her screen. 'Sunday.'

The day she'd first gone to see Gabriel. Amy felt goose-bumps rise up on her arms. 'He said he hadn't followed me.'

'I know,' said Jenna.

'That's definitely him . . .' said Lisa, staring at the screen.

Amy felt an overwhelming rush of panic. 'I was right,' she said. 'Jack must have had something to do with Gabriel's death.'

'Let's not get ahead of ourselves,' said Jenna. 'Just because we can see Jack went to Gabriel's house, it doesn't mean he murdered him.'

'But he's been *lying*,' said Amy. 'Insisting that he never went near the place. Why lie if you don't have something to hide?'

'I don't know,' said Jenna.

Amy felt a chill run through her, sharp needles prick down her spine. 'Oh my God . . .' she said breathlessly. 'The food . . .'

'What?' Lisa was looking at her, perplexed.

Amy whirled around. 'The food. Two days ago, Jack said he hadn't followed me, he'd been to Val d'Isère to get food.'

'Yes . . .'

'He didn't get it from the shops.'

'What are you saying?'

'He got it from Gabriel's house. I remember the cheese. I knew it looked familiar,' said Amy fiercely. 'It was the cheese Gabriel got for me. The rest too. He went there and brought the food back as a cover. It must have all come from Gabriel's house.' She looked up at her friends. 'Please believe me.'

Amy turned her face back to the window, everything clicking into place.

'And the reason the police haven't arrived yet is that Jack hasn't called them.'

SIXTY-ONE

2 March

Amy watched her friends' faces, bracing herself for them to tell her she was mad, she was paranoid. She wasn't either, she'd been right all along.

'Well?' she asked, her heart in her mouth.

'I think I owe you an apology,' said Lisa. 'I think Jack's not been completely honest with us.'

'Me too,' said Jenna. 'I'm sorry, Amy.'

The relief was almost a physical shock. Amy felt herself fill with emotion. 'Thank God,' she said, then held out her hands to her friends as tears filled her eyes. 'Thank you . . . you've no idea . . .' A strangled laugh escaped from her lips as they all fell into an embrace. 'I was right,' she said, half to herself. 'I was *right*.' The powerlessness that had gripped her the last few days fell away. She felt as if she could breathe.

'Something's definitely not quite adding up here,' said Lisa.

'He's not my boyfriend,' insisted Amy. 'The lying bastard is not my boyfriend.'

'No, no,' placated Lisa.

'We need to tell Martha,' said Jenna. 'I'll go and find her.' She left the room.

Amy wiped her eyes, took a deep breath. 'Oh my God, he even had me convinced in the end. But not anymore. He's dangerous, Lisa, I know it.' She looked back at the window. 'He's done something,' she said.

Lisa looked worried. 'Do you think?'

'Absolutely. We need to call the police.'

'OK,' said Lisa. 'My phone's in the kitchen.'

'Let's get it. The sooner we speak to them, the—'

Amy stopped dead as the door opened.

'Hey,' said Jack, his face alight as he came over to her. 'I've spoken to my boss. She's fairly flexible on dates, so long as they don't coincide with the Easter holidays.'

Amy stared at him. She felt empowered now. The tables had finally turned. 'We were watching,' she said, 'out the window. The police don't seem to have made it to Gabriel's yet.'

'Perhaps it's the snow,' said Jack. 'I'll call again, see if there's an update.'

No you won't, thought Amy. More lies. She felt a fire burn up inside her and it was an effort to stay quiet.

Jack was looking at her, a shadow of worry on his face. 'How are you feeling?'

Those four small words. They grated, niggled. Amy tried to ignore them but they shifted something in her. Like a wave, her anger grew bigger and bigger until a tsunami of fury rose up threatening to engulf her and then the wave broke.

'I know you were at Gabriel's house the other day,' she

said, ignoring Lisa's look of alarm. She didn't care anymore, she had to say something to him, this man who had played with her mind, her sanity.

'That's not true,' said Jack.

'Amy . . .' said Lisa.

'Oh but it is. I have proof,' said Amy.

He looked at her askance, eyes shot with despair. 'Proof?' He laid a hand gently on her arm. 'Come on, Amy, I thought we'd got past this.'

She shook him off. 'Yes, proof. A photo. You are right outside his lodge.'

A stillness settled over the room.

'You can't,' said Jack quietly. 'I haven't been there.'

Amy turned to Lisa. 'Tell him, Lisa. Tell him what we've seen.'

Lisa held her eyes and then turned to Jack. 'There is no photo,' she said softly. 'Amy is mistaken.'

It was a punch to the gut. 'What?' cried Amy, aghast. 'But you've seen it.'

Lisa shook her head. 'No. That's not true.'

Amy started to panic. 'No, no. Don't do this. You told me. You said you believed me!'

'I'm sorry,' said Lisa, her eyes cast down. 'This paranoia, it's so awful for you.'

'There's a photo,' shouted Amy. 'There's a bloody photo!'

Jack looked from Amy to Lisa.

'There is no photo,' said Lisa. Then she shook her head privately at Jack. Amy clocked it.

'No . . .' she said. 'You don't do this . . .'

346

'I think you should leave,' Lisa said to Jack. 'I think you're upsetting Amy more. Jenna's gone to get Martha,' she added pointedly. 'I think Amy could do with something to drink.'

He looked at Lisa, nodded as he understood, then turned and left the room.

Amy crumpled. 'What the fuck?'

Lisa lifted her hands, patted the air urgently. 'I know it's hard to accept,' she said in the same conciliatory tone, rolling her eyes back towards the door. 'But it will get better. I promise.'

Amy stared at her, slowly realizing.

'I'm sorry,' whispered Lisa. 'I just don't think it's a good idea to tell Jack we're onto him.' She paused. 'I'm worried about what he might do next.'

SIXTY-TWO

19 February

Tiny flakes of snow started to fall as Harry stormed down the road. He saw a bus pass him and stop up ahead. He briefly thought about getting on it but he was too angry. He wanted to walk off his fury. Everyone was ready to trip him up, grind him into the ground. Freddie Canning, Max, Kirsty. It didn't matter what he did, they saw him as someone to step on, too busy serving their own lives to give a thought for him. Someone to clean shit off their shoe, charm customers on a paltry salary while they reaped huge profits, someone to kick for fear he take their friend away. He was a lesser being as far as all of them were concerned.

The force of his rage meant he didn't feel the cold, didn't tire as he strode along the outskirts of Wandsworth and down towards Earlsfield. He was so sick of being trampled into the ground, of being shoved aside. He'd actually tried to make a go of that job but Max was a draconian wanker, giddy on his own power, who wasn't even prepared to give his staff the benefit of the doubt. Harry hadn't pocketed the other thirty pounds and that was the truth. But that was what Max was prepared to believe – wanted to believe because it re-inforced his personal bias. And Harry might have been able to persuade Max of the truth if that cow hadn't waded in. As he turned down a side street, he had a sudden thought – she'd probably interrupted just at that moment to make sure he was really screwed. She'd heard what Max was saying and she wanted to kick a man while he was down. *Bitch!*

He stumbled, almost falling. *Jesus!* What the fuck was that? A small tortoiseshell cat jumped away from him and started sidestepping towards the wall. Harry was incensed. The bloody cat had run right in front of his feet and nearly tripped him up! Everyone was out to get him. Even the fucking cat. He lifted a foot and kicked out in anger. The cat squealed and rose into the air then fell again, landing on the pavement with a small thud.

Harry stopped. He looked over at the cat, lying there in the dark. It wasn't moving. He went over and nudged at it with his toe but it lay there, its lifeless eyes open.

All his anger suddenly left him. He reached out a hand, touched the cat briefly on its head. It was just like him, people kicked him and he kicked the cat. But he knew what it felt like to be lower down the pecking order and so he felt bad. He shouldn't have done it. He picked it up. 'I'm sorry,' he said, pressing his face into the cat's body, his voice muffled by its fur. Then he looked around, saw a wheelie bin inside someone's gate and lifted the lid, but as he did so a movement caught his eye.

Harry swung round to see a woman on the phone, staring at him from across the street. She pointed her phone at him and then a flash of light caught him in the eye. It took a second and then he realized. She'd taken his picture. A photo of him holding a cat that he'd just killed. The woman's face was filled with shock and outrage. Harry put the cat in the bin and then turned to her. She began to back away. 'Hey!' he called. He needed to talk to her, to explain he hadn't meant to do it, but she'd started to run.

SIXTY-THREE

2 March

Amy crept into the hallway, Lisa following. She listened out. She could hear voices coming from the kitchen. Cautiously she opened the door and saw with great relief it was her mother and Jenna.

'Amy . . .' said Martha. 'Jenna's been telling me . . . About the photo . . . I don't understand . . .' She looked at her, unsure. 'I've made some coffee,' she said. 'One for you too.' She held out an aromatic cup, a swirl of creamy, frothy milk on the top.

Amy halted. She looked down at the drink. 'No, thank you.'

Martha was taken aback. 'But I made it specially.'

Amy searched her mother's eyes, holding her gaze until Martha became uncomfortable.

'I *know*, Mum.'

'Know what?' asked Martha but her voice tremored.

Amy looked across at Jenna. 'Do you know where Jack is?'

'I think I heard him go up to his room.'

'Are you *sure* about all this?' asked Martha.

Amy made a sound of impatience.

'It's true, Martha,' cut in Lisa. 'It does seem as if we've underestimated him.'

Amy saw her mother visibly deflate.

'But he knew everything about you,' said Martha, her voice sounding hollow. 'He knew all the stuff you said you'd made up.'

'Of course he did, Mum. I was stupid enough to put it out there, on social media. There is no such thing as true privacy anymore.'

Martha spoke quietly. 'If Jack *is* an imposter, he's certainly got some explaining to do at the very least, and if he *did* have something to do with poor Gabriel, then where does that leave us?' Martha glanced at the door as if she was expecting Jack to walk in at any moment. 'I feel like a mouse about to get chased down by a very hungry cat.'

Amy's head shot up. 'What did you say, Mum?'

'I don't feel entirely comfortable being here now . . .' Martha started, but Amy had turned away. She could remember more of the night back in London. The night she was supposed to have met Jenna. She'd caught her bus and it was nearing her stop. She pressed the bell and when it pulled up alongside the pavement, she waited for the doors to open then jumped out. It had started to snow. She headed off the main road, cutting down a small alley. Amy still felt very guilty that she'd missed Jenna at the bar. She tried to call her again, holding the phone up to her ear, her fingers smarting in the biting cold. It rang and rang until Jenna's answerphone kicked in. Amy grimaced; she sensed Jenna was avoiding her. As she left the alley and turned into a quiet residential street, she looked at her phone, contemplated sending a text.

Something made her look up. A strange sound, a high-pitched yowl. She saw a man in the shadows on the other side of the street. He was standing there. Peering at something on the ground. Amy stopped, unsure. Then she watched as he bent down and picked up whatever had been on the pavement. What was it? He held it in his hands then he looked around, his eyes settling on a wheelie bin. She looked again, not quite understanding. And then it came to her. It was a cat. He was holding a cat. And from its total stillness and the way the man kept glancing around nervously, Amy thought it must be dead, and that the man was responsible for its death. She took her phone and pointed it in the direction of the man. One tap and a bright flash broke the veil of darkness.

Shit. He was looking at her.

She moved on down the pavement, away from him, towards her own road. He was calling out, following her. She started to run. He came after her. Heart pounding, Amy picked up her pace. *Please*, she thought, *let there be someone around*. But the weather was so cold it had kept everyone indoors. The pavement felt slippery under her feet and Amy wanted to slow down but she knew if she did the man would catch her. She heard his footsteps getting louder. Only a few more seconds and she'd be able to turn into her road.

Maybe there would be someone there, someone she could cry out to and then this man would run off.

She heard him get closer, could hear his breath loud. She turned for a tiny second to see where he was and in that moment she saw his face properly.

Back at the lodge, Amy gasped and pitched forward. Her heart was trying to beat its way out of her chest.

'What is it? What's wrong?' asked Martha, startled.

It was just like her dream, the one where she was being chased down a dark, icy street. Only it wasn't Jenna coming after her, it was a man. A man who very much didn't want her to have witnessed what he'd done.

'I know,' stammered Amy. 'I know who it is.'

'Who?' asked Jenna nervously.

Amy looked at them, her eyes alight with fear. Yes, he looked a little different now, shorter hair, smarter clothes but there was no doubt.

'Jack,' she said. 'I know who Jack is.'

SIXTY-FOUR

2 March

They were all looking at her, stunned. They had listened, taken in what she'd said.

'But how did some random guy with a dead cat get from an Earlsfield street to . . . here?' asked Jenna.

Amy tried hard to think. 'I don't know . . .'

'Tell us,' said Lisa, taking Amy's hands in hers. 'What happened after you saw him?'

Amy closed her eyes, grateful for the chair that she'd sunk into. Her legs felt as if they were unable to hold her up. She shook her head. 'I don't know. I mean, I remember running and then a terrifying sense of falling and not being able to stop myself. I saw the ground coming up at me and then . . . that's it. It must have been when I hit my head. The next thing I remember is waking up in hospital.'

'So you were lying on the pavement, in the dark, with no one else around except Jack . . .' said Lisa.

Amy felt sick.

'Oh my God,' said Martha.

'Is everything OK?' said a voice from the kitchen door.

Martha yelped in fright.

Amy froze. Jack was standing just inside the room. How long had he been there?

Lisa recovered first. 'Fine,' she said. 'We're getting Amy a coffee.' She slowly pushed the untouched cup of coffee that Martha had made earlier towards Amy.

Amy stared at it, at the tempting cream swirled across the top.

Jack slowly walked into the room and Amy tensed. He was watching her. 'You should drink it,' he said, indicating the coffee.

She put her hand on the cup. Tried to relax her facial muscles but they felt locked in an expression that would betray her. She looked at her mother, saw that she too was struck mute with fright. Jack was watching all of them. In a matter of seconds he'd know. He'd know that they were onto him.

She went to pick up the cup.

'Wait,' said Martha. 'I think there's some biscuits.'

Amy started. 'Pardon?'

'Biscuits. There are some palmier biscuits in the cupboard,' repeated Martha.

'I'll have one too,' said Lisa.

'And me,' added Jenna.

Martha walked over to the kitchen cupboard where they'd stored the food packets. She opened it and there was a half-eaten packet of biscuits on the shelf.

Martha brought them back to the counter. Pulled the packet open.

'Thanks, Mum,' said Amy, taking one. Jenna and Lisa followed suit.

Martha looked up at Jack, hesitated. 'How about you, Jack?'

'Don't mind if I do,' he said, walking forward to take one.

Don't flinch, don't flinch, Amy said silently. She watched him as he came closer, took in his features, recognizing them with absolute certainty. This was the man who had chased her only a few days ago.

She wanted him to leave the room. She wanted him out so she could think clearly, decide with the others what to do.

He took a bite of the buttery palmier biscuit, holding his hand under his chin to catch the pastry crumbs. He laughed softly. 'There's no polite way to eat these,' he said, smiling at her.

She gave a minuscule nod. *Act like nothing's changed*, she urged herself. *Remember how you've been insisting he's an imposter.* 'I suppose you're going to tell me how they're my favourites,' she said.

He looked at her. 'No, I wasn't,' he said. 'That's shortbread.'

Amy recoiled. It was true. Shortbread *was* her favourite.

'Sorry, did I interrupt something?' asked Jack, looking around at them.

'Not at all,' said Lisa.

He didn't look convinced and Amy felt he was about to protest when Jenna spoke.

'Actually,' she said, 'I was just telling the girls . . . Lewis and I have split up.'

'I'm so sorry,' said Jack, taken aback.

Amy noticed that it was news to her mother and Lisa too, but to her relief they flattened their responses.

'I'll leave you to it,' continued Jack, awkwardly.

They all watched as he left the room.

SIXTY-FIVE

2 March

Jack stopped outside the kitchen door. He stood still for a moment, counted in his head to ten. There was nothing but silence coming from inside the room. None of them were speaking.

They knew, he thought.

And if not every single thing, they knew enough. *Shit*. He briefly wondered how but it didn't really matter. Whether Amy had remembered the night when she'd taken his photo or she had just managed to finally convince them that Jack Stewart didn't exist, he knew he had very little time left. He couldn't keep the game going much longer. He'd been lucky up until now. Been lucky ever since Amy had fallen on the ice over a week ago and knocked herself out. He'd chased after her because the alternative, letting her get away, was inconceivable. If she put that photo out there, if it got to the authorities then it would have been criminal damage at the very least and it would've impacted on his suspended sentence. He would have been locked up.

When he'd seen her fall he'd stalled, then cautiously

MICHELLE FRANCES

approached her. As he leaned over her he'd seen that she was out cold. He'd heard far-off voices – people were coming. Her bag and phone had been flung into the road when she'd slipped. Quickly, before anyone had seen, he'd grabbed both and run off.

360

SIXTY-SIX

19 February

Harry sat in the café in Garrett Lane and nursed his coffee, warming his cold hands. The woman's bag was tucked underneath his jacket. He'd extracted a few items: a diary, a purse with a driving licence. There was also a letter from a solicitor in Switzerland, telling the woman – whose name was Amy Kennedy – that she was a beneficiary of a deceased Esme Kennedy's estate. When he'd read the amount she was due to receive his heart had skipped a beat.

Harry looked up as the scream of an ambulance grew louder and then blue flashing lights flew past the window. He knew the woman – Amy – would be inside, would be on her way to St George's hospital less than a mile away. She was likely to stay there overnight at least. Concussion like that, the doctors were bound to want to check it out.

He looked back at the letter from the solicitor. At the top was Amy Kennedy's address. It was only a few streets away. Luckily he'd also found her house keys in her bag.

SIXTY-SEVEN

2 March

Harry paced up and down his bedroom. He was on a ticking clock. What were Amy and the others going to do now they had figured out at least part of the truth? He had very little time left.

A phone buzzed in his pocket and he felt a jolt of excitement. It had been hard getting access to Amy's room all the time, stealing her phone and hoping she wouldn't notice. He looked at the screen. Finally, the message he'd been waiting for. A request from the solicitor handling Amy's inheritance for her bank details, which they needed in order to deposit the funds. He carefully composed a reply. Pressed send. Not long now and then he could get the hell out of this place, always looking over his shoulder, wondering if he was going to be caught. It was the same as when he'd gone into Amy's flat in London.

SIXTY-EIGHT

19 February

Harry turned into the street that was written on Amy Kennedy's letter. Cars were parked up both sides and the trees were as bare as the lampposts they alternated with along the length of the pavement. After a short walk, Harry found number twenty-two, Amy's place. It was on the corner, a ground-floor maisonette with the front door of the flat above sharing the same storm porch. He looked up at the first-floor property, saw the lights were on. He'd have to be quiet. Checking over his shoulder, Harry then slowly opened the black metal gate, listening out for creaks. It was silent. He headed up the front path. He was hidden from the road now by the large hedge that ran around the edge of the property but he didn't dawdle. He untucked Amy's bag from under his jacket and pulled out her keys, put them in the lock and opened the front door. Held his breath. There was no alarm. Quietly he slipped inside and closed the door behind him.

The first thing he noticed was a strong smell of flowers – roses he saw, on the hall table, illuminated by the street lights. A card lay next to the vase: *To the most beautiful woman in the world. I know you're weirdly cynical about Valentine's but I couldn't resist. You're getting flowers whether you like it or not. Because I love you. Jack X*

Harry placed the card back down and went into the living room. He couldn't yet risk turning on his phone torch, not with the windows bare to the outside, so he swiftly closed the curtains, making a mental note to open them again before he left.

Then he turned on the torch, swung it around the room. It was brightly decorated in blue and white. Yellow cushions lay neatly placed on a deep turquoise sofa. Above the fireplace was a photo of a woman he knew to be Amy from her driving licence, flanked by an older man and woman – her parents, he assumed.

In the corner of the room was a desk on which lay a laptop. He sat down and put Amy's bag in front of him. Then he took out her phone. He needed to get rid of the photo she'd taken. He shone the torch around the desk, looking for something that might help. There was a lamp and a few pens in an upright storage tube in the shape of a palm tree. A few papers were stacked up, with a travel book for the South Pacific island of Tonga on the top with a number of pages folded down. He opened the drawer underneath the desk. Some more stationery. There was also a notebook and another mobile phone, a new one. They were bound together with an elastic band.

Harry pulled out the notebook and opened it up. It was a sort of diary. Jack was mentioned a lot, the guy who'd sent the flowers, along with details of where he and Amy had gone the last few months. Harry flicked through – it was mostly practical stuff, names of restaurants scribbled down, dates, what they'd ordered. Hardly the stuff of romantic dreams. She'd even written down his full name – Dr Jack Stewart – and presumably the place where he worked: St Thomas' Hospital. He was thirty-two years old according to the diary. Harry found it slightly creepy how this Amy woman had marked down a record of her boyfriend's personal details. It was almost as if she were stalking him. He put the diary back and kept on searching, looking over to the bookcase beside him. There was another photo of the same man that was in the picture above the fireplace. This one unframed. It was an arresting picture. The photographer seemed to have caught a real sense of the man's personality. There was a magnetism about him, a sense of a life enjoyed. Harry turned it over. There was a name and some dates on the back:

Peter: 26.07.60 – 09.01.11

Harry typed the first six digits into Amy's phone but the screen message came up 'Incorrect PIN'. He frowned. It wouldn't be the other date, far too morbid, surely, but he tried, just for the hell of it and to his delight it opened. He went into the phone's gallery, quickly found the photo and deleted it. He'd better check she hadn't sent it to anyone. He didn't think so, she hadn't really had time but he clicked on her last few messages, just in case. Nothing to a Lisa or Jenna or Jack. So the photographic evidence was now gone, but there was still the danger she'd report it to the police. She'd seen his face, knew what he'd been wearing.

Harry sat back in the chair, rested the back of his head in his interlinked hands. Thought hard about the problem. Amy was in hospital. She had seen his face. She would probably tell the authorities – after all, if she was the kind of woman who took a picture of a stranger with a dead cat, then that wasn't for her photo album, it was for the police. There was the risk that Amy had been someone who had come into the wine bar. Maybe she was one of the dozens of customers that he'd served. Maybe she knew who he was and as soon as she told the cops they would be able to find him.

Harry picked up Amy's phone again and flicked across the screen. Her Facebook page was up and he scrolled through, saw a lot of talk about Jack and the dates they had been on. Seemed he was a new boyfriend after a long period of being single. A couple of Amy's friends cropped up more than others: Lisa and Jenna – same as the two names on her texts. Both had responded to pictures Amy had uploaded of her and Jack, Lisa in particular gushing about how amazing he was. They were falling over themselves. Except the pictures weren't actually Amy and Jack, they were photos of where they were eating out and what they were drinking. There were a couple of snaps of him but without his face. Harry read on. Lisa was excited to be going to Val d'Isère with them all on 24 February to celebrate Amy's birthday. Harry looked up the date – next Wednesday. She was 'gutted' Jack couldn't make it though. Seemed he was busy saving lives. Lucky bastard had a girlfriend who didn't treat him like dirt – dump him because his job wasn't good enough. Even luckier that his girlfriend was about to inherit a huge amount of money. It wasn't like either of them were short of a bob or two as it was. This flat he was in was worth at least half a million. Jack lived in an even pricier part of London – Battersea. It was always the same, the rich got even richer while the poor were kicked off the bottom rung of the ladder, the second they managed to hang on desperately by their fingertips. Harry was reminded of the fact that now he had no job, he had no way of paying his rent. He was going to get another visit from Nick, his landlord's debt collector. How was he going to get out of a serious beating?

Harry considered looking around the flat, seeing what would be worth anything – maybe there was some jewellery in the bedroom. He could also take both Amy's mobiles. He opened the drawer and picked out the one bound by the elastic band. Out of curiosity more than anything, he typed in the same password as the other phone. It worked. Harry sat up, shaking his head at how lax people were. He went into the email inbox. At first he couldn't quite understand – they were all from Amy. Why would Amy be emailing herself? He opened one up and saw it was addressed to Jack. He read a few, smirked a little at some of the content. Harry frowned. So was this Jack's phone? Why would Amy have her boyfriend's phone in her flat? He looked at the messages again – every single one was from Amy. It was weird how there weren't any messages from anyone else. He looked in the sent box. Again, all the messages went to one person – this time back to Amy. They were a little odd;

overblown exclamations of how amazing she was. The best lover, the wittiest woman Jack had ever met. They almost seemed unreal, had a satirical tone to them. The texts were the same – only one recipient – Amy. Most of the messages appeared to be an apology – Jack bailing last minute on a dinner with Amy and her mother or one of her friends. Harry was intrigued. He recognized deception when he saw it – something about this spoke to his own instincts.

Harry decided to take a look around the flat. He went into the bedroom – there was only one set of pillows on the bed. He found the jewellery he suspected would be there. As he opened each of the boxes, one piece in particular looked pretty valuable: a diamond necklace. But for now, he left it. He carefully rummaged through the drawers but only found Amy's underwear – there was no male clothing there at all, nor in the wardrobe. There was only one toothbrush in the bathroom. He smirked. What had Amy done, killed her boyfriend and hidden his body in the freezer? He went back to the living room, picked up the phone again and turned it over in his hand, thinking.

Getting an idea, he opened up the phone and went into the location info. To his surprise, he saw that the device had stayed in the flat for the majority of the last three months. There were no records of the phone having been at St Thomas' hospital, which made no sense at all. The only time it had been out of the flat was a couple of visits to restaurants, one of which he noticed was Bentley's in Mayfair. It rang a bell. Harry quickly checked back with the texts. Jack had sent an apology to Amy on the evening of the fifteenth January saying he couldn't make dinner with her mother. He had mentioned Bentley's crab cakes. But the phone's location info placed it at that exact restaurant on exactly that date. *So if Jack wasn't at the restaurant, why was his phone there? Who had taken it there?* And then it came to him – it could only be Amy.

An idea was starting to dawn. Harry picked up his own phone and called St Thomas' hospital. After a quick conversation he confirmed what he'd suspected – there was no Dr Jack Stewart working there. Harry sat back. It seemed that Amy Kennedy had fabricated Jack Stewart for reasons only known to herself.

Harry went back downstairs, had a look around the kitchen. He wouldn't take much, nothing that would be noticed but he could do with a snack as he hadn't eaten since lunchtime. He found some biscuits – shortbread. Three whole packets of it. He closed the cupboard and turned to the fridge. Thinking made him hungry. And he had been doing a lot of thinking. If there was no Dr Jack Stewart then there was no happy boyfriend sharing a healthy inheritance after all. Somehow Harry felt sorry for him – even though he didn't exist. It seemed like such bad luck, like losing a golden ticket. More pressing was the ongoing problem that Amy would tell the police who he was and they would be able to trace him through the wine bar. Max would no doubt enjoy sticking the knife in even more – accuse him of stealing money. Harry could see a long spell behind bars.

Somehow he had to stop Amy from saying anything.

He made himself a coffee, washed down a couple of mini Scotch eggs. Then he picked up his phone.

He looked up the number for St George's hospital. Asked about the welfare of Amy Kennedy. When the nurse enquired of him who he was, he already had his answer ready – he was Jack Stewart, Amy's boyfriend. Her next of kin.

He held his breath as he waited to be told to take a hike, but the nurse softened and said that Amy was 'comfortable'. She'd regained consciousness only a short while ago and they were keeping her in for observation.

Harry said he understood – he was a doctor after all. He asked if he could come and visit. The nurse explained visiting hours and then said something that sent Harry into a spin.

'She may be confused when you come in.'

'Confused?'

'Yes. Just to warn you. She's suffering from amnesia.'

Harry's mind was racing. 'Do you mean she's lost her memory?'

'I'm afraid so,' said the nurse. 'She's currently struggling with the last few months.'

Harry was silent.

'Hello?' said the nurse. 'Are you still there?'

'Sorry . . . yes, still here. It's a bit of a shock, that's all.' Harry thanked the nurse and hung up.

It was a God-given opportunity that Harry knew would never come his way again for the rest of his life.

SIXTY-NINE

19 February

Harry got to work. He opened up Amy's phone, scrolled through her emails. Then he found it. A message from the same solicitor firm as that on the letter. This message was sent only a week ago and confirmed that probate had been granted and that the transfer date for the funds was set for Tuesday, 2 March. They would be back in touch on the morning of the second to go through the process in more detail.

Harry noted the date. It was only ten days away. Then he could be free forever. His idea was bold, audacious, but like being told the lottery numbers in advance. He knew he could pull it off. He deleted the email from the solicitor and any other correspondence he could find from them. Then he replaced Amy's phone in her bag and pocketed the one belonging to 'Jack'. He took photos of the flat on his own phone for reference. He went back up to Amy's bedroom and noted the name of the jeweller's where the diamond necklace had come from. He was so preoccupied with his tasks he completely forgot to finish his coffee. In fact when he left the flat later that evening the half-drunk mug was still sitting on the kitchen counter.

SEVENTY

2 March

Harry stood out on the balcony, letting the snow blow into his face. The cold was not helping to clear his mind. He needed a confirmation email from the solicitor that the money had been sent to the bank account. *His* bank account, as this was the information that he'd sent over. He found it hard to focus on anything else – freedom was in touching distance and yet there were four women in this lodge who had the power to undo everything he'd worked for.

Amy's phone buzzed again. Harry's heart leapt. He opened the email, read it, waiting for the euphoria as he learned he was three million euros richer.

Shit! The bitch solicitor thanked Amy very much for sending over the bank details but, as per protocol, she needed to call her to verify them.

As much as Harry had successfully duped a whole raft of people so far, sounding like a female in her thirties was not something he could achieve.

How the hell was he going to get around this?

Harry kicked out at the balcony. The frustration was

almost unbearable. So bloody close. *Don't lose it now*, he told himself. There had to be a way around it, there always was. If the solicitor wanted to talk to Amy, then somehow Harry had to find a way. Amy had to tell the solicitor that Harry's bank details were her own. He emailed the solicitor back suggesting that they speak in an hour.

Then Harry made his way downstairs.

SEVENTY-ONE

2 March

He headed back to the kitchen where he'd left the four women ten minutes before and opened the door.

The room was empty.

It was a surprise. Harry took a moment to register the silence, the vacant seats. He thought, his nerve endings pulsating. Then he went to the kitchen drawer, extracted a small folding knife. He put it in his pocket then turned back to face the door.

If they weren't in the kitchen, then where were they?

Harry moved to the living room but that was empty too. So he tried upstairs, becoming more urgent in his movements as he searched, not bothering to knock on bedroom doors but bursting in.

They were nowhere to be seen.

Harry's mood darkened. He didn't have time for this. Where were they? If he'd had any doubt that they were suspicious of him, that had now vanished.

He went back down to the hallway and flung open the coat cupboard with both hands.

Only his jacket and boots remained.

He opened the front door and immediately saw the flurry of rushed footprints. The road was still impassable and so they would have to stay on foot.

And he knew exactly where they'd gone.

SEVENTY-TWO

2 March

'Quick, quick,' said Amy, as she turned to look back at the others. They were hurrying through the woods that opened out near Gabriel's house. It was the only place she could think of where they could find relative safety – at least until help arrived. Jenna had called the police but there was no certainty of how long it would be before they could get to them. None of them had wanted to stay in the lodge.

Amy saw her mother stumble and grabbed her arm so she didn't fall. There hadn't been time to gather skis or snowshoes, so they'd slunk out of the lodge in a silent rush, desperate not to alert Jack to their departure. A few more steps and they burst into the open, leaving the lofty pines behind. Ahead was Gabriel's house.

Amy stopped for a second. She knew what lay ahead but there was no time for nerves. They had to get safely into the house before Jack noticed they were missing and came after them. She was certain he would. She forced herself to continue, up to the front path, the sleet blowing into her face. As she walked, she turned to the others.

'Don't look,' she said, her voice wavering. 'Just follow me.'

She stepped past Gabriel's body and despite her advice found herself unable to turn away. His face was uncovered as she'd left it that morning and then suddenly she couldn't bear the stillness of it, the shocking finality of a life lost and she quickened her pace, turning the handle of the front door and then stumbled into the house. She heard her mother cry out behind her, then the others followed her in, faces sombre at what they'd seen.

Amy locked the door firmly behind them. 'The back door,' she said urgently and hurried through to the kitchen where she made sure that was locked too. Only then did she feel a slither of relief.

'He doesn't have keys, does he?' asked Martha nervously.

'I don't see how,' said Amy, but Martha's comment had unnerved them all so they pulled a heavy oak hall table across the front door, wedged a chair under the handle at the back. They decided to wait it out in the living room; it had windows facing towards Esme's lodge in the far distance. It looked hazy through the sleet.

'He's going to know we've come here,' said Lisa. 'It's the only place even remotely accessible.'

Amy nodded; what she said was true. 'The police know we're here though,' she said. 'And they can't be that far off.'

'Did they give a rough time?' asked Martha, looking anxiously out of the window.

'Stay back, Mum,' said Amy. 'Just in case.'

'In case of what?'

Amy didn't know. She felt out of her depth. She didn't truly know why they were running from him, or maybe her mind refused to go into the dark places she'd have to explore in order to understand what he wanted of them and what he'd do to get it.

'The police gave no time,' Jenna said to Martha. 'They just said they would be with us as soon as they could.' She paused. 'The weather won't help.'

'So you think they're going to leave us stranded?' asked Martha, panicked.

A silence cast over the room.

Lisa clapped her hands. 'Right, we need to do something to take our minds off our nerves.'

'Like what?' asked Jenna.

'A game?' voiced Martha, seeing a pile of worn boxes next to the fireplace.

'Mum, you'll forgive me if I don't join you in a round of Trivial Pursuit,' said Amy sharply.

'OK! I was only trying to . . . Oh, I don't know. What do you do in these situations?' Martha's eyes were drawn fearfully to the window again.

Lisa moved over to where Amy was standing, her body angled away from the window, hidden by the curtains as she glanced out.

'I'm sorry,' said Lisa. 'If only I'd listened to you more, maybe we wouldn't be in this situation.'

Amy gave a tight smile. 'That's OK.'

'It's put me off posting anything on social media ever again.'

'I still don't understand how he got access to everything,' said Martha. 'Jack's phone, for example. I know you think he got into your flat, but how? Do you leave a spare key anywhere?'

'No,' said Amy. 'I mean, I have an extra inside the flat in case I lose the one in my bag . . .' She trailed off, realizing. 'My bag was handed into the hospital. I dropped it when I fell. I thought it was someone decent, the person who'd called an ambulance but . . .'

'It was Jack,' said Jenna. 'After you'd fallen. He must have taken it, looked inside.'

'My driving licence is in there,' said Amy, 'my address.' Her skin crawled, knowing Jack had had full opportunity to nose around her home, the privacy of her life.

'I need a bloody drink,' said Martha, sinking into a chair, her face drawn.

'Shall I make some coffee?' Lisa asked Amy quietly. 'If you think that would be OK,' she added quickly. But no one wanted any.

'We're sitting ducks,' said Martha, despairing.

'He can't get in,' reminded Amy.

'It's a bloody waiting game, seeing who's going to get to us first, the police or a murdering madman.'

'Mum, stop it.'

'It is though, isn't it?'

'Any sign?' Lisa asked Amy.

Amy peered out of the window again. The sleet had turned to rain and was coming down thick and fast and she could barely see across the valley. She stared hard, trying to make out the lodge, could only see a few lights in the gloom. There was no one coming across the snow, no sign of any life at all. It was eerie how it was so quiet. Surely Jack would have noticed they'd gone by now. He would have worked out they would call the police and he would know they'd make their way to Gabriel's. So why wasn't he coming after them? And what about the police? She listened out for the blades of an approaching helicopter but it was silent.

'Nothing,' she said to Lisa.

And then there was a terrible sound of glass smashing from elsewhere in the house. She was aware of Martha screaming and then Jack was in the room. He grabbed hold of Martha and pulled her from the chair, holding a knife to her neck.

SEVENTY-THREE

2 March

'I'm not going to hurt her,' said Harry, 'because you are all going to stay calm and not do anything stupid.'

He saw them all staring, stunned, fear in their eyes. Martha was as still as a statue under his grip. He kept the blade only lightly on her neck, not entirely comfortable with his modus operandi but he'd come up with no alternative. He really didn't want to use the knife. It would be messy and unnecessarily traumatic – for him as well as them. Amy was watching him, her eyes flicking to her mother. He saw her brain slowly catch up and then a minuscule flicker in her eyes alerted him to something at the side of the room: Jenna putting her hands on the poker by the fireplace.

'Don't,' said Harry warningly and Martha whimpered as he tightened his grip on her.

Jenna let the poker drop. It clattered noisily on the stone hearth.

'Any more heroics,' said Harry, 'and you'll be accountable for what happens.' None of them moved. 'Put your phones on the table,' he said, nodding towards the coffee table in the middle of the room. Still stunned, no one complied. 'Now,' he barked.

Lisa and Jenna obediently set their phones down.

'I don't have mine,' said Amy, 'as you well know.'

Harry ignored that. 'Lisa, I want you to tie up Amy and Jenna.'

'What?' asked Lisa, dumbfounded.

'Tie them up,' repeated Harry. 'And I'll be checking the knots, so don't try anything clever.' He removed his arm from around Martha and grabbed something from his pocket and threw it to the floor, all the while holding the knife to her neck.

Lisa picked up the ball of twine.

'Hurry up,' said Harry.

He watched as Lisa tied first Jenna's hands behind her back then Amy's. He then told her to tie up Martha before binding Lisa's hands himself. He picked up their phones, collecting Martha's too. 'I suppose you've called the police?' he asked.

No one spoke.

'I can easily check,' he said, indicating the phones.

'We have,' said Jenna.

'But the snow is delaying their progress.'

Their silence confirmed it.

'Right,' said Harry. 'We wait.' He saw Amy frown, not understanding why he would want to hang around.

'Who are you?' she asked. 'I recognize you. You tried to stop me after I took your photograph.'

So she had remembered. It was a shame her memory had

started to return so rapidly. It was a question he hadn't asked of the nurses; when it would come back.

'Harry,' he said. 'You can call me Harry.'

'Did you go into my flat?' asked Amy.

He looked at her. She'd worked it out. Must have remembered lots of fragments of that night.

'And the hospital,' he said. 'I wasn't lying when I told you that. Only I didn't see you, that part was true as well.'

It was the day after Amy's accident that Harry had walked into the main entrance of St George's hospital, the day after the nurse had told him Amy had amnesia. He'd headed straight for the lifts then gone up to the third floor in the east wing, following the signs to Amy's ward. He passed a number of other wards on his way and, coming upon an unmanned desk – the nurse was several metres away talking to another member of staff – he quietly slipped Amy's bag on the desktop and then continued onwards, without breaking step. He checked his watch. Visiting time had finished fifteen minutes ago. Just as he'd planned.

When he got to Amy's ward he approached the nurse on the desk. She looked up at him as he came closer, and he saw her pull her shoulders back, bracing herself for his request and preparing to deliver her refusal.

He smiled, clocking her name badge: Nurse Morgan. 'I know I'm late, but I've come to see Amy Kennedy.'

'Visiting hours are over,' said Nurse Morgan firmly.

Harry deflated. 'I know.' He hesitated a moment as if weighing up his options, then sighed. 'Don't worry, I'm not going to try and muscle my way in.' He saw her raise an eyebrow as if to say, *just you try*. 'I was on a night shift last night – I'm a doctor. Only now managed to get away. How is she?'

'And you are?'

'Her boyfriend. Jack Stewart.'

'The consultant is on his rounds now. You can come back later.'

He nodded, even though he had no intention of doing so. 'I will. Any sign of the amnesia going?'

'That's a question for the consultant.'

Harry looked downcast. 'OK. I'll come back later.' But Nurse Morgan was already moving away; overworked, she had plenty to do. Harry watched, saw another nurse approach Nurse Morgan.

'Late visitor?' he overheard the second nurse say.

'Yes, some blue-eyed boy thinks he can flutter his eyelashes and I'll capitulate.'

The other nurse laughed. 'Clearly doesn't know you.' Harry saw her glance over her shoulder and hope flared as he caught her expression: one of sympathy.

He hung around in the corridor a few minutes, pretending to get some water until he saw the second nurse appear on her own. Then he made a beeline.

'I'm really sorry to bother you . . .'

She stopped. 'Oh, it's you. I can't go against the visiting rules you know . . .'

'No, no, I understand. But I have a question . . . if you could possibly answer. I know Amy's lost her memory but . . . well, I proposed.' He saw the nurse's eyes light up in delight.

'Six months ago.' He paused, his question coming on bated breath. 'Will she remember?'

The nurse smiled. 'Let's just say,' she said quietly, 'you're going to have to get on bended knee again.'

'So she can't remember anything about the last six months? Nothing at all?'

'Afraid not. Nothing since last August.' Then she walked off.

A flare went off in Harry's brain, light cascading around his body. He kept a lid on his euphoria then turned away and allowed a huge grin to light up his face. God, he loved it when a plan clicked into place. It was so incredibly fulfilling, almost nurturing.

He was not going to be around when Nick discovered he was late with the rent again. He was going to take a trip to France. He could ski; the chalet job all those years ago that had cost him the end of his finger was finally going to pay dividends. He'd been in Amy's flat. He knew a little about her. He knew where she worked, who her friends were and what they looked like. He knew about her relationship with Jack, what he did for a living and what he wore. He knew where Amy and Jack had gone out, the texts Jack had sent. He rested a hand lightly on his pocket, where he felt the comforting bulk of 'Jack's' phone and the notebook that he'd found in Amy's desk.

Most important of all, he knew when Amy was supposed to have started dating her fictitious Jack – and it was less than six months ago. She wouldn't remember a thing.

SEVENTY-FOUR

21 February

Harry hung around the end of the street, his head down, keeping an eye on the front of Max's wine bar, the shutters still down from the previous night. It shouldn't be long now. It was a grey, overcast morning, the low cloud holding the freezing fog close to the ground. The shops weren't yet open and the icy pavements were empty. Then, in the distance he saw a man approach. Harry strode right up to Alex before his ex-colleague had a chance to even clock him.

'All right, Alex?' said Harry affably.

Alex started, then quickly recovered. 'Harry. Yeah. What are you doing here?'

'Came to see you.'

Alex nervously indicated the wine bar in the distance. 'I can't chat. Gotta get to work.'

'Must be nice having a job.'

Alex paused, seemed to weigh something up in his mind. 'Not my fault you got fired for stealing from the takings.'

Harry saw red. He pushed Alex up against the wall,

holding him close. As the bigger of the two men, he had the upper hand. He spoke softly, his breath coming in plumes. 'Do not dick around with me, you fucking arsehole. We both know it was you and I took the flak. You owe me. Now I am going to let go and we are going to walk calmly to the cashpoint on the high street and you are going to withdraw the maximum amount allowed. Once it's in my pocket, this will all be over and forgotten. Do you understand?'

'What if I don't?' said Alex sullenly.

Harry shoved him again and heard Alex grunt. 'Then Max will be getting an anonymous email from a customer who's seen you with your hands in the till.'

Harry felt Alex go limp in defeat.

Harry sat in the chair and watched the hairdresser in the mirror in front of him. She was holding up his long, dark curls wistfully.

'Are you sure?' she asked.

He smiled. The picture of 'Jack' on Facebook had been from the shoulders down and there was definitely no long hair. It had to come off.

'It's time for a change,' he said. 'A new me.'

At his feet were shopping bags. He'd thought about what Jack might wear and had bought a couple of casual shirts, some navy chinos, a soft woollen jumper that wouldn't look out of place on an off-duty doctor sitting in front of an open fire. And of course, some new socks – yellow ones. In the smallest of the bags was the most expensive item he'd bought that day. A pair of diamond drop earrings from Ruth Wood jewellers.

He was almost ready. He'd been online and found someone willing to supply him with a fake driving licence – it had been laughably easy. All he had to do was turn up at a multi-storey car park in South London in two days' time with some of the notes that were currently bulking out his wallet. He'd also booked his flight to Geneva. He still had a few days before he left – time that would be spent researching as much medical information as he could, at least enough to be able to pass as a consultant paediatrician in conversation. He would also be going over and over his story. Who he was. Who *they* were – he and Amy. He would be pitch-perfect by the time he arrived at the chalet in Val d'Isère, a 'surprise visit' that he'd managed to wangle with time off work last minute.

'I know women who would kill for this hair,' said the hairdresser. 'You have a girlfriend?'

Harry nodded.

'What does she think?'

'She likes it,' said Harry. 'In fact, you could almost say it was her idea.'

SEVENTY-FIVE

2 March

Harry looked at Amy. 'You can't blame me for becoming "Jack". You left the door wide open.'

'I didn't leave my flat door wide open,' said Amy. 'No one invited you to look through my things, steal my phone.'

'You mean Jack's phone,' said Harry.

Amy scowled. 'Why are we waiting here? What's going to happen?'

He saw the barely suppressed fear on their faces. There was nothing worse than the unknown to rattle a person. He knew it himself when he couldn't pay the rent and he waited in silence, wondering if Nick was going to come knocking, demanding the overdue rent.

'Are you going to hurt us?' asked Martha, her voice small.

He looked at her. It suited him that they were all contained for the moment. He was about to reassure her, not too much, but tell her she better not cause any trouble when—

'Why did you kill Gabriel?' asked Amy. 'He never did anything to you.'

Harry felt a twist of discomfort in his gut. His visit to Gabriel had not played out how he'd intended.

'Actually, you're wrong. He attacked me.'

'I don't believe you.'

'It's true.'

'Because you were in his house? You were threatening him?'

Harry grimaced. It hadn't been quite like that. He'd seen Amy slink out of the lodge that Sunday morning and knew she was feeling isolated. No one was taking her ranting seriously, they all thought her head injury was causing a lack of judgement, a paranoia that was off the scale. His heart had started thumping when he'd seen her leave. He strongly suspected she was going to seek an ally. He'd followed her to her aunt's boyfriend's place, heart in mouth as he tried to think through the consequences of Amy discovering her aunt was dead, because of course she hadn't remembered. It would then become clear she had been left a large amount of money. Once Amy had knowledge of this, there was every chance she would scupper his entire plan.

He'd waited outside for hours while she was talking to Gabriel, trying to keep warm while he watched the house from the edge of the woods. As she'd emerged through the front door, he'd tried to gauge her expression. She was too far away for him to see clearly. Did she know she was about to inherit several million euros? Had she told her aunt's boyfriend about 'Jack'? Had she understood what was really going on, right under her nose? He needed to find out.

Harry had waited until Amy was out of sight and then removed his skis before making his own approach to Gabriel's house. He raised a gloved hand, lifted the iron knocker and let it fall.

The door had opened and the aunt's boyfriend had stood there, surprised at getting a visitor.

Harry smiled. 'Sorry to bother you, but the binding on my ski has gone out of whack.' He indicated the ski propped upwards in his hands. 'I took a tumble and it's not right. I'm about to go down the Southern Slope but don't want to attempt it without adjusting the binding. You don't have a screwdriver I could borrow by any chance? Just to get me back down the mountain. Then I can get it fixed properly.'

'Of course,' said Gabriel, holding the door wider.

Harry stepped into the hallway. 'Sorry about my boots,' he said, as the snow began to melt on the floor.

Gabriel waved away the apology. 'Don't worry.' He indicated upstairs. 'I have a toolbox in the spare room. I'll go and get it.'

Harry watched as Gabriel headed upstairs. Then he looked around. It was a tidy place. Shoes were lined up against the wall on a small shelf. Coats were hanging on metal pegs, a mix of sporty winter jackets and something more dapper.

'It's not where I thought it was,' Gabriel called down. 'Won't be a moment.'

Harry wandered over to the stairs. 'Sorry . . .' he called up. 'I'm disturbing you.'

'Oh it's fine,' said Gabriel. He poked his head out from the landing. 'I'm sure it's here somewhere.'

When Gabriel had disappeared again, Harry started to ascend the stairs. He got to the landing and heard Gabriel rummaging in one of the rooms. He headed over and saw the door ajar. Stepped inside.

'Any luck?' he asked.

Gabriel looked surprised to see him upstairs.

'Sorry,' said Harry. 'I didn't mean to intrude. I was only going to say don't worry about it. If it's not to hand. I'll get it fixed in Val d'Isère.' He glanced around the room. It was a bedroom with floor-to-ceiling windows that opened onto a balcony. On a chest of drawers were some photographs in frames. Lots of a woman who was in her sixties and then in one picture, the woman had her arm around someone whom he instantly recognized.

'Family?' asked Harry, walking over to them, in what he hoped was a friendly tone.

Gabriel looked over. 'That's my niece. Sort of. With her aunt. Actually, she's just been here.'

'Oh?'

'Yes. Bit of a shock. She didn't know of her aunt's death.'

'I'm sorry to hear that.'

Gabriel produced a screwdriver and held it up. 'Found it,' he said.

'Fantastic,' said Harry. He pulled off his gloves and went to take the screwdriver from Gabriel's outstretched hands. As he did so, he thought Gabriel was looking at his finger, the one with the tip missing.

Harry held up the screwdriver. 'I'll just go and fix it then,' he said and turned to go back downstairs.

'It's you, isn't it,' said Gabriel. Harry turned back. Gabriel was looking at him in a way that made Harry feel uncomfortable.

'What?' said Harry.

'You're the boyfriend. The "man trouble".'

Harry's heart started to race. He gave a nervous laugh. 'I don't know what you're talking about.'

'Your finger . . . Don't lie to me. I know. What do you really want? Why are you here?'

'I told you, my ski—'

'Don't give me that rubbish.' Gabriel put his hand on Harry's arm. 'I want to know what it is that's making Amy so upset.'

Harry tried to shrug off the old man but he was surprisingly strong. 'I don't know what you mean.'

'I won't have her be hurt, you know.'

'Get off me,' said Harry.

He stared at Gabriel coldly but the older man didn't let go.

'Does Amy know you're here?' asked Gabriel.

Harry said nothing.

Gabriel dropped Harry's arm then, went to pick up his phone.

'What are you doing?' asked Harry anxiously. He started to panic. If this man called Amy, told her he was there, then it was all over. 'Put the phone down,' he said.

Gabriel ignored him. Started dialling.

Harry had no choice. He tried to wrestle the phone

from Gabriel, grabbed him by the neck and it turned into a scuffle. The phone fell to the floor. Harry felt a punch land on his jaw. He tried to scrabble backwards and felt himself hit the tall balcony window. Gabriel threw himself onto him and Harry caught the door handle as he fell, the door opening behind him. He immediately felt the cold rush of air from outside. Gabriel was still coming at him and Harry backed away. He had to use all his force to stop Gabriel from getting the upper hand. Then suddenly he felt himself gain some control and he threw Gabriel off him. He sensed rather than saw the old man tumble, heard a thud as he hit the side of the wooden balcony and another as he hit the snow below. There had been another sound. One Harry would never forget; sickeningly sharp, precise and almost with a wet twist to it. The sound of a bone snapping.

Breathing heavily, Harry stood and leaned over the side of the balcony, waited for Gabriel to get up again. But the seconds ticked by and he stayed lying face down. Harry ran downstairs and let himself out. He went over to where Gabriel lay on the snow. Harry tensed, sensing a trap. He waited longer but still Gabriel didn't move. He cautiously bent down, stretched out a hand and quickly grabbed Gabriel by the shoulder. He watched as the older man rolled over, his eyes open and dull. There was a red mark on his temple, but that wasn't what had killed him. It was the way his head lolled. And then Harry knew what the sound had been. His neck. A tiny vertebrae that had been one was now in two and less than a minute later, a human being became a corpse. *Shit*, thought Harry. *What the hell have I done?*

Back at the house, Harry took in Amy's accusatory gaze. 'The truth is, it was Gabriel who threatened me,' he said. 'We fought. It was an accident. He fell.'

'So you set it up to look as if he'd slipped on the snow outside?'

Harry didn't answer. He retrieved Amy's phone from his pocket and placed it on the floor in front of her. 'In seven minutes this is going to ring,' he said. 'It will be the solicitor handling your aunt's will. They will be ringing to confirm the bank account details that you emailed over earlier this morning.'

'But I didn't—' started Amy.

'You need to read those details back to them,' said Harry, pushing a piece of paper across to her on which he'd written them down. 'And if you say anything else then I use this.'

He held up the knife, twisted it in his hand.

SEVENTY-SIX

2 March

Amy stared at her phone lying on the floor. Then she looked back at Jack— no, what was his real name? Harry. A total stranger. Not a doctor, not a man who lived in Battersea and played rugby at the weekends. Not her boyfriend who she'd spent Christmas with in the Lake District. He was an unknown, a chancer, someone she'd had the misfortune to stumble across one cold night in February. And then he'd inveigled his way into her life like a virus, slowly taking over, attempting – and succeeding for a while – to convince her that she trusted him, that she was in a relationship with him. And now this. The real reason he'd lied and plotted. He was on the brink of syphoning off everything that Esme had left to her. In a few minutes her phone would ring and she'd have to relay a series of numbers that would divert the funds from herself to this con man forever.

He was watching her carefully. Waiting for the clock to count down. She had barely any time at all to think – mere minutes. It was unlikely the police were going to swoop in in that time. She also couldn't think of how she might be able to talk him out of it – just the notion of that was ludicrous.

It also wasn't enough time to finish loosening her binds. Because despite what he'd threatened, Harry hadn't checked the knots and Lisa hadn't tied them all that tightly. And right now, Amy was very slowly, very carefully prising them apart. A painstaking, tense task, like the game she'd had as a child, Operation, where you extracted a plastic representation of a human heart from a cardboard patient. One false move with the tweezers and the alarm went off. Harry was watching her. If he detected any movement it would all be over. She looked at the knife. It was one of those pocket ones where the blades flicked out. She got a sense he didn't want to use it. He would've kept Martha right next to him if he was a total nutcase. That blade would still be on her mother's neck.

She felt another loosening of the twine at her wrists. Maybe . . . just maybe there was a chance. She had to think about what she was going to do if she managed to get free. She had to get the knife before Harry. It was the only way. Then somehow, she had to overpower—

The phone was ringing. Its face lighting up as it pulsated on the floor.

'Right,' said Harry, holding up the knife. 'I'm going to press answer then put the call on speaker. You are going to do exactly what we've discussed.'

Amy watched as he moved to Martha again, placed the knife back at her mother's throat. She saw Martha close her eyes.

'Silence from the rest of you,' said Harry.

Then he pressed the green button.

Amy tensed. *Please stop working*, she silently implored the phone. *All those times you failed me, you can do it again now.* Suddenly she felt a kick against her leg. It was Harry.

'Hello?' she said, surprised to hear her voice sound so normal.

'Is that Amy Kennedy?' asked a woman.

'That's right.'

'This is Kim Moreau. From Vibert and Keller solicitors. How are you?'

'Fine,' lied Amy. 'Yourself?'

'Very good, thank you. As I mentioned in my email this morning, this call is just to confirm the bank details you sent over earlier.'

Except I didn't, thought Amy. 'OK,' she heard herself say.

'Could you please read them out to me?'

Amy looked at Harry, saw him nod towards the paper on the floor next to her. There was nothing she could do. She read the numbers out, heard the solicitor repeat them back to her. Kim sounded overly bright, no doubt pleased for Amy that she had reached the end of a long legal process, that she was about to receive a huge sum that her beloved aunt had left to her.

'OK, that is done,' said Kim. 'The funds should be transferred within the hour.'

'Thank you,' said Amy, feeling utterly bereft.

They said their goodbyes, then Harry hung up.

'Good,' he said. He took the phones from the table, including Amy's and went to leave the room.

'Where are you going?' asked Jenna.

He just smiled and left the room. A few seconds later they heard the front door slam.

SEVENTY-SEVEN

2 March

Amy was furious. She wrenched her arms apart, pulling and yanking until she freed herself. She leapt up, grabbed the knife that Harry had left on the floor in his haste to get away and went to her mother first.

'Are you OK?' she asked.

'Yes, yes,' said Martha, trembling.

Amy cut the bonds on her mother's hands. 'Mum, you need to be strong. You need to untie Lisa and Jenna,' she instructed.

Martha looked up, confused. 'What do you mean?'

Amy pocketed the knife and ran to the door. 'I'm going after him.'

'*What?*'

'It's my legacy. It's what Esme wanted for me. He's taken her money. You heard the solicitor. I've got less than an hour to stop the transfer of funds. I need to call her. Now.'

'Are you mad?'

'But he will have gone back into the town, to Val d'Isère,' said Jenna. 'He'll need transport.'

'I'm the better skier. I can catch him.'

'It's the Southern Slope,' said Martha.

'Yes.'

'Your father died on that run. Please, Amy, don't go.'

Amy didn't answer. She left the room and quickly searched the hall for some ski boots. Finding a pair, she dragged them on. They were two sizes too big, but she had no choice. She knew Gabriel kept his skis in a small room off the kitchen. She ran through, the boots crunching on broken glass from the smashed window where Jack had forced his way in, grabbed a pair of skis and poles and sped back. Flinging open the front door, she clicked them on and, not looking at Gabriel, headed away from the house. She could see Harry's tracks going towards the Southern Slope. She went the same way, edging along the narrow ridge, skis slow and parallel, the mountain falling steeply away to her left into an infinite sea of white. After a few minutes she stopped and braced herself.

Look after me, Dad, she pleaded silently.

Then she shifted her skis to the side until she tipped over the edge of the ridge.

SEVENTY-EIGHT

2 March

Amy knew she had to go fast if she was to have any chance of catching up with Harry. It was a challenging run, far harder than anything she'd attempted since her accident. In fact she hadn't skied this run for over ten years. Not since her father had died on the very same mountain.

Don't think about it, she told herself. *Don't think about any of it. Just keep focused, keep looking ahead*. If only she could see clearly, she thought. She had no goggles and the rain was getting in her eyes. She squinted, wondering if she'd made a terrible mistake, and then she got a sense that it wasn't as bad as when she'd left the house. The weather seemed to be easing, the clouds thinning. It was still raining but less so.

Amy could feel her feet move in the boots as she weaved down the mountain. She could handle it, she thought, she just had to concentrate. She could see a set of ski tracks ahead of her and knew they had to be Harry's. She had got up a good speed and she felt in control. Adrenaline coursed through her. *Concentrate*, she reminded herself every so often, as the fresh snow had got a little claggy in the rain and was making it harder going. Still she whipped across the slope, back and forth, feeling strong. Suddenly she caught a glimpse of a tiny figure far ahead. Her heart leapt. *Harry.* She had already gained on him, she realized. If she kept going at the same pace, she'd soon catch up with him. She snapped her attention back to the landscape, recognizing with alarm a sharp turn that was racing up towards her. If she judged this badly, she was going over the edge of the mountain into a two hundred metre drop below. In seconds she was in the turn, thighs burning, feeling for a moment as if the edge of the cliff was going to swallow her up and spit her into the empty space beyond it, and then her skis changed direction and she was back into the relative safety of the slope, leaving the precipice behind. Exhilaration soared through her. She was invincible! The gap between her and Harry was narrowing and now the slope was getting steeper. She'd be able to get up more speed. A momentary doubt flickered on in her mind but she ignored it. The rain had stopped and the sky was turning blue. She could see the elephantine grey rocks that appeared on this part of the mountain. They ran alongside the edge of the run, with one or two straying closer to her path.

No, thought Amy. *No, you are not going to get in my way. You are not going to take me down like you did my dad.* She was going too fast, deep down she knew this, but a bullishness made her keep going – she was not going to be beaten – and she skied onwards, her blades cutting up the snow as she hurtled down an eighty-five-degree gradient. She knew she had to turn at exactly the right moment to avoid hitting the rocks. She knew she had to keep her balance but her feet were sliding in her boots, making it hard to control the skis. If she fell now there was every chance she'd careen further down the slope at sixty miles an hour in a tangle of arms and legs with no control over her direction until her skull or her body – or both – were smashed against the rocks. Her mouth was dry. Her legs were burning. She swallowed down the fear, turning just before she got too close to an obstacle, again and again, and then she was almost crying out in relief as she passed them.

Then Harry glanced behind him. Amy saw him clock her and she doubled down, determined to catch up with him. *How dare you*, she thought, *how dare you think you can come here and lie to me, and take what is rightfully mine.* Esme would be cheering her on. She was almost upon him then, knew she could catch him. Somehow she just knew she was going to stop him.

Almost there. Only a few more seconds. Then she saw Harry start to slow, saw him ski off the run to one side. She frowned, not understanding. Then a movement caught her eye. A crack appeared at lightning speed in the snow beneath her, one leading to another to another until the ground under her skis was a criss-cross of jagged edges and the surface began to move, to shift, sliding underneath her, toppling her and she felt herself fall, felt the snow start to swallow her up and the sky began to disappear. A thud the weight of a truck landed on her chest and she felt herself pitch forward, or was it back? – she didn't know which way was up, snow was in her mouth, her ears, engulfing her and then she was vaguely aware she was still.

It was dark. Her lungs were gasping. The weight of the snow was stopping them from pulling in air. She was pinned on her back. Couldn't move her arms.

All Amy could think about was trying to breathe. *Don't panic, don't panic,* she told herself, knowing all the time she was panicking, she was gulping, desperate for air.

When Esme had taken her skiing as a child, she had drummed one thing into Amy's head constantly. If you are skiing with a friend and they get trapped in an avalanche, you've got eleven minutes to find them. Eleven minutes before it was all over.

SEVENTY-NINE

2 March

It was almost a pleasant feeling, calm, peaceful. A drifting sensation. Deep down, Amy knew she was falling unconscious. She also knew she had to stop herself, but it was hard, so, so hard. And drifting was so, so nice. She tried to think of things that would bring her mind back. She had to come back. She thought of her mother, sitting on the floor at Gabriel's lodge. Thought of Martha's last words to her, begging her not to go down the slope. She thought of how cross her mother would be, how she would be filled with 'I told you so's.' An age-old irritation flooded through her, then Amy found herself laughing inside. Funny how you could still be annoyed with your mother, even as you were dying. *Dying.* An urgent thought entered Amy's mind. *I have to stay here, stay focused.* It would break her mother if she did anything else. *Sing*, she told herself, *sing*! Instantly an old track from her childhood came into her mind: *MMMBop*. The lyrics reverberated round and round in her head, candy-coated, earnest and pre-adolescent squeaky, the song's jaunty record scratch an ear worm she couldn't escape from.

No, no, she thought desperately. She couldn't die to Hanson. She couldn't. She thought of her dad, of whether he knew. Was he there? Waiting? A tempting sensation of letting herself find out flitted through her mind. At least she'd made it to thirty. It was a shame she wouldn't see the summer though. Amy felt herself let go. It was so peaceful. And then suddenly she felt as if she was flying, across the mountains. Like the paragliding. She was filled with a sense of freedom, of floating in a beautiful, blue bowl of a sky.

EIGHTY

2 March

A sensation on her leg. Something pushing against it. Another near her torso. Amy felt annoyed at first; whatever it was, it was disturbing her, pulling her down from the sky. She had a terrible feeling she was going to fall, her canopy was going to collapse and she was going to die. Then a bright light hit her eyes. A gasp of air. The sky so painfully blue. She squinted. There was a silhouette towering in front of her. Someone blocking the sun. It was Jack, she realized. *No, Jack doesn't exist, remember.*

It was Harry.

She let her lids fall shut.

'Amy, open your eyes,' said Harry.

She ignored him. Maybe he would go away.

'Amy. Open your eyes,' he repeated, more sternly this time.

She did. She blinked. He was looking at her. She couldn't quite make out the expression on his face. The sun was behind him and she was blinded. *He's going to kill me*, she thought. *He thought the avalanche hadn't done the job so he's going to make sure there's no doubt.* She waited, pinned down by the snow, a growing fear rising up in her.

Then behind him, a movement. A wheeling rush of brown and gold, a high-pitched screech. *The eagle.* So it hadn't gone, it hadn't been taken by poachers. Amy felt a rush of joy. She looked past Harry, focusing on the bird, seeing its glorious flight, its freedom. She knew it had come at that moment to be with her. Esme was with her. She watched, seeing it soar, knowing now she wouldn't be afraid.

Then, a hand.

Amy ignored it at first, as confusion seeped in.

He was pulling at the snow on her arms, freeing them. Then he yanked at her wrist. Amy got a sudden rush of urgency. She used her newly freed arm to push away snow, Harry still helping her until she was standing up.

'Anything broken?' he asked.

She looked at him, unable to fully take in what he was doing.

'Is there?' he repeated.

'No,' she said. 'I don't think so.'

He pointed at the ground. 'Only one of your skis is here. The other must be buried. It's going to take you a little while.'

Then he snapped on his own skis and picked up his poles from the snow.

Stunned, Amy had a sudden flood of clarity.

'You're not going to get away with this,' she said.

'You won't be able to find me,' he said. 'You won't know who I am.'

He let a smile play over his lips and then pushed off. She watched as he skied down the mountain, getting smaller and smaller until eventually he disappeared.

EIGHTY-ONE

5 September

Harry reclined the luxury seat to a very comfortable forty-five degrees. A uniformed woman approached, sleekly beautiful with perfectly arched eyebrows. She held a small silver tray on which was a glass of champagne and she handed it to him.

'We're three hours from landing, Mr Lombard.'

As Harry took the drink he saw her eye him so subtly it was barely noticeable. But there was a suggestive glimmer that hinted at a greater interest, an offer. He didn't need it, not this time. Not now he was richer than he'd ever dreamed possible. He smiled then turned to his magazine and she glided away.

The champagne was cool against his tongue, the bubbles fizzing delightfully in his mouth. He'd had six months of fulfilling every wish that entered his mind. He had a new identity. He was exquisitely dressed and a new watch hung on his wrist, alongside the Tiffany gold cufflinks he'd coveted for so long and finally been able to buy. He had a deep tan after spending the summer in Italy, renting a villa on the shores of Lake Como where he'd swum every morning, his body kept toned and lithe. He'd drunk coffee and wine in the squares. He'd made friends – no, not friends, acquaintances. Empty, rich people he'd hung around with for a few weeks here and there until he'd tired of them, or they him. It had been a time where all his previous worries of financial hardship had melted away but despite this he'd remained restless. He had sat up on his terrace well into the early hours of the morning with a glass of wine, looking out at the still lake, the moon reflected on its dark surface, the same person occupying his thoughts. Amy.

Harry had lost count of the number of times he'd thought of her since he'd left her on that snowy slope. He could still remember the look of terror on her face as he'd stood over her, pulling her from that avalanche. It still had the power to make his guts twist with dismay. He wasn't a bad person. He didn't want her to be afraid of him. In fact it had surprised him how his stomach had plummeted with fear when he'd watched Amy get buried alive in the snow. He wondered where she was now, what she was doing. Was she still working as a lawyer backing those who were getting screwed by the big Goliath bullies? Occasionally he wondered if she was dating someone, but it wasn't something he liked to dwell on. He'd even googled her a few times but she had vanished from all social media. Something he was largely responsible for, he thought wryly.

Raising his glass, he made a silent toast to her and felt something that had been with him for a while. A pang of loss.

EPILOGUE

18 September

Amy hadn't been sure she wanted to come back to her flat, but in the end she'd relented. The idea of selling up made her angry. It was her home and she was damned if Harry was going to take that from her as well. She'd changed the locks, of course, and paid over the odds for a decorator to come in and paint every wall. It was an opportunity for a fresh start. And then, about a month ago, she'd invited someone back.

Amy had met Nathan at the local sports centre. She'd signed up for a yoga class in the hope a bit of spiritual mindfulness would help the smouldering fury that lingered in the pit of her stomach, ignited every time she thought of Harry enjoying her inheritance. Nathan had also been in the class and had seemed so chilled out, so happy with his lot, not in a weak, pushover way, but he was a glass half-full kind of guy. He placed great value on being outdoors and being lucky enough to work as a landscape gardener. He was quite a successful one too – he'd won a couple of medals in the past at the Chelsea Flower Show and this had kept the clients coming to his door.

She looked across at him now, making some sort of fruit and veg smoothie, while she scrambled some eggs. She was still discovering all the trappings of being in a relationship. How he always carried the shopping home after they'd been to the supermarket – together. Even food shopping took on a whole new meaning when you were doing it with someone else. You planned meals, and the unspoken agreement was that you would be spending the evening together. You discovered your new beau had a passion for squirty cream out of a can and tinned sardines, both of which you loathed. You bought air freshener for the bathroom, suddenly self-conscious about unpleasant aromas, something that had never needed to be considered when living alone. Weekends were a world away from what they had been before. There was no longer a struggle to motivate herself to get out of bed and find an activity that didn't make her feel like a hanger-on or lost for the day in a solitary bubble. In fact, now she often didn't want to get out of bed at all, she thought, smiling as she watched him chop apples, admiring his deeply tanned and weather-beaten skin and sun-bleached hair.

Having been single for so long, part of her wondered if all of it was real but then she remembered the occasions where she was taken aback at how easy it felt, how natural it was to be in his company, and she sensed it was the same with him. He'd met Martha and had charmed her with his knowledge of perennials and how to get the blackfly off her roses. He'd also gone out for dinner with Lisa, David and Jenna. Amy had been self-conscious at first at how

Jenna was alone, remembering all too well how that felt, but about an hour in, Amy had got a sense it was as if they had all known each other for years. At her request, no one had mentioned Harry. The money was gone forever and Amy had to get over it.

Amy buttered some toast and spooned the scrambled eggs on top, put the plates on the kitchen table. She was just sitting down when she heard the letterbox flip open and there was a pap as the delivery fell to the floor.

'Shall I get it?' asked Nathan, as he put their smoothies on the table.

'Thanks,' she said.

He came back in with a small pile of post, which he handed to her. 'I was thinking,' he said, 'do you fancy going to Kew today? We could get some ideas for your garden.'

Amy looked up from flicking through the envelopes and smiled. This was one of the best things about being in a relationship. Spontaneous bursts of fun. Things that didn't need weeks of planning because it was so natural for you and another person to want to spend time together.

'They have the tropical building, don't they,' she said excitedly. Nathan had offered to landscape her tiny garden – as a gift, he'd said.

'You're still keen on that look?' he asked.

'You think we can fit a palm tree out the back?' asked Amy.

'Hell yeah. Maybe not a coconut like that one but something for sure.'

Amy looked at him quizzically then saw he was indicating

something in her hands. She looked at her post. There was a postcard, a picture of a tropical beach. It looked like it was somewhere in the South Pacific.

'Nice beach,' said Nathan.

'Yes,' said Amy quietly, her mind spinning. She turned the card over. Apart from her name and address, written in neat, precise black ink, it was blank. She read the tiny information print at the bottom of the card, the line that told her where the photograph was taken and her heart began to thud.

'Someone on holiday?' asked Nathan.

'Actually, I think it's just a marketing thing,' said Amy, and she got up and pressing the pedal, dropped it into the bin. She put on a smile, sat back down and finished her breakfast, tried to enjoy talking about her new garden design with Nathan.

When he got up to use the shower, Amy cleared away the plates. She opened the bin to scrape away the crumbs and the postcard stared up at her. A pristine beach on the island of Tonga. She hesitated then picked it out of the bin.

The bastard, she thought, *the thieving, rotten bastard*. He'd booked it after all. And now he was rubbing her nose in it. Her beach, her dream, her fucking money. How dare he. How dare Harry spend her aunt's money, *her* money and then send her a bloody postcard from paradise. For she was certain it was from him. She thought back to what seemed like a lifetime ago now, an afternoon in a lodge in the mountains, a conversation about a recuperation holiday for her. *My treat*, he'd said. The liar.

Amy narrowed her eyes, thinking. They'd said the money was irrecoverable. But what if they were wrong? There would be records in hotel reservation lists; there might be telephone numbers, addresses. Not necessarily legitimate but there might be a lead, there would be *something* if she looked hard enough, she was certain of it.

She looked again at the postcard but instead of putting it back in the bin, she stuck it on the fridge. As she did so, she stared at the picture of the beach. In her mind she could see Harry there, lying in a hammock strung between the two palm trees. His smug face as he wrote her address on the postcard. One thought lodged itself in her mind. Solid, permanent and with a determination that would never diminish.

She was going to hunt him down and she would not rest until she found him.

ACKNOWLEDGEMENTS

I was well into my thirties before I met my husband and had wondered all of the following at several points before that fateful day: why is it so hard to meet someone who isn't a loser? Where might this individual be? Does he even exist? What is wrong with me? Why is loneliness such an endless wilderness? Along with several other soul-searching questions. And so, you could say that the idea for *The Boyfriend* was conceived in part from personal experience. It was a long, tumble-weed-filled wait and then – without any preamble – into my life he came and everything changed irrevocably. Our relationship was very different to that of the characters in this book (fortunately), but we shared the same astonishing, fast-paced change of direction when someone new is catapulted into your life and you know nothing will ever be the same again. As my grandmother always used to say: expect the unexpected.

Huge thanks to Trisha Jackson and Jayne Osborne, my wonderful editors, who went on this journey with me. Also, to all of the fantastic team at Pan Macmillan who've helped get this book edited, beautifully covered and out there in the real world. Thank you to *you*, the readers, who are with me every step of the way – your support means everything to me.

To Gaia, Lucy and Alba – what an amazing team of agents. You are always there and you have an endless supply of wisdom, advice and humour.

Ruth Wood, thank you for your brilliant insight and knowledge on concussion. Kim Thomas, the best solicitor I've ever been fortunate enough to meet, thank you for your advice on wills and sorry to make you sweat with my money transfer plans.

Lastly, huge love and thanks to my wonderful family – especially my out-of-the-blue husband.